Madge Swindells was born and educated in England. As a teenager, she emigrated to South Africa where she studied archaeology and anthropology at Cape Town University. Later, in England, she was a Fleet Street journalist and the manager of her own publishing company. Her earlier novels, SUMMER HARVEST, SONG OF THE WIND, SHADOWS ON THE SNOW, THE CORSICAN WOMAN, EDELWEISS and THE SENTINEL, were international bestsellers and have been translated into eight languages. She lives in South Africa.

MADGE SWINDELLS

Harvesting the Past

WARNER BOOKS

A *Warner* Book

First published in Great Britain in 1995
by Little, Brown and Company

This edition published by Warner Books in 1996

A CIP catalogue record for this book
is available from the British Library.

ISBN 0 7515 1676 7

Typeset in Ehrhardt by
Palimpsest Book Production Limited,
Polmont, Stirlingshire
Printed and bound in Great Britain by
Clays Ltd, St Ives plc

Warner Books
A Division of
Little, Brown and Company (UK)
Brettenham House
Lancaster Place
London WC2E 7EN

To Jenni with thanks.

Acknowledgements to Jenni Swindells, Eddie Humphries, Lawrie Mackintosh, Philip Boulton and Stephen Le Roux for their valuable assistance.

Prologue

Arion sailed for home. The sight of the treasure he carried roused the cupidity of the sailors, who resolved to kill him and seize his wealth. Arion, as a last favour, begged permission to sing a song. The sailors consented, and the poet, standing on the deck of the ship, sang a dirge, accompanied by his lyre. He then threw himself overboard, but he was miraculously borne up in safety by a dolphin, which had been charmed by the music.

PART I

Chapter 1

—— ——

As the sun's first rays lit the horizon in gold and rosy splendour the birds set up their shrill hosannas: sunbirds, weavers, sparrows, herons, flocks of red-billed queleas, eagles, until veld and forest vibrated with their morning song. The scarlet-breasted roller soared into the sky and tumbled down for the sheer joy of it. Two dainty impalas locked horns and swayed from side to side, a troop of baboons scampered out of the camel foot tree to squabble over locusts and the fish eagle screamed hoarsely as it soared down to the swamps.

There was a sudden hush, each creature poised alert and listening, but not afraid of the strange new beast that rattled and bumped noisily across the veld each morning at sunrise, but this time it stopped inexplicably and the dust rose around it. A young girl had climbed up on to the rail of the four-wheel-drive viewing truck and this was not allowed.

'Hey, get off there! You'll fall,' a man's voice shouted. As the wildlife fled, the game ranger swore.

'Mandy get down,' Hannah, her mother, echoed. Mandy was not usually so naughty. Hannah understood that her daughter's behaviour was designed to draw attention to herself and it wasn't hard to guess why. Like many second-generation Europeans in Africa, the game ranger had flourished in the sun and space. Handsome and hardy, he towered head and shoulders over everyone else and he was beautiful, with blond hair and the deepest blue eyes she had ever seen.

Mandy tossed her black hair over her shoulder, tilted her face to the trees as if engrossed in her search for birds or leopards, but remained sitting on the highest rail.

The ranger climbed out and walked to the back. Hannah held her breath, hoping for the day when a man would stay impervious to her daughter's charms, but this was not that day. He melted, his blue eyes took on a strange, faraway dreamy look, his mouth hung slightly open and he looked a little dazed as he stared for longer than was polite, obviously admiring her smooth, ivory skin, raven hair, red lips and eyes that were large and shone with love for everyone and everything. Hannah sighed. Her daughter was that rare phenomenon, a perfectly beautiful woman, with the type of sensual allure that brought out aggression in men. They had to possess her and hated her when she thwarted them. Mandy was busy discovering the power and the curse of her incredible appeal.

'If you want to see better, come on up front with me,' the boy invited her.

Mandy hesitated.

'Come on. I can explain about the birds and – and everything.' He flushed. 'I'll stop if you see something that interests you.'

She looked hesitantly towards her mother who nodded her assent. Anything was better than her daughter wobbling precariously on the top rail. Mandy was still such a kid and unable to cope with the beauty and sex appeal that had settled upon her. She was always trying her luck, testing herself, needing to find her barriers, but for Mandy there were none. She had only to smile and every man melted.

Climbing down, Mandy tried out a sultry, lingering look that Hannah had seen her practising in the mirror.

'Wow!' Sultriness fled as a cheetah loped through the tall grass beside them. 'Look! Look! There, Mum.' She was a kid again. 'Where's my camera?' she yelped, her new conquest forgotten in the excitement.

I should hang a sign around her neck: I'm only just sixteen. Their holiday to the Okavango swamps was Mandy's birthday present. But would that make any difference? She tried anyway: 'Please excuse her,' Hannah murmured to the ranger. 'At sixteen everything's so . . . so . . . exciting.' She had given him the message and her voice tailed off.

'Sixteen,' he muttered, one eyebrow raised, his mouth revealing his disappointment.

'Where does all this beauty come from?' Hannah had asked Bill, her husband, in exasperation the week before.

'She's like my sister, Rose, a rare beauty, for all the good it did her.'

Her husband was not a talkative man and the subject of his long-lost sister was forbidden territory. Hannah had learned that the hard way. When Bill was out one day, Hannah had studied the family photograph album. Despite the faded sepia tones, she could see the likeness.

How would Mandy cope with such a gift? Even old men became stupid when they met her, and this made Hannah angry. Silly fools! Behind her anger was a sense of loss for something she had never had. What would her life have been like if she'd had looks like Mandy's? Sometimes she even envied her daughter and this made her feel guilty. Over-riding these muddled emotions was her concern. Mandy was naive even for sixteen. She trusted everyone. Just look at her tossing her black hair over the seat and smiling that great wide smile of hers, while her slanted amber eyes sparkled with fun. Watching her made Hannah feel good. Truly she was blessed.

They had reached the edge of the lake where the dugout canoes and boatmen were waiting. They were to be split up – one in each canoe and this worried Hannah. 'You will behave yourself, won't you, Mandy?

'She's a bit of a daredevil. Keep an eye on her,' she said anxiously.

'Don't worry. The guides know what they're doing and we don't take dugouts near the deep water. It's quite safe in the shallows. I'll be waiting here when you get back.'

So he wouldn't be with Mandy. That was some small consolation. He hardly looked at her as he spoke. Hannah wasn't quite sure when it was she had become invisible to men, but lately the transformation was complete.

Squinting her eyes against the glare of the rising sun she gazed over the quiet grey waters, watching the birds winging past, listening to their cries. The dugouts looked insubstantial and she wondered if she would make a fool of herself and topple over, but strong hands gripped her arms and she was propelled into the canoe. The boatman crouched ahead of her, dipped his paddle, and then they were skimming over the calm water towards a bank of papyrus. Surely they would crash! She almost cried out, but then she saw the narrow tunnel through the rushes and moments later they were in another world, a place of brightly coloured water lilies, butterflies, darting birds, baby crocodiles perched on lily leaves, frogs and fish, and crystal-clear water running past.

It was paradise. Even the worry of Mandy's behaviour faded in the midst of all this wonder. Was it the silence that made it so special? she wondered. Or the beauty? It was a magical place. Their narrow dugout could just squeeze through the waterway between towering papyrus on either side. Then they emerged into a large lake and she gazed over a mass of water lilies: mauve, pink, blue, lemon and cream. A jacana bird was stepping lightly over the lily leaves searching for grubs. A baby crocodile, six inches long, saw them and leaped off his sunny perch and swam rapidly down into muddy roots. The water was completely transparent. She could see small fish, tadpoles, roots and stems. 'Amazing,' she murmured. 'Quite lovely.' The boatman paused again. Looking up she saw a stork perched on a nest. A fish eagle flashed down into the pond, leaving circular ripples glistening in sunlight and emerged seconds later with a large fish in his beak.

'Where are the others? Where is my daughter?' she asked him.

He shrugged and gestured as if to indicate Africa as a whole. 'Each one chooses his way,' he said.

They moved on, passing through long channels of overhanging papyrus, emerging into yet another lake and back into the maze of tunnels. The only sound was the birds calling and twittering and the occasional roar of a lion from the far banks. She lost track of the birds, there were so many and they were so lovely. Caught unaware, they sat bemused while she glided silently past. The overhanging trees were thick with monkeys. On a nearby bank they saw a pride of lions chasing a young zebra, and a bat-eared fox stood undecided by the water's edge, wondering if he should flee.

'Oh God! To think this has always existed and I never knew. Who could imagine anything so lovely?' she whispered.

The sun rose to its zenith, the water shimmered brilliantly, torrid air came surging out of the papyrus as if from an oven, the crocodiles slept in a torpor in their nursery shallows, not even stirring as the dugout glided close by. The boatman sweated and his jet-black skin became shimmery-shiny, while the surrounding air was filled with his musky, bitter-sweet scent. They paused for the refreshments that were stored in an icebox and then went on again. How could he possibly find his way? she wondered. Hannah nodded off and woke in a panic to find herself falling forward. She jerked upright. I would have looked a sight, she thought staring down through three feet of crystal-clear water to the muddy bottom.

Half an hour later the boat grated against the bank. She looked round, startled, to find six pairs of dark hands pulling her on to the concrete ramp. She was back in the Moremi Game Park.

'Camera? Handbag? Sunglasses?' The workers sang in unison.

Moving slowly, for it was very hot, she followed the group towards the vehicle. They sat in the shade waiting for everyone to return. It was a long wait and Hannah dozed off.

'Why is my daughter so long?' she asked when she woke. 'Is anyone else missing?'

Everyone was there. 'I expect they stopped to take pictures,' an English woman called out.

But Hannah noticed that the ranger was scanning the lake and reeds carefully through his binoculars. He frowned. 'Silly bugger,' he muttered.

Ten minutes later he was on the radio to the ranch. The guests rumbled off in the truck driven by his assistant, but Hannah remained with the game ranger and a boatman.

The main camp was sending out a search launch, he explained.

'But surely it must be safe,' she stammered. 'You wouldn't send people out into danger. Not ordinary tourists like us. Your brochures assured us . . .'

'Mrs September,' he said firmly, 'this is one of the last untouched parts of the world that's left to mankind. Naturally there are dangers in any primitive territory. If we eliminated the dangers, just supposing we could, there wouldn't be any game left and you tourists wouldn't travel all this way to see darkest Africa, would you?'

'This was her birthday present,' she whispered.

The game ranger was listening for the approaching launch. Suddenly it emerged through a break in the reeds and came skimming towards them. She was hoisted aboard to where three other rangers, armed to the teeth, were muttering in the bows.

There was something macabre and unreal about racing through the swamps at high speed. Crocodiles and hippos panicked and sank into the depths, the birds took off and flapped away, while exhaust fumes left a smoky trail behind them.

At dusk the body of her daughter's guide was found floating face down in shallow water. It was miles away from where they should have been. Police reinforcements were sent up to the swamps. By then Hannah could hardly walk, her limbs were so stiff. They transferred her belongings from the tent she had shared with Mandy to the main lodge and she was given a sedative by a doctor flown up from Maun. It did not help. She felt that she would never again sleep. Where was Mandy? What had happened to her? Visions of hippos and crocodiles attacking the dugout tortured her mind. Then she began to worry about the boatman. What had he done with Mandy?

The police arrived by helicopter and grumbled because the sedative had made her almost incoherent. She tried to talk clearly between fits of shuddering and crying as she told them all she could think of.

'What about a boyfriend?' one of them asked.

'I told you,' she said, hanging on to the shreds of her self-control. 'We don't know anyone in Botswana.'

A coldness was settling into her. She could hardly move her lips. I mustn't be sick. I must be strong. I have to force them to keep on searching for her.

That night and all next day the search helicopter and two launches mingled with the sounds of the bush. At dawn the news came that a strange launch had been seen making for Toteng. Eventually the dugout was found holed in the swamps but there was no sign of the boatman. Local Herero tribesmen near Ramsden had seen a bearded white man in a large felt hat meet the launch and carry a sleeping passenger into his truck. He had left soon afterwards, taking the road towards Gobabis across the border of Namibia. 'There's no chance of his escaping across the border,' the police told Hannah. 'We have men at every post.'

There were no more sightings.

A week later Bill arrived to fetch his wife and take her home. He'd been out at sea and unable to get there sooner. Leaving the swamps was the hardest thing Hannah had ever done in her life.

'Oh God help us,' she sobbed as they drove towards Cape Town. 'How could this cruel thing happen? Why did they take Mandy? Why her? Why . . . ? How can we leave without her?'

'We can't let this destroy our whole family,' Bill said. 'We've got to carry on.'

'How can you be so strong?'

Bill was an enigma to Hannah, as he had been ever since they married. To her and his family he was the kindest husband and father, but to others he was surly, uncommunicative and a tough man to cross. She'd married him for the security he offered. Of all the boys in the village he was the only one who owned anything at all and what he owned was considerable: his own fishing trawler and house.

Bill was tallish, sinewy, immensely strong, deeply suntanned, and lined. His arms were thick and hairy, with a tattoo, a blue anchor and a red heart with the words 'I love Hannah' underneath. He'd had it done the day he proposed to her. His hair was a shock of wavy black, with iron grey streaks here and there. His features were all too large for his face, but the overall impression was of a clever, tough, resourceful man. They would need all his resourcefulness and his toughness for she had folded. She felt unable to cope.

'Sometimes I think you have no feelings,' she sobbed. 'What's happened to our little daughter? Where is she? Is she suffering? Is she alive? What are they doing to her? Who would want to hurt a lovely girl like Mandy?'

There were so many answers to her question, she knew. Children disappeared all the time, for ransom, for spite, for satanism, for *muti* [witchdoctor's medicine], for sex, or just as a simple act of evil.

'I'm promising you now, Hannah. Somehow we'll get her back. If the kidnappers are going to contact us they'll do it in Cape Town. We'll fight this terrible thing from our home.'

Chapter 2

_____ _____

It was so dark! Mandy could not think rationally. Her thoughts raced round and bumped into each other, leaving her bewildered. Waking here had been like a rebirth into a lonely, terrifying, black world. Was she dead? Was this what death was like – darkness that would never go away? Yet how could she be dead when she felt so ill?

Days, or hours later, her memory returned with disjointed images of home and her parents. It was a time of total confusion, but slowly the pieces fitted together poignantly. Mother had always irritated her, but now she longed with all her heart for her comforting arms.

More recently she remembered her sixteenth birthday and the trip to the swamps. She was gliding through water lilies, and then the boatman turned back and smiled. There was something wrong with his smile. 'We get out here,' he had said.

She had stepped out feeling puzzled. Where were the others? Looking round she had seen a Land Rover parked nearby and this had reassured her. Calling back to the boatman, she had seen his face exploding, disintegrating, blood spurting into the air, and then he was falling back, arms outstretched, splashing into the swamps and slowly sinking. And that was all. Her memories stopped there.

Thoughts flashed through her mind of crocodiles' lairs under riverbanks, where their victims were left to rot. But there was no water here. So where was she? Sick and dizzy, her limbs turned to lead, her head exploding with pain, she had tried to make sense out of her condition. Had she, too, been shot. Oh God, help me, she prayed.

It was jacaranda time and Pretoria's sweltering streets and buildings were obscured with masses of misty mauve blossom. Inside police headquarters it was always gaunt, functional and cool whatever the month, with one exception. Colonel Greg du Plessis had been raised in northern Namibia and detested air conditioning. His office was unbearably stuffy and the dust twinkled in prisms of sunlight.

The young lieutenant standing to attention tried not to show his discomfort as the sweat trickled down his back. He was trying to make a decision which would affect the rest of his life, but this was difficult because his superior officer would not stop talking. Ari had been celebrating his coming release from the police force for most of the night and his head was hammering. He tried to switch off from his physical discomfort and think. There had been some good times, but that was before he was transferred to the Child Protection Unit (CPU). After that . . . He shuddered violently and the colonel caught the movement.

'Sit down, my boy.'

Patronising bastard!

'I want you to withdraw your resignation. One should never take important decisions when one is undergoing psychiatric treatment, or so I've been told.'

'It's over.' Ari took a deep breath. 'I'm cured.'

'You were never sick.'

The colonel was known for his ability to simulate sympathy when needed. Right now he was overdoing it, Ari reckoned.

'Merely stressed out. Overworked! That's what your file says. You became too involved with your cases. Maybe you had a minor nervous breakdown? Who knows? You are a very good policeman, St John. I don't want to lose you. I want you to withdraw your resignation. Bad timing, my boy.'

The colonel looked up shrewdly, trying to read the lieutenant's expression, but those hazel eyes were staring at a point just over his head and told him nothing. He was a tall, good-looking man, with black curly hair, a heart-shaped face and sensuous lips. His looks belied his reputation of being one of the cleverest young men in the force – and the toughest.

Ari sensed the probe and bridled. 'Beating suspects to death isn't part of the job.' He had a feeling he was being obscurely blackmailed. 'It wasn't an accident. I had to kill the bastard. That's why I'm quitting . . .'

If only it were that simple. The truth was that lately he'd been drinking, feeling depressed, avoiding friends and becoming aggressive. He knew why. He was running away from something that he did not understand and could not risk encountering ever again.

'The psychiatrist's report says you refuse to talk about it. That is, what happened.'

'Nothing happened, sir. I lost my temper and ran amok, as my father used to say.'

'Your *adoptive* father, it says here.' The colonel was leafing through that damned file again. It would give the barest outline of his life, Ari knew. At two years of age he had been adopted by Professor Duncan St John, anthropologist and author, and his wife Isobel, a botanist. His natural parents were unknown. It was all there in the file, but it would say nothing of the happiness they had given him, or his brilliant childhood in Kenya and Zambia, or the strong moral code they had taught him, or how desperately he loved them.

Concerned that they might be too old to be good role-model parents, they had trekked halfway across Africa with him, taken him on safaris into the bush and the mountains, anthropological expeditions, hunting and collecting African art. They had taught him to make detailed notes, to use his powers of observation, taught him to reason and to control his aggression, and, by example, they had taught him about unconditional love. Strange how he had imagined that a happy childhood was commonplace until he spent two years in the CPU. The only bad thing they'd ever done to him was naming him Arion Fletcher St John.

'I had a very happy childhood, sir.'

'Yet there's always that quest, I believe, that need to know your roots.'

'No, sir.' Of course the colonel was right, but he'd stifled the longing, fearing that he would hurt his parents whom he loved. All he knew was that the adoption papers had been signed in Cape Town, March 13, 1967. He had been two and a half when he was handed to Child Welfare by Father Richard Mooney, of the Catholic church.

'I'm asking you to withdraw your resignation, Ari. We don't have many officers as dedicated as you. I have a job for you. We need someone to follow up the Mandy September kidnapping. Someone reliable should be there where the family live. It's in the prettiest part of the Cape Province, a town called Silver Bay.'

Silver Bay, Ari was thinking. A strange coincidence.

'Nothing ever happens in Silver Bay,' the colonel was saying. 'It's very peaceful. There's a handful of excessively rich families who've hogged most of the valley to themselves, plus the usual horsey crowd, mainly professionals. They enjoy a record low crime rate, perhaps because there's full employment of the local coloured population and only a handful of black migrants. It's a den of liberal thinking. Easy to be liberal if there's no threat to house and home, so ninety-eight per cent of them voted for a changeover to democracy.' He glanced back at Ari's file. 'It says here you intend gaining your Ph.D in criminology, but you could do that part-time.'

'Sir, excuse me for asking this, but why are you trying so hard?'

'You were like a crusader, Ari. A one-man blitz on child abuse and cruelty. You solved every case you took on. The truth is, I need you. You headed the team that went up to Botswana and Namibia to liaise with local police. We suspect that the girl was taken across the desert *en route* to the Cape. The kidnapper might intend contacting her parents. If she's still alive, that is. They're not wealthy, but well off by local standards.

'Listen, Ari, not to beat around the bush any longer. The government is facing our first inter-racial general election soon. Certain ministers feel that we should do a few tricks so that the coloureds will vote with the whites. It's vital if we want to hang on to the Cape Province. Mandy's father is a local coloured leader. What we badly need are a few well-publicised projects to show the coloured voters that we really care, we're on their side, that they and we are one and the same.'

'A little late in the day, isn't it?'

'Let's not bring politics into this, Ari. I've heard about

your liberal views. Those wily black politicians have begun bussing in squatters to those areas where they need more ANC votes.

'I want you to concentrate on finding Mandy. You can call in the Defence Force for searches with helicopters . . . Maximum publicity – remember that, Ari. Distribute pamphlets with her photograph, organise TV appearances. Let her parents make an impassioned appeal for her return. You got that, Ari? Throw a little passion into it. As I said, the search is more important than the victory.'

'But not for Mandy, sir,' Ari said quietly.

The colonel flushed. 'Of course, these are not my personal views. I'm simply passing on the brief. I knew you'd be the right man. You really care. That's your strength and your weakness.'

Perhaps because each one might have been me, Ari thought. In the deep dark recesses of his mind were unconscious memories of earlier times. Dark times! They surfaced in his dreams, and sometimes in his work, but that was not why he was running scared. He shuddered.

'What's the subject of your thesis, Ari?'

'Child abuse, sir. I'm trying to come to rational terms with something I've seen a great deal of these past two years.'

The colonel's eyes narrowed. 'Look, Ari. You're young enough to be my son and far too good to be wasted. Take my advice. Hang on to your job and study part time.

'You'll be assisting Lieutenant Rolf Gerber,' he went on briskly, as if the matter had been resolved. 'He's in charge of admin but you're equal in rank. You'll like him. He's an easy-going fellow. Take it. A long, hot summer in the Cape will do you good. There's very little crime down there.'

Finally, after an hour debating the issue, Ari accepted,

perhaps because it was Silver Bay and there was always that longing.

Kate Palma was light-headed that morning as she galloped her stallion over the sand dunes towards home. She had ridden out at dawn and swum naked in the icy Atlantic, surging forward in a fast crawl to circle the old wreck before hypothermia set in, returning through the breaking surf, diving under the massive rollers, fighting the backwash that caught at her. There had been one nasty moment when the sea dragged her back and rolled her over the sand, but she had fought and won and coasted in on a two-metre high roller, fired with exhilaration. In her home she was so cloistered and protected. Here she was on her own, testing her mettle. Her mouth and eyes stung with salt, her skin tingled and her hair streamed in the wind as she galloped home.

Breasting the mountainside, she paused and glanced back at the sullen sea glittering deep green below. To the south-east she could see across the mountain ridge to Silver Bay's fishing harbour, and beyond to the tall granite outcrops rising sheer from the sea to tower a thousand feet or more over their shimmering reflections. To her left stood the Palma mansion, set amongst fifty acres of nature reserve. Northwards stretched the deep green valley nestling under the mountains.

Angelo Palma, her grandfather-in-law, had chosen his site with care. In a sweeping glance he could overlook his vineyards in the valley, his fish-freezing and canning plants behind the harbour, his fishing trawlers, yacht and cruiser.

Glancing at her watch, Kate saw that it was almost eight-thirty. She was hungry, but she had a meeting with their architect at nine. She smiled to herself remembering Angelo's temper when she had called in outside help to back up her intention to make yet another change to his precious castle. The old house was like a relic of a bygone age, stark, old fashioned and absurdly inconvenient. It was supposed to be a replica of Angelo's family mansion in Spoleto and he had designed it himself, which was probably the only foolish thing he had ever done, she decided, as she reluctantly turned towards home.

Ten minutes later, after handing her horse over to the groom, she ran up the steps into the main hall. Ramona, the housekeeper, was waiting for her. 'I've been looking all over for you.' As usual she managed to make a simple sentence sound contemptuous. 'Your father's on the line. He said he'd hold on because it took him an hour to get through.'

Then he must be at the game park, Kate thought, feeling surprised. Strange time for a holiday.

Five minutes later, she slammed down the receiver. Panting slightly, she rushed to find Rob, her husband, but then she remembered he was at sea with a group of scientistsontheFisheryDepartment'snewresearchtrawler. Calling for the chauffeur to drive her to the airport, she scribbled a note for Rob: *Darling, Father's in terrible trouble. Flying to see him. Back in a couple of days. Take care. Love you, Kate.*

There was an hour's delay before the first available flight left, so she paced the car park, squinting in the glare, watching the air shimmer above cars and burned grass while the heat rose in suffocating waves from squelchy tarmac. Passing men stared longingly, but briefly, at this tall, slim figure in a beige silk slacks-suit, her flaxen hair piled on her head. She was beautiful, but rich and therefore out of reach.

For Kate, the two-hour flight to Johannesburg was agonising and it seemed that it would never end. As they moved north into the summer rainfall area, clouds gathered below until all they could see was a brilliant vista of white clouds stretching to the horizon. Their descent felt like a roller-coaster ride as the plane tore through the gathering nimbus.

By the time she reached Rand Central Airport, where her father kept his private jets, her shock, anger and tension had fed upon itself until she thought she would explode. Jim, one of their pilots, begged her to delay the trip. 'Look there!' He pointed over the hangar to the east where rain clouds jostled each other, as black and menacing as a Zulu impi. Then the rain came slantwise, like a solid sheet of water, enveloping them. Kate gasped. 'Don't waste time,' she snapped.

There was something about being very rich that made you feel inviolate, Jim thought watching her narrowly. She didn't give a damn about the weather. She was as tense as a leopard, hair falling askew, long legs pacing restlessly, green eyes blazing with hot temper; even now, even when her mouth was pulled into a hard grimace of fury, she was still perfectly lovely and her large white teeth gave her a reckless, almost boyish look. Bet she's hot stuff, he thought.

'Mrs Palma, take my advice. Wait a few hours. It's not safe,' he grumbled.

'Father hired you so I presume you're good at your job.' She didn't wait for his answer as she climbed into the seat.

Bitch!

Shortly afterwards they zoomed up into writhing purple clouds, bucked and shuddered between the white-hot lightning forks, swayed and shook, soared and fell, but to Kate the storm was merely an expression of her fury and resentment.

'Broke,' Father had said on the telephone. 'Worse than broke. Insolvent! Mira and I are spending a few days at the game park – love it and leave it. A sort of goodbye to Africa. I have to get out of the country before the news breaks. I've cut a few corners . . . I was so sure I was winning . . . a week at the most . . . so this is goodbye, Kate.'

Impossible! Insane! How could someone like Father be broke? They were so rich. She could never remember a time when they had not been rich, but she had been too dazed to comment or think properly.

'Where are you going? London?' she had asked him.

'Probably not. I have to consider the possibility of extradition. We'd thought of Venezuela. Beautiful country.'

She was unable to grasp the news. How could this happen? 'Is this your idea of a sick joke? Please don't do this to me.'

'Sorry, Kate. You'll have to fend for yourself from now on.'

'You mean . . . ? Surely not my capital, too. You wiped out both of us . . . ?'

'They can't touch the lagoon. It was your mother's.'

Scalding tears of shock and anger were trickling down her cheeks as she relived the conversation. Cut a few corners? What did he mean? Had he done something wrong? And why Venezuela? Was he on the run? Surely not. Her father had always been so distinguished, so important, looked up to.

He couldn't have meant all the things he had said. She

was longing to talk to him, but the plane was taking forever and her damned tears were splashing all over her suit.

She wiped them away and glanced surreptitiously at Jim, but he was engrossed in his job. Obviously he didn't know about the forthcoming liquidation.

The storm was worsening, the lightning seemed closer, more dangerous, and it was so dark between the flashes. How small, how amazingly insignificant they seemed as they were tossed around the vast purple canvas. Jim, white-faced and shocked, fought for control and swore quietly under his breath, but she didn't care. She felt a savage desire to be dashed to the ground and annihilated. Why not? 'Why not do the job properly?' she muttered under her breath to her own demonic god. The gigantic lurches, breathless falls and surging uplifts seemed to drain some of her anger.

When she stepped out of the plane on to Wild Eden's gravel runway, she felt more resentful than furious. It was evening time, so cool and fragrant. The leaves dripped noisily and the glowing twilight suffused the veld with a soft, golden haze. For once, Kate missed the joy of it.

How could they lose Wild Eden? She had grown up here and she loved every part of it. It was her second home. It had always been a joyous retreat from the tensions of her world, but tonight nothing could soothe her. Not the graceful impalas grazing around the runway, nor the four beloved giraffe standing with their feet splayed, heads close together, staring curiously at her, nor the bat-eared fox that slunk past through the grass, nothing could penetrate her fears. She hardly glanced at the massive baobab tree she loved so much as they hurried towards the lodge. Scores of twittering weaver birds were diving into their colony in the acacias, preparing for the night. It all seemed so normal, yet her world had disintegrated.

'It can't happen. Not to people like us,' she muttered.

Chapter 3

——— ———

By the time she came face to face with her father she could only say: 'I had to come . . . had to talk to you. How could you keep me in the dark about this . . . this terrible thing?'

He was sitting in the shadows by the copper fireplace in the sprawling old lounge, as big as a house, under a high thatched roof, with sliding walls of glass which were open now. A fresh scent of damp earth and leaves filled the room and raindrops dripped noisily on to the wooden verandah. In the distance a lion roared. He looked up at her and then he looked away. She might as well have not been there.

His gesture recalled old hurts and childhood loneliness. She stared longingly, hoping that this time he would beam some love her way, if only because he was leaving, but those invisible shutters were still there.

She remembered how the house had always been full of friends, and father had been so full of fun, his blue eyes twinkling with warmth, but always for others. Never for her. Now his eyes were bleak, his blond hair fading, the skin of his face and hands was grey-tinged and lustreless. Defeat was etched in his face, but even worse was his rejection. Nothing had changed at all.

'You shouldn't have come,' was all the greeting she

received now. 'Just get on with your life. You'll be all
right. Thank God you've married into a fortune. Rob will
look after you, despite— You're part of *their* family now.'

'We won't lose this, will we? Not Wild Eden? I couldn't
bear that.'

'You're such a child. How does a girl get to be twenty-two
and still be so naive?'

'Father, I . . .' She reached forward, but he stood up
abruptly. It had always been like that. He used to say that
he hated emotional scenes, but she sensed his lack of caring.
All her life she had longed for his love, but she had never
had it. Now he would be gone forever and she was to be
deprived of her birthright. Bright temper spots appeared
on her cheeks.

'I have a right to know what's going on. I demand to
know!' She clenched her fists. 'You made me go to that
classy finishing school, when I wanted to study art. I could
have learned something useful. You brought me up to be
wealthy. You've no right to go broke. How could you lose
my holdings, too? We had so much. How could you do
this to me?'

'I underestimated the extent of Palma's spite.'

Kate stared in disbelief as her Father walked outside,
slamming the door behind him. Then she realised Mira
was standing in the shadows watching her. She had never
understood how Father could spend his life with someone
who had limited charm and even more limited intellect,
when her own mother had been so special. At least he
hadn't married Mira. She was standing in the doorway,
arms akimbo. She had always been critical and on the
defensive, but now Kate saw a secret triumph lurking in
her eyes, and a tinge of amusement. That was new. 'Let's
have a drink,' Mira said.

'No, I . . .'

But Mira was tugging hard at her, pulling her to her feet, a sign of changing times. Kate resisted an impulse to push her off. She had always found her a little unwashed. Mira's soft olive skin seemed to exude female scents, overlaid by the expensive perfume Father bought her. Her femininity seemed so contrived: a silky band around her hair, jangling earrings, chains, bracelets, a blouse, a silk cardigan with a pink satin scarf thrown over it, gold belt, long fingernails, too many rings. Despite this extraordinary coverage, her plump smooth breasts were half revealed. Kate could see her cleavage and she felt repulsed. Mira had met Father in Monaco, of all places, and she'd hung on ever since. Mother had been so gracious, intellectual and lovely, too. Mira reminded her of a sponge, shapeless and soft. She soaked up Father's humour, smiling secretly, but contributing nothing. Squeeze her and she'll ooze drivel, Kate thought, pulling her arm away.

'Your anger will hurt him even more.' Perhaps it was Mira's Parisian accent that jarred against Kate's frayed nerves. 'You must find some compassion in you. Can't you find a kind word to say to him?' she oozed. 'Some pity.'

'*Peetee*, oh God!' Kate pulled out her combs and tossed her hair over her shoulders, trying to stare Mira into silence. Was she the family mentor now? Had disaster given her status? From whore to Aunt Agatha?

'Be adult about it.'

'Oh, for fuck's sake, get off my back,' Kate snarled.

'It's worse than you realise,' Mira went on. 'We have to be in Venezuela before the news breaks or they'll take his passport. You see, he'll be arrested for fraud.'

'Fraud? Oh . . . no! And I?' Kate said brutally. 'Am I supposed to take the flak while you two hide out on your ranch somewhere pretty safe and plush? I suppose he's salted away a fortune.'

'No. Next to nothing. It was so unexpected.' She hesitated. 'Mike was set up. He doesn't want me to tell you, but I feel that you should know. There's no love lost between your father and Angelo Palma, but of course you knew that. Palma deliberately ruined Michael. I always knew there was some feud, something both sides want to keep quiet about. I think they're both ashamed. Michael won't tell me much . . . only that Angelo was paying back for an old wound. I expect your husband knew, too.'

Kate began to feel sick. Mira's words were like stabs in her guts.

'No! You're lying!'

'But it's true. It was calculated and very, very clever. You see . . .'

Her explanation seemed to be never-ending, but Kate, drowning in her own anguish, caught the gist of it: Father had wanted to gain control of a listed 'rare earth' mine in Namaqualand, but he hadn't had enough cash, so he had approached Angelo and offered him a partnership. Angelo had set him up with a confidence trickster operating from a fictitious Montserrat bank. Father was supposedly safeguarded by dollars deposited in the bank, but the bank was a sham and his dollars disappeared, together with the bank directors and the broker.

'Mike borrowed the cash from his mining company, but of course they'll say he stole it from the shareholders, and now he and the mine are insolvent,' Mira went on. 'He can't explain where the money went without being arrested for exchange control fraud. There's no way he can turn.'

'Oh God! How could he be such a fool. How could he trust this man?'

'Because Angelo Palma sent the broker to him and personally guaranteed his character. Later we found the broker had just come out of prison and Angelo knew this and deliberately passed him on to Mike. So now you know what sort of a man Palma is.'

'Is there any water here?' Kate's mouth was bone dry and she felt bilious.

Mira went to the bar and returned with a glass of iced water. 'You've always resented me,' she said. 'We've never really talked, but I had to warn you.'

'You have no proof. It's just hearsay.'

All the same she knew it was the truth almost as soon as Mira had started talking. Scenes began to slot into place: Angelo opposing their marriage so bitterly. Then there was the time she had overheard him tell Rob she had brought bad blood into the house. Too many memories. How could she live in the same house as Angelo knowing what he had done to Father? And to her? And had Rob known? If so, she would never forgive him. Oh Rob, darling, don't let it be you. No . . . Rob mustn't be involved. That would be too cruel. She loved him so much.

Kate stood still trying to look unconcerned while the knife twisted and turned. I'm going to throw up. She mustn't see how scared I am. It wasn't the deed so much, nor the ancient feud, crazy though it was, nor even her spiteful, Machiavellian grandfather-in-law that was scaring her so. It was the threat to her love. Rob was her whole world: husband, lover, friend. He was the rock she clung to. More than that, she loved him.

There was the sound of an engine starting up below. Through a break in the leaves she saw Father bent over the wheel of his jeep. He moved forward under cover of the leaves and the two women sat in silence, listening to the sound of the vehicle fade as it moved towards the northern boundary.

'He loves this place. He's been driving round all day, just staring at the bush.'

'I love it too . . .'

'I suppose they'll auction it. God knows if it will remain a game reserve.'

Kate tried to fight back her tears. 'Strange to think that animals can be bought and sold like that,' she murmured. 'I mean . . . it's like this place belongs to the game. But it doesn't. Man owns it all. I would give it back to them, if I could.'

'You make it sound as if we're different,' Mira was saying spitefully. 'Nature created her ultimate survivor, the aggressive, reasoning primate – us! You, of all people, should know that.'

Was she trying to be rude? Kate couldn't be bothered to care. She stood up abruptly and made a violent gesture with her hands, as if to push away the horror. Moving forward on rubbery legs she stumbled down the outside steps into the yard.

She stood moodily kicking at a stone with her foot. She wasn't equipped to cope with this disaster. She loved Rob dearly, but she had never truly felt a part of the Palma family. She had always longed for them to move into their own home. Until now, Rob and she had been equal partners, for she had been heiress to a fortune and she had received a generous income from shares and property. She had never worked, but she had been independent, never having had to ask for anything. She loved her husband, but she had no illusions about him in business. He used the power of money to manipulate and control. Did he truly love her? Of course, he thought he did. Nothing would change. How could it when they loved each other so?

She jumped as she heard a shot coming from the north. 'Oh God,' Mira exploded from the balcony. She had turned pale. A second shot rang out as Mira ran down the steps gripping her rifle.

Moments later the two women were racing north in the Land Rover. The last lingering light formed indigo shadows under the trees. The predators were emerging. A brown hyena panicked and raced along the road until Kate braked violently, switched off the lights and waited until it fled into the bush. What would they find? What had he done? Kate's fears were gnawing at her as she gathered speed again.

They came across Michael's jeep unexpectedly on the down side of a rocky hill. Skidding badly they narrowly missed it. There was a cheetah lying in the grass near the vehicle. It had been shot through the neck and her father was standing beside it, leaning on his rifle. He looked pleased. Mira flung herself at him and hung around his neck.

'Thank God, thank God . . . I thought you'd . . . But you're all right,' she was sobbing.

'I've wanted to shoot it for years. I'm glad I had the chance,' he said.

'But why? Why?' Kate burst out. Her pent-up emotions were bringing her dangerously close to tears, something Father would never forgive. 'How could you? You don't have the right. How cruel to destroy this beautiful beast!' She crouched beside it, stroking the fur, wishing she could bring it back to life with the force of her anguish. Poor creature. Life, that unknown and indefinable force, had fled, leaving glazed eyes, and a spotted pelt.

'If I had time I'd have it stuffed,' Father said. 'Maybe I still could. A memento of Africa.'

Whatever for? she wondered. The fiery glowing life force, that stealthy, terrible spirit had vanished. Annihilated? No, impossible, she thought. Nothing was ever destroyed. She bent over the corpse to hide her tears. 'I hate you for this,' she murmured. 'You have never loved anyone or anything.'

'Yes,' he said. 'Don't you want to go back now before I skin it?'

The following day, her parting was formal and devoid of any emotion. She stood for a moment watching the pelt swaying on the washing line where it was drying out. I will never grieve for Father, she thought. If I have any tears I'll keep them for the cheetah. I'll never return here either. Everything has become meaningless. All that he taught me has been wiped away – all my childhood. There's nothing left. Nothing at all.

Chapter 4

Kate had arrived back an hour ago and chosen the dinner table as the best place to launch her attack. Not that she had much choice, she mused, for it was the only time the family were together. Lately Rob worked all hours planning, costing, organising new schemes. Sometimes she suspected Angelo deliberately kept him working late to spite her, but Rob had explained that Angelo was lonely. I'm lonely, too, she longed to retort, but she was too proud to beg.

It was eight o'clock, dinnertime, but the vast, gaunt room was empty. She wandered around, hardly seeing the dark wooden floors, the intricately bricked walls, massive fireplace and dark-beamed ceiling. She had her own vision of what the room would look like one day. Turning to the big bay windows, she gazed over the cluster of lights around the shore. They were miles from the nearest neighbour. This was no-man's land, a large nature reserve separating the coloured village on their right from the white suburbs to the left and across the bay. She began to imagine a little house over there on the plush side of the village, perhaps a nursery, a paddock for the horses, everything normal and sane and far away from Angelo. Just Rob and she.

Then she noticed the two men on the lower terrace, sitting on a bench, talking quietly and she could sense the communion between them. They lived in a world she could not penetrate. A sudden shaft of envy made her skin tingle. She loved Rob dearly, but she had never achieved this much intimacy with him. Hurrying inside she noticed Ramona standing in the shadows by the fireplace, her impenetrable black eyes boring into her. Kate knew the old housekeeper detested her, but she had never worked out why. Not that she cared one way or the other.

'Ring the dinner chimes again, louder this time.'

'But, madam . . .' Those two words seemed to answer every order given to Ramona. In a sudden surge of impatience, Kate grabbed the gong and played *Three Blind Mice* loudly three times.

The housekeeper smiled and walked outside, leaving Kate fuming. Ramona had been in charge here for as long as anyone remembered. She was older than Angelo and should have retired long ago. She had brought up Rob after his father died and his mother left home. Perhaps she was jealous of another woman here. Shrugging her off, Kate drummed out her temper on the dinner gongs, hammering her way through *John Brown's Body*.

Her tension worsened as the two men arrived.

'You're late,' she said. 'Why are you always late?'

There was a lump in her throat and her voice came out in a growl. Turning suddenly she caught a glimpse of laughter in Rob's eyes.

'You're so sexy when you talk like that,' Rob teased in a deep bass voice. He caught hold of her arm and pulled her close to him, nuzzling her hair. 'Mmn. You smell yummy, and you taste yummier,' he whispered. 'I'd eat you on the table right now if Angelo weren't here,' he whispered. His strong fingers probed the nape of her neck searching for that secret spot which he knew was a hot line straight to her groin.

'Sh!' She pushed him away, feeling confused, conflicting emotions struggling to gain precedence. She loved him, but right now she wanted to be serious. She felt swamped with a premonition of doom. Rob would be sure to take Angelo's side, but what was she supposed to do? Take her family's ruin lying down?

Why was he trying to charm her? She could feel herself melting. His face was powerful and beautiful with his brooding coal-black, slanting eyes, his straight, short nose, his well-shaped Roman head topped with a thick mass of blue-black wiry hair. Everyone said Rob looked like Angelo, but she had never seen the resemblance. Age and grief had ruined Angelo. His face was like well-worn leather and almost as dark, his eyelids drooped, heavy with warty, lumpy skin and his brown eyes were flecked with yellow. She shuddered. When he peered straight at her from under his overhanging white hair, he reminded her of a buffalo cast out by the herd, fierce, lonely and very dangerous. It's as if he's set himself apart from others, she thought.

'Rob,' she blurted out. 'Don't joke. My father is ruined. He was set up. Mira told me Angelo did this awful thing to him. And she said you knew about it. I have to know the truth, Rob. Surely you knew that I would be ruined, too.'

She regretted her timing. No one seemed to be listening. But there was that look again, some silent message being passed from one to the other and back again.

She would try again. Angelo had said grace, which he did when they were alone together, they had been served with the soup, and for a moment Ramona was out of the room. Kate cleared her throat.

'I flew up to Wild Eden to see my father, as you know.

Father's leaving the country. He made a bad investment and his company is about to be liquidated.'

There was a glimmer of derision in Angelo's eyes. He knew. Yes, of course he did. Mira had been telling the truth.

'He borrowed cash from his company to buy another mine, but he was cheated.'

'He was cheating . . .' Angelo interrupted her, his expressive brown eyes flashing with contempt. 'He was caught by his greed. People who cheat are at the mercy of others who also cheat, but who do it better.'

'Are you accusing my father . . . ?'

'I'm afraid he's labelled himself, my dear. It has nothing to do with me,' Angelo retorted.

'Hey, wait a minute, you two.' Rob dropped his spoon with a clatter and raised his hands. He looked upset. 'Let's put a stop to this before it goes any further.' His eyes implored Kate not to speak.

'We must have this out,' she said, trying to avoid his gaze.

'Let me do it for you, Kate,' Rob said, surprisingly gently. 'We were going to tell you, but you rushed off to the game camp before we had a chance. Your father took millions of rands, twenty million actually, out of his mining company, shareholders' funds, to gain personal control of another mine. However, he never got that far. Not having enough cash, he got mixed up in a speculative scam which broke the law and he lost the lot. Perhaps I should explain more carefully,' he added patronisingly. He did at great length until she interrupted him.

'Yes, yes, I know all that. Please let me finish. The point is Angelo set up my father because of some family feud. Something both sides want to keep quiet. Mira told me everything. It was calculated and very, very devious. I want to know why, Angelo. I must know . . . really, Rob, what I really want to say is – were you involved?' Tears were burning her eyes.

Angelo's eyes were closing to slits. He nodded towards Rob. 'Ah,' he said softly. 'What could Mira possibly know? The folly of meddling women. Your father is a crook and soon he will be a convicted felon, *in absentia*.' He turned to Rob. 'People will gossip. We should suggest that Kate was his first victim. That might save you both from some of the flak. As for my role, I tried to save him, but finally I learned that the disaster was too great for my resources.'

Why wouldn't he look at her? Because he was lying? She longed to pick up the ugly silver candlestick and thump him with it. 'You haven't told me why there is a feud between you, nor why you were opposed to our marriage.'

'You're being hysterical.'

She was losing the battle. Rob was furious. He scowled at her, daring her to continue.

'I'm demanding a straight answer to a straight question. Did you set up my father? And did Rob know?' she flung at them.

'A whore would have better table manners than you,' Angelo said, sidestepping the question. He stood up and rang the dinner bell. 'Bring my food to my study,' he said softly to the maid.

'Why?' Rob asked. 'Why make a public scene? Couldn't you have spoken to me later? I can't eat.' He pushed his plate aside and stood up.

'Listen to me.' She was desperate now. 'It was Angelo who suggested Father could gain control of the company for forty per cent less outlay if he bought the shares with financial rands. It was Angelo who sent a crooked financial broker to Father. He promised to ship Father's money abroad, which I admit is illegal, but everything would have been fine in a couple of weeks. The deal was handled by an offshore bank in Montserrat.'

'Mira told you this?'

'Yes.'

'But you have no proof.'

'I believe her. Besides, Angelo didn't deny it. You know how he hates lying.'

'Even if she were speaking the truth, your father still stole the money.'

'He borrowed it.'

Rob shrugged. 'Whatever Angelo may or may not have suggested to your father, he could not force him to break the law. I'm going out,' he muttered. 'I'm not hungry. Don't wait up for me.'

Kate was left sitting alone in the midst of her disaster. She gritted her teeth. She knew Ramona and the maid were listening. I won't give them the satisfaction, she decided. Sitting very erect she finished her soup. Then she rang the bell for the next course and ate that, too, chewing each mouthful slowly, a smile playing around her lips. She would not be defeated by this horrible family, nor this cold, unhappy house, she thought as she rang the bell for her dessert.

Rob returned at midnight to find Kate lying in bed pretending to be asleep. He'd brought a glass of neat Scotch up with him. He thought he might need a drink. Kate could act up sometimes. He switched on the light and made a clattering noise throwing his clothes over the stand and his shoes into the cupboard, but she did not stir. Stupid bitch! Anyone could see she was awake. He sat beside her on the bed and took her hand in his. She was so lovely and so fierce. Tonight she had been like a wild kitten trying to corner Angelo.

'Kate,' he whispered.

He wrapped his arms around her, felt her thick hair tickling his face, pushed her hard against him until she shuddered.

He bent to kiss her, but she pushed him away. 'You must tell me,' she said. 'I must know.'

He sighed. Caressing her nipples he felt them harden and he knew that she wanted him. A wave of hot love raced through him, leaving him feeling exalted and invigorated. She always slept naked, so he pulled back the sheet and bent over to gaze at her, never tiring of her incredible beauty. 'Oh, Kate, my love,' he murmured. Her breasts were quite perfect, two swollen mounds of firm flesh with the wider circle of brown skin surrounding her nipples. He clasped his hand over her breasts and thrust his mouth on to hers.

She struggled out of his grasp. 'Tell me,' she demanded. Sitting up, looking fierce, with her blonde hair falling over her shoulders and her breasts, she looked so much like a vengeful valkyrie. He wanted to laugh at her, but sensed this was not the right time to joke. She might be right. Angelo had always hated Mike Russell, but if there was a vendetta between them Angelo had waited a long time for his revenge, but that was Angelo. He was known for his long memory, never failing to repay his debts or his grudges. He'd been paying his debt to Silver Bay all his life.

What on earth could he say to Kate? He was torn between the two of them. He loved them both. 'I know nothing about it,' he said, feeling sorry for her. At the same time, she ought to trust him.

Some of the tension seemed to drain out of her. 'If I thought you had anything to do with it I would leave you,' she said.

'And I would die of loneliness,' he said, pushing her back on the bed and stroking her breasts. He was determined not to quarrel. Just look at her hanging on to her dignity. She didn't even have the cash to buy her lipstick. Not that it mattered. She had him. He had always resented her independent means. He'd seen her fortune as a threat. From now on they would be more of a unit. She might have to climb off her high horse from time to time, but that would be all for the good.

He smoothed her damp hair from her face, feeling his insecurity seeping away. All his life he had known that money bought everything, even loyalty and love. Even Kate's love. Everything had a price, and you got nothing for nothing. Angelo had taught him that time and again throughout his childhood. He'd been twelve years old when he got his first lesson which he remembered so well.

He'd been longing to be one of the big boys and go out sport fishing with Kurt, who was three years his senior, and whose father owned a tunny boat, but of course, such an honour was out of the question. Then the invitation had been issued out of the blue, stunning him. They'd had a great time and he'd proved himself worthy, despite his youth. That night Angelo had told him how Kurt's father was angling for them to buy his freezing plant. 'We'll purchase some minor equipment, my boy, and delay the big sale until the game fishing season ends. That's power,' he explained. 'Never fool yourself. Don't for one moment imagine that people are straightforward or that they like you for yourself. They want your cash — that's the beginning and end of it all, and the trick is to get the most mileage out of your resources. Only money can be trusted, not people.' He'd been right, eventually they'd placed the coveted order, and Kurt had dropped him.

He'd never forgotten that lesson and it had served him well. Much later he'd made the mistake of falling for Kate, an heiress. God knows why she had chosen him. With his caring came insecurity, but she was irrevocably tied to him now. His hand slid down to her crotch and he began to caress her.

'I don't want to make love,' she murmured.

'I do.'

He stood up and began to take off his clothes. Kate watched him moodily. Why couldn't he take her terrible problem seriously? Was he deliberately fobbing her off with trite phrases and sex? Look at him flaunting his body. She longed to pin him down, force the truth out of him, but part of her longed to make love to him. She loved his broad shoulders, and his tough, tanned skin, and his sinewy neck, and the way the muscles rippled on his back when he moved. She loved the black tangle of hair around his groin and his succulent sweet penis and the way he smelled when he wanted her. When he bent over her, she gave up, closed her eyes and writhed with pleasure.

Watching her, Rob knew he had won. He moved his lips slowly over her body, seeking, finding, exploring. She groaned softly. At last, when he knew she was ripe and ready for picking, he thrust inside her.

He never ceased to wonder at the way she always came with him. This had never happened to him before he met Kate. It made him feel fulfilled and happy. He sat up and sipped his Scotch.

'Jesus, Kate, you're really something special,' he said.

'I'll never get tired of making love to you. And you're my wife. Crazy, isn't it?'

She was frowning as she watched him. 'Is it?' she murmured.

'Play your cards right and you'll get whatever you want out of me.'

Her eyes opened wide with shock. What the hell's got into her? he wondered. He tried to retrieve her affection. 'Fucking you is the best, Kate. You'll get everything you want, don't you worry. What's mine is yours. Bend a little, give a little, learn to please me. I love you, so you don't have a problem.' He laughed.

My God, the temperature had dropped to near-freezing. Women! He'd never understand them. He had the impression she lay awake for most of the night. Whenever he stirred she was lying rigid beside him gazing at the ceiling.

Chapter 5

———— ————

Mandy felt her body, pinching herself, but this hurt. Did that mean she was alive? Where was she – and why? How long had she lain here? She had no way of telling what had happened to her, or where she was.

She was so thirsty. Did dead people feel thirst? Perhaps she was blind and lying in hospital? She called, and called again, but there was no answer. Sound seemed to be deadened in this awful place. But surely she could hear something? A tap was dripping. Did dead people hear things?

She wanted to sit up, but she was afraid to move. After a while her thirst became intolerable. She pushed her hands into the inky blackness, but images of snakes, spiders, rats, and scorpions zoomed in out of the darkness. She screamed until she passed out.

Was it moments or hours later when she realised that she was awake again? She could still hear that tap dripping. She felt her body cautiously. She seemed to be in one piece. Nothing hurt, except her head and her dry throat. Snakes had not bitten her, rats had not gnawed at her. She took her courage in both hands and felt around her head. There was nothing there except a pillow. She was lying on a single bed, with a hard mattress and a steel frame. She fumbled around it, feeling sure that her fingers would be snapped off, but after a while she decided that she was the only living thing in this lonely place.

When she stood up cautiously, she fell. She could not keep her balance, so she pulled herself on to her hands and knees and she crawled, sliding her hands forward into total blackness, fearing that she would fall into a bottomless void.

On one side of the cell was a tap. The knowledge that she could drink water whenever she liked filled her with gratitude, for she was almost dead with thirst. She drank deeply until she felt she would burst. Beneath the tap was a drain with a grid through which the water splashed. What was beneath that? she wondered. She began to criss-cross her prison on her hands and knees, trying to work out where she was. It was made of concrete, the roof higher than she could reach. It was big, larger than a normal room. Moving round the edge, her hands encountered a smooth rounded shape. She explored until she realised she had found a toilet and the plumbing worked, she discovered. There was a wash basin, a table, a chair . . .

Reality came flooding into Mandy's mind, bringing relief. She was not crazy, or blind, or mad, or dead, or wandering in some hellish underworld, she had been kidnapped and she was being kept prisoner in an underground cell. A new strength came with that understanding. But why would anyone want to kidnap her?

'Dear God,' she prayed. 'Send help. Get me out of here.'

No one met Ari at Cape Town airport, so eventually he caught a black taxi [mini-bus operated by black-owner-driver]. It was nearly five o'clock in the afternoon and hot as an oven when the bus reached the neck of the pass and took the twisting narrow road towards the village of Silver Bay. The mountain slopes were thickly forested, dark and shimmering in the heat. On either side of the road, towering granite peaks reflected rose and purple with deep indigo shadows in the crevices. Beyond was the sea shining a deep turquoise and the mile-long, curved strip of sand shone like a silver ribbon. Lieutenant Ari St John gazed out of the bus window hungrily, longing to swim in the sea.

In the packed taxi, the torpid air was as thick with flavours as a Malay stew: cheap perfume mingled with exhaust fumes, body sweat, *dagga*, stale wine and strong tobacco. To this was added the curiously repulsive odour of the man sitting in front of him. A *Bergie* [a tramp living in caves on the mountainside], he guessed. His crinkled, unwashed body seemed to be pickled in wine and cured in wood smoke.

At the next stop the bus screeched to a halt and everyone was jolted forward. Cushioned between two massive black ladies, Ari hardly felt the jar, he simply wobbled amongst shivering black jellies. The *Bergie* began to mumble to himself, his lips and fingers moving convulsively. Ari guessed he was hovering on the edge of control, being desperate for his next *dop* [a mugful of cheap wine].

The bus gathered speed again, swaying dangerously. The women shrieked while the men sat stone still but you could smell their fear. Who needed a lie detector in a country where fear was a palpable musky odour?

They were racing past rich homes of two acres and more with swimming pools, well-tended gardens and a few tennis courts, all the required trimmings of South African middle-class professionals. Ari tried to suppress a surge of envy. He would never own a house like these. Not on a policeman's pay. Strange to see rich homes without razor-fencing, automatic gates and Rottweilers snarling through the bars. Some gardens weren't fenced at all, sure sign of a secure neighbourhood. Ari saw Afghans, sheepdogs and a variety of pets that couldn't keep a beggar at bay. And would this change if the squatters came here? He alighted in the main street, collected his suitcase from the back of the taxi and made his way whistling to police headquarters.

'Good afternoon,' he called to the back view of a large figure crouched over some fishing tackle spread over the floor.

'Hi, Rob. I reckon this reel's a goner.' The speaker looked over his shoulder and frowned. 'Your voice! For a moment I thought . . . You sound just like a friend of mine,' he said, climbing to his feet. 'Come to think of it, you look a bit like him, too.'

Station Commander Lieutenant Rolf Gerber was yet another indication of a crime-free community: he was complacent and overweight and he was panting a bit. His pale skin was badly eroded by the sun, and his nose was burned and peeling. His sandy hair was bleached almost white and his blue eyes had a metallic glint about them. 'Who're you?' he asked. Ari introduced himself.

'So you're the hotshot who's going to find the September kid,' he snarled. 'I don't believe you'll have much luck down here. You should have stayed in Botswana. The worst crime we've had in the past ten years is drunken driving.' He smiled arrogantly. 'We've got a model coloured community and there's no trouble between them and the whites. Why? Because no one wants to rock the boat. There's no hunger here. No one is homeless or unemployed and everything fits together like a well-oiled machine.

'I've been checking on you, Lieutenant. I heard you like to kill your suspects. Well, nowadays we have to toe the line. Time was when we got our confessions the easy way. Forget it! This is the new South Africa, man, and we're supposed to be synonymous with Father Christmas. You see a kid begging you give him a sweet, not a clap round the ear. You got it? That's official. Of course, we still have a few tricks up our sleeves and I have no doubt the guys will wise you up, but we never leave traces.'

Ari mentally labelled Gerber an insensitive oaf who never tackled anything unless he was sure of winning. He felt uneasy at being categorised as one of the bully boys, but he had a code: never complain, never explain, which prevented him from setting the record straight.

'First things first,' Gerber was saying. 'Here's a list of available accommodation. Check it out and take your pick. Sergeant Willis Gous put a star next to the ones he fancied.'

'Sir, my car is coming by rail. I flew down. I was told someone would meet me at the airport.' He paused, but Gerber did not attempt to explain away this lapse. 'Can I borrow wheels from the pool?'

'Strictly speaking no, but what the hell else can you do? Public transport is reduced to one bus and hundreds of black taxis. Think yourself lucky to be here, St John.' He stumbled over the words and looked up suspiciously. 'What kind of a name is that?'

'English, sir. Pronounced Sinjun.'

'Well . . .' He scowled and glanced at the letter from Ari's colonel. 'Arion Fletcher St John,' he murmured. 'I don't believe it. Mind if I call you Fletcher? Are you English?' he went on.

'No. That is, my parents are, but I was raised in

Kenya, then Zambia and later Zimbabwe. Then I came here.'

'The colonial flight down Africa.' He laughed without humour. 'Well, the buck stops here, Fletcher. Unless your folks fancy the Antarctic.'

'Sir, my father is a lecturer and author. He merely moved to new academic postings in order to further his research.'

Gerber fixed him with a steely look. 'Is that so? Well, I know what you are and I don't want any trouble. Do we understand each other? They tell me you're very bright, Fletcher. Don't flaunt it!'

There was only one address with two stars and Ari made his way there. Trendy, liberal Jack and Gillian Bronson met him in the porch, their faces wreathed in false smiles and deep anxiety which remained stuck there like a video halted in mid-frame. Jack looked fifty. He was tall, powerful and muscular, but rapidly going to seed. His bulging paunch and red-veined nose showed why, yet there was only a trace of grey in his black hair and under his puffy, red skin was his perfect Roman profile. Gill could pass for forty if she tried. Her figure was trim and her hair was dyed and highlighted to a delightful reddish glow. She looked appealing in her faded designer jeans, a yellow silk blouse, and sandals. She wasn't pretty, but she was pert and she had good eyes. She had a habit of tossing her long fringe forward and peering up from under it in the manner of the very young, which was disconcerting.

'She's down there.' She shot him a sidelong flirting glance. 'Perhaps she's still sleeping.'

'Who?'

'Our squatter. That's why you're here, isn't it?'

'I came about the cottage.'

'For God's sake, Gill, think before you open your mouth,' her husband growled.

'Oh!' Mrs Bronson let out her breath in a fierce, audible explosion. 'Oh heavens! What must you think of us? But you are from the police, aren't you? I mean, you're driving a police car. So shouldn't you just have a look at this old woman? She broke into the stables and fell asleep.'

'Gill should have explained that we used to keep horses, but right now we don't,' Jack said with false heartiness.

'It's not that we don't care, and please call me Gill,' Mrs Bronson said in short staccato sentences. 'It's just that . . . well, there's no sanitation for her. Not even a tap. Besides, we've heard the most terrible stories. Let her stay for forty-eight hours and she gets squatters' rights. After that you can't get rid of her.'

'You're rambling, Gill. The fact is we don't want her here,' Jack growled.

'Well, let's do the cottage first,' Ari said. 'With the police car outside, the other problem might remove itself.'

'You're English, aren't you, old boy? You might feel a little out of place down at the station. Come and have a drink with me when you've had a look-see. Gill will drive you batty with the inventory. Women!'

Was this some kind of a sex-war? Ari wondered as he followed Gill across a field to the cottage.

'We were expecting a *hairy back* [derogatory English term for a person of Boer descent]. We knew they were sending someone from the Transvaal, you see,' Gill said breathlessly in her nasal, high-pitched English accent, as she led the way across a field to the cottage. 'Thank God you're not. Actually we've never done this before. It's all new to us,' she explained. 'Jack was heavily exposed in the Lloyds insurance mess. We were nearly wiped out. Fortunately we managed to get a bond to pay some of the debts. We're letting this cottage for the first time. We had to sell the horses – well, just about everything, and Jack's fighting to hang on to his business.'

'That's tough.'

'Jack's a property developer,' she went on in a rush. 'I'm a freelance writer mainly for the local press. I get the odd bit published overseas and the occasional short story, which helps.'

The cottage was small, probably converted maid's quarters, Ari guessed, but it was clean and newly decorated with a good shower and bathroom, a neat kitchenette in one corner of the lounge and a separate bedroom. Gill made a big deal out of checking the inventory, right down to the last teaspoon. Once he'd signed his name, the taut look disappeared and she was all smiles again as she led him back to the bar.

The moment he walked on to the balcony Ari was enchanted. Although they were halfway up the mountain, they seemed to be hanging poised over the bay. Dusk had turned the mountain slopes to deep purple, violet mists were creeping over the bottle-green sea, and along the horizon a thick, jagged crimson stroke separated sea from sky.

'I've never seen anything like it,' Ari whispered.

'That's why I moved the bar out here. You won't see a sight like this anywhere else in the world. Heaven on earth! Or it used to be before the marmalades arrived.'

'Marmalades?' he queried.

'We've always been liberal,' Gill confided. 'We don't believe in racialism. Nor does anyone else around these parts, but you can't refer to them as people, can you? I mean, you'd never know who you were talking about. Just breathe the word kafir and you can find yourself in court. Natives, blacks, Africans, whatever – they're all *infra-dig*. We coined our own word. You know, like the golliwog on the old marmalade label. They never guess.'

'Ah!'

'You're waffling, Gill.' Jack turned to Ari with a man-to-man attitude. 'Scotch? Neat? Here you are then. The fact is, lately hundreds of marmalades are arriving daily. More and more . . . they've no money, no work, but they're everywhere. I phoned your station commander to complain, but he said they'll go away when they find there's no jobs here. What do you think?'

'I hadn't actually heard . . .' Ari lied blandly.

'We *never* agreed with false removals and all that sort of thing,' he went on gloomily.

'We've been liberals for years, but the fact is there's a problem round these parts,' Gill added, tossing down her drink. 'Scores of "*them*" are moving in.' Somehow her bar stool came close enough to Ari for their thighs to touch.

'You don't have to echo every damned thing I say.'

Gill smiled nervously. 'There's no jobs for marmalades,' she confided girlishly. 'Traditionally, the fishing boats and factories have coloured crews and workers.'

Jack poured himself another drink. 'It's like a plague.'

The Bronsons seemed embarrassed to find themselves involved in a problem which had forced them into the role of aggressor, having theoretically cheered the victims from the sidelines for so many years.

Could Jack see her knees pressed firmly against his? Ari wondered. Did he care? What exactly prompted her to flirt, with her husband standing two metres away? Putting each other down was the game they played. There was a sense of uneasiness and vengefulness between them. Ari guessed from Gill's behaviour that it was sex-based. Perhaps the shock of Jack's financial loss had made him impotent. Gill was angry and hurt and punishing him the only way she knew how.

He stood up when he had downed his drink.

'Take her with you, old boy.'

Gill? he wondered. 'Who?'

'The woman in the stable.'

'On what charge?'

'Breaking and entering, I suppose. That's more your field than mine.'

Gill led him to the stables, shoulders squared, chin jutting out, arm thrust determinedly under his.

'It looks as if the door doesn't lock. In fact, it doesn't close properly. I'll have to mend it for you,' Ari said. 'That means she didn't break in.'

'So she walked in,' Jack's voice came from the shadows. 'That's illegal, isn't it?'

Stumbled would be more appropriate, Ari decided, staring at the heap of human debris lying in the straw. He crouched beside her and shook the old woman's shoulder, talking to her softly in her native Xhosa. She sat up painfully and began to cough. She was very clean by the look of things. Not a tramp at all. Her socks and shoes, floral skirt, white blouse and headscarf were clean, but crumpled.

'What is your name, my friend?' he said gently, noting her battered old suitcase, two carrier bags and the coat she had been lying on, which presumably was her total wealth. Her frizzy black hair was grey at the temples, her face lined and crinkled and her eyes held the milky glow of an old African. It looked as if she was a recent arrival from the homelands.

'Eunice Tweneni.' She gripped his hands, grateful to find someone who spoke her language.

'You can't stay here. You are trespassing on the property of these people. This is their stable.'

She addressed him politely. 'Where can I go, my boss?'

'I don't know. I have just arrived myself.'

She sighed. 'I was so tired, my boss. I have walked since dawn, from door to door, asking for work. The white people in these parts are enough to make you cry. No one offered me bread or even a drink of water. When it became dark I saw this empty hut and I came inside to sleep.'

'Don't you have any work for her? Not even for half a day?' Ari asked.

Gill shook her head.

Turning to Jack, Ari said: 'She's desperate and she looks clean and reliable.'

Jack looked inquiringly at Gill who flushed angrily. Eunice stood up and waited, her hands folded, her eyes fixed anxiously on Gill's. She was too proud to beg, but needful just the same.

'For heaven's sake, Gill, there must be something she can do,' Jack growled.

'Can she iron?' Gill asked eventually.

'I'm sure she can.'

Eunice nodded.

'Well, all right. A half-day a week, Friday mornings.' She could not have sounded more grudging and Eunice noticed this. She bent her head. Ari guessed that she would not come back.

'Let's go,' he said. As he picked up her suitcase, he saw the look that flashed between Jack and Gill. He could almost hear them murmur 'Bloody commie', as he led Eunice to his car.

Chapter 6

———— ————

Ari sat on the edge of the quay in Silver Bay fishing harbour eating fish and chips out of a packet. From time to time he tossed a chip into the air. The seagulls dived and soared and squabbled around him until he flung them the rest. Then he sat gazing out to sea, waiting for Eunice to finish eating. As always, he was touched by the Xhosa people's simple dignity. She was starving, but she ate slowly, unwilling to show her need, sitting proudly erect. Later, when she had finished and gone down to the sea to wash her hands, she returned and sat awkwardly beside him. Ari began prising her story out of her, a little at a time and with difficulty, for she was a proud woman and unwilling to reveal her private tragedy.

It began as a very ordinary story. Eunice was a Xhosa from the Ciskei and this was the first time she had left her home. She had been married at fifteen to a man from a neighbouring tribe who had paid a *lobola* [bride price] of ten cows for her. After she had given birth to her first child, a daughter, he had gone to work on the gold mines. Year after year he returned on his annual leave and she became pregnant. She gave birth to another daughter, and then another, until she had five girls living and two who had died in infancy in the drought years when she had no milk. When she explained this, Ari felt hot with guilt, but there was no bitterness in her voice. She took hardship for granted.

'One day . . . nothing . . . no letter . . . no money . . . we were starving. Each day I walked to the post office . . . five miles . . . but nothing . . .' Her words were stilted, but her anguished eyes spoke for her. 'At the end of the year, Amos, my cousin, came back, but not my husband. He said my husband had died in a bad fight in the township. He said that it wasn't his fault.'

Ari listened in awe as Eunice spelled out her unending battle to keep her five daughters alive with no source of income and hampered by racial laws that prevented her from leaving her home to seek work in the white cities. She was deeply angry.

'Boss, listen to me. I dug my field with my hands, starting with the sunrise, ending after sunset. I had an axe on a long pole. Nothing else. Sometimes it rained. Sometimes not and the mealies would die and we would starve. Each year the grass was less until you could not see much green . . . just brown. Our cows were slowly starving. Our witchdoctor was no longer so strong. The white people's magic was winning and the rain was going to them. My daughters grew and married. Their *lobola* brought more cows and the grass vanished.' She shrugged and he noticed that her cheeks were wet.

'Oh, boss!' She shook her bowed head from side to side. 'Bitter . . . bitter days.'

Ari lay back on the sand relaxing and adjusting to her way of speech, concentrating to piece together her story, for his Xhosa vocabulary was sketchy, but he grasped the gist of her words.

One day white men had come to her village to show

the people how to grow better crops. They had asked for volunteers and she had been the first woman to accept the new deal.

'You see, boss, I knew their magic was stronger than ours,' she said simply. 'My family turned against me. When I sold our cows to help the grazing, no one would talk to me. Then, when I used the white man's magic fertiliser . . . What a fuss! The *induna* [chief] kept away, because he was afraid to make the wrong decision, but the *sangoma* [witchdoctor] threatened me.'

There was a long silence. Eunice was lost in her thoughts and Ari guessed she was trying to find a way to express herself.

'You see, boss,' she said simply, 'it was too late to turn back. The cows were gone, my family angry. I could not stop now. So when the white men said I must learn to drive the tractor the villagers would share, I learned. Yes, boss. I learned it good. It was the first. That year our crop was good and our grazing returned in winter, and the two cows we had kept became fatter. One even had a calf.'

She smiled with pride. 'Next year the other women copied me, but they had to be brave to face the *sangoma*.'

Her daughters had married young and given birth year by year, as she had, but despite her efforts the rains were miserly and the *sangoma* triumphed. Once again her family was starving, but this time she was blamed for the drought, she told Ari sadly.

The four older married daughters had set off to work in the towns, moving from job to job as the police caught up with them, leaving her to guard the children. It was not hard to imagine her life of toil regulated by the seasons, forever battling against her tribe's backward thinking and the lack of rain. She was forced by law to obey her ignorant tribal chief. Ari felt moved by her courage, knowing that she had set herself resolutely against their traditional tribal culture that saw change as a threat and an insult to their ancestors.

He looked at her, not wishing to stare, but longing to know where she found her courage. Her old, tired eyes were still glowing with hope.

'I was determined, boss. My family had to survive and grow. I want to live in a city and see my children working and thriving and my grandchildren learning your ways in schools and universities. Our ways are dead. Your magic is stronger. We must learn from you.'

Ari felt an inexplicable bonding with Eunice. She had been bound by Xhosa rituals and mysticism which had given her an illusion of security and control over her world, but she'd had the guts to break away from tradition and she had stood alone.

'Eunice, you are a brave woman,' he said softly. There was no reply. Glancing sidelong, he noticed that she was gazing blankly at the sea, her mind far away and he guessed that she was remembering home.

It was her youngest, but tallest daughter, Nonna, her favourite child, who lay moaning on the bed after thirty-six hours in labour. There were no men here, they had left as migrant workers to the gold mines. Only one of Eunice's daughters had remained at home because she was pregnant, the rest were working illegally. Her three older sisters were squatting around her daughter, bathing her face with cool cloths.

Her daughter's moans had risen to screams. Something was horribly wrong. What could she do? She could summon the *sangoma*, but she was unwilling to do this. While she trusted in his knowledge of the mind, his healing herbs and his wise advice, this year alone three women had died in childbirth under his care. No, her daughter needed the white man's magic to survive another day.

When another spine-chilling scream hurt her ears and her heart, she came to a sudden decision. She would brave the *sangoma*'s wrath. Leaving her sisters crouched around Nonna, she set off into the night for the two-hour journey over the hills, but she was in luck for it was full moon. A good omen, perhaps. Putting her fears aside, she began to run.

Dawn was lighting the distant hills when the doctor and his nurse followed her into her hut. The witchdoctor had been called by her sisters. He left in a flurry of sullen glances, waving feathers and stamping seeded anklets, muttering curses as he passed. Eunice lit the primus and boiled water, trying not to watch. Ten minutes later, when she heard the infant cry, she knew she had been right. Her daughter recovered, but the boy was born with a club foot and Eunice felt afraid for the battered little mite. They lived on the slippery slope of survival with no foothold for the maimed. I will be his strength and I will rear him, she vowed.

She called the baby Tabson and when his mother returned to her job, Eunice added the small cripple to her family, now numbering seven grandchildren. He thrived with attention, but as he grew older, she felt his loneliness and frustration. He could not even herd the cows, although he tried, but he loved every living creature and daily she marvelled at his sweetness and his intelligence. The more she spoiled him, the more lovable he became. He was a beautiful child, with a broad high forehead and

large solemn eyes. His brains were wasted here, she knew,
but he was not even strong enough to limp the ten miles
to school and back each day.

The news that his father, Monges, was returning to live
in the Ciskei was as welcome as a swarm of locusts. She
slaughtered a goat for the celebrations with a heavy heart,
for he would be bound to want his son back. Her son-in-law
was a powerful man who had been running the East London
union of dock workers and was returning to take up the post
as local ANC representative. As she had feared, he and her
daughter took Tabson back and set up home. Oh God! The
pain of it.

She became aware of tears trickling down her cheeks
and she tried to wipe them away without the white
man seeing.

'What is it?' the policeman asked her.

'I was thinking about my grandson, Tabson, boss,' she
replied sadly. 'I love that boy so much, but his father was
ashamed to have a crippled son, particularly when a healthy
daughter was born. Rather than let him live with me, which
was too close to them, they gave Tabson to a passing Indian
woman, a Mrs Desai, who paid my daughter two hundred
and fifty rands and promised to send him to school and
cure his leg. What would these people want with Tabson?
I feared the worst and waited for my chance to come and
search for him.'

But too many years had passed before her chance came.
She had the grandchildren to rear, for that was their
custom, and she was penniless. Then, only two months
back, ANC officials came looking for people prepared to
be taken to whites' towns in order to be there to vote in the
country's first multi-racial elections. In return for their free

transport, they were to settle in, search for jobs and remain in the area. Amongst the many men who had queued to go, she had volunteered and her daughter had agreed to mind all the children.

At the last moment, the *sangoma* had come to her hut, his face like summer thunder. 'Because of your faith you will find Tabson,' he had told her. 'Because of your trust in the white man's medicine, his leg will be cured by them. Because you turned your back on our ways, you will die.'

She said nothing of this to the clever young policeman beside her. He was a strange sort of a white man, for his eyes glistened with concern and she trusted him. She had poured out her heart. Instinctively she realised that she had managed to convey to him her immense and implacable faith in her quest. He would help her to find her Tabson.

Twenty minutes later, Lieutenant Gerber listened with mounting impatience to Ari explaining about the old woman's search for her grandson.

'She's not a resident here,' he argued.

'She is now.'

'But why bother? Half the black women in the cities have lost or abandoned one or another child. We'd be swamped if we tried to find them. Why doesn't she go back where she belongs? She hasn't even got a place to stay. I've half a mind to send her packing.'

He was blustering and they both knew that. Last year the Influx Control Act had been repealed and, for the first time in her life, Eunice had the right to live wherever she pleased. Silver Bay was rapidly becoming choked with homeless blacks, but everyone was waiting for orders. The new South Africa was just around the corner, but no one knew the new rules.

'Nevertheless, I'll make out a docket for a missing boy,' Ari said. 'Let's play safe and pretend that the child's white.'

'Oh, for God's sake,' Gerber grumbled. 'Don't give me that sarcastic shit. It's late. I'm going home. You handle it.'

Eunice made a statement and left. Later, around midnight, Ari saw her walking towards the beach carrying a large piece of cardboard on her head and he guessed she would make a makeshift shelter somewhere on the dunes. The sou'easter was coming up and she was having difficulty holding the cardboard. He felt such a strong compassion allied to guilt that he raced after her and tried to thrust twenty rands into her pocket.

To his surprise she refused to take the money. 'Find my Tabson. That will answer all my prayers,' she said simply.

By the following morning, the wind had reached gale force, which was normal for this was the sou'easter season. It was cold in the wind, but hot in the sun. Spiralling blasts hurled the sand over Kate as she took her early gallop along the beach. The bay was ringed with tall mountains, their peaks hidden with thick clouds that piled up higher and higher until they poured over the mountainsides, rapidly falling like waterfalls down sheer slopes, only to disappear halfway, revealing violet-tinged granite outcrops and the dark green of pine-clad slopes. The sky was deep blue, blending to oyster grey at the horizon where sea and sky merged into one. Ahead of her was the harbour where the fishing boats tossed and swayed and bumped each other in the gale. Bursts of white foam cascaded over the rocks.

Turning away from the sea, Kate rode up along the river delta, through pampas and wild strelitzias and clumps of arum lilies still in bloom, bowing and breaking with the force of the icy gale. In moments of calm came the thrilling flush of hot sun. Young guinea fowl, hamerkops and glossy ibis waded through reeds, new frogs leaped from the water and clung to waving rushes. Gulls called, circled, swooped and soared on swirls of air. Then a flock of hadedas rose from a sheltered haven, giving their loud mournful cries, and took off up the valley in search of peace. There were so many flowers: patches of delicate pink and white watsonia, lobelias, marigolds, flax, daisies, mauve scabious, delicate fairy bells amongst the reeds, clumps of wild gladiolus, white china flowers and clumps of purple pelargonium.

Kate took off her clothes and waded thigh deep, enjoying the sensation of sand oozing between her toes. The shiver of icy water brought goose pimples. She loved this place, but her pride of ownership was mixed with guilt. How could anyone own land? How could it ever be truly hers, even though it had been left to her by her mother? It belonged to the birds, and to itself, and to God. She was the custodian and one day she would have it proclaimed a bird sanctuary.

When she emerged shivering from the water, she noticed a large piece of cardboard lying over some sticks almost hidden amongst tall grasses. Strange. She pulled it aside and saw an old woman curled up on a bed of reeds, clutching some luggage, her scarf over her face. Kate tweaked the scarf away with a stick and the old woman sat up blinking.

'Oh my God!' Kate felt angry that someone should spoil this place and crush the flowers, and even angrier to be caught standing naked. She hopped into her pants and pulled on a shirt. 'You're trespassing,' she snarled. 'Who the hell are you?'

'Missus?'

'Who are you? What's your name?' she asked angrily. The woman seemed to be dazed.

'Eunice, missus.'

'What are you doing here?' Kate felt shocked and indignant.

The woman stared up, looking afraid and very sick. She seemed so cold and grey-looking. Watching her flinch, guilt surged. 'Why are you sleeping here?' Kate asked, trying to sound kinder this time. 'Don't you have a place to sleep?'

'No, missus.'

'So where do you work?' she asked, struggling into her tight jeans which were sticking to her damp limbs.

Eunice shrugged. 'I am looking for work,' she muttered.

'Do you have any references?'

'Missus?' She looked baffled, but anxious to please, for her face crinkled with concern. 'No work, missus.'

'Have you ever worked?' Kate thrust her feet into her shoes. What was she to do with her? She lacked the will to throw her off her land.

'All my life,' she said in halting English.

'Where did you work last?' Oh God, what's the use? She shrugged into her jersey and smoothed it down, ruffling her hair with her hands. If she took her home she would incur Ramona's wrath. Then she felt furious at her flash of cowardice.

'Listen. You can't sleep here. It's damp. You'll die.' Her sudden urge to help the old woman surprised her. 'But there is a place – a shelter – well it's a hut really, but it's better than nothing. It's mine, so you'll be safe there, but only until you find something better. Come . . .' The woman remained still, gazing at her with a bewildered expression. 'Come!' Kate shouted and beckoned.

The woman understood some English for she obediently hurried behind Kate and the horse.

'Stay clear of the waterfall,' Kate called over her shoulder. 'And promise not to disturb the birds. There are so many half-grown storks and herons in the reeds. Yesterday I saw a black oystercatcher, which is quite rare in these parts.'

'Yes, missus,' Eunice answered dutifully.

'And there are so many moorhens and coots on the other side of the lagoon, but you must not disturb them. Do you promise? Last year I saw an osprey here, but it never returned. I wish it would come here to breed.'

Why was she babbling on? She knew that the old woman could not understand what she was saying. Was it to drown this strange feeling of reaching out to a stranger? Whatever had got into her?

They came to a wooden hut smelling strongly of creosote, but it was sturdy and warm. Eunice examined the roof and the walls, running her hands over the structure as if she were purchasing it. It was dry and in good condition. Even the window was intact. The woman turned and smiled suspiciously.

'How much?'

She was about to say 'nothing' when she realised that this would be a mistake. The concept of kindness was foreign to blacks. They did not understand it, and it made them feel threatened.

'You must come up to the house and do some ironing every week, and maybe we'll find some more work for you. We'll pay you something.'

'How much, madam?' she insisted.

'I don't know.' Kate was feeling irritated again. 'Ask for Ramona. Tell her Kate sent you. She'll pay you. You see that big house up there on the hillside? That is where I live. You must go there.' The hut was full of spiders. The old woman put her foot on several as they scuttled over the floor, but Kate caught hold of her arm. 'No, don't kill them.'

Kate mounted her horse feeling a fool. She had conflicting thoughts about helping blacks. On the one hand, English philanthropists were fostering a nation of basket cases, Rob had told her that enough times. But then she had a strange, inbred instinct to help those who needed help. Anyway, what else could she do? Leave her to die? She was too old for sleeping out on swampy ground.

Kate felt the old woman tugging at her ankle. 'Yes?'

'Thank you, missus.' She put her two hands together in the African gesture of polite thanks and then she smiled. It wasn't a grimace of respect or the gratitude of an inferior, it was the smile of a friend.

The smile brought a lump to Kate's throat as she cantered home. Leaving the groom to brush down her horse, she sent for blankets and a thermos of hot soup. 'And a broom,' she told the reluctant Ramona. 'And while you're at it a loaf of bread. Oh yes! Why not jam, too? Or peanut butter? Yes. That would be nice. Please hurry.'

When she returned to the hut in her jeep, the old woman was still admiring her home and sweeping it out with her hands. The sweet, seductive joy of being liked made Kate feel absolutely great. She bundled Eunice into her jeep and took her home to do some charring jobs to earn some cash. To hell with Ramona, she thought.

Chapter 7

———   ———

Mandy woke to the sound of a voice whispering close beside her.

'How could you have left me for him, Rose? Why did you do that to me . . . to us . . . You smashed all our promises and our dreams . . . You lied to me, Rose? You said that you loved me.'

A hand fumbled over her breast. Terrified, she began to scream, fighting for her life, scratching at his eyes.

She was thrown back on her bed with a force that knocked the wind out of her. She heard a door slam shut. Footsteps were fading outside her cell. She screamed after them, 'No, don't go. Come back . . . Come back . . . I'll be nice to you. I'm sorry, but I'm not Rose. I'm Mandy! I'm Mandy! D'you hear me? Please . . . oh, please come back. I'm sorry, I'm sorry. You frightened me.' Another iron door clanged shut.

She seemed to fall into a void as she heard his footsteps running and fading. She sensed that he had brought food, because food arrived regularly and she had wondered how this happened. Usually it was there when she woke. She crept across the room and fumbled on the table. Something smelled of perfume and bending down she found it was a single rose in a small jar. Sandwiches, a carton of milk, an apple, some nuts, an orange, a few sweets were lying there. It was always the same. She sat on the floor shaking with shock. She could not eat now. Perhaps later.

When she had pulled herself together, she analysed her new information. From the sounds he made as he left she knew that there were two thick iron doors, one to her prison cell, and another at the top of a flight of stone steps outside her cell. Lately her ears had become more sensitive, perhaps because of the silence, and she could pick out new distant sounds: birdsong, waves thundering on rocks far below, then she heard seals barking. Was she back in the Cape? Or Namibia? If only she had taken more notice of the birds, but even she knew that owls only hooted at night. From now on she would be able to tell night from day and count the days. There was something else she had found out. He thought she was Rose. But who was Rose and what had she done to bring this punishment on her? He must be mad, she thought with mounting terror.

Hannah September scowled through drooping azaleas and ferns and was about to slam the front door in Ari's face when he flashed his ID at her. She looked relieved and led him inside. 'You don't look like a police officer,' she said. It sounded like a rebuke. As usual, Ari was wearing jeans, a T-shirt and running shoes, and Hannah was not impressed.

Sergeants Willis Gous and Albert Smit, whom he had met at the station, looked smart enough to please Hannah. They were sitting at the dining-room table surrounded by empty coffee cups, earphones, notebooks, a pack of cards and Scrabble strewn around. The recording and locating equipment had been pushed into a corner behind them.

'Nothing yet,' Willis said. He was tall, dark, and looked

freshly scrubbed and clean living. Any mother would be proud of him, Ari thought, noting his big blue eyes, curly dark hair and freshly laundered shirt, his trousers neatly pressed with a perfectly straight crease in them. He looked tired. Smit, a big, athletic man, his pin-striped shirt pulled tightly over bulging biceps, mopped his red, sweaty face and his grey eyes turned longingly to the door.

The Septembers' six-roomed home, with its slate roof, picket fence, rambling roses, small swimming pool, double garage and a bricked driveway meandering through the lavender, was a tribute to Hannah's determination to gatecrash white society. Inside, apart from the stuffiness, it seemed that every item had been chosen with conformity in mind. The passage was heaped with packing cases for they had not yet recovered from their move. 'Twenty-eight years of accumulation,' Bill September told him ruefully. 'This is the first time we've moved. There wasn't much point before.'

He meant before the apartheid legislation was dismantled, and Ari could only guess at the joy in their hearts as they kicked the dust of the coloured ghetto off their shoes forever to move into an upper-class white suburb, only to face this terrible tragedy.

Hannah was still a handsome woman, but now she looked on the point of collapse. Nevertheless, she had dressed carefully in a pink silk cardigan, pearls and pleated linen skirt. Her dark straightened hair was cut into a fashionable bob. She kept fingering the pearl necklace as if to reassure herself that her prim personality was still in place. Ari felt that he had her neatly pigeonholed, but her husband, Bill, bothered him, for there was an impenetrable barrier about him. His eyes missed nothing and gave nothing away. He was like the sea, deep and unfathomable. He could be dangerous if sufficiently roused, Ari surmised, but what would stir him to violence? His family? Or his boat? And why was he so cautiously watchful?

'What is it you want to know?' Bill asked, his voice emerging like a growl. 'What else can we possibly tell you? You must realise we've gone over everything, time and again. It's distressing for Hannah.'

Ari hesitated, looking from one to the other. 'Strange business,' he said. 'No ransom demands, no contacts, she just vanished.'

Hannah gave a long shuddering gasp. 'Excuse me,' she whispered as she fled.

Bill scowled at him. 'Let's get on with it.'

'I'll wait,' Ari said. 'I need you both. Of course it's distressing. What else could it be? A mother loses her only daughter and the possibilities are . . . well . . . disturbing, but hopefully not as grim as those she imagines in the small hours of the morning.'

Bill gave him a sad smile. 'She wakes screaming several times a night.'

'Of course. She's a mother. Could I see any photographs and of course I'd like a full description . . .'

'We've done this time and again.'

'I'm sorry. I've just arrived . . . You see I was on this business up there. I've been sent down . . .'

'I understand.'

Bill went outside and came back with an album of photographs.

As he leafed through them, Ari felt stunned by the girl's beauty. She was tall, graceful, beautiful, poised and photogenic. Could she have run away with the man who had been seen by the tribesmen? She looked older than her sixteen years. He chose one good studio shot and took her passport for the description.

Shortly afterwards, Hannah returned carrying a tray with biscuits and coffee. Even in her grief she had not forgotten the lace tray cloth, and the best china. Respectability had been ironed into her at a very early age.

'If I sound unfeeling, believe me, I'm not,' he said to Hannah. 'I have a number of avenues to exhaust. The sooner we start the better. I'll be back time and again. Maybe we'll have to go over the same ground. If you cry, don't run away to hide your grief, it's normal. I'm amazed at your control, but let's get on with it. I want to list the possibilities to you.

'Someone might have a grudge against you and be hitting back through your daughter. Her boyfriend might have kidnapped her. It could be ransom. Then, she might be mixed up in the drug scene. We can't ignore the white slave angle, although they usually go for blondes. We can rule out one common motive for these disappearances and that's satanism, or *muti*. The kidnapping was too planned and it was a very costly exercise for the kidnapper. It cost more than she would be worth for *muti*. It also rules out casual killing or rape. This was a well-planned exercise. The reason why I have been sent to the Cape is because it appears that the kidnapper knew your movements. He knew she was going to the swamps for her birthday and he had the cash to go after her. Mr September, who do you know capable of planning this kind of exercise, who has a grudge against you?'

'No one,' he said promptly.

'Have you made any enemies lately?'

'Only them.' Hannah gestured towards their front *stoep*. 'Take a look here.' She pushed back the sliding glass doors and moist, warm air filled with a cloying stench flooded into the room. Ari could hear the babble of voices, babies crying, women muttering. A sea of canvas, cardboard, corrugated iron and branches stretched before them, not far from the Septembers' house. He had not realised the extent of the camp, but now that they looked down over the bushes they could see hundreds of shacks.

Ari was shocked into silence. Refugees from eroded homelands, the squatters had surged into the towns, but there were no Red Cross parcels, no tents supplied, no blankets, no soup kitchens. Was there any country unkinder than this one? he wondered.

'Good God,' he said eventually. 'So many of them.'

Bill got up with a scowl, switched on the air conditioning and slammed the door shut.

'You see, we sealed off the garden tap,' Hannah said.

'Yes, here's why,' Bill said. '. . . Our water account, two thousand rands.'

'We've worked all our lives to move into this up-market house, amongst professional people.' Hannah never said 'whites', Ari noticed. '. . . And now we're surrounded by "them" and they steal our water, so we are enemies, I suppose, but how would one of them get up to Botswana?' Her voice tailed off.

'Let's get back to drugs. Did she or her friends ever—'

'No!' Bill snarled. 'I told them and I'll tell you, she was a well-brought-up girl and only sixteen. She didn't go out nights. She was always here if she wasn't at school.' He had an explosive type of anger like a semi-dormant volcano that bubbles up meanly now and then, but at most times remains quiet.

'And her friends? She might have known something. Perhaps one of her schoolmates got mixed up in the drug scene, pushing, or smoking. Nowadays they mix in all kinds of stuff, just to get the kids hooked. Maybe she heard something.'

Bill sighed. 'I suppose you have your job to do, but what you're saying is offensive to people like us. She was a well-brought-up young girl, no drugs, no boyfriends, no skeletons in the cupboard. Just a nice kid who was doing well at school. We kept an eye on her.'

'There has to be a reason for this kidnapping, Mr September. I have to ask these questions,' Ari said firmly. He stood up.

'I think we may as well remove our team from your house. A ransom demand is looking unlikely after all this time, but if you hear anything call us at once. There'll be a reward posted, and several TV spots asking for information – you'll be asked to appear, by the way. That sort of thing. We're doing our best, but there doesn't seem to be much to go on.'

As he left, Hannah muttered that he should wait outside for her.

Ari hung around behind the house. Dusk fell and soon he was rewarded by the sight of Hannah hurrying down the pathway. 'Look,' she said, flushing heavily. 'This might be important. Mandy had a boyfriend, a white boy who went to the same school. She was quite keen on him, but Bill broke it up. He forbade the boy to see her – he even went to the boy's mother.'

'Why should he do that? It's only natural that she should go out on dates. She was sixteen after all.'

'We knew he was on drugs,' Hannah said. 'And I can tell you one of the suppliers. It's old Tom up in the village. He's legless, but he used to be a skipper of one of the trawlers once. They treated him shabbily and he didn't get a pension.

He's got to do something to earn a living. I wouldn't like to get him into trouble.'

'All right. You can trust me,' Ari said. 'My job is to find Mandy.'

'The boy's still at school. I went there yesterday. He hadn't heard from Mandy. You see, I thought . . . Well, nothing.' Her face twisted with grief and she turned and hurried back to the house.

As he drove back to the station, he went through the possibilities in his mind. It was ten days since Mandy had been kidnapped and a ransom demand no longer looked likely. Too many young girls had gone missing recently, but they were mainly blonde, blue-eyed and lovely. Mandy, with her black hair and amber almond-shaped eyes was not a candidate for the thriving Arab white slave trade, but he could not yet rule out this possibility. Children were kidnapped daily for sexual perversions and this prospect was still high up on his list of possibilities, but even more likely, to his mind, was drugs. He intended to pursue that angle vigorously. She might have seen something she should not have seen, or threatened to report a pusher.

Every day children went missing in the townships where witchdoctors would pay a fortune. The children's body parts were used for various types of *muti* and they weren't always killed first. It was macabre. He shuddered as he remembered the foul den he had eventually uncovered in the back of a disused Soweto workshop. He had killed the *sangoma* and he didn't have an ounce of remorse. He shuddered. As long as he lived he would never forget the smell of death and the one toddler who was still alive.

As he made his way back to the station, he wished he

could shake off these unwelcome memories that foisted themselves on him from time to time.

It was past 9 p.m. but Ari, who was on call, was sitting in the office watching *Police File* on television. When Willis came in carrying his chess set and two cups of tea, Ari was hoping that an ex-girlfriend, now a programme director on SATV, would manage to graft a last-minute spot announcement into the *Police File* programme.

'Thanks! Just hang on a minute, Willis, while I watch this,' he said. First came Mandy. The girl's photograph would stun viewers, Ari reckoned. Then the blonde announcer smiled winsomely into the camera and described Eunice's grandson and his club foot. 'Tabson Tweneni was last seen in the company of a Mrs Desai from Cape Town,' she said. 'A reward has been offered for any information. Please contact Lieutenant . . .'

Ari jumped up and switched off the set. 'Okay,' he said, feeling pleased. 'That's it! Let's have that chess game you were threatening.'

'Reward?' Willis queried. 'How the hell did you organise a reward for a black kid who was dumped by his parents?'

'From a certain political party's public relations fund,' he replied smugly. 'They want to look to be caring for everyone.'

Lieutenant Gerber strode in, his face twisted with temper. 'What the fuck's going on? Are you crazy? Are we supposed to fork out for every runaway kafir kid? Who gave you the authority to offer a reward? You're supposed to be looking for that September girl. I told you to forget about the black kid. Every second Xhosa woman dumps her child on one or another relative and they go missing all the time. Millions of them! We'll be inundated.' His lips curled into a sneer. 'What are you, some sort of a commie?'

That was the ultimate insult, Ari knew. He stood up. 'Not your problem, Lieutenant. Child Protection took over the case as from yesterday and I am temporarily assisting them . . .'

'Like hell you are. You're under my command here.' But Gerber wasn't looking for a confrontation, merely letting off steam. The door slammed shut again.

Willis stood up. 'How come, Ari?'

'For politics there's all the time and the cash in the world. One of these days we'll be fighting an election down here. Both sides want to show they care. I asked and they said "yes". Now, are we playing or not? I've put a couple of Cokes in the fridge and there's some cold pizza. One of these days we ought to pass the hat for a microwave.'

Ari waited until 2 a.m. but to his surprise there were no calls about the missing Tabson. He hadn't expected to hear about Mandy, but he had been so sure the Indian family would want to collect. He might as well go home, he decided.

It was a strangely seductive night with a hot wind blowing from the north-west, a berg wind they called it here. He took a circuitous route around the suburbs and the harbour, telling himself that he needed to get to know the place, but the truth was he was unwilling to face his empty room. This was a special night, a night for romance, or dancing by the sea, or walking barefoot in the surf, or almost any damn thing except going to bed alone.

The sound of distant laughter and music was coming from a brilliant haze, like a star, on the beach. Ari drove towards it, drawn by a human need to be part of a group. He had been an outsider for far too long. Soon he realised he was approaching Sands, the élite nightspot perched on the edge of the beach. Spotlights lit the outside dance floor where a good jazz band had reached the dreamy stage, with more than a touch of Africa in their technique. Hot music! Hot night! Oh, for someone to love.

The balcony was thronged with dancers, but as Ari slowed to park, he heard a man's voice raised to a shout. A woman shrieked her furious retort and a lithe figure in a long white dress split to the thigh ran out of the nightclub, her glittering hair streaming behind her.

A bright red Porsche started up, jerked forward and zig-zagged along the dead straight road while gathering speed alarmingly. Ari set off in pursuit, but the girl kept ahead. He couldn't match the Porsche. Siren blaring, he raced up into the mountain pass. There were no street lights and the overhanging trees turned the main road into a dark tunnel through which they were speeding. Ari frowned as he watched his speedometer.

Now he was losing her. He swore. The Porsche was out of sight when he heard it skid off the road. The sound of the smash seemed worse than it was. Moments later he caught up and saw that the car had tunnelled into dense bushes and landed in a ditch. The woman in white had managed to climb out and she was hanging on to the bank and trying to climb up. He switched his torch on, dazzling her, and gaped. She was so lovely. He had never seen true beauty in the flesh. She might have walked off the screen to tantalise him. What on earth was this vision of perfection doing in the ditch? Her hair gleamed, her large, slanting eyes glittered with temper, her perfectly shaped nose was covered in mud.

'Help me up, for God's sake. Don't just stare.'

Then he noticed her sad, grieving eyes and the pouting mouth. She was spoiled, rich, drunk and beautiful. Worse still, she had got through to him with her incredible appeal and this annoyed him. He hauled her up by her wrists and examined her for bruises and cuts, but miraculously she was only shocked. Gripping her arm, he saw the glitter of her wedding and engagement rings in the torchlight. Moments later he was manhandling her towards his car.

'Who the hell d'you think you are? Let go of my arm!'

Tripping badly, she recovered, turned and pushed him away.

'You're in big trouble, ma'am,' Ari assured her. 'Speeding, drunken driving and resisting arrest.' He gave her a sharp push and she sprawled awkwardly over the back seat.

'Damn you. Wait until you hear who I am.'

'If you don't shut up, I'll handcuff you,' he said in a low, furious growl. 'Behave yourself.'

'You can't talk to me like that,' she said, slurring her words. 'Oh God. I feel vile.' Then she passed out. Ari radioed headquarters to send someone to tow her car back and to call the district surgeon to the station.

Nearly an hour later Ari was still waiting for the district surgeon to arrive and do the blood tests. Why was it taking so long? This place needed some shaking up, he reckoned. His spoiled brat had recovered enough to pound out her rage in the cells.

'Where the hell is that surgeon?' Ari asked Willis. 'Give me his address, I'll go fetch him.'

Willis shrugged. 'Relax, man. He was out on a call. He'll be here soon. I'm going to make coffee.'

He returned with three mugs and took one of them to the cell.

'Are you trying to sober her up? What's got into you, Willis?'

Willis picked up his book. He was being mulishly uncooperative.

It was 3 a.m. when an unshaven, dishevelled Lieutenant Gerber lurched in, rubbing his eyes and swearing at everyone.

'Thanks for calling me, Sergeant,' he said to Willis, but his fury was directed at Ari. 'What sort of a fucking idiot are you? Don't you know who she is? The Palmas own this town . . . the vineyards, farms, the fish factories, they supply all the jobs. They even own the fucking fish, they've got all the concessions. Sometimes I think they own the government. One word from them and your career is kaput, finished, ended. You understand? Lay off the Palmas. I'm warning you, Lieutenant. Besides, there's no harm in Kate, she's just a little high-spirited. Rob will get her in shape one of these days.'

It sounded like training a dog to Ari. He tried to sound natural, but his voice came out like ice. 'She was speeding and she was too drunk to stand, let alone drive. When the district surgeon gets here I'll prove it to you.'

'So what? They were celebrating her husband's birthday, but the two of them had a fight. Rob's already called me. Look here, Lieutenant,' he grabbed the charge sheet. 'I'm taking over this case. Leave it to me. I like to think I temper justice with mercy.'

'I noticed that with Eunice Tweneni and her grandson,' Ari said cuttingly.

'Watch yourself, Lieutentant. I'm taking Mrs Palma home.'

Two minutes later he led Kate to the charge office, which was the only way out. Her hair was messed, her face mud-streaked, her dress torn and her eyes mirrored all the sorrow of the world, or so it seemed to Ari. She was so lovely. Naturally she would have married a rich bloke. Were all women for sale? he grieved.

'Hang on here, Kate, I want to get your file,' Gerber muttered.

She hung on to the counter and scowled at Ari. She would fight her way out of there if she had to, he guessed. Yet he could almost smell the shame which oozed out of her. She wiped a hand over her sweaty forehead. 'Here.' He handed her a handkerchief. 'Not even a Palma has the right to endanger other people's lives,' he said quietly. 'If you don't care about your own, that is. Women should have more decorum. Have you any idea what you look like?'

'No one was hurt, you chauvinistic pig,' she said. 'And I wasn't speeding much.' She looked him up and down with total contempt. 'Who the hell d'you think you are? My husband can send you packing just like that.' She snapped her fingers.

'But that's your husband, not you. How about you? What can you do – other than getting drunk? If you don't like MCPs then don't hide behind your husband's power. I promise you this, Mrs Palma, next time I'll see you in court.'

Her eyes filled with tears, but she stepped forward and slapped his face hard all the same. Gerber came at a run. 'She doesn't know what she's doing,' he said as he pulled her to the car.

'Bullshit,' was the last word he heard. Then the car door slammed shut and Ari heard them drive off into the night.

What did Rob Palma have over Gerber? he wondered, trying to control his outraged sense of morality. The answer was provided by Willis.

'I guess you're wondering why I called in the commander,' he said, looking shamefaced.

'You could say that.' Ari was tense and cold.

'Gerber fancies he's in Rob's league. Of course he's not, but Palma lets him think that he's one of the men. He goes up to their house to dinner once a month. He and Rob go game fishing pretty often. Sometimes they fly up north on a hunting trip in one of Palma's private jets. We all get boxes of crayfish and snoek or prawns sometimes, but that's not the point. Gerber would never hear the end of it if you disgraced Rob's wife in public. Furthermore, Angelo Palma has enough clout to get him transferred. I felt maybe you didn't feel that strongly about justice, to ruin Gerber's life. He's not such a bad guy.'

'But that's not the point.' Ari felt amazed that Willis should imagine it was. 'Doesn't anyone here care about the law? Isn't that what we're here for?' Willis looked miserable so he let him off the hook. 'Why does Palma soft-soap the police?'

'Dunno! It's not that he needs us, it's just that he likes to have us in his pocket – just in case, know what I mean? He's like that. He flew the bank manager and his wife to the Comores last winter. I guess a guy like that doesn't need overdrafts, he just likes to have control over people. Rob Palma has a real problem: he's in competition with his grandfather. Not much chance of him winning. Times have changed. It's hard to become a living legend nowadays.'

Ari watched Willis with interest. He wasn't as green as he looked and he had a deep intuitive understanding of people. His expressive eyes seemed to mirror his soul.

'So why does a woman like that go and get drunk? She's got everything, it seems, plus a brand new Porsche which she doesn't give a damn about.'

'Everything has its price,' Willis said. 'She's going through a rough patch. Her father's skipped the country and left her destitute, apart from her very rich husband, that is. The news is about to break in the newspapers. She'll be on the receiving end of a lot of flak because it seems her father, Mike Russell, defrauded his company's shareholders. Personally, I wouldn't like to be in her shoes, and I sure as hell wouldn't want to live in Angelo Palma's house.'

'Want some more coffee, Willis?' Ari asked.

'Aren't you off duty now?'

'You've got me interested. I wouldn't mind catching up on local gossip.'

'It's not me that's got you interested. It's her. You'd better forget her. Funny thing is, you look a lot like her husband. I wonder if she's noticed that?'

Ari was hunched over the makeshift kitchen shelf making instant coffee. Boiling water splashed his hand and he swore. That was the second time he'd been told about the resemblance.

It was after 4 a.m. when Ari left the station. He drove along the main road and up the valley to the base of the mountains where he parked and sat on a grassy bank, enjoying the warmth of the wind and listening to the night. The full moon was hovering over the western peaks, casting her sensual light over the forests. A black man came walking down the mountain track strumming some weird toneless musical instrument and singing sadly. The sound clung around him as he passed, mingling with the scent of wood smoke, *dagga*, and the musky tang of his body. Was he a squatter? And did he long for his distant family?

Ari felt tormented by the beauty of the night. Suddenly he felt more alone than ever before. He longed to be part of the valley, to belong in some way, but how? He wondered

at the diversity of the people here and at his own unknown
heritage, for it was here in Silver Bay that Father Richard
Mooney had handed him to welfare for adoption. Did fate
play a hand in one's future? Had he been sent here for
another more subtle purpose? Were his natural parents
living nearby? It was a night for strange imaginings. Again
the owl gave its haunting cry and a night jay screeched as
it soared overhead with a thrilling rush of wings.

After a while he started the engine and drove back to
the coloured village and parked there. Here were smaller
homes, stark apartments and hostels, a school, a church,
a mosque, all mushrooming up the mountainside and
glistening white in the moonlight. A low rumble of voices
came from a nearby house. A cat cried and passed swiftly.
A voice yelled in anger followed by a swift sharp cry and
then silence. He could see the phosphorescence glittering
in the moonlight and hear the murmur of the waves. Then
came the melodious Arabic chant of the muezzin from the
mosque on the hillside calling the faithful to prayer, his
voice reaching far out over the village: '*In the name of God,
the most gracious, the most merciful . . . thee do we worship and
thee do we seek.*'

With the coming of the squatters, the town had become
a microcosm of South Africa, all peoples, all religions,
co-existing by ignoring each other. The whites hung on to
their land and their wealth, the coloureds hung on to their
jobs, their humour and their families, while the blacks hung
on to survival with all the pitiful means at their disposal.
Moslems, Christians and Jews were hardly aware of each
other's religions. Live and let live reigned, but the town
had no cohesion, no togetherness. No soul!

He sat on, wondering, thinking, longing. The wind
caressed his face and ruffled his hair. He could taste

the bitter veld herbs and the dry soil from the dust-driven northern deserts. He ran his tongue over his lips, tasting, smelling, experiencing something which he could never fully understand – his love and his hatred for this tormented land.

Chapter 8

———— ————

The newspaper had been folded and placed beside her plate so that the headlines were clearly visible. TYCOON FLEES DEBTS AND ALLEGATIONS OF THEFT. Kate raced through the report and began to feel very hot. There's no air, she thought, glancing at the windows, but they were wide open. Her chest was tight, her stomach hurting. She felt the hostility surrounding her and glancing up saw Ramona hovering in the doorway. Her eyes mocked her and she was smiling softly.

Grabbing the newspaper, Kate fled to the garden. Had everyone read it, even the servants? Naturally, she thought. Everyone knew of her downfall. How could this happen to her? It was like a nightmare that wouldn't go away. A deep shame spread up through her, like poison threading its way through her body, coursing through her veins, until she was tingling with self-disgust.

If only she could go away, she thought as she re-read the worst paragraph: 'It is believed that twenty million was stolen by the chairman and transferred overseas . . . over one thousand employees have lost their jobs and hundreds of retired investors have lost their life's savings. An inquiry will be held . . .'

The small child in Kate surfaced. She had to go home

and cry out her grief. Discarding the newspaper, she drove to the only place she had ever acknowledged as 'home', her mother's old house. The sight of the silverleaf trees, and the pool where they had spent so many carefree summer holidays, and the summerhouse where they had tea on fine days, brought tears to her eyes. She could hardly see to drive as she sped past the lawns and drew up in the courtyard. Parking beneath the larch tree, she half ran to the porch, but stopped, gasped and almost gagged at the sight of the bars nailed across the door. A liquidator's notice was pinned there, giving the date of the auction as February 13. 'Household effects, furniture, antiques, paintings, toys . . .'

'I must go inside,' she insisted to the security guard sitting on a bench near the door. 'I have so many personal items to collect.'

'Get permission from the liquidators. The address is up there . . .' He pointed to the door. She couldn't get another word out of him. He was like a mute, staring stubbornly at his feet.

She drove to the nearest public telephone and called her lawyer.

'They can't touch your inheritance from your mother, that's the wetlands bordering the lagoon and the river delta, including the old lighthouse,' her lawyer advised her. 'I don't have to remind you of your mother's wishes concerning the wetlands, but the trust was never set up before her sudden death. Some clever dick could probably wipe out that codicil, but I wouldn't want to help you do that,' he said sternly. 'If you want any personal effects from the house I'll gladly ring the liquidators, but they would want to accompany you when you go there. Let me know, but don't just call, come and see me, Kate.'

Kate replaced the receiver and walked slowly back to her car. She drove around the village feeling numb with delayed shock. Somehow her father's disgrace and flight had seemed dreamlike in quality. Today's headlines had made it real. She felt so alone, and now she must face the scorn of the locals. Instinctively she knew that anything she had ever learned would be useless to help her through this crisis.

Her car was running out of petrol. She turned into the petrol station and filled up. She was signing the book when the proprietor, Jim Dawson, came out. 'Hi, Kate, morning to you,' he said. His smile seemed rigid and forced. 'I've transferred your account to that of your husband. That okay? Just ask him to confirm it, please.'

'Oh God,' she whispered.

Her bank card produced no cash. Her stomach turned to lead as she walked in and demanded to see the bank manager. 'Mrs Palma. I was expecting you. Please sit down,' he said, his face a picture of misery. 'Your account is overdrawn. I contacted your husband, but he hasn't rectified the matter yet.'

She stood up wearily. 'Thank you. I'll speak to my husband and sort this out.' His eyes shied away as he stood up.

Rob was in the library talking on the telephone. She waited five minutes while he discussed the cricket. He seemed to be doing most of the talking.

'I must speak to you,' she whispered. He held up his hand and scowlingly indicated that she should keep quiet, while keeping up the same bantering tone to Gerber.

She was starting to get the hang of this power game.

Some strutted and some crawled, depending upon the size of their bank balances. Looking at him, Kate wanted to hate him, but Rob looked pale and tired and more handsome if that were possible. His hair was growing longer, which she loved, but he would have a crew cut soon, she knew. His nose was short and straight, but there was that slight curve where it had been broken in a skiing accident. They had had such good times together. Remembering their last skiing holiday, and the wild times they had had, made her weaken. She smiled at him, loving the look of him, his large expressive brown eyes and his full sensuous lips. Just looking at him always gave her pleasure, but today his sullen, brooding scowl was intimidating. His long brown fingers drummed on the desk as he spoke and his eyelids were slightly lowered, giving him a sinister appearance, like Angelo. Yes, he will look like Angelo one day, she decided.

Eventually the conversation ended.

'Rob, why didn't you help me out with my account?' she asked, a red spot appearing on either cheek. This was the first time they had ever discussed money.

'The manager gave me your bank statement. In the past twelve months you've got through more cash than most people see in a lifetime.'

She felt so shocked, she opened her eyes wide and gaped at him. 'Huh?' She didn't believe what she was hearing. 'But you know that I spent the money on this house. You liked it. You said so. Everyone has said so. I was rich, or so I thought. Practically all my year's income went on this house.'

'More fool you. Angelo won't thank you for it.'

'The paintings are worth a great deal.'

'Try selling them and you'll find out how much they're worth.'

'Surely you could have put cash in my account?'

'I could have, but you didn't ask me to.'

'Must I ask for everything?'

'Well, I don't have a crystal ball, Kate.'

'You didn't need the crystal ball, because the bank manager contacted you.'

'For God's sake don't start a confrontation. I'm busy.'

'I'm broke.'

He took out his cheque book. 'How much d'you want?' he asked coldly. From his tone she might have been collecting for charity.

'Two million,' she retorted.

He flung down his pen in disgust. 'Don't waste my time, Kate.'

'You could at least pay me for the paintings and redecorating . . .'

'Nobody wanted those damned paintings.'

'For the first time in my life, I hate you,' Kate said. The words tumbled out before she'd had a chance to think about them. 'I never knew you before, not really. You're a bully! You never showed me your true side. Now that I'm down you're kicking me.'

'Thanks for your vote of confidence, but you couldn't be more wrong,' he told her coldly. 'I'm working on a scheme to make you independent again, so you can have your own private income. Meet me at my lawyer's office at two. I can't drive you there, I have a lunch appointment in town. Meantime, work out what you need for pocket money and clothes per month and I'll consider it.'

'Consider? You bastard!'

He smiled at her. 'We're an economic unit right now, Kate. You're extravagant.'

Oh, how she longed to punch that superior smile clean off his face.

'Listen, Kate,' he called as she was about to close the door. 'You've been running a bit wild. It has to stop. That's why I'm holding the purse strings from now on. If you want to buy something ask me. Here's some cash to tide you over.' He took out his wallet, shed some notes on to the desk top and left them there. Then he picked up the telephone and dialled. She stood in the doorway, rooted with shock.

'Would you like me to kneel or something?'

'I'm talking, Kate,' he said, his hand over the receiver. 'Grow up, and don't be late for the meeting.'

'Remember, Kate – he who pays the piper calls the tune.'

That worn-out cliché came as a vicious blow beneath the belt – and from Rob of all people. Momentarily Kate's body went into shock while her mind panicked beyond control. She turned towards the window to hide her face. They were at a meeting with Rob's lawyer, Dan, their architect, Bailey, and the quantity surveyor. All three men were looking embarrassed at Rob's temper. The meeting was turning into a nightmare.

Was she powerless because she was broke? And was it always like this for couples if only one were wealthy? she wondered. Perhaps it was just Rob's way.

He mustn't know. He mustn't see my hurt. A month ago he could never had said such a thing. God knows, he'd been trying to get his hands on the lagoon and surrounding wetlands ever since they were married. Now he thought he had the power to force her to give in. Perhaps it had slipped out, she thought grasping at straws. Perhaps he was sorry. She glanced towards him, not pleadingly she hoped, but gazing at him fair and square, but she could see that he was set against her. His face was moulded into sullen fury.

Squaring her shoulders she turned and faced his team of stooges. 'You know my intention with the wetlands and the surrounding fields. They will stay as they are – my father promised Mother. She had planned a bird sanctuary.'

'Spare us, for God's sake! Your father's word is an embarrassment right now. He's caused enough anguish.'

Dan stood up looking upset. 'You're so pale, Kate. Are you feeling all right? I suggest we adjourn and carry on after a break. I've discovered a great little tearoom and it's not far—'

She shook her head. She hadn't realised Dan was kind. In all the devious deals he and Rob had envisaged and put into action she had never seen this other side of him. Bailey, their architect, was looking agonised, too. Rob looked furious, but lately he usually did.

'I want you to understand clearly what I'm trying to put together here, Kate.'

Now Rob was trying another tack. His soft voice was wooing her, but his expression was still moody and with-drawn. He could never hide his feelings, his eyes mirrored his soul. She flinched, thinking that betrayal by those you love was the ultimate anguish.

'You're penniless, except for these damned swamps. The liquidators may try to get them out of you, but if you sell them to the consortium, they can't touch you and you'll have a forty per cent stake in a very profitable venture.'

She shook her head, unable to look at the fixed, aggres-sive, burning need in Rob's eyes. He had to dominate, had to have his own way. Look at him trembling with rage because she dared to thwart him. He always fought dirty.

'For God's sake, grow up, Kate. All this fuss over a few scraggy birds.'

'We're not talking about a few scraggy birds,' she said in a deceptively calm voice that masked her disgust and inner fury. 'We're talking about power – you did all this behind my back.' She gestured towards the meticulous plans drawn up for the deeds office. Months of work. How many months? Three, she guessed. Rob had set his plans in motion and waited for the day when the scandal broke. 'You're not getting the lagoon and that's final. You can tear up those plans.'

For a moment he was too angry to speak. His eyes flickered towards her, momentarily revealing his hurt pride. She had thwarted him in public. He would never forgive her.

'Well, if you want to live on charity all your life.' The hardness was now becoming ominous. 'I guess you'll still expect to get to Europe in July, and go skiing in December. God knows I'm paying a fortune to Avril Pearlman since your account dried up. That's one you're wearing now, isn't it?' He gazed at her suit, and she felt naked. Quivering inwardly, she squared her shoulders.

'Two thousand rands I seem to remember. Be my guest, Kate, sit on your backside at bloody tea parties in your latest Pearlman creations. I'll carry on footing the bills, but I'd have thought you'd have more pride.' Rob looked hard and mean. His brown eyes were glinting with hurt pride, his face white with anger.

'Knock it off, Rob,' Dan said angrily.

Kate blinked back her tears. He was sneering at her. Yes, he was. There was no other word to describe that spiteful leer. What must they think of us?

'Come on, Rob. Kate is your wife. You're being ridiculous,' Dan said. Bailey was staring at the papers he was carefully rolling, while the quantity surveyor gazed at his feet, a picture of misery.

It was starting in her toes and moving up through her legs to her thighs and stomach and way up, engulfing her, a strange indefinable feeling. Self-disgust was the closest she could name it. She had to get out of there fast because she was going to vomit and that would put a cap on her humiliation.

How dare he . . . how could he . . . oh, how dare he? She rushed to the loo and heaved out her loathing and her frustrations together with her lunch. Crouched over the wash basin, trying to rub the splashes of vomit off her Avril Pearlman powder blue suit which had suddenly become a major liability, an awful thought surfaced from the depths: *it was over!* He had pierced her inner secret self, her love place. She knew she would stay for a while. She would fight and plead and try to hang on to her love, but it was over all the same and the sooner she accepted this the sooner the wounds would start to heal. Her knowledge made her angry. If he wanted a fight he could have one. War had been declared.

She stared in the mirror, noting the taut lines around her mouth and the shadows under her eyes. She felt so afraid. Father had always advised her on anything important. Since her marriage, she had looked to Rob to make their serious decisions. Never once had she taken charge of her own life. But Rob was wrong and she was obliged to confront him on a major issue. He would get his own back on her, she knew. For the first time in her life she had to stand on her own feet. But could she? What sort of a person was she really? At that moment she did not know.

She dried her hands and made her unsteady way to Dan's office.

'What are my legal rights concerning my land around the lagoon now that I'm a pauper and dependent upon my husband's charity?' she began.

'Come on, Kate. Relax. Don't make things worse than they are,' Dan said. He wouldn't look at her. Instead he was shuffling files and piling them up, doodling with his pen, anything rather than look at her.

'Rob got a bit uptight, but can you blame him? He's set his heart on this property development – and he's right, it will remake your fortune, well some of it – enough! I'm sure he feels sorry.' He was speaking as if Rob weren't there.

'Are you sorry, Rob?'

'Sorry for what? You don't need legal rights,' he countered. 'You need some common sense. I've had enough of this. She'll come to her senses. She'll have to.'

He went out, slamming the door. Bailey muttered something and left the room and Dan sat gazing at his hands as her dreaded tears began to trickle down her face. She stood up quickly. 'Goodbye,' she choked.

'No, wait!' He sighed. 'You asked me a question. The land around the lagoon is yours and can't be touched by anyone. Rob's wanted it for years, as you know, because he owns the adjoining smaller strip on the west side. Put the two together and you're sitting on a gold mine. As to your rights as a married woman, it is Rob's duty to look after you. However, you are married by ante-nuptial contract, the basis of which is to protect what is yours rather than to compensate you and protect you, should the marriage founder, if you know what I mean.'

'No,' she said.

'Very little would come to you in the unlikely event of a divorce. Now, Kate, don't take it hard. You know Rob.

Once he gets an idea in his head he hates to be thwarted. He loves you and he'll get over this.'

She waved him aside and stumbled out into the glaring sunlight. She had a real need to go home, but where the hell was home? she wondered.

Chapter 9

In the face of this unknown, tough, manipulative Rob, Kate
was beginning to accept the prospect that he and Angelo had
jointly ruined her father. Lunch had been a miserable affair
while Angelo and Rob talked business and ignored her. Rob
was still furious with her. Obviously he intended to punish
her until she gave in over the wetlands.

She cornered him in his library after dinner. The sight
of him looking so remote and unkind hurt so badly. She
longed to throw her arms around his neck and beg him to
make friends, but that would be a tactical error, she knew.
She would be rejected and land up looking a fool.

'I'm busy,' he said.

'I don't care. How dare you treat me so contemptuously.
Neither of you spoke to me all through lunch. You can't
expect me to live in Angelo's house after what he's done
to my father and to me. And what about you? Now that
I've seen your tough side in action I'm wondering if you
were involved in the scam. What was it all about, Rob?'

She waited for an answer, but Rob picked up his
calculator and began pressing the knobs.

'I'm waiting for an answer.'

'I'm waiting for you to get the hell out of here.'

'What's the good of talking to you? Don't you care what

happens to our marriage? Don't you care if I love you or not? I've a good mind to leave.'

He looked up, his eyes blazing with suppressed fury. 'You can't leave, Kate, and the sooner you realise that fact and learn to trust me, the better.'

'Trust you!' she said incredulously.

Was Rob right? Was she locked in here forever? Kate took her notebook and sat outside. It was a lovely summer's day, cicadas chirped shrill and compelling, frogs croaked in the river, the sun blazed overhead and the heat rose from the earth filled with the scent of herbs, flowers and grass, but Kate did not notice. She was scribbling in her notebook. She could probably raise ten thousand rands from selling her jewellery, she thought. If she sold her horse she could pull in a little more. That would last for a while. But then? She would have to get a job. What could she do?

Thoughts of turning to her friends were quickly banished. Really, who was there? The wives of Rob's business colleagues had been pushed together by their husbands and they'd tried to group, but not one of them had contacted her since her father's disgrace.

What if she gave in over the swamps? From then on, she would be totally disciplined by Rob. She would be Rob's puppet. Could she live a life of pretence for the sake of her social position and security? Did she have a choice?

Kate was hurting badly and like a wounded animal she needed to get away. One place that had always been a haven was the lagoon. As kids they'd gone canoeing on the lagoon and picnicked in the gardens. As a schoolgirl she'd held dancing parties there. Mother used to paint in the summerhouse there, too. How kind the world had seemed until she died.

Changing into riding breeches and a T-shirt, and sad-
dling Ponty, her horse, she took a roundabout route over the
sand dunes, letting off some of her frustrations in the thrill
of speed until Ponty's black coat was flecked with foam.
They galloped down to the sea on the rocky side, where
an underground spring of pure water came bubbling out
of the slopes amongst a grove of gnarled milkwood trees.
Ponty knew exactly where to find it. Then they trotted up
the steep slope in the oppressive heat of the afternoon sun.
The horse lathered and floundered until she dismounted
and walked beside him. Crossing over the crest of the
ridge, she turned towards the bay and soon they were
cantering in and out of the sea along the beach towards
the river delta.

Turning upstream, she became aware of noisy activity
ahead. A powerful engine was stopping and starting.
·Shielding her eyes from the glare she peered over the
dunes and saw the head and shoulders of a man driving a
large vehicle backwards and forwards, east to west, in short
bursts of monotonous activity. With each spurt a larger part
of him disappeared from sight. Why was he digging down
into the sand?

Drawing closer she saw that he was cutting a deep trench.
Was Rob going ahead with his condominium, using his side
of the dunes? Strange place for foundations, she thought,
unless he was walling his property from hers? A gang of
labourers was removing roots, shrubs and stones to help
the bulldozer on its way. She trembled as she moved
closer. The bank was changed beyond recognition, shrubs
and flowers were cleared away and part of the wetlands
had been drained. But why had he cut a long trench to
the sea?

He was draining the lagoon. The knowledge came like an

icy blast. Even in Rob's wildest flights of money-grabbing he had never suggested draining the lagoon. All her pent-up aggression came surging out as she gathered speed and raced towards them. The bulldozer ground to a halt as Kate galloped into its path, showering sand over the driver as she blocked his way. A worker moved forward as if to grab her horse, but she threatened him with her crop. The horse reared and the man darted back swearing at her.

The driver recognised her. He flinched as she urged her horse too close for his comfort, waving her crop in front of his nose, almost incoherent with fury.

'Who gave you orders to drain the lagoon? You must stop . . . right now. I insist.'

The driver jumped down. Looking old and shabby in his overalls, he shuffled his feet humbly, peering up at her with anxious eyes.

'Your husband, Mr Palma, begging your pardon, ma'am. He knows what he wants and he issued clear instructions. He told me to cut a channel linking the sea with the lagoon. We've been working on it for seven days. He's been down here every night, so I can't see there's a problem with it.'

Seven days! She felt astounded that he would cheat her so. She could fight him in court, but maybe she would be too late. By tonight they might have cut through, and then . . . ?

'I am ordering you off the land,' she said firmly. 'Leave the bulldozer where it is. Or do you want me to fetch the police?'

She held out her hand for the key, quelling the rebellion in his eyes, willing him to obey. 'Give me the key.'

The driver sweated with embarrassment. He knew his orders, but he was old. He came from the days when non-whites were reared to obey whites – any whites. The labourers had already turned round and were trudging over the dunes towards the estate manager's house.

She stared coldly at the driver and he raised his hand in a gesture of capitulation. She took the keys imperiously.

Wiping his face with his handkerchief he climbed down from the bulldozer and turned away, pausing, uncertain . . .

'Go!' She waved her hand towards the house.

He set off at a trot and soon disappeared behind a clump of trees. She waited another two minutes and then dismounted. Climbing up into the seat, she started the engine and moments later she was driving the heavy digger over the bumps into the lagoon. A thrill of triumph surged through her as the lumbering machine moved deeper into the water. In next to no time the bulldozer was over its tread. 'Keep moving, keep moving, keep moving . . . Ridiculous, but keep moving,' she urged herself.

The water swirled and rose. Eventually the engine spluttered and cut out. She could feel it slowly sinking beneath her, down and down. Still she sat there, trembling, feeling shocked and unreal, but something had changed. She had changed. She had made a statement, perhaps the first major rebellion in her life. *She'd done it!* Okay, so it was mad, crazy, but she'd done it. The water was lapping around her feet and it was hard to stay on the slippery seat because the vehicle was tilting over. She was knee-deep and hanging on. Finally it toppled and she slipped into the water and set off for the bank, trying not to stand until she was in the shallows, because she knew from experience she would sink into smelly slime, it had happened so often when she was a kid.

Some youngsters were dog-paddling out now and clambering on to the sunken bulldozer, yelping with joy.

Heady with triumph she remounted her horse and moved downstream to the sea.

It was then that she heard the poignant pained cry of an Egyptian goose. Searching through rushes, knee-deep in mud, she found the bird caught by one wing in a trap. She freed it, holding its head carefully for its neck was strong and its beak sharp.

She was bent over it, trying to bind it in her T-shirt when the blow came. The pain was vicious, momentarily stunning her. The bird escaped, fluttering into the bush, and as it fled, a filthy, undernourished squatter raised his knife to pin the maimed bird. She struck up at his arm with her crop, knocking the knife from his hand. As the bird scurried into thick bullrushes, the man grabbed the knife and turned on her, wild fury in his hungry eyes. With surprise she realised that he wanted to kill her. Impossible! She had been expecting an apology. As the blade flashed down, she hung on to the hilt, using every ounce of strength she possessed, his hard hands against hers. She could feel the blade cutting against one palm. Her hand was slippery wet with blood, but she was strong, too. She panted with the effort of grasping the weapon. How he stank. She pushed him hard and he stumbled backwards, taken by surprise. Now she had the knife. She lunged at him in a fury, hitting his arm, and his blood spurted from a bad cut.

'Keep away!' She climbed painfully to her feet, feeling weak and giddy, but as she stepped forward she saw that she was surrounded by squatters and they were angry. One of the women stepped forward, her face a mask of envy and hatred.

'Necklace her!' she shrieked. 'Necklace her . . . necklace her.' The cry was taken up. A ragged boy ran forward and flung an old tyre towards her.

For a moment she was paralysed with fear. Then she ducked, fended it off and grabbed her horse. Leaping into the saddle she used her crop and the horse reared up over them as she tried to frighten them into making a gap in the circle. If she could force a path through to the lagoon she could swim for it, but they were circling like wild dogs.

Two shots cracked nearby, followed by a sudden silence. The mob began to disperse as a man approached. It was that bossy policeman. He looked so authoritative, despite his jeans and T-shirt. Suddenly he didn't seem so bad.

'Thank God you came,' she called out.

'Don't panic. It's not over yet,' he said as he came closer. 'Some of them have firearms. Say nothing. Get off your horse quickly and keep between it and me. Take my arm.'

He walked her towards the sea, and now, for the first time, she saw the extent of the new squatter settlement. How did this happen so quickly? she wondered, feeling depressed. Virtually overnight. Despair was settling in as she kept walking, hanging on to the policeman's arm, and her horse. Hostile eyes, grim mouths, wailing babies and the stench of sewage. 'Oh, how terrible,' she muttered. 'Where will they all go? How can I get them off my land?'

'You can't. This is our latest problem and no one knows how to cope with it. They have squatters' rights, you see. No one knows what to do. We have no instructions to act.'

A stone fell and the lieutenant stopped and shouted at them in Xhosa, their home language, lecturing them, calming them as he walked her through the shacks towards the sea. At the edge of the settlement he paused. 'There! You're quite safe now. You can ride home. I'm sorry for what happened, Mrs Palma.'

How did he know he was needed? And why was he apologising for *them*?

'I'm coming to the station. I want to lay a charge. My husband is trying to drain the lagoon . . .' Her story spilled out in breathless gasps. Then she asked: 'How did you know I was here?'

'Your husband's driver ran all the way to us. He's too afraid to go back to the manager. He wanted a witness to prove his innocence. I came because I was afraid you might run into trouble. You see, your husband ordered several shacks to be destroyed this morning. You didn't see them?'

She shook her head.

'About fifty shacks were knocked down nearer to the road beyond the trees. I think he did it as a test case to see if he could get away with it. The situation is a new one and times are changing. No one knows what's right and what's wrong. Tempers are running high in the camp. War has been declared. Until the squatter matter is settled I must ask you to keep away. If you want to go there, I'll provide a police escort.'

'Can I lay a charge? I have to get a court order preventing my husband from draining the lagoon and trespassing on my side of the river,' she hurried on. She knew her actions would lead her into chaos, but she was afraid to hold back. Once the lagoon had been drained there would be no wetlands. Nothing to fight for, no birds, no shrubs, no need to have a sanctuary.

He frowned and cleared his throat. 'It's a civil matter, Mrs Palma,' he said. 'I expect the council and the environmental blokes would come out on your side. It would be costly. Let me speak to your husband.' His face was impassive as he stared at her. 'Are you sure you understand the implications of all this? If so, I feel I can persuade him not to continue.' He looked over his shoulder, scanning the bushes, but the danger seemed to be over. 'In the long run he can't win. The case would probably take two years and cost you both a fortune. Meanwhile your private squabble would become public property.'

Just like that? Could she really take refuge behind a stranger? Why not? Besides, he didn't seem all that strange any more. 'Yes, please speak to him,' she said. 'Tell him I approached you to lay a charge of trespassing and despoiling my property.'

'If that's what you want.'

'Yes,' she said firmly.

Rob was in a temper as he watched Kate ride her horse into the stables. He had endured an embarrassing ten minutes on the telephone being lectured by someone he considered both intellectually and socially his inferior.

'For God's sake, Kate, grow up,' he snarled. 'Did you have to involve the police? Look at you. You're covered in mud. You've been brawling with a squatter . . . I hear you attacked him with your crop and knifed him. Whatever plans I may have to get rid of the squatters have been ruined by your public brawling. Why can't you leave things to me? Do you think you can drive them out single-handed? Are you crazy or something? D'you know what that bulldozer cost?'

'He tried to kill me,' she said. 'He trapped an Egyptian goose and I let it free. So he attacked me with his knife.' She held up her hand. 'I need stitches. Do you think I go around armed with a knife to attack people?'

The fight went out of Rob like air out of a pricked balloon. He became deathly white as he grabbed her hand

and called Ramona to fetch a doctor. Then he rocked her in his arms. 'Oh, my God, you could have been killed. Keep away from there. D'you hear me, Kate? I forbid you to go there. You might have been killed. Don't fight me, Kate. I'm doing this for you. Don't you understand? It's for your own good. I want you to be rich in your own right. Leave everything to me. I'll turn you into a millionaire. I'd do anything for you.'

'I won't let you drain the swamps, Rob. Believe me, I'll stop you. Don't you see the swamps are only part of our problem? You are denying me my own individuality. Can't you see that?'

He let her go abruptly and stood staring at her, his eyes filled with anguish and bewilderment. 'Don't fight me, Kate,' he whispered. 'You don't know what you're up against. You see, I have this problem. I never lose.'

Chapter 10

———— ————

Mrs Allingham from the Wellington retirement home was eighty if she was a day, everyone said, but she acknowledged only sixty-nine years and refused all help with her shopping. She set off on Saturday morning, wheeling her basket on wheels, her handbag hidden under a blanket. She had hardly gone halfway when a black man leaped out of the shrubbery by the river, knocking her down. Grabbing the blanket and the bag, he ran off towards the shops. Mrs Allingham scrambled to her feet and set off after him screaming: 'Stop, thief! Stop him. He's got my bag. Stop that man.'

Jack Bronson was buying meat. He and Robin, the butcher, came running out of the shop. A quick glance set Jack's adrenaline surging as he leaped forward to floor the man with a flying rugby tackle. The squatter scrambled to his feet looking dazed. He made a quick lurch to escape across the road, but a young, long-haired student sent him reeling from a punch to his jaw. He fell to the ground and tried to rise, but Jack kicked his feet from under him. At once he was surrounded by a jeering mob of hating whites and coloureds. The terrified squatter pulled out a knife as he backed to the wall.

'He's got a knife!' Jack yelled. 'Look out everyone.'

Jack's world had turned a hazy red. 'Fuck you, man,' he

roared. He kicked at the knife in sudden rage, and followed up with a hard punch to the squatter's stomach. The black keeled over, gasping. Seconds later Jack was on top of him, backed by a shouting, kicking mob bent on murder.

'Kill the bastard!' the cries rang out. Everyone had his own personal vendetta against the squatters. They all fought to land a kick or a blow on the crouched figure.

Emanuel Fernandes, sitting opposite on a park bench, stood up with a sigh. He retrieved the blanket, bag and basket and returned them to the old lady. She was leaning against a tree trying to get her breath back. She looked all out, so he offered to help her to the shops, sensing her reticence.

Mrs Allingham was not used to associating with riffraff stinking of *dagga*, but her heart was palpitating, her breath almost gone, and the truth was she felt a little dizzy, but she wouldn't like anyone to know that, so she hung on to his arm and put a brave face on it.

Ari, who was driving back from the harbour with Willis, braked and came running. He caught a few punches as he fought his way to the centre of the mob. Pushing the bloody, pulped mugger between him and the wall, he fended off the attack.

'Let him go. That scum deserves what he gets.'

Someone punched him hard on the shoulder. It was Jack, looking swollen and ferocious. He'd gone crazy. All of them had; their faces were gargoyles of fury. All their pent-up frustration at the unwanted invasion was focused on beating the squatter.

Ari grabbed his gun and fired into the air. 'Come on, guys,' he shouted. 'Back off! Are you crazy? Let's find some sanity around here.' He let out his breath with relief as the villagers backed off.

Robin was the first to recover. 'He mugged Mrs Allingham,' he told Ari. 'That's her bag there. Knocked her clean over. It's a wonder she didn't break her hip.' They were harmless now that the anger had been shocked out of them. Ari had seen it all before, the crowd mentality that could turn a man into a mindless cog in a hating machine. Moments later they were laughing and clapping each other on the backs. They moved as a body to the nearby café, and Ari, who was holding the skinny, moaning squatter in a half-nelson, took him back to his car, handcuffed him and drove him back to the station. Leaving Willis to charge him, Ari went back to rustle up a few witnesses.

Meggie's Tea Room was just around the corner from the station, and the crowd had gone there. He squeezed into a space by the door and saw Mrs Allingham munching a cream éclair, a look of contentment on her face. A swarthy man with a ponytail and weird clothes was sitting opposite her looking bemused by his sudden acceptance. About a hundred locals had pushed their way into the café and they were either sitting or leaning against the walls.

Meg, the proprietress, was leaning over the counter, grey hair smoothed back, her chubby red face wreathed with concern as she listened to her customers' woes. She had taken on the role of chairman of this impromptu meeting, between making tea and totting up bills. Her two young student waitresses were looking hassled by the unaccustomed pressure.

'What are we going to do – there's hundreds of them,' Robin called out.

'More like thousands. From my stoep I can see the full extent of the catastrophe.' It was Hannah September who spoke and a sudden silence followed her words. Everyone knew the Septembers were the first coloured family to move into the most exclusive area in Silver Bay. Those from poorer parts resented this, while her neighbours shunned her.

'They've been stealing water from my hosepipe,' she went on bravely. 'I didn't mind at first. I thought the poor people have got to have water, but my bill was over two thousand rands. I've had the outside tap cut off. My husband's thinking of building a wall.'

Meg passed her a cup of coffee and she sipped it, wondering if she had said too much. Cecilia de Beer, painter and sculptor, one of the bay's famous inhabitants, looked up at Hannah and smiled sadly. 'I'm sorry about your daughter. I hope they soon find her,' she said. 'Come and sit with us.' The women shifted up to make room for Hannah at their table.

Roger Binks, estate agent, stood up. 'Listen, we have a real problem,' he said in a strong cockney accent. 'Perhaps you don't realise that it can get much worse than it is. I've heard the council are considering finding a permanent place to house the squatters. Silver Bay would become a no-go black spot. For those of us who love this town it would be the end.'

'Jesus! What would that do to house prices?' Bronson groaned.

'My house is my pension,' Ruth, a widow who worked as the hotel's receptionist, called out. 'All my savings are bound up in it. I can't afford a property crash.' A chorus of voices murmured their agreement.

'My daughter was scared half to death when they stole her bike and dumped her off it. She was badly bruised,' Meg put in. Now the babble of voices had risen so high no one could hear anything.

'One at a time,' Meg called out, banging a spoon on the counter.

'Did you hear about this morning's rape?' Barbara Jones, local Animal Welfare representative, stood up and the women sighed. Once Barbara started you could never shut her up, but this time her words were riveting. 'The horse was injured and it had to be shot. That's why I was called in. A young girl of eighteen was dragged off her horse halfway up the mountain and raped by four men. She's suffering from shock and trauma. She's not from Silver Bay, merely riding here. She's in hospital, I believe. Look, ask him. He should know,' she added, pointing at Ari.

Ari stood up unwillingly. 'The young woman claimed to have been raped by four men,' he said. 'We haven't found them, yet. I must advise all of you to go walking and riding in pairs at the very least. If you have guns take them with you – if you know how to use them, that is. This morning Mrs Palma was attacked near the beach, but she fought off her attackers and escaped.'

'What are you going to do about it? That's what the police are for, isn't it – to protect us? So turf them out.'

It was a question Ari had been dreading. He understood their fears. The town was like an over-heated boiler ready to blow. Right now the locals would do anything for a posse of old-style Boer police with their clubs and guns, the ones they had vilified in the past. They were all suffering from the trauma of multiple losses. Overnight, their way of life had vanished. The present was scary, with muggings, rapes, murders, housebreaking and overcrowding on beaches and parks. Children could no longer ride their horses and bicycles up and down the valley, the beaches stank, the mountainsides were littered with tins and empty bottles. Fires were a daily hazard to the wild life, housing prices had fallen dramatically, and no bonds were being granted until the 'squatter problem' was clarified. Even shopping was hazardous as hungry beggars hung around outside supermarkets. Shop owners kept their doors locked and barred and shoppers rang to enter. Virtually overnight, Silver Bay had become a 'no-buy' area.

The rich would survive as they always did, but his heart went out to the poorer whites, for they were trapped in South Africa. No one knew what the future would bring, everyone dreaded the inevitable changes. Apartheid had been swept away and no one knew what would take its place. Ari felt their fear and their insecurity, but as the law stood now there was nothing to stop half of South Africa from camping on the mountainsides if they wished.

'It's no good calling for help. We have to defend ourselves.' Dave Craw, the dentist, stood up on a chair and called for silence. 'I'm for driving them out of town.'

'Hey, Dave, get down. I spend my life looking up your nostrils,' Roger yelled.

Dave stepped back on to the floor. 'Listen to me. We're not the first town to be targeted like this. It happened up north near Randburg in the Transvaal. The council had an empty farm designated for almost a million blacks. Didn't any of you guys read about it?'

'Yeah, I read about it,' Bronson called out. 'White residents blocked the only road to the camp and manned the blockade day and night. After a couple of skirmishes the blacks and the council gave up.'

'There are only three roads into Silver Bay,' Dave went on. 'We could guard our town so easily. I'm for action. I'd like to get a crowd together to drive the buggers out. You all know where to find me.'

'Burn them out.'

'Kill the bastards.'

'Contact me,' Dave called. 'We'll make a plan.'

Pandemonium broke out. Meg called for silence.

'Listen,' she yelled. 'We need to have a formal meeting, a chairman, that sort of thing. This place is too small. We must get all the ratepayers together – the sooner the better, so keep in touch. Jack, will you find a venue?'

He nodded. 'I'll be in touch.'

As the impromptu meeting broke up, Ari ordered a cup of coffee. After a while Meg came to sit next to him.

'I'm in a lather,' she said. 'I've never done anything like that before. What are we going to do? If they turn the lagoon into a black settlement I'll go bust. The tourists wouldn't come here. Most local businesses would go bust, too.'

Ari had no answer for her. 'Change is the only sure thing in life and it's seldom painless,' he said, squeezing her shoulder. He insisted on paying for his coffee and left.

Chapter 11

As the days passed, Mandy's hearing grew ultra-perceptive. She could hear the engine of the vehicle *he* drove from far off, and from the revving, she knew that she was hidden in some remote bushy place, which could only be reached by driving over difficult terrain. She would hear the vehicle being parked somewhere far above, then the doors would be slammed and there would be nothing more for almost fifteen minutes, until the birds stopped singing. Then she would hear footsteps, heavy breathing, the top door opening, heavy feet descending, her hatch would be flung open and bread and milk and sometimes apples would be thrust through.

When would *he* come next? 'Please come, please come,' she whispered into the darkness. What if *he* never came? What if *he* were killed in an accident? She began to pray for his safety. *He* was her lifeline. She felt like a foetus connected to *him* by some weird umbilical cord. Why? Who was he? And why had he called her Rose?

The next time the voice came whispering to her in her sleep, she lay very still, trembling, but not fighting as the hand explored her body.

'I love you, Rose,' a hoarse voice whispered.

'Who are you?' she said.

Silence, and then the hand was pulled away.

'Don't stop. I like being stroked,' she forced herself to say. 'Who are you?'

'You know who I am.'

'How can I know for sure in the dark,' she said. 'Bring some light so I can see you.'

'I am your fiancé, but perhaps you had forgotten.'

'How long are you going to keep me here?' she asked, trembling as she felt his hand on her breast again.

'Until you love me as you used to. Until you swear that you are sorry. Until you promise to marry me and go away with me. But first you have to be punished for what you did.'

She began to cry. 'Please don't hurt me,' she sobbed.

'Oh, Rose, I would rather die than hurt you.'

'But you *are* hurting me. I shall die here. I hate the dark. You must let me go. You must. I'm not Rose. Surely you realise that.'

His knees cracked. She heard a swift intake of breath, like a gasp. The rustle of fabric was moving away. There was a footfall closer to the door. 'No . . . No . . .' she screamed. 'Don't leave me.' She flung herself towards the sound. As she fell forward, her hands felt something soft. She hung on and heard fabric tearing. 'I shall die here. Take me with you.'

The reply struck terror into her. 'Our little game can only be played in the dark, my Rose. Outside, you would be Mandy and I would have to kill you. Do you remember the boatman?'

The door slammed shut, the footsteps left.

She began to tremble at this new concept of her kidnapper. He was not mad, just evil. He knew in his heart that she was not Rose. 'Why? Why? Why are you doing this to me?' she shouted, beating the door with her fists.

'You have to be punished,' the voice called mockingly through the door.

Chapter 12

———— ————

Over the previous two weeks Ari had spent every spare moment questioning Indian leaders in temples, mosques and community centres. Why should an Indian woman foster a black boy, a non-believer and cripple into the bargain? they had asked. That was the question that plagued Ari, too.

Willis had spent his day off checking non-white schools and Ari had spent the afternoon questioning Hilda Ackerman, mother of Simon, whom Hannah had named as Mandy's ex-boyfriend. Ari had felt amazed at Hilda's degree of denial as she flatly refused to accept that her son took drugs of any kind, yet Simon was clearly exhibiting withdrawal symptoms. Pale and defiant, he had remained firmly behind his mother's chair, clutching her shoulders, his dark eyes glittering with fear, his body shuddering every few minutes. Ari sensed their fear, but he could not get through to them.

'I don't want to punish you, Simon,' he had said. 'Loosen up. I can help you get out of this mess.'

Eventually the tension of their situation, whatever that was, had got to Hilda. 'Leave us alone,' she had screamed. So he had left, but he was still wondering if he should have stayed. Something was badly wrong.

*   *   *

The trouble was, he was tired. At St Patrick's church orphanage, his last call, the principal suggested the boy might be living on the streets as so many were, so Ari drove to Home Shelter, a charitable house set up in Cape Town to provide a twenty-four-hour shelter for young vagrants.

It wasn't difficult to find the long barnlike building at the top of Cape Town near the Malay quarter, but it was past 9 p.m. by the time he got there. A crowd of skinny, scruffy kids was hanging around outside and a fat, friendly woman was trying to shoo them in.

Ari wandered in and gazed round the long room lined with bunks on either side. There was a canteen at one end and a makeshift office at the other. Sitting behind a trestle table was a man who looked as if he belonged behind a bank's boardroom table. His face was long and bony, his brooding grey eyes peered myopically through thick lenses, his blond hair rose up in a frizz from a widow's peak. He looked very bright indeed and his voice was cultured as he introduced himself as Archie Goodman, the manager. He'd gained his Ph.D in sociology recently, Ari soon learned, and he planned to devote the next few years rehabilitating street kids. In next to no time Ari had parted with forty rands. 'The church supplies the building, but we exist solely on charity,' Archie explained apologetically.

The street shelter was an open house. Kids came and left as they pleased. To Ari, the sight of them was like a punch in the guts: glazed old eyes, snotty noses and voices that could only whine. At least here they could eat without prostituting themselves, and sleep in safety. Food and a bunk with a blanket were always available, day or night, he was told. Their conversation was interrupted scores of times by new arrivals and kids fighting.

'I'm worried because no one's come forward to claim the reward,' Ari explained in a sudden lull. 'Tabson wasn't kidnapped so there's no crime involved. Why don't they come?'

'So you fear that he's seen or heard too much to be handed over to the police and that you might have endangered his life with your spot announcement on the TV?'

'Exactly,' Ari said slowly, unhappy to hear his fears voiced so succinctly. 'It seemed a good idea at the time, but now . . . But there's still the hope that he's run away, or that they've moved up country.'

'We had a boy with a club foot. I'd only recently arrived at the time. Give me a few minutes . . .' Archie opened a cupboard and brought out a shoe box. 'These cards are for the unknowns,' Archie told him as he fingered his way through them.

Ari was so tired. The squatters had brought a spate of housebreaking and muggings and he'd been working all hours. He began to nod off.

'Are you listening, or what?' Archie said.

'Sorry.'

'Late one night about eight months ago a boy with a club foot asked for shelter. He was suffering from malnutrition and all the attendant ills that go with it. Next morning an Indian woman pitched, claiming to be his mother's friend. She said she'd been asked to mind the boy so that he could go to school. I warned her of police action if she didn't feed him properly, but I had to let him go.'

Ari felt a surge of hope.

'I was worried about the woman. Something didn't ring true – but I didn't have time to do anything positive. I tried to check on him later, but she'd given a false name and address. The trouble is, I'm short-staffed, there are only three of us and we don't have any state subsidies. It's bloody impossible. To tell the truth, I spend half my time on the telephone begging for donations.'

He sighed. 'I made a note here that the boy had mentioned that he often went over the rocks at night collecting mussels when he was hungry. He said he could see because of the lighthouse. I assumed that he lived somewhere near Kommetjie.'

Ari left feeling elated. At last he had a lead.

Ari had to sleep. He went home and called Willis to get over to Kommetjie and check on the Indian community. Then he threw himself on his bed. He woke unwillingly to the sound of the telephone ringing. It was Willis.

'I think we're on to something,' Willis began, while Ari struggled to pull himself together. 'There's only one Indian woman here and her name is Patel. Her son, Sam Patel, is a nasty hybrid from a half-Zulu, half-Xhosa father, whom she never married. Sam's disliked by everyone, from what I've heard. He owns a grocery store supplying the local coloured areas, but this seems to be his cover. Lately Sam's got very big, new car and a motor launch. The neighbours claim he's into drugs while his mother runs the shop. They had a crippled boy working there. Evidently he helped push *dagga* plugs on street corners, pretending he was begging, but he hasn't been seen for the past two weeks. Sam left his house at midnight and drove to Silver Bay harbour where he keeps his big game fishing launch. He saw a local drug pusher called Tom and left a few minutes ago. I'm waiting here at the yacht club. I guess you'd like to pay Tom a visit.'

'You're a genius. Yes, I would. Thanks, Willis. Be right with you.' Ari glanced at his watch. It was three-thirty. He couldn't believe he'd slept five hours, it seemed more like five minutes. Thrusting his legs into his jeans and pulling on a T-shirt he left. He needed a shave and a shower, but it would have to wait.

As he approached Tom's cottage, which overlooked the canning sheds, he heard the muezzin's chant calling the faithful to prayer. The hut was pitch dark, the door unlocked. Ari flicked on his torch and walked inside.

'Under the bed . . .' a sleepy voice muttered. 'Fifty rand a plug.' A match flared and the lantern was lit by an old man blinking and tired. He pulled himself to a sitting position by holding on to a rope dangling from the ceiling above him. Then he fumbled to rearrange the pillows behind his back. Ari guessed he had a gun there. He pounced, seized the gun, and put it on a table at the end of the bed.

'You'll get this back when I leave,' Ari said, pull-ing out the box. He studied the plugs of *dagga*. They were beautifully bound in leaves and shaped like small Christmas crackers. He smelled the leaves. It was good stuff, not home grown, but probably from Lesotho. He broke one open and scattered the contents on the wooden table, scraping it aside, sniffing cautiously, then he turned to Tom. 'I'd like something stronger . . . Where d'you keep it?'

By this time Tom was sitting up and watching him with a puzzled expression. His face was square and very lined, his bluish-brown eyes were set wide apart and he was very near to white, Ari saw with a shock. There was a large cyst on his forehead and his hands were gnarled with arthritis. The expression in his eyes bothered Ari. Like a child he put his trust in strangers. Even now, when he realised he had made a mistake, he had not extinguished a glow of hope. Yet there was sadness, too, and the grief of innocence. He had to be pushing eighty. What a life, Ari thought and compassion surged.

'You've been misinformed, sir. Pure *dagga* . . . the best. That's my line. It's costly, but it's pure. You want something stronger try someone else. You owe me for that one you've just ruined. By the way, who are you?' He had a soft voice and he spoke beautifully with a strong Irish brogue. Tom puzzled Ari.

'A friend.'

'A friend with an official expression.'

'I could still be your friend.' Ari stared at him meaningfully. 'I'm very good to my friends,' he said reaching for his wallet and ostentatiously taking out some notes.

'Don't play games with me. I'm too old. Besides, I'm not the talkative type.'

'Listen,' Ari moved swiftly to catch hold of the old man's artificial legs. He swung one round. 'Make a good cosh,' he said. 'I could do with a cosh.'

The old man bit his lips, but his eyes were watery red. 'I sit around watching people,' he said, 'and I make my own inferences about them. I'm hardly ever wrong. You will never break that leg. You couldn't do it. Not unless you lost your temper.'

Ari glanced at him in surprise. 'Listen, Tom. Help me. You've had your life, or just about. When you lost your legs you got a raw deal and I guess you've had to battle to survive. But you can look back on better times, times when you had your legs. Not so? Now this kid I'm after has been crippled from birth. His family chucked him out because they were ashamed of him. I want to find him. I think some Indian is using him as a pusher and I think they're about to bump him off. I may be too late.

'I look at life this way, Tom. There's two sorts of people

in this world: those who care and those who don't. The first kind are my friends, talkative or not, and the rest are my enemies – and I demolish my enemies. Which side are you on?'

'Put those legs down, for fuck's sake.'

'Tabson delivers this to you, doesn't he?' Ari fingered the dried leaves.

'No.' Tom looked genuinely affronted. 'He's Patel's boy and Patel's stuff is questionable. I wouldn't touch it.'

Inferences! Questionable! Strange words for an old, legless coloured pusher. Ari longed to know more about Tom.

'Tabson comes here when Patel wants information, but this time he came himself, I expect you know that.'

'Yes.' Ari felt a bolt of fear surge through him and Tom saw it and frowned.

'He was looking for a skipper who'd keep his mouth shut and do a special job – no questions asked.'

'You knew someone . . . ?'

'Of course. If you ever let on I told you anything about him, that will be my lot. He's a nasty bastard. Savage as a mamba and twice as slippery.'

Ari put some notes on the bed. 'I know a man makes better stuff than this,' he said, running his hands over the rough wooden legs. '. . . padded, no pain, special joints. Costly, but for friends that's a small consideration. Of course, it would take a bit of saving.'

'What's your name, boy?' Tom asked hesitantly.

'You can call me Ari.' For some reason he wanted to befriend the old man.

'Well, Ari, I told Patel that Jean Graux would be down at the quayside mending nets on the *Enterprise* fishing trawler. The gale will be too strong for them to put out today. Graux is on contract to Palma's outfit. As I once was. Listen, boy,' he said, his blue eyes wide with concern. 'Be careful. Patel is treacherous and dangerous.'

'Not as dangerous as I am,' Ari said, meaning it. 'Where does Graux live?'

'On his boat, eight metres, green bows and it's called *Tralee*. It's out in the bay. Jean can't often afford harbour dues. He's from Mauritius and he's a fine sailor.

'Remember what I said about Sam Patel. Watch out!'

Chapter 13

The sky was lightening over the eastern horizon and the awakening wind was whipping the dark sea to a frenzied white foam. Dense clouds piling up on the mountaintops warned of a bad gale.

By the time Ari had commandeered a dinghy with an outboard, the first sun's rays were turning the clouds crimson. The boats in harbour strained at their moorings and twanged and knocked as wires were stretched and metal knocked against metal. He zoomed out through a flock of seagulls circling over a shoal of fish. The waves splashed in his face and he was soaked by icy spray within the first few seconds. He saw a great white mass of a whale looming up and he gave it a wide berth. As he tied the rubber duck to the bows of the *Tralee* a face peered down and a hand waved a wooden club in his direction.

'What the fuck d'you want?'

Ari couldn't place his accent. Jean Graux was burned almost black and his skin contrasted strangely with his bushy white beard. He looked a fit fifty. His eyes were huge, lustrous and of a deep blue colour, his features were European, a long bony face, pinched, pointed nose, thin lips and prominent cheekbones. He was wearing a red vest and khaki shorts.

'Police,' Ari said, waving his ID. 'Can I come aboard?'

'I suppose so.' He stood back and scratched his beard and then he stretched. He'd just woken up after a hard night's solitary drinking, Ari guessed. 'What's the problem?'

'Papers. Just checking. Yours in order? D'you have permanent residence here? Work permit?'

It was just a guess, but it seemed to hit the target. Graux turned pale.

'They're somewhere around,' he said.

'I can check on the computer back at the station.'

'Look. Can't we talk? It's just a case of a renewal . . .' Graux was sweating despite the cold.

'I'm a friendly sort of guy,' Ari said. 'You help me and I'll help you.' He pulled out his hand gun. 'Put your hands behind your head and go down first,' he said. 'Sit down.' He handcuffed him to the back of a chair.

When Jean had quietened enough to listen, Ari pushed his gun back in the holster. 'You aren't going to get hurt. I just want you to listen to reason. You ever met a guy called Sam Patel?'

'Dangerous son of a bitch.'

'Tell me more.'

'Why should I?'

'Maybe because I can have you deported, or perhaps because he's waiting to see you down at the harbour. He's going to put a proposition to you that will involve murder. I'm after him and if you agree to help him, he'll think you set him up when I pitch. If you say "no" to his proposition he'll have your number anyway. Best thing is to let me go in your place. Now tell me all you know, even hearsay.'

'It's all hearsay because I never met him. Patel's grown very rich lately taking out consignments of drugs to boats going up the east coast, I've been told. Mozambique,

Uganda, Kenya, et cetera, a huge market. They say he ships the stuff in from Lesotho and other places, perhaps the East. Who knows?'

'There's more than drugs involved this time. I need to be you for twenty-four hours. That's all. You're going to get paid for a job that I'll do. I'll even hand over the cash to you, or as much as he gives me in advance.'

'You don't have to handcuff me.' His gaze was steadfast and there was a hint of humour in his eyes. Ari liked him. 'I wouldn't get mixed up in something like that. Go ahead, but unlock these damned things first.'

'Can't do that,' Ari said. 'You might tip him off. There's too much at stake. See you later.'

'And if the boat founders. It might hit a whale – even a storm . . .'

'I'll see you later,' Ari called. 'That is, if the boat doesn't founder.' A string of curses rang in his ears as he clambered down the ladder and started his outboard engine.

Mending nets was a job Ari knew nothing about. After fooling around for a while, he decided he looked as stupid as he felt. He'd do better to clean the deck. He was swabbing down when a short fat figure hailed him from the quay.

'Jean . . . Jean Graux?'

'Who wants him?' Ari frowned at the man standing on the quayside. There were times when Ari felt he could smell evil. Perhaps he'd developed a sixth sense, or was he cracking up as the psychiatrist had warned he might? He could not shake off a sense of fear and revulsion. Patel's features showed his roots, his skin was almost black from his Indian side, his nose was pure African. His hair was greasy ringlets hanging around his face. His lips were thick, his face long and bony. A weird concoction of diverse races.

'Are you Jean Graux?'

'I'm busy,' Ari said turning away.

'Too busy to earn five hundred rands in your spare time?'

'Maybe not.' Ari put down the bucket and swung his legs over the gunwale to land on the quay. Patel came up to his shoulder. His breath stank of ginger, curry and garlic. He was polluting the fresh sea breeze and his gold tooth flashed in the first sunbeams.

'I have to meet a boat three miles out at midnight and my skipper's sick. I don't have the know-how.'

'Plenty of skippers for hire around these parts,' Ari said. 'Why come looking for me?'

'I heard you're discreet and reliable.'

'I try to keep out of trouble. If trouble comes looking for me it's costly. You don't look rich to me. You can fuck off.'

'One thousand,' Patel said, his fierce Zulu eyes flashing fire.

'What's the job?'

'I told you. Take me out to meet a boat and keep your mouth shut and your eyes on your work. Okay?'

'For a thousand?' It wasn't difficult to sound contemptuous.

Patel hesitated, turned away and walked off, but after a few minutes turned back. He really was a *nasty*, Ari decided.

'I'm not a rich man,' he whined. 'The job's not that profitable.'

'Five hundred now and a thousand at the end of it,' Ari murmured.

Finally Patel brought out his wallet and counted the notes, his fat little fingers caressing each one.

Ari thrust the wad into his pocket and they arranged to meet on the quayside near Patel's game fishing launch just after dark. Ari waited an hour and then bought a couple of Cokes which he took out to Graux with the cash. 'Quit moaning,' he said. 'It's good pay for sitting on your arse all day.'

'You going to leave me tied up here?' he grumbled.

'Yes.'

'Then fuck off,' he said.

Ari lay on a sandy ridge overlooking the harbour, toasting his half-naked body in the fierce heat. He was off-duty, but a nagging worry kept him on a high dune overlooking the bay. He could see the only entrance to the harbour and the quayside where Patel moored his deep-sea, game-fishing boat, the *Arabica*. At 1 p.m. he was surprised when Patel's van arrived. Two men unloaded some heavy sacks and carried them on to the deck. They were sweating and straining in the hot sun. Two minutes later Patel emerged from the van and went on board. Suddenly the boat shuddered, moved and parted from the quayside. Minutes later it was zooming towards the harbour entrance.

Stumbling through sand dunes towards the car park, Ari struggled to make his brain think clearly: what have I done wrong? How did he get on to me? Where the hell is Tabson? His frustration was overladen with guilt.

Reaching his car, he switched on the two-way radio to headquarters. How can I expect them to send a police launch and a helicopter for an unknown black child? I can't even prove he's on that boat, and even if I could . . .

Moments later he was speaking to Gerber. 'There's a massive drug cache *en route* to East Africa aboard the *Arabica* which just left harbour. I need help.' Gerber was both angry and unwilling to stick his neck out. 'An informer. Yes, I'm quite sure . . . They'll probably liaise somewhere outside the three-mile limit . . . Contact the drug squad. They can pick me up in the car park opposite the harbour entrance. I counted four sacks of it. Yes, a fortune. Absolutely sure, Gerber.'

Each second passed with agonising slowness as he waited. He felt sick with fear for letting Tabson down. And if there were no drugs, what then? Who cares? Just let me get Tabson back.

The call came. A helicopter would pick him up shortly. A police motor launch was coming round from Cape Town. He must pinpoint directions. 'It's on your head, Fletcher,' Gerber's voice boomed.

'Right,' Ari whispered, switching off the set. He had to trust his instinct. Tabson was on that boat. He knew it.

The pilot and two police officers picked him up a quarter of an hour later. Were they too late? The thought was almost more than he could bear. They wanted to talk about the drugs, but he was terse and uncommunicative. After all, he was only guessing. They swung out over the bay, looking down on clear turquoise waters with darker patches here and there. They sighted the fishing launch at ten minutes past two, approximately eight nautical miles north-east of Silver Bay. Ari let out a whoop of triumph. The police boat was fast approaching, still out of sight, but in radio contact.

'Keep away until our guys move closer,' Ari told them. 'Then you'll have to let me down quickly.'

'Why risk your life? We have competent men in the launch. They can handle it.'

'He'll ditch the load. Besides, there's an informer. I must get to him first. I can't take the risk . . .'

'We'll have to drop you damn fast or they'll wipe you out. Give it a miss. Far too risky,' the police officer said. He looked concerned.

Ari donned the harness and shortly afterwards fell through the trap door. For a moment he lost orientation tumbling and spinning madly out of control, completely unaware of the sky or the sea or how far he had fallen. The wind tore at his face and forced open his mouth and eyes, searing him with cold. He wanted to scream, but the wind knocked his breath back. The rope straightened and the jolt seemed to hammer his body to a pulp. He was sure every limb had been torn loose. Something had gone wrong. Had he jumped too fast or too soon, or what? One of these days, he thought, I must learn how this is done. Moments later he hit the sea with a stunning crash but the rope snaked up and he caught hold of the boatrail as he shot up past it. He was yanked up further and his arms almost left their sockets. Then he remembered the lever and as the harness fell away he landed with a massive jolt on the deck.

They hadn't shot him. Why? Logic told him he should be dead. He sprawled crablike to the nearest shelter fumbling for his hand-gun. Feeling the familiar smooth barrel lent him some security. Where the hell was everyone?

Down in the hold, destroying the evidence? That thought propelled him to the hatchway. Ducking and diving, he leaped down, scrambling behind the nearest cover, hearing the plops of bullets hitting the wood panelling behind him.

There were three of them. He fired in rapid succession and two fell. Patel was bending over a trapdoor set into the deck trying to force a sack down. Moments later Ari was dragging him back, whipping his face with the pistol.

His hands were round Patel's thick throat, choking the life out of him, fumbling for the sack, *but the sack had gone*.

'Where is he?' he yelled.

'Who?'

Patel screamed with terror as he pushed him headfirst down into the trapdoor, thrusting his head under the sea. He hauled him up choking.

'Where?'

'Who . . .' he gasped, pointing to the hatch.

'Where's Tabson?'

'Never heard . . .'

Madness set in. Ari brought his pistol down with a sickening crunch on Patel's forehead and the blood spurted. In a curious, enforced slow motion, Ari began to punch him, feeling the tacky flesh squelch under his fists.

'Where's Tabson?' he yelled at the pulp. 'Where is he?'

Then Ari heard the police boarding the boat. Taking a chance he dived through the trapdoor into the sea.

Icy cold shocked him, but a split second later he forced his eyes open. He was floundering too near to the surface, unable to go deeper, knowing he was too late. Then he caught sight of a dark shape slowly drifting, caught along in the boat's momentum. Ari propelled his body downwards with a massive surge, grabbed at the sack and caught it. It was heavy, lumpy, like the body of a boy. He fought to get it to the surface.

Moments later he was screaming up to the deck. 'Help me. Help me.' He kicked frantically like a snared fish, trying to hold the sack out of the water. 'Will somebody up there help me!'

A shout came. Then a rope. He grabbed it with one

hand and moments later, two guys were down in the sea with him, holding the sack until it was hauled up.

By the time he reached the deck, the boy was out of the sack. One of the men was giving him the kiss of life while the other cut the ropes that circled his body. He must be Tabson, Ari thought, seeing the deformed leg and foot. 'Too late,' a policeman grunted, but then Tabson's body was gripped by a convulsion.

'Try harder,' Ari gasped.

Tabson took the first shuddering groan and soon he was vomiting up sea water. As relief set in Ari began to swear quietly. He made his way stealthily down to the hold where Patel was coming to. 'Sam Patel, you're under arrest for dealing in drugs, kidnapping and attempted murder. This is from Tabson.' He gave him one massive punch and cut his fist on Sam's gold tooth. Sam's head snapped back and he fell unconscious.

He heard shouts behind him. His arms were pinned. 'I needed to hit the bastard,' he muttered.

His hands were so swollen, it was difficult to write up his report. When he did he was cagey, not wanting to lie, but grateful that the cargo had contained crack, mandrax and *dagga*. South Africa was rapidly becoming the drug centre for Africa. Consignments were being loaded on to vessels going up the east and west coasts and Patel was one of the large-scale operators. Of course, he was out on bail.

Eunice came to collect Tabson. She took Ari's hand in hers and said, 'Thank you. I never thought that I would ever learn to love white people.' Tears were running down her lined old cheeks as she took Tabson's hand in hers. He saw them walking along the dunes to a cave, or a bush, or wherever she'd found a little shelter.

Chapter 14

——— ———

It was New Year's Eve, but there was no joy for Kate at the dinner table. Angelo ate in sulky silence, but from his baleful eyes Kate gathered that he was in a towering rage and that she was responsible. Rob took up the cudgels on his grandfather's behalf.

'You gave that old squatter woman blankets!' he accused her, his eyes red with fury. 'And food. And you told her she could stay on our land.'

'My land,' Kate murmured.

'It's the same thing.' His eyes were daring her to contradict him. 'You even gave her a hut to sleep in. Did you know what you were doing? You were giving her and her bloody tribe *squatters' rights*!' The last two words shot out like bullets from a cannon.

He leaned forward, brown eyes glazed, staring at the candle as he often did when deep in thought. He looks like a Roman gladiator in one of those old Hollywood epics, she thought. Give him a whip and he could drive the Christians to the lions.

No one was filling her glass, so she reached for the decanter.

Rob turned to his grandfather: 'There are hundreds of blacks there. The police can't do a damn thing and neither can we. Last week I demolished fifty shacks, but they rebuilt.'

He sighed. 'I've seen the Minister. The situation is fraught with hazards.' He scowled as he tackled his steak. 'Squatters can only be evicted if you find alternative accommodation and pay for their transport. Every damned item they own has to be packed, transported, listed, down to the last stick, and moved. The trouble is, there is no alternative land. We'll have to find a way to drive them out,' he said without a tremor of hesitation.

'This is all your fault,' Angelo said, turning to Kate.

'It was one old woman – and she was supposed to stay for a week,' she whispered. She frowned at him. 'I was helping her . . . but only until she found work.'

No one was listening. Is compassion a crime in this household? she wondered moodily. How had they found out about the old woman? Obviously Ramona, her *bête noire*, had told them. Just look at Angelo's face. He's gone purplish with rage. How can his face turn dark like that? Look at his eyes! They're almost hypnotic. She drained her glass again, wishing she could stop feeling like a whipped dog.

'You didn't think,' Rob said. Then he sighed. He was always making allowances, as if she were a child, and this hurt more. 'She brought her friends, relatives, tribesmen and their friends and relatives. She had no choice in the matter. The blacks think "group", not individually. Besides, she has to obey her *induna*. If you can't think for yourself, then for God's sake, ask me.'

He was so damned patronising.

'Why should I? It's none of your business,' she said as icily as she could. 'It's my land. Mother left it to me.'

'She wanted a bird sanctuary,' Rob said. 'She sure as hell didn't want the place full of migrants. They're trapping all the birds and eating them. I doubt there's one left. It's prime land, worth a fortune.'

'But it's mine.' She slammed down her glass and the wine made a purple splash on the tablecloth. All at once Ramona was there shaking salt on to the stain. The old bitch had been watching and listening to everything. 'Go away,' Kate snapped.

'What about our land on the other side of the lagoon? D'you think we're not affected?' he went on pompously. 'We're at risk. The council intend to buy up so-called "suitable land" at municipal valuation, which means for a song.' He looked genuinely hurt. 'When I asked for a definition of "suitable land" they said places where the blacks have settled in. This would create black spots in the midst of a luxury suburb. Those civil servants don't live around these parts, of course, or they wouldn't dream of choosing Silver Bay. If this happens, all the surrounding areas will lose their value. Billions of rands are at stake. The government has abdicated all responsibility. They're running scared. The blacks have all the power. Imagine putting a permanent squatter camp in the midst of a high-class area. So there you have it.'

'Nevertheless, you can't run my conscience for me. I was brought up to help people . . . to care . . .' It sounded trite, even to her own ears.

'For God's sake, Kate, stop canting. And don't push your father's caring down my throat. A whole lot of shareholders found him most uncaring.'

'You fight dirty . . . yes you do,' she said unhappily. 'What has all this to do with my father?' She lit a cigarette, deliberately breaking the Palma law of no smoking at the table, enjoying the expression of distaste that spread over Angelo's face as he stood up. He gave a funny sort of half-smile, as if to acknowledge her declaration of war, then he left.

'Fuck you, Kate. You're a walking disaster area. You know smoke gives Angelo asthma.'

'Good. Hope he chokes to death.'

'I find you disgusting. We won't go to the Lilfords' party.'

She had forgotten. She glanced at her watch. 'I'm going. You do what you like.' She stood up. 'Okay, Rob, so I made a mistake,' she acknowledged with a bitter smile. 'I'll tell you this for the last time. You and your vile grandfather are not going to change me one little bit.' She thumped her fist on the back of her chair. 'I may be Mrs Palma, but I'm still me. I'll never become so poor that I'll let a poor old woman sleep out on swampy ground. She would have died soon. D'you understand, you self-centred pig? Some people think of other values besides money.'

She turned to glare at him, but suddenly he was smiling, and so sweetly. That was the bitter bloody end. She burst into tears, which spoiled her line, she thought sadly, as she struggled to pull herself together. Finally she fled to the bedroom.

Watching Kate's pathetic exhibition, Rob felt pity stirring. Poor little thing. He guessed what had suddenly brought her tears. Only yesterday she had begged him to pay for three paintings she had purchased some time back for the lounge. He had tried to work out how to temper power with mercy, so he had examined them at great length, paid for two and returned one to the art gallery. This way she had her way, but she learned who was the boss. In future she'd remember to ask for his approval before spending his cash.

She had sat on her bills for weeks until the tradesmen

became threatening. Then she had dumped them tearfully on his desk, explaining her predicament. As if he cared. It was his husbandly duty to pay her bills, but she had to acknowledge the cost of their marvellous lifestyle and understand that *only he* could provide it for her.

Her tears had moved him, for he had never seen her cry before. At the same time he realised that he'd hit on her Achilles' heel. She had been brought low by her loss of financial independence. Funny that! Most women would spend all your cash without giving it a second thought. He decided to give her a few minutes to recover. Then he followed her upstairs, hoping they would make love.

Why was she scowling at him? She looked so cold. 'I paid all your bills,' he flung at her. Adding: 'You might say thank you.'

She gazed at his reflection in the mirror, her face a mixture of humiliation and rebellion. 'Thank you,' she said.

'What are you going to wear tonight?'

'Does it matter?' she asked, suddenly quite sad. Triumph shot through him and became a physical urge.

'Oh God, Kate. It matters to me. Why d'you think I paid your dress account? Ten thousand rands! And I gave them another ten to last you a while. I want you to look good. I want every man in Silver Bay to lust over Mrs Kate Palma, the best-looking bird in Africa. You'd better find something pretty sexy for that much cash.'

She looked away.

'Come on, honey. Pull yourself together. Don't give the squatters another thought. Don't worry about it. Just call me "the fixer". Yeah! Worry about me. That's your job – looking after me.'

Rob watched her carefully. She was the most beautiful woman he had ever seen. Sometimes he thought he would die of anger when she took it into her silly head to take risks and endanger herself. Take the time they were scuba diving in the Pacific. She'd gone right up to a scorpion fish to take a picture and afterwards she'd swum off into the wreck alone and he'd lost sight of her. At the time he had worried about that scuba-diving instructor. Had she? Did she? Did she ever?

He felt himself slipping fatally into his fears and suspicions. This always led to a fight, and invariably he was wrong. He shuddered at the force of his jealousy. She was his. Yet lately Kate seemed to be on a mission to self-destruct and this worried him. Equally crazy was her desire for a child. He wouldn't let her have one. He couldn't bear the thought of that marvellously smooth, unblemished belly getting daily more swollen, and her perfect breasts being ruined with milk. She had to stay as she was, perfect in every way. Even her toes were lovely, but her looks wouldn't last long if she persisted in smoking and going in the sun.

He walked up behind her and began to massage her neck and her shoulders. He slipped her gown down to her waist and kissed the nape of her neck, cupping his hands around her breasts.

'Let's make love, Kate.'

'I don't want to make love,' she said. Reaching for her hair dryer, she began to shape her hair, giving him a blast of hot air.

'I hate women who use sex to get their own back.'

'Sex is part of love,' she retorted. 'How can I feel sexy if I don't feel loving? How can I feel loving when you're such a bastard?'

'It takes two to fight, and I can't see what the one's got

to do with the other. You've got fuck-all else to do besides screwing me,' he said, his face a picture of childish temper. He stood up, baleful and sulky. 'It's your duty. What else do I ask you to do? I work like a dog for you. Good God, I just paid twenty thousand rands to Pearlman. Doesn't that deserve a fuck?'

'You want me to whore for my clothes and my keep?'

'Your terminology, not mine. I don't give a damn what you call it. I want to make love to you and I think I deserve it.'

She dropped her gown and walked naked across the bedroom. She lay on the bed, opened her legs and closed her eyes. 'Twenty thousand rands is a lot of money. You better enjoy it,' she whispered.

Watching her, Rob felt a surge of alarm. What was happening to them? He loved her so much, but still, maybe she should learn who was boss. Yet, all his instincts told him to back off and leave her be, but the sight of her naked body turned him on and now his need was uncontrollable. She was so lovely, and she was his. Even lying down, her breasts stood up full and lovely with rosy nipples and perfectly soft white skin. He adored her slim brave waist, those beautiful square shoulders, her long white neck and her silvery blonde hair lying all over the pillow. He put one hand over her left breast and felt her shudder. She began to tremble.

'Little goose. We're married. How can you talk about whoring?' He stared down at her and she opened her eyes and looked into his. Once again he felt that he should not, but he wanted her badly. He sighed and clambered over her.

Kate was filled with a sense of self-disgust, but even worse was the way her body reacted to him. She fought to dampen her ardour as Rob thrust into her, but soon she could stand it no longer, an unquenchable need was driving her into a frenzy.

'Oh, Rob . . . Oh, Rob . . .' she heard herself mumbling. However much they fought, the sweet thrust of his love still moved her traitorous body to untold heights of rapture.

Astonishing bliss, each time it was unbelievable – each time always like the first time. She began to move, thrilling to the rhythm of his lovemaking as he nourished her with the maleness she craved. At last he gave a long shuddering sigh and she felt his body stiffen. She came with him and then she was crying softly on his shoulder: 'Oh, Rob . . . we mustn't fight, we mustn't spoil this. Oh, Rob . . . Rob . . .'

She curled up beside him, but he fell asleep. Soon he was snoring. Kate sat up and looked at him wistfully before getting out of bed. It would be so easy to capitulate. But if she did she would become a mindless zombie, a decorative asset to hang over Rob's arm, a mere extension of him. She felt heavy with sadness. She still loved him, but war had been declared.

Chapter 15

———— ————

It was New Year's Eve and Ari was frustrated, lonely and homesick. He had come to the Lilfords' party with Willis, but he was a stranger here, and he didn't feel like making the effort to pick up a girl. He was in a bad mood, trying to cope with a feeling of inadequacy. Willis soon found a partner and dumped him. Ari preferred to drink alone. He had no idea of the whereabouts of Mandy, nor any idea why she had been kidnapped, and he was frighteningly aware that he had nearly lost Tabson. Just seconds later and he would have been too late.

He had bungled the entire search from beginning to end, endangered the boy's life with his TV spot and arrogantly believed that Patel had been taken in by his act. Lastly, he had been forced to hand over a starving boy to his penniless grandmother. They were without shelter, sanitation, or food. God knows if he'd survive. He shuddered, tossed back his drink and took another.

But that wasn't all of it, he knew. He could sense his nightmare creeping up on him, setting his skin crawling, his gorge rising, his hands sweating and his whole being clogged up with shock. He shuddered. He could smell the damp leaves, see the dark hole. But why was it always the same dream? A dream or a memory? He knew he was going to have a bad night.

And Tabson? Would he ever recover from the shock of being bound and tied into a sack and flung into the sea? Or would he carry the memory of Patel's greedy eyes for the rest of his days? As Ari stared at his glass, he felt his temper rising. It was always the same when his black moods took hold of him. He wanted to hit out and fight back . . . Longing to fight off the despair of feeling helpless in the face of evil. Why was he like this?

Moody and depressed, Ari began to probe his failures, prodding at the pain, unable to let go . . . the kids he hadn't saved festered like abscesses in his memory. Which was worse, he wondered, the deliberate cruelty of whites, or the mindless ferocity of the blacks' witchcraft?

Someone was staring at him, willing him to look up. He felt this so strongly that he scanned the faces along the bar. 'Oh fuck!' he muttered. There was Mrs Palma. Her clinging designer dress, low-cut and shimmering, glowed lustrous and vaguely green in the light, as her eyes did. There was something so unashamedly sensuous about her. Yet she was so young and healthy and sort of pure-looking. Her beautiful, haughty face seemed angel-like compared with the other women. The contrast was baffling.

Some oaf had his hand on her shoulder and he was bending over her, peering down her neck. So where was her husband? She was beginning to look nervous. She beamed him a glance of coy invitation. A flirtatious come-and-get-me expression flitted slyly across her face. This annoyed him. Why did she feel that sex was her only appeal?

He stood up, feeling sad to leave his drink and his planned night of forgetfulness. As he walked over to her she smiled, but she seemed to be looking past him towards the night, longing to get out of there. Relief showed in her eyes, but her mouth curled into a derisive smile.

'Like the genie in the lamp you always appear when needed,' she said. She shot him a sad smile. Why sad? he wondered.

'Where's your husband? I haven't met him yet,' he said.

'Sleeping,' she said briefly in a tone of voice that told him to let that topic alone.

'Hey, Kate,' her companion said. 'Come and dance with me.' He caught hold of her arm and she lurched, off-balance, spilling her champagne on her dress.

'Leave her,' Ari said. He pushed the man back, took Kate's arm and led her out of the french doors to the garden.

'Oh,' she breathed in deeply. 'Wonderful fresh air. I hate parties.'

'Then why did you come?'

She turned, looking surprised. 'It was a matter of honour,' she said.

Her companion followed them out. He stood there watching them moodily, as if making up his mind. He was tall and powerful, but grossly overweight. His face was a fat podge, but out of it his large and shrewd blue eyes burned with jealous indignation.

He put his hands in his pockets and rocked on to his toes. 'Hey, Kate. I thought we were going to even up the score . . . you know, pay me in kind.'

'What score, Jim?' Kate asked stupidly.

'I lost a packet through your old man's scam . . .'

She gasped. Her mouth was still open as Ari pushed the hulk back fast. He lost his balance and tumbled into a large flower pot.

'Why you . . .' He stood up, wiping his backside, mustering his energy to make a lunge.

'Don't bother,' Ari told him. 'You might get hurt.'

It was a deliberate taunt and he felt bad about it, for the bull-like figure complied by charging him, head down. Ari sidestepped and brought the heel of his hand down hard on the back of his neck. The hulk looked puzzled and rubbed his neck, blinking and seemingly dazed. Then he threw a punch that caught Ari on the side of the face and really hurt. Next moment they were at each other's throats until the hulk collapsed with a sigh on the floor, ruining Ari's revenge.

'Oh God! They all blame me,' she gasped.

'He's jealous. That's all. He was looking for a way to wound you because you dumped him inside. I guess he won. You're wounded. Silly to let him get through to you,' he growled.

'Let's get out of here,' she said.

'I'm going home.'

She stood staring at him anxiously. 'I have to talk to someone.'

'Why not try your husband,' he said angrily, not really sure why she made him feel so antagonistic.

'Whenever we meet you're in a temper. What are you like when you're not?' she asked.

'The way you carry on you'll never find out,' he said gruffly. 'Why does a girl like you come to a party without her husband?'

'We'd arranged to come together, but he wanted to sleep. Why are you so old-fashioned? Why shouldn't I?'

'I was brought up old-fashioned,' he said.

'I don't want to go home, Lieutenant,' she said. 'I'd better go back inside. I need to find someone to talk to. I just don't know what to do any more.'

'I'm a good listener,' Ari said, regretting his brusqueness, 'why don't you pour it all out on me? Perhaps we could get some coffee somewhere.'

He drove her around Silver Bay, but it was 1 a.m. and everything was closed. Finally he dropped by the station, where he had stowed some sparkling wine in the fridge for the guys on duty. There was one bottle left. He took it back to the car.

'Over there,' she said, pointing across the bay, 'is a lovely place to park.' He started the car and drove in that direction. 'I came out to think,' Kate said. 'You see . . . it's like I'm at war with everyone – even Rob – it's almost as if Rob's glad I'm broke and squashed because it gives him all the power . . .'

Ari was only half listening. The night was fabulous and so was the view. He took the narrow road cut high into the mountain, overlooking the bay. The moon cut a silver swathe into the black waters, and the granite peaks were darkly silhouetted against the moonlit sky. Occasional sandy coves shone in the moonlight and he could see ships' lights twinkling in the bay.

Kate was intent on pouring out her life's history, he noticed, for she began at the real beginning, when her father met her mother. It's going to be a long night, he thought.

'You see,' she turned towards him and he saw that her cheeks were wet, but her eyes were wide open and she was making an effort to pull herself together. 'I never really had a home life and I don't know quite how married people act. I have to find someone to talk to, someone ordinary, not rich or anything like that, just someone who's . . . To tell the truth, I was planning to ask that man – I want to know, is married life always a power game? What happens when a wife gives up her job to have a baby? Does she lose all rights? Just how do people operate if they're not rich? D'you know what Rob told me tonight? He said: "Twenty thousand rands deserves a fuck, don't you think?" That's what he'd paid to my couturière. How do your folks operate?'

He parked on the side of the road overlooking the bay.

'I can't imagine Father ever entertaining such a thought,' he said. 'That's if he'd ever had twenty grand to blow. They're a unit, sort of bonded.'

He told her about them and she listened so quietly he thought she'd fallen asleep, but it was good to talk. He began to throw off his tension and the unanswerable questions. Remembering that world made him feel good.

'Sometimes, particularly when I was in the CPU, I used to have to go home to replenish my soul. Know what I mean?'

'I was happy, too, when Mother was alive . . .' She was off again.

A long while later, a tribe of mountain baboons, long-haired and shabby, came stalking round the car. One of them began to play with the windscreen wiper, so he started the engine and drove slowly back to Silver Bay. Kate began to tell him things no woman should, perhaps the wine had loosened her tongue, but Ari sensed Rob was turning her into a whore. And she, the poor little thing, was trying to sort things out for herself, so he said almost nothing. He'd always been a good listener.

He was tired. He glanced at his watch. Almost 4 a.m. and he had to work tomorrow.

'Shall I take you home?'

'No,' she said fervently.

Finally he took her to his place because there was
nowhere else to go, and because he was so damned tired.

'Listen,' he said as he drew up outside his cottage. 'There
are some men who only feel confident when they pay for
what they get – love, sex, social position, friends. Rob
sounds like that to me. It doesn't mean he's a bad guy, or
that he doesn't love you, it's just that he can't cope with a
relationship unless he's in charge, and he buys his power
with money. That's all he's ever known, by the sound of
things. You understand? It's not a reflection on you. If he
did have a part in Angelo's revenge, maybe it was to secure
you by buying you, because he can't bear the prospect of
losing you.'

It was the best he could do. He didn't reckon anyone
was around as they crept inside. He gave her the bed and
she curled up under the duvet and didn't stop talking once,
not even when she sipped coffee and nibbled biscuits. He
lay down on the sofa under the window and half listened
while she rambled on. She was hyped up and unable to
relax. Eventually she ran out of steam.

'You're a strange guy,' she whispered. 'Everyone knows
about your drug bust. People are saying you're some sort
of under-cover agent for the drugs squad. Are you?'

'No. Child Protection. I wasn't even sure about the
drugs. It was something quite different. Go to sleep.
I'm tired.'

'You're not the goody-goody genie you pretend to be,'
she murmured. 'I watched you at the party. You downed
three drinks in quick succession and you were planning to
get drunk. Why?'

He couldn't explain . . . kids sold for *muti* and dismem-
bered while still alive, kids used for sex slaves, little blonde
girls sent up to central Africa, kids brutalised, sodomised,

flogged, raped, starved, burned or half drowned for fun. *And buried alive* ... He shuddered. Why had he thought that? He'd never had a case like that, but still there was that awful nightmare of his.

It was a night for talking out trauma and anyway she was asleep, or close enough to make no difference.

'I'm trying to get to grips with evil,' he told her. 'I want to know what it is, how it operates. Some strange things have happened ... So now I want to know, is evil like darkness that doesn't exist when the light is switched on? Or is it an outside force, some dark and dangerous current, waiting its chance, contaminating, corroding, a savage cloying intelligence engaged on its own fight for survival, like a bacterium? Are we at risk? I have a memory of evil, but I can't quite grasp it. It comes from way back. I remember a large black hole, and beady glistening eyes watching me, and the knowledge that I was helpless and in the grip of terrible evil.

'Something strange happened in Soweto one night,' he went on. 'I was after a missing kid. An informer told me about an old *sangoma*, an old man, who made potions for sex and sold them for a fortune. I got there too late. I won't tell you what I found in his unbelievably evil place. I beat him close to death, which didn't take long because he was old and weak. Then I took out my gun to shoot him. He opened his eyes and said, in perfect English: "You don't know what you're up against. You can't beat me. I have millions of homes." He smiled and suddenly his eyes changed. He looked at me and cried out in Zulu. He couldn't speak any English. He begged for mercy and I said I'd spare him if he spoke in English, *but he could not*. Then I killed him.

'You see, there was a toddler lying there who was still alive. Is still alive. They're doing a series of sex change operations to turn him into a girl – since he can't be a boy. He'll be on hormones all his life.' He shuddered.

'Oh God! I'm probably crazy, but I fear the corroding power of evil and I abhor the violence that surges into me when I'm close to it. I seem to catch it. Perhaps I'm weak. Easy prey.'

'Perhaps you're talking shit.' Her voice came sleepily through the darkness. 'There's no such thing as evil. Only love, or the absence of love. You're right. Like darkness and light. Darkness is merely the absence of light.'

Her words calmed him. He fell asleep and later woke to the sound of sobs. For a few seconds he could not remember where he was or who was crying. He got up and lay beside her, cradling her in his arms, stroking her hair, feeling a surge of protectiveness while she sobbed.

'Oh, Ari,' she whispered. 'I love my husband, but I have to leave him. You see, if I remain with Rob I'll become a whore. I'll lose myself. I don't know how to explain, but I know it's true. Could there be anything more terrible than having to leave the man you love? The strange thing is, you remind me of Rob. I don't know why, but it's the reason why I feel so close to you. It's like you're the man he could have been, but isn't.'

She fell asleep snuggled up beside him, her head on his shoulder. Later he began to want her. His sexual desire was a burning, tearing agony. He hesitated, then he leaned over her and pushed his lips over hers, tasting the saltiness of her skin and feeling the softness of her tongue. For a moment he lost himself in the wonderful oneness of kissing her.

'Oh, Rob,' she whispered.

He turned his back on her and Kate snuggled behind him, still sleeping.

Chapter 16

————— —————

Deep inside the crippled boy was a voice calling out to be healed. Tabson could not hear his own inner plea, but he recognised it in the distant cry of a hurt animal, a maimed bird or a wounded dog. He had a strange, intuitive, almost psychic awareness of an animal in need. Then, with a compulsion that was bigger than himself, he became the healer, thrusting all the fervour of youthful faith into finding, guarding, feeding and nursing the maimed creature. Sometimes he failed and then he cried bitter tears for the victim and for himself, although he did not understand this. Only that the world was a harsh place and he and the maimed were on the same side, and his compassion was infinite.

So when he heard the far-off cry of the female Egyptian goose, urging her mate to fly away, and the pained croak that came in reply, he understood the situation. Waiting until Eunice fell asleep, he crept out of the hut and made his way slowly upstream, listening, whistling softly under his breath, creeping along the bullrushes. Sometimes he sat and quickly puffed at a joint and as carefully pinched it out. Then it would seem that the cry of the goose came from within his soul, and it hurt more.

The bird had moved far away from the settlement, but

that would not protect it from marauding dogs and hungry people, he knew, so he plodded on.

A man came stealthily from the road and passed Tabson so close he might have touched him. Shuddering, the boy shrank into the shadows and watched as the man moved purposefully down towards the shacks. He was fit and powerful, but heavily laden and his breath came in short sharp gasps. At the edge of the encampment he lowered his sack and took out a bottle. The liquid shone translucent in the moonlight. Stepping back a safe distance he paused, watchful and intent. A match flared, the fuse was lit and the bottle soared on a high arc to crash down on the roof of a shebeen. Breaking glass, and the plop of igniting petrol came simultaneously.

Smiling softly, he waited until he saw the flames and smelled the smoke. He lobbed another bottle to be on the safe side, and passed on to the second shack. Seven petrol bombs, six fires. Good going, he reckoned. Already the flames were erupting. There was a sudden nearby shout and the man ran off, leaving his sack and the last bottle on the ground.

The homeless, the jobless and the dispossessed squatters were sleeping like babies under their ramshackle canvas and wood shelters around the lagoon. Like all down-and-outs, they had little to lose, but they had hope, for around them lay plenty such as they had never seen in their lives and they knew that sooner or later they would share in this feast. They were here – step one had been accomplished – and that was truly good. Besides, the night was absolutely perfect. A lustrous full moon had soared into the black sky, the berg wind warmed them, the marvellous bounty of water lay wastefully about them, and they were surrounded by the twinkling lights of rich homes. Jobs were there for the finding – wages, food, life!

A whiff of smoke came sneaking over the sand, creeping under canvas, caressing the trees; a sudden spark flared and died; some grass began to burn. They, who had always lived by open fires, cooking on them, harbouring the embers, blowing them up at daybreak, saw no danger in the scent of smoke; they lived their lives within this scent and it was a part of them, so they slept on.

The neighbouring shacks went up in a blaze, like a firework display, as the paraffin stoves and lanterns caught and splattered fuel on stacks of wood and canvas. Now the people began to emerge screaming, and their cries woke others. The camp struggled awake and people began hurriedly to dismantle their homes, but they were too late. The berg wind was strong and hot and it fed the embers as it carried them over the settlement. There were a number of small explosions under piles of wood that went up like blazing stars, as if petrol cans had been hidden there. The women found themselves trapped in circles of fire, so they hung on to their infants and rushed for the lake.

The first victim was an old farmer from the Ciskei. He had filched a few chunks of polyurethane foam from a furniture factory where he had begged a labouring job. The fumes from the foam poisoned him in his sleep. He did not wake as his makeshift home burned to cinders.

More explosions showered the terrified people with burning debris, leaving them screaming and writhing. The settlement went up in a scorching blaze with sparks like a firework display as stored petrol ignited. The squatters were panicking and screaming as they fought their way through the fires blazing around them. Some fled to the sea and soaked their blisters in ice-cold water. Their screams woke others and the camp struggled awake, babies crying, women screaming for their children and husbands. They were scorched and scared and choking on smoke which teased them, circling, spiralling, racing from all directions as the wind got up. The port jackson and eucalyptus trees around caught light, and their oily boughs and leaves flared and crackled and fed the blaze.

The wind was strong and hot and it fed the embers and whirled them over the settlement. There were a number of small explosions under piles of wood, that went up like blazing stars. Boysie, the unauthorised but generally acknowledged leader of the camp, suspected that petrol cans had been hidden under logs, but there was no time to think now. A wet sack over his head, he raced through the blazing huts, ushering groups of bewildered women and children to the lagoon where they stood wailing and coughing, up to their necks in water, unable to see more than a red haze through smoky vistas.

Eunice was dreaming that she was trapped in a circle of fire. The *sangoma* screamed his curse and she woke to the reality of it. The roof was alight. Grabbing her bucket of water, she flung it over Tabson's smoking bed. Grovelling in the scorched blankets, she realised he was missing. At that moment a fiery wooden beam fell in and struck her on the back. She fell forward, pinned to the ground, screaming in agony as her flesh began to burn with the beam. Through the shock of her excruciating torment she saw the *sangoma* beckoning to her. Her last thoughts were for Tabson.

In the shebeen, a drunk who had become entangled in fallen canvas, was screaming and dying as melting rubber burned into his skin. His small toddler died with him.

Ari, a light sleeper, was wakened by the smell of smoke

drifting through the window. He shifted Kate gently off his shoulder, stood up, and went to the window. There was no sign of fire on the mountains. He ran out barefooted to the summer house. It took only a second to grasp the scale of the disaster below. Most of the bush behind the beach was burning, a circle of fire ringed the lagoon, and the sound of distant screams was carried in the wind. The fire was already dying down, the damage done. How long had it blazed before he woke? he wondered. Deep inside him another fire took hold, fuelled on resentment. He was going to get the bastards who had done this thing.

Moments later, Jack joined him. 'So they drove the squatters out of the wetlands after all,' he said with a tinge of awe in his voice. 'The Palmas stop at nothing.'

Gill was running towards them across the lawn, wearing a satin nightgown which shimmered and glittered in the moonlight. She'd had time to brush her hair, but not to put on a robe, Ari noticed. He had to go down to the fire, but what would he do about Kate now that the Bronsons were awake? At that moment Kate emerged from his room and he heard Jack gasp, while Gill's face was a mixture of fury, envy and amused malice.

'I must go.' Ari grabbed Kate's hand and pulled her to the car. 'Don't you care what people think?'

'Not really,' she sighed. 'What difference does it make? I'm dirt in this town.'

'You're being absurd,' he snapped. 'Businesses fail every day, but Mrs Palma can't spend the night with every Tom, Dick and Harry she meets. I'll drop you at your car. I'm going to the lagoon.'

Now he was absorbed with his work and Kate noticed that his face was set in grim, angry lines. As they raced downhill the fumes and smoke from burning debris became unbearable. Kate held her handkerchief over her nose. They could hardly see through the smoke. He parked outside the Lilfords' house where Kate had left her car and gave her a strangely affectionate look.

'You're a great person. Keep out of trouble, Kate. If you need me you know where to find me. Good luck!'

Kate drove home feeling apprehensive. The lights were blazing and she began to tremble. Had they been looking for her? She walked inside and saw Ramona sitting upright in the antique chair by the front door.

'Where's my husband?' she asked.

'He's gone out,' Ramona snapped.

'And Angelo?'

'Out.'

She let out her breath in a swift, audible sigh and went to change into a tracksuit and sneakers.

'I've been watching the fire,' she lied to Ramona. 'I'm going back there.' The old woman did not acknowledge her words, but remained staring stiffly at the opposite wall. Kate stifled her surge of dislike as she ran lightly down the steps.

A grey light was filtering on to the scene as dawn broke. Kate parked in a side road that led to the back of the lagoon. Trying not to throw up at the fetid stench that made her stomach crawl, she watched the raggle-taggle mob limping past on blistered feet, thin shoulders hunched against the misery of existence. Wary eyes, faces dark and blank, hardly a gleam of anger was left. They were shocked, apathetic, dejected. All the fight in them had gone up in smoke with their meagre possessions. A burned child writhed and screamed, its mother cradling it in her arms. Everything was black – that was her first impression. Trees, grass, flowers, shacks, beams, cartons, everything was carbon now. 'Next year,' she whispered softly as she got out of her car. 'This place will burst out with fresh life, but I wonder if the birds will ever return.' She moved forward into the barrenness, feeling unreal.

Kate had had her own way all her life, and now she had no resources to cope with setbacks, let alone the disasters that were hammering her from all sides. She felt dazed as she gazed at the destruction of her beloved wetlands.

'How could they? Oh, how awful.' Fists clenched, biting her lower lip, her pale cheeks wet with hot tears, she looked with disbelief at the rusty tins, bent iron bars, fragments of wood and canvas, old rags, broken shoes and thousands of empty wine bottles strewn everywhere. Beyond the marshes lay a filthy jungle of smouldering blackened ruins, the smoke still rising. The thick port jackson trees had been burned to maimed blackened stumps. She saw a corpse of a man lying under a burnt iron sheet, his legs protruding. Her stomach heaved, and she was too shocked to feel compassion.

Oh God! How could this happen? So much and so fast.

She wandered through the ruins towards the lagoon, scorching her shoes, choking on the acrid fumes. A whole encampment of homes, shebeens, and shops, a complete township of canvas, iron and sticks had sprung up in the shadows of the concealing trees and no one had known just how extensive it was. Now that the trees were burned and blasted, the whole catastrophe was laid bare, witness to her stupid blunder in taking Eunice there.

'Hey there! Get back.' Glancing around she saw the police standing in a group near the lagoon.

'There's a corpse over there,' she called to the ambulance men.

Ari was hurrying towards her. He pointed towards the sea and she saw more ambulances parked there and men in white carrying stretchers. 'I've seen the corpse. They'll take him in a minute, but first they're looking for survivors.' Ari's face was twisted with grief and anger and she felt surprised. Why should he care?

'Is he the only victim, or were there others?' she asked without really listening.

There was a shout and a tall figure leaped out of the bushes. 'Don't shoot! It's only Frikkie,' Kate called as a policeman aimed his revolver. 'Frikkie, come back here,' she commanded. He turned and walked towards them with a curious shambling gait, and Ari watched him curiously. He looked like pictures of primitive man with his sloping forehead, jutting brows, and small, deep-set eyes set close together, almost hidden under a mop of black hair. His arms hung forward from powerful shoulders and they were longer than was usual. From the way he moved and his strange expression, Ari assumed that he was simple-minded.

'He's burned. We must get him into an ambulance.' Willis went racing after him, but Frikkie fled over the dunes.

Kate walked on and suddenly cried out.

'Oh! How horrible,' she cried out, gazing at four blackened corpses.

'I'm sorry. They're going to the mortuary, but we have to deal with the injured first.' Ari had come up behind her. He wound his arms around her.

'And a child! Oh, how terrible.' Tears were trickling down her cheeks. 'And I know this woman. I let her sleep in my hut by the lagoon. Oh! How dreadful. Then I killed her. Yes, I did, I couldn't have known that such a thing would happen, but I didn't think.'

Gerber had overheard her. He was staring hard and looking hostile.

'You see,' she whispered to Ari. 'I brought her here. She brought the others. It's all my fault.'

'You didn't kill her, Kate, but someone did.' There was that anger again. 'Her name was Eunice and I have to find her grandson, Tabson. He has a club foot. Could you look around for me?'

She left him, pushing her way around scorched ruins, avoiding the fires. She reached the lagoon where the water was grey and unruffled. God knows what rubbish lay under the surface. More burned debris lay steaming between the rushes and lilies and tall buffalo grasses, but there were no birds at all. Kate sat on a tree stump and put her face in her hands.

It was then that she heard the strangled cry of an Egyptian goose coming from a clump of thick reeds on a sand bar near the edge of the lagoon. Could it be the bird she had freed from the trap? Wading into the water, she felt afraid of what she might find. Knee-deep, she pushed through reeds and lilies to reach a sandy ridge that formed a small, hidden island. A boy sat crouched on the ground and he was holding the Egyptian goose in his arms. Its shattered wing had been set in a rough plaster of sticks and mud and it hung awkwardly over his arm.

'Oh, goodness!' She bent down to take the bird, but the boy shrank away.

'No, missus. Don't hurt it. It's going to get better, missus. I'm looking after it. Please, missus. Leave it be.'

He stood up and backed away and now she saw his bare,

deformed foot splayed inwards. He had to stand on tip-toe for the crooked leg appeared to be shorter than the other, and he walked with a pronounced limp, his back curved, one hip pushed out, his face twisted with sadness and fear. How strange he looked with his huge eyes, his skull-like face and thick mass of crinkly hair. He was shivering badly and she guessed he was in shock.

'You must be Tabson,' she said. 'I think you should go to a doctor. I'll take you home with me. Give me the bird.'

He backed into the reeds.

He looked up at the pretty woman and shook his head. People were bad news for Tabson. He had learned to trust no one. Yet the white policeman had saved his life, he knew. So what did this woman want, and why did she want his goose? Perhaps she was hungry.

Tabson did not like white people. They seemed disgusting to him with their raw pink skins like pigs. They smelled like pigs, too. When he was a child he had been taught how the white people had first come to their country. There had been a period of heavy rains and the ground had become mushy and boglike. Then a great black fly had flown into the mire and laid its eggs everywhere. Weeks later white maggots had emerged from the earth and eaten every green thing. When the people were starving and the maggots bloated with fat, they had formed larvae under the earth's crust. Out of them the blustering, bullying white men had crawled. Whenever he saw one sweating or shouting, he remembered the story. But this woman looked like an angel in the book he had seen at the local mission school. He was torn halfway between distrust and his longing to be cared for. Why was she trying so hard to get him? She was white and therefore selfish. Why was she offering shelter? 'Tabson, Tabson,' she was calling and holding out her hand. Instinctively he felt he could trust her.

Saying his name seemed to calm him slightly, Kate noticed. He looked about eight years old and he was emaciated and dirty, his clothes muddy and torn. She sat on the bank beside him, wondering what to do or say to gain his confidence. Ari would know. 'Tell me how you found the bird,' she asked softly. 'You see, I found this very same bird two days ago. Its wing was caught in a trap. I freed it, but it escaped when one of the squatters attacked me. I must take it to the vet.'

'No!' Now he was ready for flight.

'We'll go together,' she said reassuringly.

'I shall feed it,' he said obstinately. His voice was husky, half-broken, and sounded older than he looked. His long, delicate fingers were stroking the bird's neck. He kept making strange clicking noises of endearment, but the bird looked frantic.

'It will die,' she said.

'No, missus.' His hands clutched harder and the bird squawked.

And who will look after you, you silly boy? she thought. How odd that he should care so much. She had always thought that blacks were entirely lacking in compassion. 'Sell him to me. I'll give you twenty rands.'

'No, missus.' He looked away and she could see that he was trembling.

'Tabson. You must come with me. I have a dry safe place for the bird and food. You don't have food for it. I'll feed you, too. Aren't you hungry?'

'I must stay here. Someone will be looking for me.'

'Eunice is dead, Tabson. I'm very sorry. Come with

me. I'll look after you.' Now why had she said that? she wondered.

'Yes, missus.' His head was bowed and tears were running down his cheeks as she led him past the police. When Tabson saw Ari his eyes glowed with the recognition of a friend.

'So you found him,' Ari smiled sadly at the boy. 'I'm afraid . . .'

'I told him,' Kate said, blinking back her tears.

'I'll find a safe place for you to go to for a few days, Tabson,' Ari said.

'He's coming with me.' Kate surprised herself with her resolve. 'At least until you trace his parents. He does have parents, doesn't he?' she went on anxiously.

'Yes. I have their address. I'll get on with it.'

Ari's face was puzzled. There was a question in his eyes, as if he couldn't quite pigeonhole her, Kate noticed. He thinks I'm some kind of a good-time girl, she thought. Perhaps I am.

'You'll have to call the doctor. He needs care.'

'I can cope,' she said defensively. She could not understand why she felt a curious identification with the crippled boy. Was it because he longed to help the maimed bird, as she did? She took hold of Tabson's hand firmly. 'He'll be fine with me for the time being,' she said. The truth was, she was already regretting her impulsiveness.

Her apprehension grew on the drive home. She hated the brooding, watchful house with its overhanging jutting rooms. It was a cold, unhappy place. Someone was watching her, but who? Then she saw a curtain move in the diningroom. Ramona perhaps? Rob would have something to say about this, she thought with a shiver of apprehension. Tabson seemed numbed by the sight of the house, stables, rose garden and swimming pool. He was so vulnerable and distrustful. He looked as if he might try to run away. What on earth was she supposed to do with him all day? Perhaps she could feed him up and teach him to swim and play.

The wild goose was a simple matter – she knew exactly what to do. She told Rob's secretary to call the gardener to make one of the stables secure with a run outside. The vet was summoned, and Tabson watched wonderingly as the bird's wing was re-set in plaster. An hour later he was hobbling round his enclosure. Tabson looked happy for once.

So far so good. She couldn't face Ramona, so she handed Tabson to the assistant housekeeper, a capable Malay widow.

'Bath him, clothe him, feed him and teach him how to eat properly,' Kate said. 'Oh . . . and call a doctor.' Once again the necessity of wealth hit home as Kate realised how simple it was to cope with all one's problems.

Rob was sitting at his desk. He had spent the night supervising the fencing of his land by the lagoon and now he wondered whether or not to snatch a couple of hours sleep before work, or drink a stiff brandy and get on with it. He was fit and he could manage without sleep for days if necessary. He'd proved that to himself enough times in the Namib.

There was a light tap and Ramona walked in without waiting for his reply. This always annoyed Rob, but he stifled his irritation. Instead his eyes gazed intently at his fingertips, which were pressed so hard together they had turned white. Ramona had brought him up as if he were her own. In his pre-school days, he had seldom been with anyone else. Later, she had shielded him from his grandfather's rage when he had done wrong, helped him with his homework, lied for him, protected him, and once she had even stolen some cash for him. He could never describe the bond between the two of them, but it was there and it was real. Nevertheless, it was irksome to be treated like a child, and sometimes she forgot she was only a servant. As she sat down, he sensed her fears and he felt vaguely troubled. He had never known Ramona to be scared of anything. Inexplicably, he felt depressed, and obsessed with a premonition of doom.

'Listen to me, Master Rob,' she muttered. 'That new police lieutenant is your *doppelgänger* and fate has sent him to Silver Bay. This means the worst kind of misfortune for you. Get rid of him quickly before it's too late. He brings bad luck – evil times. He can destroy you. Believe me! Get him transferred.'

Rob scowled at her, trying to intimidate her, but Ramona was never intimidated. She could act crazy at times, but he'd never known her predictions to be wrong. He tried to laugh at her, but she leaned over him, her black eyes burning with passion. 'You know me, Master Rob,' she hissed. 'You know I'm always right. Get rid of him. Another thing, Kate spent the night out while you were down at the fire. She was still in her evening dress when she came home at dawn. She was seen leaving the Lilfords' party with this lieutenant. Now will you get rid of him?'

She went out leaving Rob a prey to his own vicious jealousy.

Chapter 17

——— ———

Gerber's fury was comic and tragic at the same time as he replaced the receiver following a call from a senior prosecutor at the Cape Town magistrates' court. He was a man who avoided problems simply by refusing to accept them, Ari had noticed. Everything was all right and would remain that way if you left well alone. Silver Bay was a great little town and crime had no place here. His denial was bordering on pathological, Ari reckoned, watching Gerber carefully.

The lieutenant was turning purple with rage, his eyes watered and twitched. It had something to do with an inability to lose, Ari realised, which was probably why he liked hunting with telescopic sights or a night-scope. Ari had wanted to open a murder docket for the four squatters burned to death in the fire. Gerber had insisted on writing them off as accidental deaths and he had aired his views boringly for the past two weeks. Ari had said very little, but the way he had worded the documents handed into court had encouraged the prosecutor to insist that they open a murder docket on four counts. Gerber had only just heard the news and he was unable to contain his temper.

'It's all yours,' he said, scowling at Ari. Then he did what he always did, packed up and left, this time for the Grants' party, where everyone important was going, leaving the five remaining police on duty to cope with the spate of crimes that nightly plagued Silver Bay.

On board the Grants' yacht, the music was magical, the lights twinkled invitingly, and anyone who was anyone was there, but the favoured few were gathered around the bar on the top deck.

'After you've been in Ethiopia for a while,' Rob was saying loudly, 'you can't bear to give another cent towards black welfare. Africa is fast becoming one big basket case. Ethiopia has become a desert region. Its population must either be resettled or abandoned. Their country will never sustain them and the sooner we walk away and let nature play her age-old role, the better.' Kate listened and cringed. She had the feeling that a man of his intellect should know better than to talk like that.

They were celebrating Dave Grant's birthday. A glass of whisky in her hand, Kate glanced around at the nude shots of blondes in sailor hats. Dave, their host, a copper millionaire, had his hand stuck between the closed thighs of a beautiful young girl who closely resembled the girls on the posters, if you overlooked her fragile G-string and a tiny ribbon bra. She looked embarrassed, but determined to stick it out, and she was superciliously ignoring the rest of the company. Dave, once an athelete, but now overweight and middle-aged, was very red in the face, and beginning to snort, which he did when he was drunk, for his sinuses seemed to collapse.

Was she after Dave, or the thirty-odd million that went with him? Kate wondered. Where the hell was his wife, Melissa? The yacht was crowded with friends of the Grants, most of whom were Rob's friends, too. There was George

Rockwell, an American mining magnate based in Namibia, the de Villiers who owned most of the diamond concessions up the coast, Don Cohen, a property millionaire, three American visitors, who were claiming to represent several billions of US investment money, plus a few Silver Bay residents: the local doctor, John Flanagan and his wife, Sigal, the dentist, Dave, and his wife, Lynette, and the Bronsons. Cecilia, the artist, a couple of writers, a sculptor, an opera star, and a poet were thrown in to show that not only money counted here, which was a lie anyway, Kate thought.

Rob, looking marvellous in a blue and white striped jersey and white pants, his dark, square face glowing from the wind, held forth, as usual, swaying, cajoling and offending them all in turn with his clever, acid tongue, black eyes gleaming. Claude de something-or-other, who had written several books on conservation in Northern Africa, was hotly contesting Rob's statement.

'I think it utterly disgusting that we should condemn millions of people to die a terrible death by starvation while sitting down to a gourmet's feast like this,' he said, glowering at the dish of heaped, steaming prawns and langoustines.

'Don't spoil everyone's appetite,' Grant roared from his comfortable settee. He hauled the bare girl closer to him. In the sudden silence that followed, they heard the strumming of guitars coming from the top deck. Claude's eyes were glittering with fury.

'Aren't you the fellow who wants to save the Sahara Desert's wild dogs, amongst other things?' Rob said, a curious glint in his eyes. Kate felt a surge of sympathy for the writer. When Rob's mouth twisted with amusement someone was about to come unstuck.

Not everyone was here for fun, Kate noticed. Cecilia was attempting to sell her latest painting and she'd persuaded Melissa to hang it in the stateroom. Jack Bronson was trying to persuade Rob to amalgamate their beachside properties in order to build Rob's coveted condominium. Gill Bronson wanted to write Angelo's biography, but he was fending her off gallantly. He could be charming to women he liked. For the first time Kate got a glimpse of the charming, handsome man she'd heard he once was. She felt surprised.

Richard Mooney, their retired Catholic priest, was here to whip up some support for his 'feed the squatters' campaign, and the sculptor was here because he needed the meal. Just about everyone wanted a share of the Americans' billions. They were hovering, waiting their chances. Everyone was getting drunk or high and masculine laughter swamped the shrill feminine voices.

Kate found Melissa leaning over the railing, a cigarette in one hand, a glass in the other.

'If I were to fall overboard I don't suppose anyone would notice,' Melissa said, without turning her famous profile towards Kate. Studying her, Kate could see why she had once been a world-famous beauty, but now she looked ravaged. Her ash-blonde hair glittered in the moonlight, and although a recent facelift had pulled her neck to a youthful smoothness, her eyes glistened tragically above puffy bags. She was forty-eight years old and she looked her age.

'If I died it would save Dave the trouble of a divorce.' She slurred her words slightly. 'I pitched earlier than he expected this evening and caught him in our cabin rutting with that bitch. D'you know what he said? He said: "Listen here, lady, I'm a free agent. I made a pile and I don't owe a cent to anyone. No one keeps me, and you, for one, aren't going to tell me what to do. If you don't like it, look the other way, or sue. Yes, why don't you? You've never done a day's work in your bloody life and it's beginning to show. Your tits are empty and your buttocks flop down to the back of your knees. When women reach fifty they should be lined up against the wall and shot. Now fuck off." That's what he said – verbatim. I'm still in shock. I don't know whether to sue him or my plastic surgeon.'

'He was drunk, I'm sure,' Kate said, putting her arm around Melissa. 'You know how belligerent he gets when he's drunk.'

'Yes, and truthful. I won't give him the pleasure of getting rid of me. He's always been a swine, but he used to be besotted with my looks. Now he's crazy about hers. He's always thought of me as an expensive possession, but I've been written down, depreciated.'

'I'm sure she's only temporary. He'll come to his senses.'

Mel gave a snorting laugh. 'Are you crazy? Somehow she gets it up for him, even when he's drunk. Besides, she offers him youth. He looks at her and feels young. Silly old fool.'

'You have all your friends and your children. We're all on your side, Mel,' Kate said in a futile effort to calm her.

Melissa laughed briefly. 'The kids have grown up and left home and my friends would drop me if I left him. I've always been lovely, Kate. That was my life, being lovely. I'm forty-eight and I could easily live another forty years, but everything I've ever lived for has evaporated, because my looks have gone. I'm telling you, Kate,' Melissa went on, her voice cracking, 'if I had anything meaningful in my life, I'd leave him, but what the hell am I supposed to do with myself for the next forty years? Why should she get his millions? I aim to stay here like the proverbial spoke in the wheel. Now that I'm thwarting him, he sees me as a real person for the first time in our lives and he hates me. That gives me a sort of sick satisfaction. At last I've become real.'

Kate longed to flee, but friendship demanded her futile attempts to coax Melissa back to some degree of composure. A difficult task with that young nubile cuckoo upstairs. 'You must be dignified. Let her think she's the hired body, a lifesized Dutch wife. Yes, why don't you?'

'Oh, Kate, don't stand there with that delicate peaches-and-cream skin, and those youthful shining eyes, and preach to me. You look a lot like I used to. What d'you know about bitterness, or being overlooked? Lately men ignore me. They aren't horrible or rude, they just don't see me. You've got it all, I've got nothing, so stop preaching to me. Go away.'

Oh God, Kate thought. She's me in twenty-six years time. She tossed off her drink and returned to the bar to down another. Melissa had got through to her where it hurt.

Rob was moving in for the kill, she could see that by the glint of mockery in his eyes. One hand was resting on the luckless author's shoulder. Claude was blabbing about the lack of land available for wildlife, the poaching, over-grazing and insecticides making inroads into the Okavango swamps. 'We white Africans,' Claude lectured, 'are the custodians for one of the world's last great natural continents. History will show how well or badly we did our jobs.'

'Nourish the Ethiopians and all the other basket cases, or protect nature's balance and thereby save the wildlife, eh, Claude? With the soaring birth rates, this is probably the very last century of co-existence. Make your choice as we all have to. So what's it to be, Claude?' The silence was painful.

Melissa, who had joined the party, gave a sudden shriek. 'Oh heavens! What's this horrible thing crawling down your neck, Rob? It came out of your hair.'

The shriek became agonised when the 'thing' leaped on to Melissa's white dress. It looked like a minute black spider.

'A louse!' Rob said. He picked off the offending insect and studied it. 'It's gone jet black, camouflage. Third generation here, I should say. I've been itching like crazy, but I never gave lice a thought . . .' His eyes, now brooding and furious, sought out Kate's and promised her a lifelong sentence of retribution.

'To my wife, the social worker,' he said, lifting his glass. 'She, like you, Claude, believes in helping the underdog. She has her little pet. He's crippled, dumb, stupid, black, ignorant and now we know he's lousy, too. You see, Claude,' he said, dropping the louse on his head, 'you're not the only one who wants to save Africa and its creatures.'

Relieved laughter echoed around the bar as Claude swung forward to hang his head between his knees while he beat his hair with his hands. A circle of space had cleared around the two men.

'Kate,' Melissa called, in a vain effort to improve the mood. 'You're an enigma – so beautiful, yet you care. I envy you. I've never cared for the poor. They're always ugly. Tell us how you do it, Kate. Stand up here.' She pulled Kate on to the raised dais around the bar and thrust a glass into her hand.

For Kate, the evening had taken on sinister undertones. She looked around at the stern mouths and predatory eyes. Her thoughts went back to her father and the cheetah. Then she remembered what Mira had said: 'We are nature's ultimate survivor, the aggressive, reasoning primate.' Was that all? If so, the cream of *Homo sapiens* was gathered around her, glaring at her, wishing she'd get on with the toast so they could get on with hard lobbying or drinking. 'It's not our problem' was their motto and the only sin they acknowledged was losing the money stakes or the beauty stakes.

'I want to know if there's anyone here who's truly happy,' she murmured in a small, lost voice.

No one answered. Then the priest spoke out. 'The squatters are often happy,' he said. 'But then they have so much more than you people have.'

'What could they possibly have?' Melissa sounded anguished, her eyes looked haggard.

'Kindness, my dear. Respect for the aged . . .'

'Aged,' Melissa croaked.

Rob chuckled. 'Come, darling. Let's say goodbye before we infest our friends.' He grabbed Kate's hand and pulled her off the boat. Moments later they were hurrying along the quay. Kate looked up and sighed. Above them the yacht bobbed gently in the light swell, the music was divine. Seen from a distance the party looked highly desirable.

Chapter 18

_____ _____

Rob's anger was feeding on his resentment. He started the
BMW coupé and it surged forward, tyres squealing, and
mounted a concrete ledge with a wham-bang that hurt.
'Fuck!' Rob swore. He reversed noisily, careering over the
gravel car park in a circular route until he hit a hole. The
car came to a shuddering noisy halt, but moments later they
were racing forward towards the highway.

'You're speeding!' Kate yelled.

'Shut up.'

'I'm scared.'

'Shut up.'

'Why should I?'

'You want to live, don't you? I'm telling you, I've had
enough. Shut up.'

They drove home at maximum speed in a series of
lurches, bumps and squealing tyres, stopping _en route_ at the
twenty-four-hour chemist for two large bottles of anti-lice
shampoo and then racing off into the night.

Where's Ari? Kate wondered. I'd like to see him book
us now. Rob would explode and when the bits of him
splattered down they'd burn like acid.

They almost crashed into the back of a police van that
was racing up their driveway towards the house.

'What the hell . . . ?' Rob muttered.

As they drew up, pandemonium broke out: the house blazed with light, a barrage of shots rang out, figures jumped out of the windows and ran in all directions, whistles blew.

A tall boy raced by, head thrown back, skinny legs working too fast as in an old silent movie. They could hear his rasping breath. Rob raised his handgun and fired in a single swift movement. Then the boy lay writhing and screaming on the ground. Sergeant Smit came running down the path. 'Good shot,' Smit yelled. 'At least we've got one of them.'

'Call an ambulance,' Kate shouted up at the house. She held the boy in her arms. He was only sixteen by the look of him and he seemed to be bleeding to death. The bullet had entered his buttocks. His face was contorted and he was crying for his mother. Kate sat on the ground, cradling his head on her lap. The next few minutes seemed like an hour, but then the ambulance arrived and the boy was bundled on to a stretcher and driven off into the night. The last thing she heard were his cries.

Shocked and dazed, Kate walked wearily to the house. Could anyone lose this much blood and survive? she wondered as she threw her blood-soaked clothes into the bath. A debilitating depression was seeping through her. She could hardly move her limbs, but Ramona came knocking on the door. Kate must come downstairs to see the police, she called.

Willis Gous seemed to be in charge of the team. There had been six youngsters, aged between fourteen and seventeen, wearing gloves and balaclavas, they told her. They had driven a stolen car up to the house to off-load the goods beforehand, then broken into the house and grabbed most of the silver as well as the jewellery that Kate had neglected to lock in her safe, plus Rob's expensive cameras and video equipment. Everything had been recovered from the boot of their car. Ramona had foiled their getaway by quietly calling the police without raising the alarm.

'Will Rob be charged?' she asked Gous.

'There'll be an inquiry, but no, he won't be charged. You see, it was the only way of catching any of them. All the rest escaped, but we have their car and all of the loot. I'm afraid you won't get your jewellery yet, Mrs Palma.'

Kate shrugged. That was the least of her woes in a long tragic evening.

'These boys have been successfully operating in Camps Bay,' Smit said. 'This is the first time they've come here. The last, too, I should think.' There was a tinge of satisfaction in his voice.

Strange how Rob was so different in front of other people. He was all smiles, joking, entertaining, clapping Smit on his shoulder, but the moment the door shut his face became bleak and cold.

'How could you shoot that boy?' Kate asked sternly. 'Did you think you were hunting impala?'

'Resisting arrest,' Rob said briefly, but she could see that he regretted his action. He looked sick.

'That's it,' Rob told her, his voice rising to near breaking point. 'I have no doubt that Tabson tipped them off. First thing in the morning he goes. I'd throw him out now, but I'm scared he'll return under cover of darkness.'

'Is it your fault you have lice?' she asked.

'No, it's yours.'

'Well, it's not his fault. Someone infected him – some- where. You're being hysterical about it.'

'You are. I'm telling you now, Kate. Get him out, or I'll throw him out.'

'He has nowhere to go until his parents arrive,' she said quietly.

'Who cares? He's not our problem.'

'Would you throw him out knowing that he has nowhere to go?'

'What do you think?' He smiled a strange, lopsided smile. 'If you thought you married a saint, Kate, I'm sorry to disillusion you. I don't ever want to hear his name or see him again.'

There was no help for it, Kate decided. No matter what Rob had threatened, Tabson would have to stay here for the time being. This morning, Ari had called her and told her that he had located Tabson's parents who didn't want the boy back. 'He's eleven years old,' he told her. 'Hard to believe, isn't it? Obviously starved. He needs a lot of care. I've been in touch with Welfare who are looking for a foster home,' he added. 'It won't be easy because he's crippled. Hang in there, Kate. I'll be in touch.'

No one wanted to wash Tabson's lousy hair, so eventually Kate did it herself, feeling strange, new, maternal feelings as she hugged him against her to dry his head. The housekeeper dressed him in his smart new clothes and sent him to play in the garden.

She found Rob in his office. 'The CPU are finding a foster home for Tabson. He'll have to stay here for a couple of weeks,' she said casually. 'Right now there's nowhere else for him to go.'

'They must look after their own,' he repeated stubbornly. 'Last night he brought in burglars. Next time it will be murderers. They'll cut your throat as you lie sleeping. If you're for *them*, you're not a part of me and mine.'

'Why?' She felt amazed. 'I never knew you were so racist. All these years and I didn't realise . . . What's it all about? I've never known you to be cruel. How could you have shot that boy last night?'

'He was resisting arrest. For God's sake, Kate,' he shouted. 'They were stealing our things. What d'you want me to do, hold open house for the locals to help themselves? Sometimes I doubt your sanity. Good God, Kate, even his own parents don't want him. Doesn't that tell you something about him, and them?'

For the first time she realised the extent of Rob's power. She threatened to leave and tried to tempt him with promises, but Rob was not prepared to house the boy, nor to pay a cent towards his keep. She had nothing of her own, no power, no cash, no prospects.

She summoned their Malay assistant housekeeper. 'I'll pay you well to look after him until I find a permanent home,' she said, wondering where she'd find the cash.

'Heavens, madam,' the woman replied in her sing-song accent. 'It's more than my life's worth to take that boy home. You see, we're very light-skinned. My husband wouldn't have him.'

Kate was in a mess. She stood by the window contemplating this strange society where skin pigmentation set the standards that were as rigid as any Indian caste system. She felt dazed and incapable of any action. With a feeling of dread, she watched Tabson limping around the garden behind the gardener. As if in a dream, she saw Rob walk outside, take some money out of his pocket and thrust it into the boy's hand. Then he pointed downhill towards the main gate. The boy looked puzzled, but the gardener understood. He smacked the boy on his backside and pointed down towards the village. Tabson looked up at the house and then he limped off.

She stood rooted to the spot. Her tension seemed to have immobilised her. So this is what she had come to! She ran down the front steps and called Tabson, but he seemed to have disappeared. 'Where is he?' she asked the gardener, who pointed to the back of the house.

'Getting his goose,' the man mumbled, looking away.

She passed Rob at the door. 'Bastard . . .' she said. 'I hate you. You have no compassion and you're a bully. You think you can change me into someone I don't want to be. You want to make me as hard as you are. You want me to be a part of you.'

'Pull yourself together,' Rob snapped. 'If you could just see what you look like. You look mad.'

'I was mad. Suddenly I'm sane,' she said softly, as the tension fell away from her. 'I alone am in charge of my own fate. I, not you, will decide if I'm to be a kind or cruel person. Do you understand?'

'I understand that you're hysterical.'

'You're driving away someone who really loves you, Rob. Think about that. Is that what you really want?'

'If you leave here now you'll never come back.'

'So be it,' she said. As she ran to the back of the house, her chest was pounding, her ears were singing, her mouth was dry and she was breathless with fury. Tabson had the goose under his arm.

'We're leaving here, Tabson. Put the goose back.'

'But who will look after him, missus?' he asked, his eyes bright with tears. 'Can't it come with us?'

'Of course it can,' she said. 'But first we must make a place for it.' She wondered at Rob's curious logic, for she knew he would never be cruel to an animal. 'He'll look after the goose, don't you worry.'

She put Tabson in her car and went back to collect his few clothes. She packed an overnight bag for herself and fled.

Rob was standing there, stiff as a statue, his eyes cold with fury. There wasn't much point in saying goodbye, she reasoned. The last few weeks had been one long goodbye.

Chapter 19

As she walked into the dusty lighthouse a blaze of sunlight hit her head-on. Like a flaming torch, freedom was exploding in her face and the tears that welled out of her eyes split the sunbeam into prisms of brilliant colour. 'Free . . . ! I'm free!' She lifted her face towards the splendid glass dome high above and shuddered at the impact of her amazing reality. 'I've waited all my life for this day.' She began to laugh, and Tabson laughed with her.

Seconds later, the feeling passed and Kate stood dazed in the middle of the floor, her chest heaving, her senses churning, battling mid-way between triumph and fear. Looking around she saw the dusty, dirty room, the peeling paint and decaying wood, the broken windows and the rusty staircase.

'Oh God! How awful!' A sense of loss began to creep up quietly. It was all so quiet, terrifyingly so, like a calm backwater beyond the mainstream. The world was moving on, but she had opted out. She could sit here alone forever and who would care? It was all very well to have reckless moods of independence, but now came the time to pay for them. Just what was she going to do for a living?

For a panicky moment she wanted to run straight back and beg Rob to be kinder. She shuddered. Was Melissa right after all? Should she stay with Rob? But no! She could not become the sort of person who abandoned the Tabsons of this world.

'Just how low can you get, Kate?' she lectured herself. Besides, what would be the point of going back? The same old torments would start again. Rob held all the power and the purse strings and he intended to extract the maximum obedience for his cash outlay. What was the point of luxury if you couldn't call your soul your own? At the same time, she could not survive without an income. Thoughts of slowly starving in peace and quiet crossed her mind and were as quickly dismissed.

She would have to find work. But just imagine getting up early and being caught up in that terrible rush hour to reach some drab office where she would be bullied and dictated to all day, and then back again to cook and clean, and all to get a modest living? Her senses rebelled against such a fate. How could she waste her life like that? Other people did! Then a worse thought came – could she even get a job? She knew nothing about business. She couldn't even type!

So what did people do if they had no work, no cash and no food? 'Look at the squatters, my girl,' she whispered sternly. She could starve like them, or huddle under a piece of cardboard in swampy land, like Eunice. Suddenly the lighthouse seemed a little more attractive. After all, it was dry, it was shelter, what's more it was hers.

But where could they sleep? How would they wash? There must be some facilities for basic existence, she reasoned, since her grandfather had once lived here.

Tabson was limping up the rusty spiral staircase and waving down at her, laughing with pleasure. The thump of his footsteps on the steel stairs echoed in the silent building. Round and round he went. She heard him stamping somewhere up there. After a while he came down. He crossed the floor, pushed open a door and disappeared. Moments later she heard him calling her. She found him in an empty room with an old shower and a washbasin. He was turning on the taps.

'No water, missus,' he said in his strange, hoarse voice. 'How do we get the water to come, missus? Look! There's lights, but they don't work.' His eyes mirrored his disappointment.

'Oh God!' What on earth could she do with this big gaunt empty lighthouse? The building was shaped like a gigantic thimble, each floor being a large room, connected to the one below by a steep spiral staircase right in the middle. The top floor would be private if she designed a door of some sort. She went up there and gasped at the panoramic view of the sea, rocks, beaches, fishing harbour, mountains surrounding the bay, and the crooked valley snaking between the three towering granite ranges. She spun around until she felt dizzy. How can I curtain all these windows, or perhaps it's not necessary? There was so much room, just this one floor would give her a studio, a bedroom and a dressing room. She began to visualise it as it could be – if she had the cash, the energy and enough time. She half closed her eyes, tilted her head to one side and thought about colour. That was about all she could afford. But the dirt! How would she ever get this place clean?

She hurried downstairs and went outside, turning her back on a task which seemed beyond her. Feeling nervous, she sat on the old stone step at the door. Two dassies scampered through the reeds around the rocks and disappeared under a bank of tangled agapanthus. A fiscal shrike screamed its coarse cry from the tangled thorn bush by the stream, and then she noticed a pair of hadeda ibis gleaning insects in the grass. Tabson came running outside and the birds rose heavily into the air, protesting loudly.

Could she live here? Perhaps she could. Then she must make it a happy place. But how? She had so little money it would hardly cover essentials, and even that precious store wouldn't last long. At least Tabson would be safe here. She turned and looked at him – seeing his malformation as something apart from him. He was not a cripple, but a boy with a crippled leg. His questing, alert, distinct intelligence shone in his eyes. And he was kind, too. 'Tabson,' she said, 'you mustn't call me missus. You must call me Kate.'

'Yes, missus Kate,' he called back. He found the fuse box, but looked disappointed when the lights failed to materialise.

There were some tall, stately trees around, syringa, wild fig and acacia and the grass was full of pretty blue irises, daisies, orchids and ericas. They were all so brave, she thought. All struggling for survival against the thick sturdy grass and rushes. Everything struggled for life and growth, as she would, too.

As she sat there, the strangest feeling came over her, a sense of being at one with the trees and flowers. They and she were indivisible, part of a living force of love that surged around her. The experience faded, but she retained a feeling that she was not alone. She had linked her soul with some indefinable force around her. What was it? Who was she? She had a feeling she had been tested in some way and that she had the strength to survive. Then a heaviness sank into her. She snuggled into the grass against a rock and fell asleep.

She woke to the sound of a small boy calling: 'Missus . . . missus Kate . . .' Where was she? Her misfortune came flooding back and she almost cried out, as the reality of her plight hit her with a body blow. Tabson held out his hand and emptied some coins into her lap. He was clutching a loaf of bread which he solemnly tore in half. Handing her the larger half, he sat in the sun and munched the bread, looking pleased with himself.

'Where did you get the bread . . . and the coins . . . ?' She closed her mouth firmly. There was no point in asking. Clearly Tabson had been begging in the village. It was her fault. She should have made an effort to feed him. But how? She had nothing to cook on and no fuel, nor even a table.

'You must never beg. Never! Promise me, Tabson. You will not do this bad thing again.'

He looked up, startled by her tone, and then his eyes filled with tears. She reached forward and took his hand, squeezing it in both of hers. 'Tabson, all the while you have no family to care for you, you can count on me,' she said. She felt better. Something had been finally decided upon. 'And I shall feed you,' she added. Fumbling in her handbag she took out a notebook and pen and wrote . . .

Problems . . . 1 – Short Term . . . 2 – Long Term . . . Short term was straightforward. She needed food, electricity, running water, furniture, paint, curtains, and cash to pay for all of this. *Solution* – sell her jewellery and her horse. Anyway, she could not afford to feed Ponty and she had no stable, so she stifled her regrets. Under *Long Term Problems* she wrote – a job. Then she crossed out the word job and wrote 'income'. Then there was Tabson. She underlined his name and wrote underneath: doctor, vitamins, school, and a specialist for his leg. Listing her problems made her feel better.

First things first. Calling Tabson to the car, she drove to

the village to find out how to get the water and electricity connected and to buy a few essentials.

She returned to find Frikkie sitting on the doorstep smoking a cigarette. From the pungent smell of the smoke she guessed it was *dagga*. Then she saw his dreamy eyes and his sloppy smile and she knew she had been right. He was on a high.

'What are you doing here, Frikkie?'

He scrambled to his feet and stood there swaying. She had seen him working around the garden, but she had never really looked at him. For the first time she saw why they called him *bobbejaan*, a baboon. His eyes were so dark they were almost black, deep set and close together and you saw them indistinctly through a tangled fringe. But she could see how nervous he was and he kept blinking. There was a puzzled look about him. He was too baffled to cope with life, she decided.

'I need work. And food. Help me, Miss Kate. That Ramona has thrown me out.' His voice was so soft, she strained forward to hear him. 'She's angry. She blames me. She won't give me anything to eat.'

Rumour had it that Frikkie was Ramona's son, but she always denied this. How thin he was. Ramona was cruel to him. They were two victims of Ramona's spite.

'Let me work for you.' His voice was like a soft growl or a purr.

'What can you do?'

'I could clean up, maybe paint the place, mend the glass.' He looked around. 'Catch some fish, make a garden.'

'I don't have much money,' she began hesitantly.

'Just food, Miss Kate. That's all anyone gives old Frikkie.'

'Oh! How wicked! That's completely unfair. I shall pay you, and of course I shall feed you. Right now you can help me unload the car.'

She rifled in the boot for a box of provisions, but when she carried it inside and opened the door of a wall cupboard, a field mouse ran out. Frikkie captured the mouse in his big hands and reverently carried it outside. She watched in wonder as he soothed the creature with his gentle voice and let it go free in the long grass.

Suddenly she was in a frenzy of planning. She must have a table and a knife. But no, much more than that – knives and forks and plates, a table. Oh heavens! The list was endless. There and then she decided to put her pride in her pocket and cadge whatever she could from her father's liquidators. Perhaps she could even get some cushions and curtains. Who knows what she might be allowed to take?

'You can start work today,' she said. 'Just as soon as I've fed you.'

Frikkie stared blankly at her, but now there was something new, an impersonal curiosity. 'I intend to live here,' she told him. 'With Tabson. And if we can find a suitable outhouse, you can stay here, too.'

The next few weeks were filled with activity. The walls were cleaned and painted; the floors scrubbed, the roof cleared of cobwebs; the kitchen floor re-cemented; the outhouse made habitable for Frikkie, a carport built under the trees, ceiling timbers varnished, floors sanded and polished. Home was emerging right under their eyes.

With Frikkie's help she planted and fenced a field for vegetables. After weeks of frenetic energy, the lighthouse was clean and freshly painted, and the repairs were finished. She had been given 'basic necessities' by the liquidator and his idea of 'necessities' had been lavish. He had decided that her own paintings and linen were personal effects. He'd thrown in some cutlery and crockery for a minimal price, so they were fully equipped. She even had her mother's old sewing machine, and the curtains had been altered to fit.

They had beds and two couches, a table and chairs, cushions and even quilted duvets, vases, rugs and books. After some hassles, the water had been switched on, but they were still cooking on a primus and using candles for light. Nevertheless, their home was looking cosy, a little nook of their own, nestling down by the trickling stream, amongst the rocks and rushes. She had picked armfuls of strelitzia to brighten the lower room.

Frikkie had finished the walls and now he was painting the staircase dark green. Luxuriant plants were placed around in earthenware pots, with the taller ones grouped around the bottom of the stairway. A table made of smooth railway sleepers polished to a fine pale beige filled one side of the room with benches on either side. The more she gazed at their home, the more she loved it. Each area came under her careful scrutiny. It had to look exactly right and aesthetically balanced. Frikkie never complained as he moved the furniture and plants this way and that way, and repainted ledges and walls, experimenting with colour until she was totally satisfied.

One morning a funny floppy puppy with huge paws and jutting ribs, a skeleton walking on four stilts, arrived trailing behind Frikkie. They called him Dopey and he stayed.

Each day, around noon, they would light a fire and Kate and Tabson would sit on a rock overlooking the sea and watch Frikkie flick his hand line down amongst the green shallows, as he crouched on a rock immobile, statuesque. The swift jerk was always astonishing and moments later a fat fish would be jumping and gasping until Frikkie took his knife and cut off its head and gutted it, while Tabson watched and learned and *braaied* it on the fire.

Some days they had a pan full of harders and pilchards, which they ate with mealie pap flavoured with tomato and onion gravy. Kate would eat and sleep in the sun, and wake to stagger down to the ice-cold water to swim, and later she would take her paintbrush and tackle another wall, and the funny floppy puppy would squat beside her, being very serious about its self-appointed role of guard dog.

If she was not happy, she was at least content. She had no one to fear, no one to impress. The days passed in a blur, time became muddled.

Only at dusk could she find the time to wander round the lagoon and see how much Frikkie had done to clean up the mess. Would the bush ever recover from the fire? Would the birds ever return? Then one evening she saw some turtle doves, and a malachite kingfisher sitting on a blackened bough searching the shallows for minnows and frogs, and she felt there was hope after all.

Her first visitor was Melissa Grant. She walked in one afternoon carrying a bunch of flowers. It was the first time anyone had come and Kate loved her for it.

'I bought you a vase, too,' she added in her deep, cultured voice. She handed over a long box. 'I thought you might need it, but I see you've coped rather well. Better than I had imagined, but then you were always a genius at this sort of thing. Look how you transformed Angelo's dreary castle.'

She spent a long time examining the room and Kate wondered why she didn't say anything. Had she been a little too lavish with the paint? Was it too colourful? But no! It was absolutely right for the building.

'Why take so much trouble for something that's so temporary?' Melissa said finally. 'Well, you've had your fun. You've tarted up this old place and shown Rob you can survive a few days without him. It's done him good. He's lost at least five kilos. Serves him right. He came down to the boat yesterday. He expects that you'll be back any day now.

'Oh, by the way, the Palmas have decided to give your little black pet a bursary. Anything to get him far away. I don't know why you waste your time with him,' she whispered, looking at Tabson shrewdly. 'All the care in the world won't make much difference. He'll never be accepted by his family because he's crippled.'

She sat down and crossed her beautiful legs. 'Ramona's found a black family prepared to foster him. Professional people. Rob asked me to drop by and tell you to return to your conjugal bed with all haste.'

Kate felt disappointed. So that was why Melissa had come. 'I'm not going back to him, Melissa,' she said. 'I'm going to get a job soon. I've sold a few things and raised enough cash to last me a few months. I want to find out who I am. I'll never know if I let Rob make every decision for me and run my life.'

'I thought you loved him.'

'Yes, I do . . .'

'There's your problem, darling. It's so much simpler when you don't. Then you know where you stand. I dislike my husband,' she went on. From her tone she might have been discussing the weather, Kate thought. 'He's pompous, ugly, disloyal, mean, greedy and old, but there's some very good reasons why I should stay with him.'

'Such as?'

'Continuity, my social position, not having to find out

which friends will dump me, not having to diet, just not being manless.'

'Those things may seem important to you, Melissa, but not to me.'

'You're crazy, Kate. Rob's worth fifty million or more.'

One side of her mouth had twisted down to form a permanent disfiguring line, Kate noticed. 'D'you remember what you said at Dave's birthday party?' Kate said. 'You were so unhappy. It made me think. I don't want that sort of life.'

'We'll see about that, Kate.' Melissa's eyes filled with tears. 'I've just heard Dave's got cancer. They've given him a year at the most. He wants to marry her, but I'm hanging in there. He hasn't got time to divorce me, even if he could succeed.'

Looking at her ravaged face, and the spite in her eyes, and sensing the bitter, wasted years, Kate felt sadness sinking into her, and this made her angry. She had battled so hard to keep her spirits up.

'So you're waiting for him to die,' she accused Melissa.

'What do you think?'

'I think that you're far sadder than you like to pretend.'

'Fuck you,' Melissa said, her voice trembling. 'Oh, by the way.' She stood up and made for the door. 'Rob gave me a message for you. "*If you aren't coming back, fetch your damned goose.*" That's it.'

Later that afternoon Kate went to fetch the goose, but as soon as she came in sight of the house, butterflies started whirling in her stomach, her heart began to pump faster and suddenly she was out of breath.

She was catching the goose when Rob came hurrying from the house. He'd been looking out for her, presumably.

She should have expected this, she thought. He grabbed her by one arm and began pulling her towards the end stable. She gasped as Ponty neighed and stretched his head forward to be stroked.

'Oh, Rob! Since when have you started riding?'

'It's your horse, Kate. I didn't buy the damn thing for me. Take it. I don't want it.'

'How did you know Ponty was for sale?'

'Mary from the stables phoned me. She said: "I have your wife's horse here. I expect you'd like to buy it. One of these days she'll want to ride it again." Then she doubled the price, the bitch. Why did you sell Ponty?'

'I need the cash, I can't afford to feed him and I don't have a stable.'

'If you need cash all you have to do is tell me.'

'I need cash for Tabson's leg.'

There was a long silence. 'All right, I'll pay.'

'You just have – by buying Ponty. Thank you, Rob. Be gentle with him.'

'Kate. Please! Don't do this to us. Come back.'

'No. I can't, Rob.'

'You must come back.' He pulled her towards him, clumsy in his agitation.

'Let me go, Rob. You can't always have your own way. I have to be alone, to think things out and learn to fend for myself. I want a divorce, Rob.'

'Living on alimony is not independence.'

'That's why I don't want any.'

'Idiot!' He tried out a laugh, but it failed miserably. 'Okay, so I was a bit brutal over Tabson. I've reconsidered and decided to forgive you.'

'For what?'

'For being so headstrong and wilful. Now let's stop this

silly game. You've won. Okay? Are you satisfied? A total capitulation on my part. I love you, Kate.'

'Oh, Rob. Don't make it worse for both of us. I'm not coming back. At least, not for the foreseeable future. You'll only dominate me again, and one day I'll find I've become your shadow.' She sighed.

'So you're running away. I must say there's a lot of your father in you.'

'You can't hurt me any more, Rob,' she said, knowing that she was lying, because she was deeply hurt.

'I'll settle a private income on you. You'll never have to ask for a damn thing, but only if you come back. I'm not prepared to keep your lover.'

'I don't have a lover and I don't want your cash,' she said.

She wondered why Rob turned so pale. 'Don't lie,' he snarled and she felt afraid. He seemed to be running out of control. 'I know you spent the night of the fire in that policeman's bed.'

'But that's not true,' she burst out. 'Who said that?'

'I have my sources.'

'He is not my lover,' she said quietly. 'He might have been. I was willing. I wanted to give my love to almost anyone, just as long as it was given for free, instead of selling it for designer clothes and holidays overseas and all the other luxuries you've been holding over my head. I wanted to stop being a whore. Can you understand that?'

'Damn you, Kate.'

The push that was almost a blow, took her by surprise. She sprawled back on the straw and Rob threw himself down on to her. While she struggled to fight him off, Ponty began to rear and kick, but Rob didn't care.

'You're my wife. D'you hear? For all time. I'll never give

you a divorce.' He thrust his mouth on to hers, forcing his tongue between her teeth.

Using all her strength, Kate tried to push him off her. Any moment now, she thought, Ponty will trample us. 'Let me go. You can't force me.'

'Bitch!'

While one hand gripped her throat, squeezing until she was nearly throttled, the other ripped her panties down with violent, powerful movements. She heard the fabric tear and felt the straw against her naked skin. When he loosened his grip on her throat she screamed at him, but he was beyond hearing. He was mumbling: 'You must love me. Don't you know how I miss you? You bitch, you never cared for me, only pretended. How does he fuck you? Is it so damned fantastic that you can throw away millions? Just what has he got?' His hands were gripping her wrists and forcing them together above her head. He pressed his full weight on her until she could only take shallow gasping breaths. Kicking at her knees, he pushed her thighs open.

Kate fought back. He's gone mad, she thought. He might kill me. She bit him hard on the cheek, tasting the blood.

Rob thrust hard and deep inside her, grunting like a pig, muttering: 'You're mine . . . you always have been. Don't leave me. I'll kill him.'

She could not believe how ineffective her strength was. She nearly choked in the dust as he pounded her. She was beginning to panic.

He came, writhing and groaning, rolled off her and began to cry. It was the most pathetic sound she had ever heard.

'You hurt me badly,' she said, trying to get to her feet. Her ears were ringing, there were black spots dancing in front of her eyes, and she felt heavy with pain. Worse still was a sense of physical loathing for herself. She felt dirty and contaminated, her skin crawled with disgust, her limbs were heavy.

'I'm sorry,' he groaned. 'I thought that when we made love you would remember that you love me.'

'You dare to call that love? That was war,' she muttered.

'Have you thought for a moment what I'm going through?' Rob said quietly.

'Buy a Dutch wife that looks like me, Rob. She won't argue and you'll be happier. You don't want a real person. The truth is, I still love you, but you have all the power and you use it crudely and cruelly. That's why I had to leave.'

Noticing that she was half-naked she tried to pull up her pants, but they were in shreds, so she took them off. Her jeans were torn, but no one would see in the car. She soothed the horse and turned to Rob, who was crouched in the corner of the stable, his head in his hands.

'Grow up, Rob. Learn to cope when the terrible power of your wealth and your strength fails you. Try to understand that you being rich has nothing to do with my feelings for you. You might still turn into a real person.'

She gathered up the goose and put it into the box and limped to her car. Then she drove home.

Rob listened to the sound of her car fading out of hearing. Why couldn't she understand how much he loved her? He did not know how to cope with his anguish. Never before had he lost something so precious. It seemed that he was enduring the very worst that man can endure. All that was meaningful was gone. He had tried to bind her to him and she had slipped away. He should end it all. Blow his brains out, but would she care? She would marry her policeman and they would live happily ever after on his money. What should he do? He squatted in the corner of the stable, his head in his hands, thinking.

Every hard-earned lesson of his life had taught him to fight for what he wanted. That was how he had always operated, that was his life. He had learned the power of money in his childhood. Perhaps money could still buy him back his wife and get rid of his rival. What if he put a contract out on St John? These things could be arranged. But murder? God knows he hated enough. One thought obsessed him, he loved Kate and he must regain that which was his. Since she had left he had not once lost the image of her face, her beautiful eyes, or the sensual feel of her soft hands on his body. Making love to Kate had been like a gift from God, but today's sorry affair had been a mockery of his love.

'Oh God!' He muffled his groan with his hands, using every ounce of will-power to hold back his tears.

Chapter 20

———— ————

Meggie's Tea Room opened at eight sharp and Ari was there as Meg opened the door. She was dressed in a green floral overall, her hair tied up in a yellow turban with the shape of rollers protruding through the silk. She looked younger without make-up, he noticed, and without her grey hair showing she could have been thirty-five. Funny how she'd looked pushing fifty the other evening. She lavished fresh cream into his coffee and gave him a toasted egg sandwich which she insisted was on the house. When she'd finished cooking she came and sat next to him bringing her coffee. She smelled of *eau de Cologne*, and her presence made Ari feel relaxed.

He looked around appreciatively. She'd turned the corner shop into a cosy, homely place, but right outside he could see several dozen squatters, hunched and hopeless, crouched in the corner of the car park area. Then he saw Meg's kitchenmaid, together with the cook, carry out a big urn of soup. A waitress followed with a tray of loaves cut into halves.

'Poor sods,' she said. 'I can't tell you how heartsore I am. It's not their fault. They should never have been brought here. They were promised the earth: houses, jobs – everything! They paid up to thirty rands each for their bus fares, and then they were dumped on the pavement with no hope of finding jobs or homes.'

'Hm! Probably there are enough jobs around these parts if only the locals could get over their fear and antipathy.'

'If you hear of anything, let me know. They pop in here looking for work and I'm keeping all inquiries. The church is running an ironing and mending depot, so some of the women earn a bit there.'

A station wagon drew up outside and a boy of about twelve ran up the stairs and paused in the doorway. 'Mum wants a guy to cut the lawn,' he said.

'Hang on.' Meg stood up. She went outside and called. 'There's almost a thousand of them,' she said when she returned. 'The fish-canning factories have taken on some as cleaners and upgraded the coloureds to better jobs. About a hundred women are charring around local homes, but there's a long way to go.'

She was a good woman, Ari decided. He began to sound her out gently. 'Terrible the way they lost all they own.'

'Yes, awful, truly awful. Some of them were badly burned.' She flushed and tucked a wisp of hair under the scarf.

'Four of them died.'

She shuddered. 'As if I didn't know. Don't tell me again. Things like that upset me.'

'I guess we all feel responsible after that meeting here.'

'What do you mean?' Her face became very red, while her eyes flashed warning signals.

'Well, let's face it, jointly and severally we all wanted them thrown out. Some were more outspoken than others. D'you know how many of the locals joined Dave's committee to throw them out?'

'What committee was that?' she murmured.

'You were there and so was I, Meg. Who exactly was on Dave's side? Did he come up with a plan on how to shift them out of the dunes?'

Meg's face became impenetrable. The warm glow petered out, her lips folded into a straight line and suddenly she looked fifty again. 'Why don't you ask him yourself? I know nothing about it. I don't think anyone spoke up about pushing out the squatters. Not that I can remember. In fact, no, definitely not.'

'It was murder, Meg,' he said gently. 'You're not the type to get involved with murder, are you?'

'You're talking rot. One of their paraffin stoves turned over, I shouldn't be surprised. They're always burning themselves out. Happens all the time.'

'The fire was caused by petrol bombs. We have the evidence and we've opened a murder docket. We intend to get the culprits. It's no secret. You can tell your customers, Meg. If folks around don't speak up they could find themselves arrested as accessories to murder. That applies to you, too.'

'Are you threatening me?' she asked. She put one hand on his arm. 'Don't, Ari. I like you. It was accidental, there was no such committee. We're all liberals here, we always have been. No one would harm these people, but they shouldn't be in Silver Bay.' She stood up and went behind the counter, her expression stiff and unapproachable. Ari turned his attention to his egg sandwich, wolfed it down and ordered another. The only real fight they had was when he insisted on paying.

Ari found Jean Graux cleaning the trawler. There was a big swell even in the harbour and Ari had difficulty keeping his footing for there was nothing to hold on to within shouting distance of the man.

'Thank God I spent my life at sea,' Jean said. 'I'd hate to blunder into the incestuous disaster they call Silver Bay. They're all interdependent, you know, and most of them have skeletons in their antique cabinets. They'll cover up for each other.'

'Why?' Ari demanded, but Jean had turned away. He was bent over the hold of his fishing trawler, holding the end of a powerful hose. In his thigh-length rubber boots, old T-shirt and shorts, he could have been mistaken for one of his crew.

'What is it with you?' he shouted, ignoring Ari's question. 'You have this compulsion to punish the guilty, but who can point a finger at anyone in particular and say that he made himself what he is – that we are blameless and he is guilty? We're all in this together, or didn't you know that? Of course, that's why you're a policeman. You don't get much pay, do you? Why do you do it? You have this compulsion to find the truth – and when you find it what are you going to do with it?'

'As you said – punish the guilty. I like to think I represent law and order. It's all we have – the sum total of our fight against savagery.'

'The beast within . . . ?'

'I suppose so.'

'And your beast? There must be a reason why you have this desire to hit back.'

Ari sighed. He had talked about his work over the odd pint in the pub. Jean knew too much about him, but he never talked about current cases. Ari switched the question on to 'hold'. It would be there waiting for recall on one of his darker nights. He sat watching the stormy, dark green sea, and the frenzied gulls, who were circling, screaming and diving.

'What are they after?' he called out to Jean.

'Same as the tunny are after, it's the tunny that are churning up the water – sardines. In the sea everything feeds on smaller fry, just like this bay. They and it . . .' He grinned delightedly at his philosophical outburst. 'Ultimately it all boils down to the poor, bloody sardines. All that!' He gestured towards the richer suburbs.

'So you, Ari, are threatening the town's idol, squatting up there in his quasi-Spoleto castle.' There was a hint of malice in his voice that puzzled Ari. 'Can't you see him up there with his binoculars sizing up the shoal? He probably knows how many tunny I'll catch before I even net them. Can't you feel your skin prickling? I bet he's watching you right now and wondering how to get rid of you.'

'Why should he want to do that?'

'Because you're like a seal. You hang on and you won't let go. You'll shake your victim until he spills his guts.'

'You think he's guilty of the dunes' murders?'

'Don't worry, he keeps his hands clean. He pays others to do his dirty work. Look at me, up to my thighs in fish offal, doing his dirty work.'

'He pays you well.'

'Yeah! And I bet he paid some poor sucker to burn out the squatters. Look here, Ari . . .' Jean jumped over the rails and perched on a bollard. He fumbled for a cigarette, but couldn't get it alight in the gale. 'After all, it's his land – well, his and Kate Palma's. They're all in the same family – or were.' He gave Ari a searching glance and burst into harsh laughter. 'I'd watch out if I were you.'

Ari felt his cheeks flushing. So all the village knew about

Kate spending the night in his room. He hung on to his dignity, ignoring the innuendos.

'I can't see the Palmas' motive in burning the squatters out. They're rich and they have so much power. Others stand to lose much more, relatively speaking.'

'The word's been getting round that the squatters found ruins under the dunes. There must be a reason why Palma had the former house buried under the sand.'

'Are you sure about this?' Ari asked curiously.

'I listen to the gossip in the bars. The fishermen are great talkers when the wine gets into them. If I were you I'd sound out about how Bill September got to be so rich. He's worth close on half a million. There's some rumour about Angelo recompensing Bill for the death of his father. Old man September was Angelo's first skipper when he bought his first trawler. He's one tough bastard,' Jean said. 'Believe me!'

'Yes,' Ari said. 'The gale's worsening.'

Jean frowned. 'It'll be a bad trip, but I'm going anyway. See you tonight at the Humber. Okay?'

Jean climbed down the hold. Five minutes later he emerged in oilskins. The boat shuddered and began to move away from the quay. The crew were jumping around, winding ropes and battening down.

Was there any other country in the world where fishermen faced such hazardous conditions? Ari wondered as he watched the trawler moving head-on through the gale towards the harbour entrance. Five minutes later it was heading out to sea through the massive swell, rising on pyramids of water and falling out of sight. So Angelo had started off the hard way. Obviously he knew how to gamble against tough odds, and he wasn't short of guts either, but would he risk murder for the sake of money? That didn't seem to ring true. He decided to drive on up to Tom's place. He knew everything about the past.

Tom was not in, but his neighbour, a widow, came running. 'He's in hospital,' she said. 'Someone wanted to kill him. Three boys tried to necklace him. Why should anyone want to kill that poor old cripple?'

'Oh God! Is he badly burned? Which hospital? Why didn't someone tell me?'

'It only happened this morning. I believe he's okay. Why don't you leave him alone?'

'Do you know which hospital Tom's in?'

'Somerset.'

'Why would anyone want to pick on Tom?'

'The squatters might. They might think he's responsible for burning them out.'

'A man with no legs?'

'Tom has a lot of power. He's always been the unofficial union leader of the crewmen on company's trawlers. He got a bad deal from the company when he had his accident and he tries to make sure they don't. Last week he organised a strike of the locals to force Rob Palma to turn the blacks – mainly squatters from Ovambo – off the boats. Tom knew there weren't enough trained blacks to crew the entire fleet. Rob was all for flying in new teams of Ovambos from up-country, but his grandfather stepped in and forced him to sack the blacks. Old man Palma has always been in favour of keeping the jobs and the money in the village. God knows why. It would pay them to take on blacks, they're cheaper and they work harder.'

'So you think Tom was trying to force black labour out of this area and that he might have got some blokes to burn out the squatters?'

'I don't think so, but some might. Why else would they want to kill him?'

And why would they go to such lengths to try and make it look like a black vendetta-type killing by necklacing? Ari wondered silently. Anyone could have crept in on that old man in the night and bumped him off with a brick or a knife.

Ari had a present for Tom. He carried it carefully into the ward and laid it on Tom's knees. Tom looked older and more battered, but his eyes blazed with childlike indignation. There were dressings on his hands and face, but he was not badly hurt.

'Help me up, Ari. I want to sit up straight. I've been ringing the bell, but these flighty nurses only come when they feel like it. Without my piece of rope I'm lost.'

Ari put his arm under Tom's armpit and hauled him to a sitting position, feeling surprised at the steely muscles in his arm and his back which were as hard as iron. He pushed the pillows behind him. 'Okay?'

'That's fine, thank you.'

'So how did this happen?' Ari asked, pointing to Tom's bandaged hands.

'Gang of hoodlums. Luckily for me my neighbours were home. They rushed outside and drove them off. Someone threw a match, but they weren't set up for their fireworks display and I'd wrenched the tyre off my head, but my hands got it, as you can see. I reckon I'll have the bandages off and be out of here within a week.'

'You didn't lay a charge?'

'I guessed you'd get here sooner or later. What's the point of laying a charge, my boy? It was Patel's hoodlums and Patel is out on bail. What the hell is the good of you fellows? Can you tell me that?'

'Not really,' Ari said. 'So Sam Patel tried to make it look like a black vendetta. Well, I'll get after him. Open your present.'

Tom opened the package with difficulty. Ari wanted to help him, but he waved him off. Eventually the paper came off a bottle of rum.

'There's this, too, Tom,' Ari said, handing him an envelope. Tom opened it with the help of his teeth and a cheque for 10,000 rands fell on to the bed.

'What's this then?' Tom asked, his voice quavering for the first time.

'Maybe you didn't know there was a reward offered by the CPU for information leading to the rescue of one Tabson Tweneni. This is the reward.'

Tom looked up, his eyes shining with tears. 'You take this, my boy,' he said. 'You'll have more use for it than I. You can get around. I heard the story of how you got him out of the sea. You're famous round the village, Ari.'

'Tom, it's yours. It will ease your old age. For instance, you could buy two better legs and what's more, I reckon I could get another subsidy towards paying for them.'

'Let's drink to this, Ari. Will you join me?'

'Sure will,' Ari said. He was on duty and he hated rum, but what the hell. It was the right time and place for a celebration.

Tom sat stroking the bottle, a soft smile playing around his lips. 'I admire you,' he said. 'There's no nonsense about you. You remind me of someone I used to know well. I'm going to give you some information. This business of burning out the squatters could be a whole lot more complicted than you realise, Ari.' He pronounced his words so clearly and there was that trace of an Irish accent again, which always became audible when he drank.

'Why don't you go and see Emanuel Fernandes, who lives up the top of the village? He has something you should have. Tell him I said he should hand it over. He might be a little unwilling to do this, you see. And give him my regards.'

When Ari said goodbye, Tom was sitting up in bed smiling happily. Ari tried not to show the old man how worried he was. If Patel had decided Tom was responsible for tipping off the police, leading to Patel's charge of attempted murder and kidnapping, then Tom was in big trouble.

Chapter 21

―――――   ――――

By the time Ari arrived at the Fernandeses' house in the
coloureds' village, he had put in an hour of research
and discovered that Emanuel Fernandes was Spanish,
but he had applied to change his racial classification in
March, 1961, in order to marry his beautiful, half-French,
half-Ethiopian woman, Juliette, and live with her in the
coloured village. They were both Rastafarians and saw
themselves as self-appointed missionaries, but so far they
had few converts to their faith.

Rastafarians, he had read, worship Haile Selassie, the
former Emperor of Ethiopia, under his pre-coronation
name, Ras (Prince) Tafari, whom they consider to be the
Messiah and champion of the black race. They believe
that blacks are reincarnated Israelites, subjected to white
domination as divine punishment for past-life sins. When
they are redeemed, whites will be compelled to serve them.
They are vegetarians and smoke *dagga* as part of their
religion.

The Fernandeses had a pretty pink house at the end of a
tree-covered, cobbled cul de sac, overlooking the harbour.
Emanuel had long greying hair tied in a pigtail, a long
beard and soft brown eyes. He earned a living producing
beautiful stained glass. Ari was fascinated by a cockerel

with fiery colourful feathers, a butterfly in shades of purple, mauve and crimson, and a pelican standing in a turquoise swamp.

It took Ari some time to convince them that he was not going to book them for having the largest and most vigorous *dagga* bush he'd seen, growing in their backyard beside a crimson poinsettia. Then, while Juliette made him black tea with lemon and honey, and brought biscuits, Emanuel slyly offered him a joint, which he accepted. Ari was delighted with them. He made up his mind to win their confidence.

'That bush has a story,' Emanuel told him. His face took on a poignant expression, but Ari did not prompt him. He sensed he only had to wait.

'It was planted nearly thirty years ago by a close friend,' he said, the tears rolling down his cheeks. 'We used to have some mad times in those days. All-night parties, dancing by moonlight, and the drinking. He should have been spoiled, he was so damned wealthy, but he was the kindest, sweetest person you'd ever want to meet.'

Ari decided to wait for the *dagga* to take hold of Emanuel. 'Tom sent me to you,' he said eventually. 'He thinks you have something I should have. He suspects that Mandy's kidnapping and the dunes murders are connected in some way to something that happened thirty years ago. Do you know what he's talking about?'

Emanuel turned pale and lit another joint. He called Juliette back and they argued in Spanish. Ari wished he could understand what they were saying as he surreptitiously switched on his tape recorder. They went on arguing for quite a while. Juliette seemed to be winning.

Emanuel was on his fourth joint and his eyes were rolling wildly. 'Too many deaths, my friend,' he said. 'And they all sprang from love. Strange, that, don't you think? The death of my friend was only a part of it. Juliette feels you should have this evidence. I shall not tell you anything, because I don't know what happened and that's the truth. Just in case my fears were based on firm evidence, I buried this box beneath the tree. I felt it was a fitting place for it.'

He went outside and took a spade and dug down three feet to a wooden box which he had buried there. The soil was loose, Ari noticed, so it hadn't been there long. He brought the box inside.

Juliette shuddered and hurried outside as Ari opened the box and unfolded the plastic sheet. He swore quietly at a skull lying there. The back of the skull was broken and the neck vertebrae snapped off. The bones were smooth and white and it looked very old.

'D'you believe this skull is that of your friend?' Ari asked.

'No. He's buried in the Palmas' private cemetery. Whatever I say to you will be guesses. You must make your own investigation. It's better this way.'

'So where was it found?'

'One of the squatters, his name's Boysie by the way, was acting as a sort of leader. He feared a dysentery outbreak so he called for volunteers to dig a row of latrines on the western side of the lagoon. They started on an eight-foot-deep trench where one of them unearthed this skull amongst a good deal of building debris. He didn't know what to do with it, so he tried to sell it. I bought it.'

'Why didn't you contact us?'

'I don't know why. Perhaps I am afraid of resurrecting old hurts. Perhaps I'm wrong in my suspicions. Would the police be interested in a twenty-eight-year-old death? It might be accidental. Who knows?'

Ari took the skull and left. Fernandes had said

twenty-eight years. Obviously from something that happened then. And the *dagga* bush was almost thirty years old.

His curiosity stirred, Ari drove straight to a Spanish restaurant in town and bribed the waiter to listen to the tape and translate the conversation while he made notes.

Fernandes: 'It was all settled long ago and he paid . . . God knows he paid enough.'

Juliette: 'Can money pay for a life?'

Fernandes: 'We don't know it's her. We haven't the proof and even if it was, who's to say she was murdered?'

Juliette: 'What if she were your friend, or your sister? Wouldn't you want to do something about it?'

Fernandes: 'We don't even know if it's her skull.'

Juliette: 'Of course it is. I always knew she wouldn't leave without saying goodbye to me. They killed her.'

Fernandes: 'He was my friend. What would *he* have wanted us to do?'

Juliette: 'That's obvious. He loved her.'

Fernandes: 'He loved his father, too.'

Juliette: 'Give him the skull. What will be, will be.'

Ari drove back to the station and sent the skull to forensic in Pretoria. There were three new cases on his desk – all breaking and entering in areas near the beach. It would take up the rest of the afternoon. He sighed, hunted in his desk drawer for his sandwich, and drove to the first address.

It was almost time to go off duty. Ari was tired, but he decided to question the Bronsons. He arrived at that precise moment when the sun, tonight a massive red globe, was sinking below the turquoise sea. In that ephemeral moment a flash of green seemed to light the sun's descent.

'Did you see that?' Jack said, sounding awed. He turned to Ari for the first time. 'I've never seen it before. I've looked for years.' His hands were shaking, Ari noticed. 'When you see that green flash, it means your dreams come true.'

Could a businessman like Jack really believe that? Ari wondered. Or was he in deep financial trouble and grasping at straws? What if it were true? What would he wish? Ari had a sudden longing to find his roots, and with this feeling came the most extraordinary affirmation that he would succeed here in Silver Bay. His conscious acceptance came like a bolt from the sky, yet intuitively he realised that he had always known this.

The two men sat in silence, watching the mountain peaks, still brilliant with sunlight, shed their bright images into the dark reflecting sea. Purple shadows crept up from their base in dark water, while violet mists stole across the sea from the darkening horizon. As the last transient light vanished on the horizon, sea and sky merged into an indeterminate grey. The magic was quite lost.

'I sit here every night and watch the sunset,' Jack said after a long silence. 'It's like a sort of a drug. I have to be here. Of course, I can't always make it.'

At that moment Gill tripped in wearing ultra-high heels and a very short skirt and carrying a tray with snacks and ice. She must have seen him come. The lights from the passage silhouetted her figure and formed a golden light around her hair. Her face seemed soft and appealing, her figure youthful. She was still a beautiful woman, he acknowledged, and she dressed for men in soft clinging fabrics that showed her rounded thighs. How old was she? he wondered. When she stooped over him her dress fell forward showing her naked breasts, and her musky perfume drifted round him. At that moment she seemed like a part of the night: sensual, sultry, highly desirable.

'Hi, Gill,' he said, standing up slowly. He turned away deliberately, for something in her eyes showed she had seen his need.

'What about a Scotch?' Jack asked.

'Actually, Jack, I'm still on duty. To be precise, for the next five minutes, so if you'd pour a Scotch I can gulp it down shortly. It will be very welcome, I've had a frustrating day, but I have a few questions to ask you.'

'Sit down,' Gill said. 'I'm going to be popping in and out. I have some jobs I want to do.'

'Questions in the line of duty?' Jack asked looking apprehensive.

'Yes. It's about the fire.'

'Oh that. Well, I suppose one of them pushed their primus stove over. Happens all the time. Blessing in disguise really. God forbid a squatter camp were to take root right under our noses in our little corner of heaven. For starters, we'd lose our property values. Can you imagine the views? Iron huts and wood fires, the smog, the sunsets would be ruined, and the beach would be unusable – for whites, that is. Most of the shops down there rely on tourism. They'd go under in no time.'

'I'm a stranger here,' Ari said. 'I've no idea what a house like this would sell for. I hope you don't mind my asking.'

'Before the recession a couple of million. Right now it's valued at one and a half million. With a squatter camp down below I wouldn't be able to give it away. Same goes for every other house around here. Then there's the tea rooms, the restaurants, the little boutiques. If those squatters realised that collectively they were costing us around a billion they'd have put the squeeze on.'

'But you, individually, stood to lose almost two million rands if the squatters stayed where they were?'

'Yes.' He stood up looking worried and poured himself another drink. Ari began to feel convinced of a conspiracy existing between the major ratepayers. Perhaps the committee organised by Dave was responsible for the fire. Had they paid someone to burn out the squatters? Would Jack admit to anything? Probably not, but he decided to give it a try anyway.

'So you and that so-called committee stood to lose a fortune if the squatters remained?'

'Good God! We're not murderers you know. As I said, one drunken fool knocked his primus over and the whole camp went up like a fireworks factory.'

'That's because most of the shacks were doused with petrol bombs while everyone was sleeping, and more bombs were hidden around the place. The place was torched with petrol bombs.'

Gill, who was standing in the doorway, dropped her tray with a clatter. 'No! I don't believe it. How can you prove that? The petrol would have burned away.'

'But not the evidence. Nowadays it's easy to prove. Besides, a crude type of petrol bomb was left on site.'

'They should never have come here. No one wants them.' Gill broke off and swore. Then she poured herself a drink.

'Gill, you have to understand that Silver Bay is no longer the isolated colonial haven we once had here,' Jack began.

'In a way it's a microcosm of South Africa,' Ari took over, 'because we have everyone here, all races, all social levels. They are here because they are here, because they exist, because they have to survive and grow. We've kept them apart from us for fifty years. Hidden out of sight. In times of drought the children died like flies. Now they've joined our world and we have to learn to accommodate them. That's it, quite simply.'

She shot him a look of pure poison and Ari wondered if Kate's visit had something to do with that. Afterwards they spoke about mundane things and Jack became maudlin and spoke at great lengths about his time in America. He brought out the photograph album. Ari excused himself as soon as he could and went to bed early.

Around eleven, Gill knocked quietly at his door. She was dressed in a transparent negligée of black nylon. He could see the outline of her breasts which were fuller than he had imagined and her skin looked soft and inviting.

'We can't do this to Jack,' he said, blocking the doorway.

'Oh, for God's sake! I just want someone to talk to,' she said, pushing past him. 'I slipped out to warn you.'

'Of what?'

'Not to make a fool of yourself. You're a nice guy, but you don't understand the people in this town.'

'That's true,' he said encouragingly. 'Have a drink?'

'Oh yes, please.' She sat childlike on his bed, her knees under her chin and her arms wrapped around them. 'I want to warn you that you're going to make a lot of enemies if you pursue this case,' she whispered.

That's exactly what Gerber said, Ari thought.

'I want to tell you about us. Jack was wiped out. You know how Lloyds underwriters work. You have to pay jointly and severally. Jack's share was more than we owned. At the same time Jack has a good property business, so Angelo Palma lent him the cash to pay his debts. This way Jack had a chance to get on his feet again.'

'Why did Angelo do that?'

'I don't know,' she said. 'Everyone in this town owes him something. In a way, he's like a benevolent Godfather. Not the evil Mafia sort, but everyone's benefactor. I suppose he wins our allegiance that way.'

'Why should he want it?'

'I don't know. It's almost as if he feels he owes all of us a debt. If so, he's been paying back for a very long time. Not that it makes much difference to him, because he's so incredibly wealthy. I sometimes wonder if it really helped Jack. The embarrassment of being helped has made him strange. He's sort of not very manly any more.'

'Impotent?'

'You said it.'

'You can cope, can't you? It's not the end of the world, is it?'

'It's his spitefulness that I can't cope with. He seems to blame me. God knows, but I tried to keep him out of Lloyds. And then the lack of love – not just the sex. Sometimes, on nights like this, I can't bear it.' She stood up and leaned out of the window. 'Just smell the night, the wonderful, hot, balmy scent in the wind. This is a night for love.' She unfastened her gown and it fell in a shimmering nylon heap. 'Please love me, Ari, just for tonight. Please.'

What else could he do? Ari wondered. He had never ever refused a woman. It would be so impolite.

He took off his pants and folded her in his arms, but where was his libido? He felt embarrassed. When he felt her naked flesh writhing against his hips and belly, he gasped and suddenly needed her. He picked her up and carried her to the bed and pushed into her. His passion was released as she began to move, gyrating her hips, clutching his neck and whispering in his ear: 'I knew you'd be like this. Oh, darling, darling.' Exquisite pleasure was flooding through him. She was all melting and molten inside, merging and flowing with his will, her gasps and shudders dependent upon his thrust and pull. Now her low moans were egging him on to take over while she lay helpless and softly clinging. He heard her cry again and again. She was skilled, and fragrant and sensual and she hadn't been screwed for a long time. She wanted more, and still more and she came often with deep, shuddering sighs. Ari came three times, feeling guiltier each time.

'Remember,' she whispered around 3 a.m. when she left. 'We are just two desperately lonely people reaching out for comfort in the night. I still love Jack.' She burst into noisy tears and fled.

Ari tried to get some sleep, in the three hours or so he had left, but he tossed and turned. He couldn't help thinking about Mandy and her plight and his inability to find any clues about her kidnapping. And then there was Eunice and her terrible death. It hurt that he was unable to find those responsible. What was it Jean had asked? What is it that drives you to get your revenge? Was he right? What crime took place in his early childhood that he had pushed out of his conscious mind? He had a pathological fear of evil, he knew, allied to an unreasonable aggressiveness towards cruelty. Was some dark act hidden in the deep recesses of his mind?

After a while he got to think of Angelo. What sort of a man was he? Good or evil? Philanthropist or power mad? Manipulating the locals with offers of cash, or genuinely wanting to help them? Who was it who had burned out the squatters? Had they heard the screams, seen the corpses? And if so, did they care?

At precisely 4.30 a.m. he thought he heard footsteps creeping towards his room. He froze. Yes, there was no mistake, someone was at the window. His heart jolted as he fumbled for his gun.

The window was slowly sliding down, but as yet he could see nothing. Then there was silence and he guessed that the intruder was listening to hear if he was sleeping. He tried to stop holding his breath and breathe heavily as if he were sleeping, but thoughts of a petrol bomb kept him rigid with fright. Slowly a head moved up until it was silhouetted against the moonlit sky. It was larger than life, like a gorilla, with a mass of tangled hair. He almost yelled out, but then he remembered Frikkie. The massive bulk was amazingly lightfooted as it climbed in and approached the bed. Ari brought his gun slowly round to point at a spot between the man's eyes, but he turned away and began to search the cottage.

Ari waited until he was in the kitchen and climbed out of bed. He aimed his gun and switched on the light. Frikkie wheeled round and tried to bolt for the window, but Ari tripped him as he lunged past.

The demented man lay blinking, spittle trickling out of one corner of his mouth, his eyes shocked and blank. He was quite old, Ari realised, fifty at least, but his vacant expression made it hard to pinpoint his age.

A quick frisk made it clear that Frikkie had no weapon, not even a knife. His hands were still blistered and burned and he was mumbling incoherently. 'You have no right . . . no right . . . give it to me,' he begged.

'Give what to you?'

Frikkie became evasive, but Ari caught one sentence – 'She should get a proper burial.'

Life was getting interesting. There was no point in

booking Frikkie, Ari decided. He was harmless and witless. No point in trying to get to sleep either. He dressed and drove Frikkie down to the all-night café for fishermen in the docks where he bought them both thick toasted egg and bacon sandwiches and strong sweet coffee.

Frikkie gobbled his like a starving man.

'You're a good bloke,' he said in a hoarse, soft voice. 'You could have put me inside. Ramona's a terror when she's angry. She's got it into her head that I lied to her. It's all because of you coming here. But it wasn't my fault. She's wrong to blame me. The dolphin took him. But she won't listen to me.'

'Why were you searching my room, Frikkie?'

'She sent me,' he said evasively.

'What were you looking for?'

His eyes began to flick wildly from side to side. 'Wasn't my fault,' he said.

Ari decided to get a skilled psychiatrist to question Frikkie and see if they could get any sense out of him.

'It wasn't me, it was the dolphin,' he muttered craftily with a mouth full of egg.

He was getting nowhere, Ari decided impatiently. He ordered another sandwich for Frikkie, paid and left.

Dawn was breaking above the craggy peaks and the sky was turning from pale green to rose. The air was cool and faintly fragrant, smelling of the sea, wild herbs and damp earth. There were no puffs of clouds above the mountains, a sure sign that the gale had blown itself out. They were going to have another lovely day. What a place! As he walked into the station he thought about Gill and Kate. Two lovely women who couldn't be more different. He'd fucked one of them. He couldn't help wondering about the other one. Pity they were both taboo. He felt a sense of lingering regret, for Kate specifically, and for all the beautiful women he was never going to love.

Chapter 22

Tabson was strangely quiet on the way to the hospital, his small hand gripping hers. On impulse Kate stopped at a toyshop in town. There was a huge assortment of weird gadgets. Toyshops had changed since she was young and that wasn't so long ago, she decided. Tabson refused to accept more than one item, and finally picked a contraption of Perspex balls, rods and bits of electrical wiring. 'I'm afraid this is a bit advanced for his age,' the shop owner said apologetically. 'You can make all sorts of vehicles that move and do things, but I don't think he . . .'

Tabson grabbed it harder.

'We'll take it,' Kate said.

Dr Jones, worried, frowning and intent, said very little until he had taken Tabson away for an examination and X-rays. He returned much later and explained the position at length. He was the best orthopaedic surgeon in the country and Kate intended to take his advice. While he examined his theatre appointments Kate made a mental note of the bottom line . . . a minimum of three operations would be necessary, including skin grafts, and there was no guarantee of success, but even a failure would leave Tabson far better off than his present condition. The possibility existed that he might become almost normal. They must start immediately because his spine was badly affected and becoming curved.

'I realise you're doing this for philanthropic reasons, Mrs Palma,' the doctor said in his grey colourless voice, 'and I shall assist you by operating at a minimal charge. However, there will still be the theatre costs, hospital, tests, X-rays, remedial treatment, et cetera. I'll speak to everyone, but you won't get away with less than three thousand Rands.'

'Thank you, Dr Jones,' she said, feeling strangely moved. 'Please go ahead.' It was far more than she had expected, but somehow she would find a way to raise the extra cash.

'Go and get his things and bring him back,' he said gently. 'He must be admitted before four o'clock. Now that he knows, the sooner we get started the better. It won't be easy for him.'

What a rush! They bought new pyjamas and books and the rest of the things he would need, went home to feed Dopey and say goodbye to Frikkie, then back to the clinic. Ten minutes later Tabson was sitting up in bed, looking dazed and scared, but very determined.

'Listen, Tabson.' She held his hand, smoothing the rough skin. 'God will look after you. Do you believe in God?'

'God, missus?' His brow wrinkled. Oh goodness, how could she begin? The gap between them was like an unbreachable chasm. Yet he was so compassionate. Surely there was some innate part of God within each living creature?

'Just like you wanted to heal our goose, so the doctor and I want to heal you, just because we love you, like you love the goose. Okay, you got that?'

His hand tightened on hers. 'Stop worrying, missus,' he

said in his husky voice. 'I want my leg to get better. I want to play soccer and I don't care if this hurts.'

She left with a lump in her throat.

Arriving home, she found the telephone department installing her telephone. Her first call was to reassure Tabson and tell him the good news.

Three days ago their electricity had been switched on. She couldn't believe it had happened at last. She had spent days plaguing the electricity department to lay a new cable to the lighthouse. She'd had to pay in advance for the work, but now, at last, she had water, electricity and a telephone. What a day! What bliss! But it had all cost so much and the knowledge that she was fast running out of cash was like a dark shadow that followed her wherever she went. Most times she battled to keep her fears at bay.

When the telephone rang for the first time later that evening, she leaped with joy and grabbed the receiver, feeling sure that it was Rob.

'Darling, thank God you have a phone at last. I've been plaguing them for days. I need you.' It was Melissa's deep, cultured voice. 'Dave is sinking fast. Only a matter of days, they say. Isn't it tragic?' She gave a little sob. 'We have to be brave. I know he would like that. Darling, about that silly old house of ours. I've wanted to refurbish it for years, but Dave had an attachment to all the junk we've collected. Quite honestly, Kate, you're the best person to tackle the job. Now don't say "no", or you can't, because it's a matter of great importance to me. I want you to get over here first thing in the morning. Turn this house upside down, throw out the furniture, everything, even the paintings. Of course, you'll get a good price for them and I'll give you a cut. I'm going away, darling. By the time I come back, I want this place to be livable. I don't want a single damned item left that reminds me of Dave. And nothing nautical either, I'll never forget that bloody bitch in her sailor hat and just about nothing else.'

'What about Dave? Doesn't he have a say in it?' Kate asked quietly.

'He'll never know. He's sinking fast. That's why I want to throw out grief and create a wonderful atmosphere. You did that with your absurd lighthouse. Did you know that, darling? You threw out sadness and created joy . . . with colour and plants and God knows what else. I don't know how you did it, Kate, but now you must do it for me. I want it finished by my birthday.'

'When's that?'

'In a month's time.'

'You're crazy, Melissa. Be reasonable.'

'This is business, darling. Name your price. Just do it! See you in the morning. Bye, darling.'

A sharp click terminated the conversation.

I suppose she's rich enough to have her own way now, whatever the cost, Kate thought. So Dave's dying. What if it were Rob? Oh God! No! Tears started burning her eyes and she clenched her fists. She still loved him, she thought regretfully.

How could she be alone tonight? She drove around the village and parked for a while near the Grants' home, but decided against going in. Next she drove towards Cecilia's studio, but changed her mind again. She had such a longing to see Rob, although she knew it was madness, but eventually she succumbed and drove up the windy deserted road through the nature reserve to Angelo's house.

She parked and noticed that Rob's car was there and

not in the garage, so he was home, but going out again. Presumably Angelo was in, since there was a light in his study. She paused and looked up at the house. She had always hated it, perhaps because she had wanted them to have their own home, but looking at the building with new eyes she realised that she had never appreciated the masterly way it was constructed, with rounded turrets and jutting ledges.

It was then that she heard a giggle coming from the pool room behind the swimming pool, followed by the deep boom of Rob's baritone voice. Shivering with tension and anticipated hurt, she crept towards the sounds.

Rob was making love, that much was clear. She had to get out of there, but her feet would not obey her head. Instead she kept walking towards them as if mesmerised.

Blunderingly she leaned against the wall, setting off the burglar alarm. The lights switched on, dazzling her. The noise seemed to numb her mind. Rob raced out, gun in hand, followed by a tall thin girl with a towel around her. She recognised the face of a local TV star before she turned away.

'I'm sorry,' she said. 'I just . . . I felt . . . I don't know why I came.' She began to run, blinded by her tears.

'What the hell did you expect?' she heard Rob roar behind her. 'I'm not a eunuch. Come back here. Come back, Kate.'

She was driving blindly down the driveway, hitting bumps, tyres screeching around corners, panting with hurt.

'Oh God, oh God,' she was repeating obsessively. The drive to the lighthouse was a nightmare. Memories of Rob crowded in on her: Rob with his black hair glinting purple in the sun at the helm of his skiboat, his eyes alight with excitement; Rob naked in the tub, his broad strong shoulders rippling wet and soapy, Rob's bottom lip so sensuous and full, the way he kissed her. In spite of everything that had passed between them, Kate knew that she loved him still. Now he had this woman . . . She gritted her teeth. Had the two of them made love even when she was living with him? 'God damn the bastard,' she muttered. Her eyes clouded with tears, she missed the path and swung into loose sand. The wheels turned loudly and futilely. She rubbed her eyes and got out of the car. Frikkie would dig it out in the morning. She walked the rest of the way. Rob was right, she thought, as she flung open her front door and collapsed weeping in a chair. He wasn't a eunuch. Far from it! She should have known, but that did not dull her pain.

Night fell bringing loneliness. How empty the lighthouse seemed without Tabson. Even Dopey whined around unhappily. Kate walked outside and sat on the rock overlooking the sea. The full moon was rising from behind the mountains and the sea was glittering with its countless reflections. She could see the lights of the rich homes twinkling halfway up the mountain. Far off on her right a cluster of dimmer lights shone in a dull haze from the coloureds' village.

At that moment the carefully created wall she had built between herself and her present chaos crumpled. Why had it happened? What trauma had led Rob to crave power and mastery over everyone and why did she crave her freedom? The tragic collapse of their love seemed to twist like a knife in her stomach. 'Oh God,' she wailed, suddenly frantic as fear and loneliness swelled through her. Even those fisherfolk knew how to love, how to fight and forgive and start again. At that moment she longed to be one of them, bedded with her husband, bodies entwined, safe in their traditional roles, not questioning, nor rebelling, at peace with one another.

She listened to the waves washing the sand, and the murmur of the stream trickling down the rocks. A night jay was calling in the trees behind, and a dikkop, lonely since his mate was killed, came hopping through the grass and screeched at her. Poor lonely bird! There was the sudden call from an African owl and then a piercing shriek. She shivered and silently wept.

I am cursed, she thought, her mother dead and her father gone and now Rob lost to her forever. All her dear memories of Rob were hopelessly contaminated. The lights in the village went out, the moon rose, but Kate, filled with a deep sense of loneliness, sat motionless.

Ari had got in the habit of checking Kate's lighthouse nightly, just to make sure she was all right. Tonight he saw that there were no lights on, but the door was open. He heard a dog growl and saw a figure sitting silently on the rock. Then the dog, which was just a starved puppy, flung himself at Ari, barking ferociously.

'Hey, boy! Where d'you come from? Easy there, easy now. I'm a friend. I won't harm you.

'You shouldn't be sitting out alone at night,' he called to Kate. 'You know it's not safe. This crazy mutt is not enough protection. Next time I come, I'll bring you a hand-gun and teach you to shoot.

'Kate,' he called again. 'That's you, isn't it?'

She stared eerily without answering him.

He jumped on to the rock and shook her and she gasped.

'Oh, it's you. Hi, Ari,' she said breathlessly. 'I'm so cold. I was just sitting. What time is it? What are you doing here?'

Ari frowned at her, sensing her loneliness and rejection and this brought a strange sense of relief. She was fallible and scared, just like everyone else, despite her incredible appearance. Come to think of it, she didn't look all that marvellous right now. Her face was pale and blotchy, her eyes swollen, her hair was dry and in a mess, there were tears on her eyelashes and her cheeks were pale. He watched her thoughtfully, wondering what would cheer her the most.

'Hey now. Any guy coming new into a town without knowing anyone would be proud to call you their friend. How about it?' She smiled gently and rubbed her nose against his T-shirt. He could feel the warmth of her body, but she was still shuddering. 'Why're you shivering, Kate?'

She shook her head stubbornly. Ari put one arm around her shoulders and drew her gently towards him. For a while they sat close together watching the phosphorescence glitter in the waves, warming each other with the nearness of their bodies.

'What a night,' Ari said.

The flea-bitten dog stirred and crept jealously between their feet and tried to nudge his way upwards.

I must get some flea powder, he thought, or she'll be eaten alive.

'Ouch!' he said, pushing the dog away. 'You ever heard of things called fleas? Let's go inside. Where's Tabson?'

'He's in hospital.'

'Heck! You should have told me. What's wrong?'

She sighed. 'To tell the truth I'm a bit scared. The

specialist has embarked on a series of three operations to improve his right leg. It might not be one hundred per cent successful. He has to have a bone graft, and skin graft and so on.'

'You took such a chance all on your own?'

'Who else is there?'

'Me!'

'And what would you have said?'

'I don't know. But why you?'

'Because no one else cares, because his life is not worth living as a black cripple, because he's in the hands of the best orthopaedic surgeon in the country and at least there will be some improvement, even if the worst happens . . . and because someone has to care . . .'

'You're a good person, Kate,' he said. And I was entirely wrong about you, he thought guiltily. I thought you were vain, and spoiled and too used to having your own way. Maybe you were all those things, but underneath is a truly generous person. He watched her thoughtfully, understanding her loneliness and her fear. She was so forlorn. Compassion flared.

'You don't have to be alone,' he said and pulled her closer against him. 'I'm here. Remember that.' He touched her neck and ran one finger down her cheek, and leaned forward to kiss her forehead. His lips moved over her brows and down the line of her cheekbone to her mouth and softly met hers, his tongue caressing her lips.

She reached up and caught hold of his neck and pulled him fiercely closer. He felt desire rising, but behind his lust was the feeling that she was too vulnerable and he should not take advantage of her hurt. He must care for her.

'Shall we go inside?' he asked softly.

Tears were trickling down her cheeks.

'Hey, Kate, what's wrong?'

She shook her head. 'I can't tell you about it,' she whispered. 'Don't ask me. Just hold me, Ari. I need you. I need someone to love me, please.' She was trying not to cry.

'Since I met you, Kate, I've had such a longing . . . but are you sure?'

She looked up at him silently pleading and he noticed the shadows under her eyes and her pallor. 'Yes,' she muttered so quietly he could hardly hear her. 'I'm very sure. I want you to make love to me. Can you stay until morning? I don't want to be alone.'

He stood up and pulled her to her feet. He guessed what had happened as he led her upstairs. With a strange obedience she stood still and allowed him to remove her shorts and T-shirt, shuddering as his hands touched her body, lingering there with gentle stroking movements. He coaxed her with his hands, stroking her breasts and stomach, smoothing her hair. He understood that it was not him she craved, but love, any love from any man. Just to be wanted, to shut out the hurt, just for one night.

He vowed that he would win her, eventually, as he made love gently, teasing her, coaxing her, and bringing her to a climax. When she came, she cried out, 'Oh, Rob, Rob,' without even knowing.

Ari tried to ignore his hurt. 'Kate, I care for you,' he told her. 'You're the loveliest woman I've seen in my life. I've longed for you since the moment I set eyes on you. That night when you drove into a ditch, I couldn't stand looking at you, knowing you were married to someone else. You still love your husband, but I suppose it's only natural. I'll wait.'

'No. I detest him. That's why I left him.' She fell asleep in his arms.

At dawn she sat up, looked down at him fondly and smiled.

'Thank you,' she said. 'Thank you for being here, for caring, for making me feel loved, thank you for being you.'

She bent over and kissed him soundly on his lips. 'And now! Are you hungry? I am.' Moments later she grabbed a gown and disappeared down the stairway.

Patience and loving would win her, Ari decided. Eventually she would divorce her husband and be his.

In summer, Ari discovered, the Cape goes slightly crazy with joy. Each day is more perfect than the previous one, for the sou'easterly gales have mainly blown themselves out. Northern holiday-makers throng the streets and beaches in bright Bermuda shorts and shirts, the shops are full to overflowing with grapes, cantaloupes, spanspeks, mangoes, water melons, figs and olives, the stalls buzzing with persistent bees. Flocks of brightly coloured birds gorge on ripe berries. The mountainsides are thick with massive protea blooms, yellow and purple, pink and red, and the brilliantly coloured sunbirds and Cape sugarbirds dart from flower to flower. The paradise flycatchers hover and dart after swarms of midges, trailing their tails like kites. Sidewalks and fields are bright with wild carnations, daisies, lilies, orchids and geraniums and the trees blaze with summer blossom: hibiscus, bougainvilleas, jacarandas . . . Sunshine lasts for twelve hours a day and the nights are hot and balmy. Nights for beach *braais*, for sleeping out in the mountains and bathing in ice-cold mountain streams. Nights for love . . .

At the end of February, the weather changed abruptly

during the night and by morning low clouds and thick mist had set in. When Ari woke and reached out for Kate, she had already left. Damn! He had slept late because it was dark. Fortunately he was off-duty. He clattered downstairs and found she had taken Tabson with her.

He knew where to find her. As he'd thought, Kate was at Melissa's. He walked in and sneezed. At first he couldn't see for dust. Then he saw Kate directing her workmen, as they stripped off plaster and wallpaper. The carpets were being pulled up, ceilings were being scraped and sanded. Kate was wearing dungarees with braces, an old T-shirt, and rubber-soled canvas shoes. She was covered in dust, and her bloodshot eyes peered from her dusty face. Her nails were short and black, her hair was tied up with a scarf and she looked happier than he had ever seen her. She was arguing with Fernandes. 'No, I told you, no red, absolutely no red. Turquoise, blue and green. White? God, no. Listen, Emanuel, be a dear, just follow my sketches, please.' She squeezed his hand and smiled appealingly and Fernandes melted.

A young girl with fabric samples took her place in the front line. 'Why didn't you say you were short on this colour? No, we can't take another colour. Let's choose another fabric.' Moments later they were huddled over a trestle table. She hadn't noticed him yet.

Kate had spent days on her sketches, working all hours deep in concentration. Now she had to turn her ideas into reality, it wasn't as easy as she'd expected, for she was reliant on finding the fabrics and colours she had dreamed up.

She saw him and rushed over to hug him, leaving him as dusty as she was. 'How will I finish in time?' she wailed.

'I have the greatest faith in you,' Ari said. 'If it's humanly possible, you'll do it.'

He knew that Kate had obtained a down-payment from Melissa's lawyer and engaged a gang of workmen to help her. Each day new ideas came flooding into her mind, and each night Ari was asked to view the rooms, and study her drawings and think about colour and light and space. He had suggested a few stained-glass windows and taken her to see Emanuel. The two had hit it off at once. Now she had a new dimension to work with.

For Kate, Ari sensed, this was a time of hard, creative and physical labour and deep sleep. Emotionally speaking, she was resting. She had become very thin, but in some strange, triumphant, creative way she was happy.

He found Tabson in the garden. 'Did you have breakfast?' he asked.

'Yes, but I'm hungry again. As fast as I eat, I'm hungry. There seems to be a big hole inside me.'

'That's because you're growing so fast. I bought you some chocolate.' He fished two bars out of his pocket, and sat on the grass to watch Tabson play. He was a clever boy. He created and re-created wondrous moving toys with his Perspex globes and bits of wiring. Right now he'd made an earth-moving machine and he was manoeuvring it around the garden by remote control, picking up gravel and tipping it out again.

'That's amazing, Tabson,' Ari said, meaning it. He was learning to love the boy. Kate and Tabson filled his world. Lately, his dream of marrying Kate seemed so much more attainable.

He decided he might as well lend a hand with the work. He volunteered. Minutes later he was driving unwanted carpets and curtains to the squatter camp.

Chapter 23

The forensic laboratory in Pretoria had sent back details of the skull Emanuel had dug up from under his *dagga* bush. It was of a coloured woman of approximately twenty years of age and it had lain in the dunes for about thirty years. Her skull had been cracked open and her neck broken.

'Who cares how she died?' Gerber said when Ari applied to open a murder docket. 'Ancient history! We have enough problems coping with the here and now.'

'But I have a hunch,' Ari argued. 'I believe that some of the crimes plaguing Silver Bay are linked, and go back in time to a previous crime. Something bad happened twenty-eight years ago, sir, and I believe that Mandy's kidnapping is linked to that event, whatever it was. I'm also guessing that the arson that killed some of the squatters was intended to drive them out before they dug down too deeply and found the skeleton. Whoever it was didn't realise that the skull had already been removed from its sandy grave. Well, that's my guess, sir.'

'Get out of here, Lieutenant, and keep your guesses to yourself.'

Later that day, Smit borrowed an old skull from the museum and the guys left it on Ari's desk with a label tied on which read: 'Homo Neanderthal, murdered plus-minus forty thousand BC, murder docket to be handled by Lieutenant Ari St John.'

Ari didn't mind the ragging. They were great guys, with the exception of Gerber.

Ari was still smiling about that when he reached the Fernandeses' cottage. Emanuel was on the front porch working on his latest creation. 'Amazing how you seem to hang right over the bay,' Ari said. 'You've got the best views up here. Look at the sea. It's sort of turquoise and lime today. Lovely, isn't it?'

'Lovely and always different,' Emanuel said. 'Sit down. You won't mind if I carry on working, I hope.' Juliette brought him strong black coffee and cakes and Emanuel offered him a joint, but they both switched off their friendliness like a light when he began to question them about the skull.

'You're wasting my time,' Ari growled after ten fruitless minutes. 'You know what happened. You both know – I'd bet my last rand on that. I'll be back, believe me.'

Emanuel showed him to the door and followed him to his car.

'Ari, my friend, leave it alone, why don't you? Juliette doesn't agree with me, but I think you're making a mistake. Raking up the past will hurt a good many people.'

Ari shrugged him off and drove towards the quay where the fishing trawlers were unloading.

Bill September was downright rude when Ari began to question him about the skull. He ushered Ari on to the quayside away from the crew and spoke hurriedly.

'Stop wasting my time. Leave this shit alone and find my Mandy. You seem to see yourself as a knight-in-shining-armour carrying the law to primitive outposts. Let me tell you something, Lieutenant. Thirty years ago, Silver Bay was the prettiest place you could imagine, with farms all the way up the valley, a small fishing community and full employment from the Palmas' fish-canning plants. We didn't know what crime was. This woman, whoever she was, could have come from anywhere. Perhaps she was a prostitute. Perhaps she fell down the mountain. Who knows? Who cares?'

'D'you know what I think?' Ari said, scowling at him and feeling furious. 'I think everyone knows and everyone cares a great deal that the past should remain conveniently buried. To hell with the lot of you. What about the woman? Time doesn't diminish a crime one bit.'

Ari strode back to his car in a temper. It was beginning to seem like a personal feud – himself against an entire village.

Gill and Jack Bronson were on their balcony sipping sundowners, as usual. Ari handed Jack a bottle of Scotch, a regular weekly routine. Then he sat down and tried to relax.

'God, what a day,' he said. 'Listen, Jack. Perhaps you can help me. Search back in your memory. As far as I can make out, about twenty-eight years ago, the entire village conspired together to break the law – but how . . . ?'

There was a loud crash beside him. 'Shit,' Gill swore. A jug of ice had slipped out of her hands and smashed over the tiles.

Ari helped Gill to sweep up the ice and splintered glass and mop up the water. A jagged end cut his hand and it bled copiously, despite a plaster Gill gave him.

'As I was saying,' Ari said gruffly, determined to push

home his advantage. 'How could a group of villagers conspire together to commit a joint crime, which culminated in the murder of a young coloured girl?'

'You tell me, old man. You're the sleuth,' Jack said, trying to force out a laugh.

'Well, I've learned something tonight,' Ari said. 'You're covering up, too. Strange!'

'Oh, for fuck's sake, you're way out of line, Ari.' Jack stood up and poured himself a neat Scotch. 'You see things that don't exist, you make problems out of nothing. Relax a bit and start enjoying life.'

'He's doing all right,' Gill said, and then bit her lip.

Jack scowled at her. 'His private life's his own business,' he said, 'or perhaps it has something to do with you?'

Gill flushed and Ari stood up abruptly.

'I'm leaving. Getting an early night. Good night.'

Ari had a boring day ahead. He intended to check all Silver Bay births from fifty years back against deaths, the voters' roll, and emigration. The truth was, his role would probably consist of a few calls to the relevant computer experts at headquarters, plus a day of waiting by the telephone. The South African population was well documented and everyone carried ID cards.

The information Ari needed arrived at 5 p.m. the following afternoon. Of the fifty women born in Silver Bay during the relevant three-year period, there was only one who was not either on the voters' roll or who had not left the country, or married, or for whom a death certificate had not been issued – and that was Rose September, Bill September's sister and Ramona's daughter.

*　　　*　　　*

The following day, Ari spent a boring eight hours going through statistics of the Insurance Registrar. He discovered that 1964 was a significant year for Silver Bay. Eight coloured people, including Ramona, took possession of their previously rented company houses, and that included the Fernandeses, who had married a couple of years earlier, Fernandes having been swiftly reclassified. The transfer was organised through a newly formed employees' home-ownership scheme, created by Palma Fish Processing Ltd in that same year.

Six months later, Ari discovered, Bill September bought his fishing trawler, with a 'nil' deposit, the trawler to be paid for out of profits over the next fifteen years. A pretty good deal, Ari realised. Was this a massive blackmail pay-out, or bribery on a grand scale initiated by Angelo Palma? And where the hell was Angelo's son, Rob's father? Why was he never mentioned? What was it Emanuel had said? His best friend was buried in the Palma cemetery.

The Home Affairs office again supplied the statistics. Trevor Palma died in June 1964 at the age of twenty-four.

'Curiouser and curiouser,' Ari murmured.

When he returned to the station, he pulled out the file and re-read the transcript of the Fernandeses' conversation when they gave him the skull.

'It was all settled long ago and he paid . . . God! But how he paid.' 'Can money pay for a life?' 'What would he have wanted us to do?' 'He loved her.' 'He loved his father, too.' 'Give him the skull . . .'

Ari was so full of conjecture he felt he could burst, but as yet he had no hard facts. He'd need more than suspicions to open yet another murder docket and to question Angelo Palma.

*　　*　　*

Friday nights, Ari usually met Jean Graux in the Humber Bar, and tonight Jean was waiting there. His brown eyes were alight with fun as he teased the new barmaid, a lovely half-Chinese student who, Jean told him, was working her way through university. Jean was all spruced up, his beard trimmed, his hair cut and he was wearing a smart checked shirt and mohair trousers. He looked pretty good for his age, Ari thought.

'How's it going, Ari?' Jean's voice boomed across the bar as he ordered drinks and introduced him to the girl, who was called Susan Lo. 'Have you found out where Mandy is yet? Or who set light to the squatters?'

'No,' Ari said slowly, 'but listen to me, I have a theory that this crime is linked to a previous murder which took place on the same site. The skull of a young coloured woman, plus-minus twenty years old, has been handed to me.

'Twenty-eight years ago, Jean,' Ari went on thoughtfully, 'a crime was committed. I don't know what it was, but I know that many of our locals were involved and it led to the death of a young woman, or so I believe. I sent her skull to Forensic two weeks ago. She had a broken cranium and neck.'

He went on talking, needing to voice feelings that were more intuitive than proved.

Eventually Jean shuddered violently. 'You're giving me the creeps, Ari. Lay off, won't you? Hey, another round,' he called loudly.

'My turn,' Ari said.

'No. This one's on me. I've had a good week, a good sea harvest and now I have the 'flu and I'm going to get drunk, at my own expense. It always works. I wake up feeling better.'

He did look a bit pale, Ari noticed for the first time.

'Will you see me back to the boat?'

'Sure I will, if that's what you want,' Ari said.

'And what happens to this skull you sent to Pretoria?' Jean asked morbidly.

'They'll keep it.'

'Doesn't it . . . she . . . get to have a Christian burial?'

'Eventually, but only when we've finished with it. We'll probably have to make more tests.'

True to his word, Jean became extremely drunk and finally Ari had to manhandle him into his car with the help of the barman. Parking at the quayside, he noticed a strong smell of smoke and, looking up, saw a thin strip of bright red flames running along the mountainside. He dropped Jean into his dinghy and jumped in after him. Jean sang loudly and drunkenly all the way to his yacht. Once there, Ari realised how difficult it would be to hoist him aboard. He battled and cursed, while Jean kept singing in his ear and wobbling the dinghy until Ari felt sure they would capsize.

Eventually they did. Ari fell, with Jean over him, knocking his head hard against the bows. He was only half-conscious as he fell, but the ice-cold water revived him. He surfaced under the dinghy and stayed there feeling dizzy and gulping in the trapped air. He was listening intently to hear where Jean was. Relief set in when he heard Jean swimming. Still singing, Jean climbed the rope ladder and made fast the dinghy. He was so drunk he hadn't even realised Ari was missing.

Ari was wet through so he might as well swim back and leave the dinghy where it was, he thought, since Jean would need it in the morning. He set off across the dark bay.

As he walked up to his car, he noticed that the fire had spread to a far larger area and the smoke was drifting over the water bringing a sharp, pungent smell. As he tied up the dinghy he heard the strains of 'Rose of Tralee' wafting over the water. Jean had a fine tenor voice, he noticed, despite his being very drunk.

Fanned by the wind, the fire spread over the surrounding slopes, burning the trees and shrubs in a fifty-metre high blaze. On Saturday, residents of homes situated high on the mountains had to be evacuated. Police, local volunteers and troops fought side by side to quell the flames while helicopters hovered overhead, dropping their water loads on to the blaze. Like many others, the Bronsons had been saved by sheer luck. They had lost the wooden hut at the top of their garden, but otherwise the shrubs were only scorched, the house untouched.

As always, rain followed excessive heat and after a twelve-hour downpour all that was left of the fire was the smell of sodden burnt vegetation, huge black scars on the mountains, and smouldering grass. The locals, who loved their mountains, put on old clothes and boots and trekked up to beat the smouldering embers and search for burned tortoises and buck.

'This is too much,' they grumbled. The disaster had been caused by an old squatter who had lit a fire to cook his breakfast and let it run out of control.

A whole way of life had gone up in smoke and now their beloved mountains were going the same way. 'This is just the start,' they told each other grimly.

Mandy had stopped counting the days and nights. She huddled on her bed waiting for the end. She would not eat. She could not carry on. She could not even be bothered to kill herself. She was going to die here and no one would

ever know. She wanted to die. Let *him* come and stroke
her skeleton and not even notice that she was dead. He
was crazy and she was in his power, like a fly dewinged
and imprisoned by a small child. She was doomed and she
could not stand her fear and physical tension any longer,
nor the bitter loneliness. There was no point in hoping. No
point in eating. She was lost in this suffocating darkness
and she would never be released. She curled foetus-like on
her bed, and lapsed into silent despair.

Sometimes she felt someone shaking her, sometimes she
seemed to hear a voice whisper: 'Who are you?'

'Mandy,' she would mutter, and then he went away.

Days or weeks later, she felt someone stroking her. 'Rose,
why aren't you eating? You're getting so thin. If you don't
eat you'll die.'

She would not speak. Why should she? Lately she was
lapsing in and out of a trancelike state, which was some
small comfort.

'Why are you doing this to me?' she whispered, the next
time he came.

'You have to remember that you are Rose. You cannot
run away from who you are. You always tried, but you have
to learn.'

'Yes. Perhaps I am Rose,' she said, drifting back into
that other world where *he* could not follow her.

She came to, days later, to find that she was choking.
Raw, burning liquid was being spooned into her mouth.
Her body was coming back to life painfully. A soft light
was glowing from the corner of the cell and everything
was shimmering out of focus. The light hurt her eyes at
first. A man was sitting beside her, holding a mug and a
teaspoon.

'Come, open your mouth,' he said. 'Just a little more.

There's a good girl!' His voice was deep and familiar. It was the voice of her dreams. Another spoonful brought her coughing and spluttering back to life again. She stared hard at his wavering hand and eventually it came into focus. Tears of gratitude were trickling down her cheeks. Light! She could see. 'Thank you, thank you,' she muttered. His hands were beautiful: long, supple fingers, sun-tanned and roughened skin, such strong hands! She longed for his strength. 'Let me lie down,' she whispered. 'I feel dizzy.'

'No, Rose. You must eat. If you will do as I ask, I shall leave the light on for you. Try!'

He pushed a plate of soup towards her, but she shook her head. 'I can't!'

He began to feed her. She gagged on the first mouthful, but swallowed it obediently. He fed her like a child, spooning each mouthful towards her, wiping her mouth with a tissue. The soup brought back her strength and as she recovered she became hungry and began to wolf down the chicken broth.

'Put your arm around my neck,' he said. Gripping her shoulders, he pulled her to her feet and led her round the room. Round and round they went, and all the time he was explaining: 'You have been very ill, Rose. You wanted to be someone else. You wanted to get away from me, but now you know who you are.'

'Yes,' she whispered. With jerky, despairing movements she stumbled around the cell.

Later, when she was tired, he tied her to the bed while he left the door open to drag in a galvanised iron tub which he filled with warm water he had heated somewhere outside. He undressed her carefully, and lifted her into the tub, and she stood there, immobile, her cheeks hot, full of conflicting thoughts, being washed as she was once washed by her mother, feeling just as close to him, as he wiped her ears and her eyes, and carefully washed every intimate place. But still he was not satisfied, she must kneel over the tub while he washed her hair, which he rinsed with fresh water. When she was wrapped in a towel and patted dry, her hair towel-dried and combed, he kissed her face, her cheeks, her lips and her eyes. And then he gently lowered the towel and kissed her breasts and her belly and the cleft of her venus mound.

'My special Rose,' he whispered.

She had not yet dared to look at him, but when she did she gasped. He was quite old, and rough-looking, but compelling. His eyes were startling blue, his features regular and he was a strange combination of brutality and compassion. His white hair was cut in a crew cut, but those curious eyes beamed love to her and she felt entranced by them.

'I seem to know you,' she said, puzzling over this. 'I have seen you before.'

'Yes, of course you know me,' he said with a laugh. 'I am your fiancé, Jânek József. You mustn't be afraid any more. I shall look after you forever. I won't punish you any more. You have been punished enough for leaving me, but now we are together again.'

He poured some more brandy into the enamel mugs and they sat solemnly side by side on her bed, sipping the hot liquid. He lit a cigar and soon the air was full of the smell of him. It was a familiar odour, for it was always clinging to him, but now she was breathing in *him*. He had invaded her life, her body, and her lungs, and there was nothing she could do, she was overpowered by him. She was his, yet she still fought against this terrible possession.

She pulled the blanket off the bed and wrapped it round her. 'Still fighting?' he asked with a smile.

She was thinking: You won't succeed. I'm still me. Call me what you like, but you won't conquer me.

She waited for him to go, her stomach knotted into cramps of fear, longing to be free of him, but dreading his leaving. But then, when he made as if to go, she caught hold of him and begged him to stay.

'If I stay, will you stop fighting me?'

'Yes, oh yes,' she sobbed.

But he went anyway. 'I will come back soon, and I will stay a while,' he said.

He returned much later with boxes of food, a mattress and blankets. He made himself a bed on the floor. Then he stripped off his clothes and stood in a tub of cold water, sponging himself.

'You want to wash me?' he asked.

She shook her head sulkily, but could not tear her eyes away from his rippling muscles, the hard biceps and smooth, tanned skin.

He was soon snoring, but she could not sleep. In the morning she was heavy-eyed, but he seemed not to notice. He stayed for the day, nursing her, feeding her, bathing her, massaging her limbs back to life and always watching her, whatever she was doing, tying her when the door was open.

When he lifted her in his arms, she wanted to scream at him to let her go. But when he let go of her, she longed for his touch.

That night she felt tortured by her conflicting desires. She wanted to kill him, or perhaps she wanted him to rape her. She was not sure what she wanted, but he filled her universe. There was no room for anything besides him.

That night he fell asleep again, and she stood up and stripped naked and tiptoed over to him. She crept under the blanket behind him, feeling his back that was like an iron board.

He turned over. 'What took you so long, Rose?' he asked softly. 'Kiss me!'

She had never kissed before. The feel of his soft and sensuous lips on hers was like nothing she had ever experienced. Swords of pleasure were stabbing at her, in her belly and her groin, his lips seemed to join with hers, his tongue caressed her mouth, she put her arms around his neck and pulled him closer. Pushing her thighs against his body, she flung one leg over his hips, licked his face and ran her tongue over his eyelids. How strange his penis felt, pulsating against her belly.

'Who are you?' he asked roughly, pushing her away from him.

'Rose. Your Rose.'

'Yes,' he whispered. 'I thought you'd never regain your senses. Love me, Rose. I've missed you so much.'

'Yes,' she whispered. 'As long as you stay. Please, never leave me again. I'll do anything, anything.'

Chapter 24

———— ————

By Melissa's birthday, February 25, her house was ready, which was a minor miracle, Kate acknowledged. Melissa was thrilled and suddenly Kate was richer by twenty thousand rands.

From then on she knew exactly what her future career would be. But she was in no hurry to begin. She spent the last week of February lazing around at home. The sunlight flashed around her, the sun's heat burned down and through her and she welcomed it like an old friend, and the heat rising from the earth came up through her feet bringing its own special energy. Sometimes it seemed she was only a shadow moving, transient and insubstantial, ephemeral, drifting, through an illusion while most of her was somewhere else. So she was content to wait until her life unfolded itself without her assistance. Only the nights brought problems, for then she missed Rob bitterly, but she kept her longings to herself and waited for time to heal her wounds.

Arriving at the lighthouse on Sunday morning, Ari was surprised and pleased at the way he had become part of the family. Kate flung herself into his arms. Dopey leaped all over them both, Frikkie looked up and gave a toothless smile before bending over the embers to contemplate the ten fish he was *braaiing*. Then Tabson came limping up from the sea.

'Uncle Ari. Look at my leg!' He strutted up and down, bashing his cast on the ground with each step. 'Look here . . . They are both the same length.' He fished a tape measure out of his pocket. 'Auntie Kate gave this to me,' he said shyly. He shot her a glance of pure adoration. Then he carefully measured his left leg from the knee down.

'He does this several times each day,' Kate whispered in his ear. Her breath tickled him and he had a sudden desire to make love to her, but Tabson was there so he would have to wait. He put his hand over hers and squeezed hard.

'You see this,' Tabson said in his hoarse, half-broken voice. He held up the tape, his thumb marking the measurement. 'Now watch!' He solemnly measured his right leg. 'They're both the same length,' he concluded. Then he smiled, a happy, carefree boy's smile and for some reason it brought a lump to Ari's throat.

Ari was tired, having been up for most of the night in a gun battle with three squatters who had been caught red-handed robbing a supermarket. Lying prone in the hot sand, he dozed while waiting for Frikkie to finish cooking. A gorgeous smell was drifting round him. He was so hungry, but the fish were taking forever. Kate was in her kitchen making a salad, the potatoes were baking in embers, Tabson was throwing a ball around for Dopey to chase. The boy looked so confident nowadays. Kate was good for him, Ari could see.

Even the goose seemed strangely happy and excited this morning. He kept stretching and flapping his one good wing and looking around the sky. Then he would go back to grazing the grass in his long run that encircled three quarters of the lighthouse. He seemed so restless.

'When does his wing get unbound?' Ari asked. 'He wants to fly.'

'Who doesn't,' Kate said. 'The vet's happy with him. He popped round yesterday. Maybe a couple more weeks. We're eating out here. It's such a lovely day. Look!' She pointed out to sea. 'There's a dolphin.'

'A school of them,' Ari added. The sea was a deep turquoise, but against the morning sun, each breaker was translucent, a shimmering mass of pale green water through which the dark shapes of the fish were twisting and leaping and playing the fool with each other. Sometimes one misses the moment, he thought. One's always thinking ahead and behind, but all we have is the now. One can lose one's whole life this way. Imagine dying and never having experienced a true moment of the here and now. Except sex, he thought. Then one was riveted on each molten moment. Would they make love tonight? he wondered. He laughed at himself. He was off into the future again, forgetting to watch the dolphins – forgetting to live.

Kate was quite a girl, Ari thought, watching her run down with paper plates and mugs and plastic cutlery. She was a real gypsy. She could make a home anywhere and be happy with very little. Already she had a garden growing, she managed to look ravishing without visiting a hairdresser's or wearing make-up, and she was kind. She was a good woman, he told himself. All his life he had yearned for a girl who was both good and lovely. There was only one thing wrong, she still pined for her husband.

Did he love Kate? Ari had to admit that he did and he longed for her to be his for once and for all. She was seldom out of his mind. Just look at her poking at the fish, nearly naked in her tiny bikini, her flaxen hair falling over her tanned shoulders, her long, smooth legs half covered in sand. Watching her sent his libido soaring, but it wasn't just sex or looks that attracted him, he knew. He'd fallen deeply in love with her and he admired her more than any woman he'd ever met. Her looks no longer counted.

'Kate, what are we going to do?' he whispered, brushing his lips against her cheek. 'I love you, Kate.'

'It's hunger talking,' she said laughingly.

'You'll never go back to Rob, will you?' he persisted.

Kate remained silent, avoiding his eyes as she laid the table.

'Tell me you'll never go back to him.'

'Oh, Ari. All I want right now is an emotional truce,' she said. 'What's the good of talking about things like that? I'm not even divorced.'

Frikkie caught his attention by pointing up into the sky and making excited noises: 'Honk, honk, honk. I knew, I knew,' he cried. Bent half over, his arms flapping wildly behind him, he mimicked the goose hopping over the sand. 'Look at him. He knows she's there.' Looking up, Ari saw a bird circling high above them, so high it was hardly more than a pinprick in the dazzling blue sky.

His mind turned guiltily to his studies. He'd done no work on his thesis since he'd been here, which was hardly surprising since he worked all hours. The crime rate was soaring. Statistically speaking Silver Bay would soon rival the Transvaal cities. He had so many cases and most of them were unsolved. And then there was Mandy. Ari scowled and began to assemble all the known facts in his mind.

'Ari, enjoy the day,' Kate commanded. 'You're working, aren't you?'

He laughed. 'Perhaps if I put on my trunks I'll feel off-duty.' He went up to the lighthouse.

When he returned, the fish was cooked and Kate had

brought the paper plates and salad and a bowl of steaming piquant sauce. Ari opened the wine he had brought, and a Coke for Tabson, and Tabson retrieved the potatoes from the embers and rolled them out of the foil. 'Ouch! Ouch! Ouch!' he squealed as he burned his fingers, but he wouldn't let Frikkie do it.

The four of them ate hungrily. 'You know how to cook,' Ari called out to Frikkie, who was sitting some distance away in the shade of the milkwood trees. 'Fantastic. Number One!' He stuck up his thumb in a sign of ultimate approval, and Frikkie's eyes flashed while his mouth split into a broad grin.

They ate and drank and later, half dizzy from the baking sun and the raw red wine, Kate and Ari fell asleep on the sand and woke feeling roasted. Running into the ice-cold surf they set off on a lazy crawl around the bay, keeping pace with each other and back again to bring their frozen limbs to life by basking in the late-afternoon sun. Ari fetched another bottle of wine from the boot of his car and opened it.

'What a life,' he said, lifting his glass in a toast.

'For us,' Kate frowned. 'For us everything is perfect, but what about them?' She frowned moodily and he wondered why.

Them? Ari frowned. Why must she spoil the day? Time enough to think about 'them' on Monday morning. He told her as much, but that annoyed her.

'Surely you realise most of them are starving. Yes, right there, along the end of the beach. They exist on scraps and the free soup Meg hands out. Frikkie catches them fish, but it doesn't go far amongst so many. A few residents have given them blankets and when it rains they pack themselves into any old space they can find, like the toilets at the end of the beach. It's terrible that human beings should live like that. No one cares,' she flung at him. 'I tell you, no one. Do you care?'

'I suppose so, but I don't see . . .'

'That's the problem. Everyone thinks the same. They can't do much, so rather do nothing. But they're suffering bitterly.'

He grunted, longing for her to give over. He wanted a day free of crime, sordidness, and the endless social iniquities he dealt with on a daily basis, but she could not let go.

'I telephoned the council on Friday and spoke to the regional manager. D'you know what he said? "This is not a welfare state, Mrs Palma." Her voice took on his rough accent. "And until new legislation is passed concerning vagrancy, the squatters can sit on a beach, or the mountains or any place they like and we have no legal way of coping with them." I wasn't trying to cope with them, I was wanting to help them,' she said indignantly.

'I reminded him that the council was supposed to be providing land for them. D'you know what he said? All those promises have fallen through because local residents have lost interest and they aren't pushing the council any more. And why?' she demanded angrily. 'Ari, listen to me,' she urged him, 'you aren't listening. D'you know why the locals have lost interest?' He pretended to be asleep, but she shook his shoulder. 'Because the squatters are no longer threatening local property values. When they were sitting right behind us, bang in the middle of the most valuable part of Silver Bay, most people were prepared to make a sacrifice to supply alternative space. People were prepared to do something.' Her voice was shaking with the passion of her convictions. 'But now they're scattered over the beaches and mountain slopes, or any odd corner, they can exist or starve without doing much financial harm.'

'Spoken like a true liberal,' he said laughing at her.

'Oh for God's sake try to care.' She was working herself up into a fury. 'Did you know that some of their children have that awful stomach parasite that only Third World countries get – but I can't remember the name – and three have died of pneumonia?'

'Yes, yes, yes!'

'Don't you care?'

'It's happening all over, Kate. Perhaps here the contrast is scary. The rich and the very poor are so close together, but go to the Cape Flats and you'll see hundreds of thousands of poor, homeless people.'

'I've decided to do something about it,' she said. Her eyes had taken on that obstinate glint he was getting to know so well.

She didn't mention the squatters again and Ari was relieved. Tabson went inside to play with his newest electronic gadget and they were alone, so he stroked her back for an hour, feeling her twitch and shudder and sometimes she groaned with pleasure. 'You didn't answer my question, Kate,' he grumbled, wishing he could stop himself. 'I want to know where I stand. Do you still love that terrible husband of yours?'

She shrugged. Then she sat up and stretched. 'It's too hot to be serious,' she countered. 'Let's swim.' She ran down the beach, but Ari pretended to fall asleep. Not for anything would he let her know how hurt he was.

At sunset Frikkie came running with Tabson limping behind him. He was pointing up to the sky where they could see a large bird was circling, but much lower now. There was a sudden swoop, a thrilling rush of wings and the bird rocketed down like a falling stone. There was a strange whirling sound as the wild Egyptian goose landed with a thud right next to Tabson's pet. Now there was such a commotion, the geese honking and calling and dancing around each other, Tabson hopping with joy, and Frikkie grinning and rushing off to get some mealies. The female took off several times and sat in a nearby tree calling furiously, but her mate could not fly and each time she returned and fought with him. Kate was totally engrossed and thrilled with the united pair.

He might as well go home, Ari thought sullenly. Kate would be preoccupied for hours and if he stayed they would fight.

'I'll be getting along,' he said. 'You seem very preoccupied.'

She looked surprised and then she laughed at him. 'Oh, Ari, this is not like you,' she said. 'Jealous of a goose? Or am I reading you wrong?'

'Wrong,' he said. 'I go on duty soon.' What was the point of nagging her? She had answered his question her way. 'Be seeing you.'

At seven o'clock the following morning, Ari got an urgent call from the station. He dressed hurriedly and drove down. Gerber was already there in his tracksuit looking bleary-eyed and still unshaven.

'Silver Bay residents are in a frenzy,' Gerber told him. He reached into his drawer and took out his shaver. 'Just about anyone who lives within a mile of here has called us since four this morning. The squatters have moved back on to Mrs Palma's land by the lagoon *at her invitation*. Can you believe it? The bitch has gone cuckoo. She even unlocked the gate for them. As you know, Rob had fenced off the place, razor wire, everything. I wish to God those two would keep their matrimonial squabbles to themselves.

Talk about cutting off her nose to spite her face. You see, Rob has a dream of creating a lush, ultra-luxurious housing project there and she wants—'

'I know what she wants,' Ari said, cutting in on him. 'But do you?' He watched Gerber go bright red with temper. 'She wants the Bronsons and the Septembers and the Palmas and the rest of the ultra-rich who overlook the beach and the lagoon to get together to push for alternative accommodation for the squatters. She hinted to me that she would do this. To be honest I didn't think she'd go through with it. I hope she thought it out properly. She's going to be in a lot of trouble from residents.'

He grabbed a paper cup and thrust it into the machine. He'd got a headache from too much wine and sun and maybe frustration, too.

'I've never known Kate give a fuck about anyone and I've known her for some time,' Gerber said, rubbing his chin where he'd cut himself with the shaver.

Ari sighed. 'She's a mass of contradictions, but her heart's in the right place.'

'That could be temporary. They'll skin her alive in this town. Somebody burned out the squatters in the first place, so she had better look out for herself. Not that she doesn't deserve all she gets.'

Ari shot him a curious glance. It was the first time Gerber had acknowledged the dunes fire as being deliberate arson. 'Perhaps you know something I don't know. Perhaps I should be questioning you . . .' Ari began.

'For fuck's sake get off my back. I know as much as you know, and that's precious little, except I know when to let sleeping dogs lie. Where's your meddling got you so far? Half the town hates your guts and you're no nearer to solving anything. You haven't a clue where that September girl is.

'Now listen, Ari, I called you in because I need you. A few hotheads have manned a road block near the intersection leading to the back of the lagoon. They're trying to stop the squatters from getting on to Kate's land. Perhaps they're your murderers, who knows? Get down there and talk them out of it. We don't want a major clash erupting here. Tell them the squatters are moving in by invitation this time. They might not believe you. I find it hard to credit myself.'

Gerber was right, Ari found when he raced there. Dave, the dentist, and Jack and six other professional men were holding up the road like ancient highwaymen. They were armed to the teeth and furious and they all lived above the lagoon.

'Come on, guys,' Ari began calmly. 'Come on, Jack. You can't win.'

Jack danced forward, fists held in front of his face in an outmoded boxing style. 'I don't want to hurt you, Ari, my friend,' he said. He looked absurd as he began to shadow box in front of Ari's nose.

Ari stifled a grin. 'I'm not here as a friend. I represent the law,' he said sternly.

'Fuck off,' Dave said, 'or you might get shot by mistake.'

'Must I call up reinforcements? Do you want to go down to the station in the back of a van? Did you know that our prisons are multiracial now? Do you know what would happen to you lot during the night?'

'You bloody commie!'

'You don't live here.'

'Yes – fuck off! This has nothing to do with you.'

'Keep out of our business if you know what's good for you.'

Dave pulled a gun on him and waved it dangerously around. I could disarm him, Ari thought, but tempers are running high, and anything could push those lunatics over the edge.

They were circling him, grim-faced, looking like 'extras' in a corny cowboy movie, but Ari was aware of the danger. If they attacked together, he might get one or two, but he'd be dead by then. He could see from their eyes that they were running out of control.

'Shut up and listen, you morons,' he said, fingering his gun and backing against a convenient oak. 'Mrs Palma has kindly lent her land until alternative space is supplied by the council, which they have promised won't be long. As an ecologist, she is anxious to prevent further fires on the mountainside.'

'Hah! She's a bloody commie, like you . . .' Dave broke off and turned round. In the distance they heard voices and shuffling bare feet on the gravel road. A group of women was approaching.

'They're not breaking the law,' Ari said quickly. 'They're invited and there's nothing you can do about it.'

'Piss off!' Dave walked up too close to him. Ari saw the punch coming and hesitated. He didn't want to shoot him. The blow knocked him off his feet. He fell heavily, hurting the back of his head. Fortunately his gun was still in his hand and unfired.

Jack pulled him to his feet. 'You all right, Ari?' The men were shouting at him, picking up stones, their faces twisted with rage, but Jack screened him.

Ari pushed him aside. 'Talk some sense into them, Jack,' he said. 'And thanks.'

The women had paused, afraid to go on. One of them called behind to a man who was carrying a load of corrugated-iron sheets. He threw them down and picked up a strong stick. His face was threatening and ugly as he stood there. Others were approaching from behind.

Dave and his friends were undecided, muttering to each other. 'Dave, listen to me,' Ari said quietly. 'You can win this round, you can even kill me, but you can't win in the long term. You guys have got to find another way to do what you have to do. It's too late for force.'

After a couple more nasty moments, they turned tail, grumbling about bloody commie policemen and their whores. Ari reckoned he was lucky to get off with a swollen jaw.

He sat in his car, rubbing his sore head and watching the tide of men, women and children pass silently down the road and into the wetlands. 'What have you done, Kate?' he whispered. 'It's you against Silver Bay. I hope you're as tough as you think you are.'

Chapter 25

———— ————

Kate was getting dressed when she heard a brick smash through a ground-floor window. Dopey began to snarl and bark. Shock and anger surged through her. Her breath was rasping, her hands shaking as she grabbed her gun and raced down one floor to Tabson. He opened his eyes.

'What's wrong?'

'Go back to sleep and stay up here,' she said.

As bricks and debris were hurled through her broken windows she flung herself down the spiral stairway on wobbly knees, shouting: 'No . . . No . . . !'

'Dear God, don't let Dopey be hurt,' she murmured as she ran. By now, her lounge was a mass of splintered glass and broken bricks. Dopey was frenzied, but unhurt. She pushed him into the pantry and locked the door.

An angry face leered from the window as a stone came skidding across the table towards her.

'You bastard,' she yelled and fired over his head. The shot was dangerously low and she gasped. How could she have done that? He yelled and ran. Kate raced to the door, her shaking hands fumbling at the chain. She was muttering 'Bastards . . . bastards . . .' and sobbing with rage. As the door burst open she fired once more over the crowd of running boys.

Who were they? She hadn't recognised any of them. Not locals, surely. Had someone hired a gang of toughs to frighten her?

'Oh shit,' she moaned, looking at the debris.

When Kate went to the shops later that morning to buy some glass and putty, she found that the shop proprietor was unwilling to serve her.

'I'm next,' she snarled, but he ignored her.

'I demand . . .' she broke off and looked around at the customers who were doggedly staring at the floor.

'You must serve me, since I pay cash and I am a good customer here.'

'Wrong, Mrs Palma. I have the right not to, and I choose not to.'

'You are short-sighted fools,' she snarled. 'You won't see me here again.'

'Good,' she heard as she strode out of the shop.

'Who cares?' she whispered. 'He's not the only hardware store in Silver Bay.'

In the afternoon, Tabson was set upon by some local children while he was waiting for her to fetch him from school. He didn't seem very concerned since he had beaten them off. 'I kicked them with my cast,' he said. 'They squealed.'

'You must be more careful with that leg,' she said, more sharply than she should have.

Kate began to panic. What could she do? Where could she send Tabson for safety? Would Melissa take him for a week?

She was sitting at home guarding him and Dopey when the dog started barking hysterically. Looking outside, she saw a group of uniformed men climb out of a van and surround the lighthouse, but they didn't look much like police to her. Was she being besieged? She strode outside.

'What the hell . . . ? Who are you . . . ?'

'We're here to guard you and the lighthouse, Mrs Palma,' one of them said, touching his peaked cap. 'Mr Palma took out a contract with our firm. We're to stay for the foreseeable future, or at least until he thinks you're safe, ma'am. Not just from the locals, he told us, but from the squatters you've put on your land there.' Relief surged through her and with it an emotion so strong, she had to rush inside and burst into tears.

Why? Why am I crying? she wondered. I wasn't that scared. But she felt as if she had been reborn. Rob still loved her. He cared. He cared enough to employ guards to look after her. Then she thought: wasn't that why I left him – because he wanted to run my life for me? Minutes later she was on the phone to Rob. 'Stop interfering in my life,' she said firmly. 'Thank you for caring. I was glad about that, but I have to look after myself.'

'I aim to get out of your life forever,' he said. 'I've started divorce proceedings. But I'm not prepared to sit back and see you harmed. I still care, Kate. You've just made yourself the most unpopular woman in town, so the least I can do is make sure you're safe.'

'You and Angelo made me the most unpopular woman in town when you disgraced my father,' she said, replacing the receiver.

Kate almost buckled under the torrents of abuse that landed on her over the next few weeks. It came by telegrams, anonymous callers at dead of night and hand-delivered letters of rage. She had no idea people could hate so much.

When the editor of the village rag arrived to interview her, she was terrified. Was she to be vilified in the local press?

'Mrs Palma? Pleased to meet you. I'm running a story on the squatter problem,' he said. 'Would you care to add your comments to a short article we're publishing in the next issue?'

'I suppose it's all right,' she said nervously.

He handed her a copy of the proposed article:

'The fight over the wetlands which split the Palma family and sent them careering towards the divorce courts has reached supreme court level,' she read. 'Mrs Kate Palma applied recently to have the wetlands around the lagoon proclaimed a bird sanctuary. Strangely, she has now voluntarily let almost a thousand squatters on to her land. So much for the birds' safety. Is this a case of cutting off her nose to spite her face?'

'Oh,' Kate reeled with shock and the room began to spin. 'Horrible! You are so wrong. All you people are so petty and so selfish.

'How could you write those lies? There are two thousand starving homeless people in Silver Bay and all you can think about is writing scandal,' she flung at him. 'Get out of here!'

He turned bright red, took out a tissue and mopped his head. 'You seem so sincere, Mrs Palma. You're not at all as I'd imagined you would be. Please give me a chance to make amends. Let's start again.'

Kindness always unnerved Kate. She could fight meanness, but suddenly her eyes were burning and threatening to make a fool of her. 'I'll make tea,' she said, rushing off to get a tissue and blow her nose vigorously.

'Of course I long for the wetlands to become a bird sanctuary,' she said, a few minutes later. 'But these people have nowhere to go. No one seems to care. But they did care before, when the squatters were right under their noses. D'you see what I'm trying to do? I want them to be reminded that the problem still exists.'

'Yes,' he said. 'I've got the picture.' He left, looking thoughtful.

On Friday Kate could hardly bear to collect the newspaper from the supermarket. She pushed it into her bag and read it surreptitiously in the car.

'Against a backdrop of smashed windows and brick-scarred walls, courageous Kate Palma spelled out her vision for a new and caring Silver Bay,' the article began.

What a cheek, she thought. I've mended all the windows. Nevertheless, he'd reported almost word for word what she had said. At the end he had written: 'We happen to be the first. If we can cope, other towns will learn from us.'

It was late that night when she heard knocking on the door. She was alone because Ari was on duty. She went down feeling anxious and peered over the chain Frikkie had installed.

She opened the door and saw Rob. The sight of him sent her body into action stations: heart pumping, mouth drying, knees weakening and she had to stifle an impulse to throw herself into his arms. She had forgotten how aggressively male he was: his black hair, longer than usual, was tousled by the wind, his mischievous eyes gleamed as he grinned sardonically.

'Well, well, Joan of Arc herself. Are you enjoying your martyrdom? You didn't seem to like it much with me.' He pushed past her, while she feebly blocked his way, and stood gazing round the lighthouse.

'Hm! Melissa said you'd done well, and you have, but you could do with a TV set. I'll send one round.'

'No thanks. I don't have time to watch,' she said.

They had got off to a bad start, which she regretted. 'Do you want a drink?' she asked. 'Why don't you sit down?'

'Are you alone?'

'Yes.'

'I'll have whatever you've got.'

Kate poured him a glass of wine, noting the changes. His eyes looked tired and there were deep black shadows under them. His skin looked pallid, almost dead-looking. Where was that healthy glow? She had never seen him like this and she felt worried, but she forced herself to remember him screwing the actress, and hardened herself.

'You've split the town in half, Kate,' he said. 'You're famous. Or should I say infamous? Fights in clubs, half the people collecting blankets and food and cooking utensils for the homeless, the other half plotting how to drive them out. Meetings, endless talks . . . The local priest came out strongly on your side. Did you know that?'

She shook her head, thinking even his voice is different, softer, a little hoarse. What's happened to you, Rob?

'Gill Bronson's spent this week getting signatures for a proper home for the squatters. By "proper" she means far away from her views. She's got thousands of signatures. Even the government's had a meeting on the "Silver Bay problem", as it's called.

'I've got to hand it to you, Kate, you took a gamble and it paid off. I've been told that some of the Forestry Department's land will be made available within a week,' he went on.

He was looking smug. Kate could tell from his expression

that he'd had something to do with that. 'Thank you,' she said.

'Don't thank me, Kate. I'm kicking myself. You see, I never took the trouble to get to know you. I just adored your looks. You won't have much of them left soon. I'd watch out if I were you. Your skin will be leather in twenty years time. What happened to your hair?'

'Nothing. I've tied it up.'

'It used to shine.'

'I've given up hairdressers, along with drinking, smoking, travelling and fighting. I'm much happier now.'

'Good for you.' His mouth set into a grim line. 'You've grown a little pompous since you left, Kate. You need putting down from time to time.'

'Is that why you're here?'

Rob's eyes flashed with temper. 'You're playing with fire with that police lieutenant.'

'I don't want to discuss my private life with you.'

'As for Tabson! He'll never fit into white society and you're ruining him for anything else. You're making a big mistake there, Kate. He'll be a fish out of water all his life. Like a *Hansie* lamb, he'll never go back to the flock.'

'But he won't be a cripple,' she said defensively. 'As a cripple he was an outcast even with his own parents. If you came here to criticise my life, I think you should go, Rob. Last time I saw you, you raped me and I was hurt for a long time, both physically and mentally.'

'I was overwrought.'

'You always make excuses for yourself, but never for others. The fact is, you like to have your own way and you can't cope when you don't.'

'Perhaps I'm changing. Please give me another chance. I'll give you a private income.'

'I'm not for sale, Rob,' she said, feeling insulted. 'You're right. You don't know me.'

'Oh, Kate!' He caught hold of her and pulled her tightly to him.

As she smelled the familiar smell of him and felt his strong arms around her, she was caught up in an unbearable longing to turn back the clock.

'You must go,' she said firmly. 'I've put the past behind me. I'm not the Kate you think you know. I'm someone altogether different.'

'Is there no way out of this bloody mess? No way we can be together?' he asked wistfully.

'Perhaps when I'm independent enough to stand up to you.'

'You mean I have to wait for you to make a million? I should live so long.' He looked so amused that she pushed him out and slammed the door shut. Then she fled to her bed and she cried herself to sleep.

Chapter 26

——— ———

Ari was on standby, but sleeping at home when Willis telephoned to tell him that there was a fire on Bill September's trawler and that arson was suspected.

He glanced at his watch: 4 a.m.! 'I'll meet you there in twenty minutes,' he said. 'Bring the bust from my desk, but don't bash it around. It's breakable.'

He thought about the fibreglass bust while he hurriedly dressed. It had arrived yesterday from Pretoria and the features bore a strange resemblance to photographs of Mandy, yet the eyes were blank and the features too smooth and perfect to be lifelike. In fact, it was the reconstructed face and head of the dunes' skull which he had sent to forensic. A note attached to the bust had told him that this was the first example of a 'breakthrough' in forensic technology. The skull reconstruction could be relied upon as giving a sixty per cent likeness of what the girl had looked like, he read. He had ordered photographs to be taken the previous day.

Bill September's fishing trawler was badly gutted, but Ari guessed that insurance would cover the loss. It was still dark when Ari jumped on board and peered down into the hold. He shone his torch to where a group of workmen were pouring water on smouldering wood. Despite the wet handkerchiefs tied over their mouths, they were choking on the acrid fumes while Bill hoarsely growled commands. He looked up suspiciously. 'Don't shine that blasted torch in my eyes,' he snarled. 'What is it now?'

'I'm not staying long,' Ari said. 'Just hoping you'll change your mind and tell me what the hell is going on?'

September waved impatiently. 'If only I knew . . .' He grimaced nastily, poking a rod into the charred wood. 'If I knew who it was, you'd have another murder on your hands.' He clambered out of the hold and jumped down on to the quay.

'You're insured, I assume?'

'Of course, but it never covers the loss of earning power while the boat's in drydock and all the other peripheral items and nuisances. Just when the tunny are running. Fuck them all! Tell you one thing.' He paused and lit a cigarette, cupping his strong, gnarled hands around the flaming match. 'This was done by someone who knows boats and my boat in particular. I have guards on board always, but the buggers slipped off for a drink in the bar over there and someone must have seen them go.'

'That narrows it down a bit,' Ari said. 'I see you've made a good job of washing off fingerprints and that sort of thing.'

'D'you expect me to leave my boat burning while you sods get your act together?'

Ari shrugged. 'Did your crew see anyone suspicious?'

'No, and neither did Jean. Luckily, he saw the fire through the portholes and raced in on his dinghy. There was no one here when he came aboard. By the time the crew pitched, Jean'd got the hoses out and the pump working.'

'The hold cover was off?'

'Yeah. We'd been cleaning out after the last trip.'

'The petrol bombs could have been thrown down by anyone passing by,' Ari said. 'Three or more I'd say by the look of the damage.'

'Seems so.' Bill gazed out to sea longingly. 'Goddammit! We should be out there.'

'Just come over to the car, please,' Ari said.

Bill looked afraid as he followed Ari to the car. 'Is it about Mandy?'

'No. It won't take a moment. Take a look at this.' Ari pushed the bust under Bill's nose.

'I'm looking. So what?'

'This is a reconstruction of the skull found in the dunes. You'll note the strange resemblance to your sister, Rose, who you said left for America, but whom I believe was killed and buried right over there. There is also a strong resemblance to Mandy.'

'You're fucking mad,' Bill said.

'How did you get to own your own boat and house? Why did a dozen families in the fishing village suddenly achieve home ownership? Why did at least ten whites and ten coloured youngsters suddenly get bursaries from the fishing company to study overseas? And lastly, what happened to Rose? You know, don't you? Why do the locals gang up on me? What are you all trying to hide? What possible crime could link you all together?'

'Look here, Lieutenant,' Bill said, turning away angrily. 'I didn't like Rose. She was a whore. She disappeared and I didn't care tuppence where she went or what happened to her. Nor do I now. It's so long ago I don't even remember what she looked like. I'm sure she deserved whatever she got. Whores usually do.'

He jumped on the boat and disappeared down the hold

leaving Ari feeling strangely elated. For once Bill had lost his composure. He was getting somewhere.

By the time Ari approached his office, the eastern mountain peaks were starkly silhouetted against the salmon sky. Geese and cormorants were winging their separate ways up and down the valley and there was a delicious tang of ozone and sea weed. Ari's happy mood changed abruptly when he caught sight of Kate looking dismal and crushed in Gerber's office.

'What the hell . . . ?' he growled.

'This has nothing to do with you, Lieutenant,' Gerber said.

'Are you kidding or something?'

'Mrs Palma has been detained for questioning concerning arson and murder which took place on her lagoonside property on the night of . . .'

'For fuck's sake – we all know what night it was and anyway this is my case.'

'I have information from a reliable source that Mrs Palma and her gardener were seen there when the fire started.'

'She was with me the whole bloody night and I have a feeling you knew that, Gerber.'

'I'll need a sworn statement from you before releasing . . .'

'So that's your game. I've got your number, Gerber. When we're off duty . . .' He let his threat hang in the air and noticed how Gerber's eyes began to blink rapidly. Despite his bulk, he was a nervous man. 'You'll get your sworn statement if and when I decide it's necessary. D'you think Kate would burn the squatters out and let them back on to her land again?'

'Yes, if she's scared enough.'

'You're not after Kate, you're after the sworn statement, aren't you? D'you always do Palma's dirty work?'

Gerber's eyes showed his guilt and his cheeks flushed.

'Come on, Kate,' Ari said, pulling her to her feet. 'I'll take you home.'

'Does he truly suspect me?' Kate asked as he drove her along the beach road. She looked scared and shocked.

'No! That's not what this is all about.'

'So what is it about?' she asked plaintively.

'About you being divorced . . . about me being cited as co-respondent and perhaps sued for alienation of affection . . . and me being rapped over the knuckles by my superiors and possibly being transferred. Now I come to think of it, that's the bottom line. Someone wants me out of here.

'Ramona gave a statement, I saw it on Gerber's desk. She claims you came home at dawn covered in soot and dirt, together with Frikkie who was badly burned and that subsequently a woman in the camp told her you were there when the fire started. Who d'you know can make Ramona say whatever they want, even to the extent of incriminating her own son?'

'I'd never have thought Rob would stoop to lying. I don't believe he'd do this.' She caught her lip in her top teeth and began chewing it.

'Don't do that, Kate, your lip will bleed. Perhaps it wasn't Rob. Perhaps Ramona wants to see the last of both of us. Or perhaps Rob thinks you'll come running home scared.'

'That's crazy!' She glared at him, daring him to contradict her. 'I'll never go back to him.'

'You may be kidding yourself, Kate, but you sure as hell aren't kidding me. You're still in love with your monster.' He drew up in the side street behind the lighthouse. 'You going to invite me in for coffee?'

'Sure,' she said listlessly. She sat as if dazed and then got out in a swift, defiant movement, slamming the door. She exuded defeat as she stumbled to the lighthouse. It was something to do with her sloping shoulders and head hanging forward and the way she moved her feet. He watched her sadly and followed behind.

'Kate, listen to me. It may seem like the end of the world, but it's not. Life has a habit of kicking you when you're down. I used to think that someone up there was spiteful, because it always happens that way. Later I realised that like attracts like. You are so sad and beaten that you are attracting your own misfortune. So cry it all out and be done with sadness, Kate. You're young and lovely and there are so many good times waiting for you – marriage to someone who loves you, seeing your own babies, creating a home and family, building your own career. It's all out there, believe me, but it won't come until you are receptive. It can't come until you allow it. Let go of the pain, Kate. Just let it go.'

Her sobs began slowly at first. A couple of shudders while she boiled the kettle, then some tears came trickling down her cheeks as she stirred the instant coffee. It was enough to form the first crack in the massive dam she'd been constructing since her private disaster began, Ari reckoned. The crack widened, the dam wall crumbled and the deluge was like nothing he'd ever experienced.

Kate collapsed on a settee and mourned for her father, for her failed marriage and her lost home, and her fears for Tabson, her grief for Eunice and the squatters and fear of Gerber and how he had looked when he had dragged her out before dawn in her pyjamas and dressing gown.

'Just like you read about but you don't think it could ever happen,' she sobbed, reliving her humiliation. She tried to explain, through her sobs, how people had changed towards her when she became poor, and how contemptuous they had been.

'When you're rich you see people through rose-tinted glasses,' she wept. 'Happy smiles and sweetness wherever you go, but just see them when they aren't trying to impress you. I can't believe it's the same people, or the same world.'

When it was clear that she was not going to stop crying, Ari picked her up and carried her fireman-fashion to bed, no mean feat, he thought proudly, reaching the fourth floor.

He pulled off his T-shirt and her pyjama top so that her naked breasts were hard against his skin. Would fucking her help? he wondered, and then guiltily put the thought aside. Yet he couldn't help wondering about all that had happened to Kate lately. It was strange how her arrogant, tough, thorny exterior had been ripped aside to reveal the sweet tenderness and caring that she nurtured inside. Did her ordeal have to happen, just as the mountain fires had to happen to release the seed pods from their shucks? Was there any meaning in this misfortune for her, or for anyone?

He sat soothing her, stroking her back, fetching a cold wet towel for her face, letting her weep it all out on his shoulder until her face was swollen and she could hardly see out of her eyes, but he sensed that much of her grief had washed away.

Eventually she stopped crying and sat up. 'Goodness! I'm sorry. I don't often carry on like that. What must I look like? Crying never suited me. I thought I'd given it up.'

'You look good to me,' he lied. 'Tell you what! Tonight we're going out. We're going to Sands nightclub. We'll show off together. Brazen it out and show them how happy we are.'

'Oh, no,' she murmured as she clung tightly to him.

'We'll dance all night, and smooch on that dance floor under the stars, and gobble prawns and crayfish, and drink too much red wine.'

'No, white wine, idiot,' she laughed. 'If we eat shellfish it has to be white wine, ice cold and very dry.'

He felt offended, but he was determined not to show it. 'We'll give the locals something to talk about. How about it?'

At last there was a glimmer of a smile lurking in her eyes. 'You're on,' she whispered. 'They can go jump. Every last one of them.'

She was going to be all right, he thought as he left later. Kate was a fighter.

Ari had insisted on fetching Tom from the hospital, hoping to pick up something that might help him with his investigations. Anything! He'd reached a stalemate over Mandy's disappearance. He could not understand Bill September's attitude.

He's a cool customer, Ari decided. He isn't panicking despite the loss of his daughter, and arson on his boat. He keeps a cool head and says little. He and Ramona are two dark horses.

Am I right? he wondered. Is Mandy's kidnapping linked to Rose's death? What if Angelo Palma had killed Rose? Then why would Ramona stay on as his housekeeper? Admittedly, her son got a trawler and she got a house and a safe billet for life, plus a cottage on the Palma premises and a home for Frikkie. But would this compensate a mother for her daughter? Commonsense said 'no'. What if Rose had been given a new personality and had emigrated? No! This morning's facial reconstruction had put paid to that theory – it was Rose's corpse that had lain in the dunes for twenty-eight years. Was that why Frikkie had been sent to recover the skull? And Mandy? What was her fate? Would he get to her in time? The trouble was, the whole damned village was set against him.

Silver Bay had become a detective's nightmare. There was so much crime, so little time to cope with individual cases – muggings, housebreaking, shoplifting and nightly fights amongst the squatters, usually terminating with stab wounds or death. There were rapes, incest, robbery with violence, arson, an endless list of local cases. So far none of the local police force had been killed, but the recent spate of attempts on their lives meant they had to work in pairs at night and this wasted time, too.

Anger kept Ari's foot pressed hard down on the accelerator as he sped towards the hospital, cursing the whole damned village. Did no one care what happened to Mandy? For days and nights he'd been obsessed with horrid imaginings. Where the hell was she and how could he get a lead? Was she alive? Was she being abused or tortured or raped in some dark festering hole? Was she terrified? Or was she dead?

Then there were those other terrible imaginings, when he himself was incarcerated in a dark hole and buried alive. When evil seemed to creep up around him and he saw those glistening, dark, beady eyes. Then the dread began again as some ancient, subconscious memory hung around him like a shroud. Now it was her turn. He had to find Mandy.

Joy in the morning! Looking at Tom walking proudly though stiffly down the hospital driveway strapped into his new legs, with admiring nurses cheering him on, Ari decided that at least something good had come out of his time here.

'Things change,' Tom said, when he'd been helped into the seat and buckled up, 'and nothing is ever the same again.' He looked happy enough about his changes. The reward money had paid for his new legs and they had been fitted while he was recuperating from his burns. Now he was far more mobile, walking slowly but steadily with the aid of two sticks.

Tom was in a philosophical mood. 'Life pushes you through change at breakneck speed. The trick of surviving is to be a deft hand at the tiller. To do that you have to know where you're going and how to get there. Where are you going, my boy?'

'Darned if I know.'

Tom sighed. 'That makes navigation difficult. Are you in love with that girl Kate?' he asked in his soft, precise voice.

Ari felt uncomfortable. Obviously their affair was public property. 'Yes,' he said, after a pause, 'but I think she still loves her husband.'

'On the whole, women usually stay put unless they're abused in one way or another. The Palma women have a long history of unhappiness.'

Ari remained silent, hoping that Tom would tell him more about the Palmas, but Tom was engrossed in noisily sucking his hollow tooth.

'Tell me about Frikkie,' Ari said after a while. 'He doesn't seem to be mad, but rather disorientated. He's never quite aware of what's going on.'

'Simple-minded describes him well enough,' Tom said.

'Have you any idea why Ramona threw him out?'

'No.'

'He keeps blabbing about a boy on a dolphin. D'you know anything about that?'

'It's just a legend. He's been muttering about it for years,' Tom said. 'By the way, there's a sardine run in the bay. They're piling up on the sand, thousands of them. It's quite a sight – kids with buckets and women with their skirts tucked up round their waists scooping the fish out of the sea.' He chuckled happily to himself, but Ari sensed that he was deliberately changing the subject.

'Frikkie claims that a dolphin rescued a young boy in the bay and brought him to the shore. It seems to be an obsession with him.'

'If you'll believe that, you'll believe anything. I find that most of Frikkie's stories boil down to his getting out of trouble with Ramona.'

Tom could be downright irritating at times, Ari thought, but glancing at his face twisted with pain, he felt ashamed of his impatience.

'Do you believe that Frikkie has something to do with the dunes' murders?'

'Frikkie's no murderer. Quite the reverse. His mother, Ramona, is another matter. I should watch out for her, if I were you.'

'Is she really his mother?'

'Yes. She had twins. Bill was bright and Frikkie was dense, poor sod. She's a very ambitious woman, you see.'

By now they were driving up the winding cobbled street towards Tom's home. 'I have a feeling that everyone knows who burned out the squatters and who murdered Rose September, but I can't prove her identity and I don't have a motive, so I can't even open a murder docket. As for this terrible business of Mandy . . . there's no clues, nothing, but I have a feeling that it's linked to the murder of Rose September. And even you . . .'

He broke off thinking that he should not be seen talking to Tom. 'Someone tried to kill you because they thought you would tell me something – but who? Why don't you tell me all you know? That would be some form of protection.'

'Well, here's some hard facts, but they might lead you astray. Sam Patel is blackmailing the parents of most of the kids he has hooked on drugs. Mandy's ex-boyfriend is one of them. Sometimes the kids even stay up in a house Patel owns on the mountainside overlooking the bay at Kommetjie. They're not kidnapped, don't think that, they go there of their own free will. Patel scares the parents into making regular monthly payments to ensure that their children are kept off the really hard stuff. Mandy is not there. Patel would never risk that.'

'Why do you think Bill's boat was torched?'

'September's made a lot of enemies lately. He's been employing blacks, mainly Ovambos from Namibia. Local fishermen are up in arms because it's taking the jobs away from this area. The villagers have vowed to get him back, but they wouldn't tackle him face to face. I've seen him knock three men senseless when they jumped him on his boat and in a matter of seconds. The skippers of the Palma trawlers hate Bill because he earns huge profits selling his fish to the company while they only get a living wage.'

'Keep your ears open,' Ari said. 'There's more where this came from.' He passed a bundle of notes to the old man. 'In future, Tom, I'll come in the night. I don't want you to be seen talking to me.'

'A little late in the day for that. Don't you worry

about me. Some things are more important than an old legless fool.'

Refusing help, he got out of the car and hobbled to his front door leaning heavily on his sticks. He went inside and shut the door without looking back, as he always did.

Chapter 27

——— ———

The moment Ari walked into the lighthouse, he realised that they weren't going to the nightclub. Kate was wearing the old T-shirt and shorts she kept for gardening and she was sitting on the floor surrounded by papers. Her hair was plaited, her eyes still swollen, and she was sneezing from the dust.

She looked up, smiling faintly. 'Sorry. I don't want to go out and sorry about all the fuss this morning. I've made a casserole for supper. My first, so don't criticise. By the way, Tabson's last operation is scheduled for the day after tomorrow. There's a chance that his leg will be completely normal, but the doctor can't be sure, at least not until he operates. I'm so scared, Ari.'

Looking at her Ari thought that he would like to marry her. The desire was so strong that he blurted it out without properly planning his strategy.

'Have you ever thought of settling down with a plain, straightforward, ordinary guy with a mediocre salary, Kate?' he asked. Try as he might, he couldn't look at her; instead he began to tidy the papers on the floor. There was no answer from Kate.

He decided to shrug off his question. Kate looked so vulnerable he wished he could cheer her up. What a fool he was to try proposing at this time. 'I guess I spoke out of turn and chose the wrong time,' he said, looking shyly towards her.

'Something like that. I'm not free, not at present. It's easy to forget that I'm married. Besides, I don't even know who I am. That's the truth.'

'But I guess you know that I love you.'

'Oh, Ari. You mustn't love me. You see, I need time to sort out who and what I am. First I have to learn to know myself. I have to learn to love myself, too.'

'I love you enough for both of us.'

'Do you love *me*, I wonder, or the way I look?'

'You don't look as good as you used to, but I still love you.'

'Thanks for the compliment.'

Oh heck! He'd definitely blown it now. 'What's this then?' He shuffled through some of the debris.

'Father's private papers. I'm trying to sort them out. Oh, what a mess! He left in a hurry, as you know, and the liquidators dumped what they don't want here this afternoon.' She pointed to a large tin trunk standing open by the table.

'I'll give you a hand,' he said.

There were dozens of files dating back to Russell's pre-mining days, Ari discovered. 'Let's get on with it,' he said briskly. 'Are you filing it all, or what?'

'I'm throwing away everything unless I can think of some constructive reason for keeping it, like photographs of my mother. You know the sort of thing one keeps.'

Switching his mind off girls and love and things he had no right to think about, Ari began to sort, label, punch and file. Oh God, what a bore, but since they weren't wining and dancing at Sands he might as well make himself useful.

Around midnight he came upon a sealed envelope marked CONFIDENTIAL. Inside was a bank deposit slip, so thin and yellow with age that he had to hold it to the light to read the faint ink which had turned pale blue. It was for two hundred thousand rands, dated February, 1964, drawn on the account of A. M. Palma, at a local Silver Bay branch. The slip was stuck on to two sheets of cardboard taped together. When he cut them apart several photographs fell into his hand.

He whistled as he shuffled through them. In one, Mandy stood tall, naked and proud, together with three other naked figures whom he could not identify. Turning it over, he read: 1964. (L to R): Trevor Palma, Rose September, Emanuel Fernandes, Juliette Fernandes. But surely this was Mandy, not Rose? The likeness was remarkable. Uncanny! He took the pictures to the light and studied them for a long time. There were about twelve of them and they showed several young white men in various stages of undress, dancing and swimming with a selection of beautiful young coloured girls. There were several close-ups of a couple making love in the dunes. Judging by the shadows, the pictures had been taken at different times.

In 1964, he remembered from Gill Bronson's catty stories, Mike Russell, Kate's father, had been a journalist. It seemed that he had taken these nude photographs of Ramona's daughter, Rose, together with Rob's father. Ari studied the pictures again. From the position of the mountain backdrop it seemed that the shots had been taken from the Russells' side of the lagoon, not far from here.

'I'm going out,' he told Kate. 'Back in five minutes.'

She was so engrossed she hardly heard him.

It was a clear night with a full moon lighting the veld. It

took him only five minutes to walk to the edge of the lagoon. Gazing over the still waters, he matched the view with the photographs, noting the dimensions of the stark black mountain ridge silhouetted against the lighter sky. Clearly the pictures were taken from here with a telephoto lens. The villa shown in some of the pictures had been on the Palmas' side of the lagoon, but it was gone now. Presumably the ruins were buried under the sand. And what else would he find there? More bones? More secrets?

One thing was clear, he thought as he walked slowly back to the lighthouse, Mike Russell had made a quick coup by blackmailing Angelo. Publication of these pictures would have meant imprisonment and disgrace for all the young people involved. They had been breaking the Immorality Act which forbade sex across the colour bar, just when it was most stringently imposed. Presumably this was the cash which had set Mike up in his first mining venture, and which started the feud between the two families, ending in Mike's ruin.

He would have to break it gently to Kate and he would have to keep the photographs as evidence. This new revelation would hit her badly. Her old man seemed a bit of a bastard. Poor Kate! She'd take it personally, as usual.

Finally he waited until they were sitting on the dunes after their late supper. It was a glorious balmy night. He could hear the night jays calling in the trees behind, the murmur of the stream and the gentle splash of waves on the sand. The soft breeze was carrying the fragrance of sea air mingled with the pungent scent of the veld behind them. He heard an owl cry.

He was about to tell her the news when she sat up, scowling. 'How could Father commit fraud? He was always so selfish, but he had no right to take such a chance. All these weeks I've stifled my anger, but now I can feel it surging out of me and I can't contain it any longer. I despise him.' She got up abruptly, raced to the beach and set off into the dark waters.

Idiot! he raged. Surely she knew sharks had been sighted in the bay that morning. He set off after her, churning the water in his frenzy to catch up with her and at last he did. She was floating on her back, arms outstretched, rising and falling over the gentle swell, gazing at the moon.

'It's not safe here,' he began.

She looked over her shoulder. 'You will never know the wonderful feeling of not caring whether you live or die,' she whispered.

'What about Tabson? Doesn't he count for anything?'

Evidently he'd said the right thing for once. Moments later she was swimming strongly back to shore.

At dawn the next morning, armed with warrants and an order, Ari began to excavate the dunes with a posse of workmen borrowed from the town council, plus several police constables. Half the village had turned out to watch, and gangs of small boys kept creeping up and making nuisances of themselves.

Backed by the wide powers given to him to aid his search for Mandy, Ari rode roughshod over the Palma family's objections. The bones he was so carefully packing and preserving were Rose's not Mandy's, but the publicity satisfied both the press, the villagers and his colonel.

At noon, leaving the team to continue their excavations, Ari drove to the Septembers', but Bill was out at sea.

'He should be back by dusk,' Hannah said. He noticed her eyes were red with weeping. 'You must tell me, you must.' She hung on to him with hands that were wet and slippery. 'What makes you think my Mandy is buried beneath the dunes. You have information, don't you? You know she's dead.' Her face was screwed up in anguish.

'No, Mrs September. I don't know where Mandy is, but I think there's a possibility that her kidnapping was a reprisal for Rose's death. I am searching for the remains of Rose, not Mandy. Look here. This is a reconstruction of the skull found in the dunes.' He produced the photographs of the mask.

'If it's true,' she sobbed, 'then Bill kept this hidden all these years. Bill's told me time and again that Rose went to America. Now I'm going to force him to tell you the truth. I have the means to make him talk. There's a few things I know about his business that he wouldn't want you to know. I want my daughter back and I'm putting my faith in you, Lieutenant. Be at my house at six this evening. That's about when he'll get back. He'll tell you all he knows, I swear to God I'll make him. Just find my daughter. Don't let me down.'

He left her and made his way to the Palmas' mansion. It was time to tackle Angelo Palma, but he knew that this powerful family would attack him with all the resources at their disposal. From now on it would be a bitter fight.

The paintings, sculpture, intricate brickwork, antique marble floors and furnishings took Ari's breath away. He announced his police identity to a black-coated manservant and after waiting only five minutes was led into a spacious office.

Angelo Palma was an intimidating figure. He was over six feet tall and he was broad, but emaciated, with no trace of a stoop to his shoulders. He had a thick shock of curly white hair which contrasted strangely with his brown skin.

He certainly wasn't the monster that Kate and Jean had described to him, Ari decided. On the contrary his eyes looked hurt and vulnerable. Ari took to him immediately.

Nevertheless, he sat down and went into his attack without wasting time. 'You must have got a lot of satisfaction in getting back at Mike Russell after waiting almost thirty years,' he said, facing Palma across a vast expanse of polished yellowwood.

Angelo's face remained expressionless, but his hooded eyelids could not entirely hide the shock in his eyes. He did not reply.

'I'm here, sir, to ask you questions relating to the death of Rose September. What exactly was her relationship with your son Trevor?'

Angelo scowled at him. 'There was no relationship,' he muttered and Ari noticed that he looked ill at ease. 'How could there be? In those days the law expressly forbade all such unions across the colour bar.'

Ari spread the old photographs over the desk. 'These pictures tell a different story, Mr Palma, and you paid two hundred thousand rands for them in 1964. How much are they worth today?'

Sly contempt was glinting in Angelo's eyes while his mouth curled into a sneer. 'How did these photographs come into your possession?'

'Let's say I came across them in the line of duty.'

'From Mrs Palma obviously . . . and you and maybe Mrs Palma, too, thought . . . Well, she's an expensive woman to keep, Lieutenant, as you've discovered by now. Your pay won't go far. So you want to sell these to me?'

'I asked you what they're worth to you? I'm still waiting for your answer.'

Angelo reached into his drawer and drew out his cheque

book. 'This is a seller's market, Lieutenant,' he said in a gruff voice. 'You may not know what that means, but I'm sure you've worked out what you want. I thought you were too good to be true.'

'Fifty thousand . . . ?' Ari voiced the words tentatively.

Palma began to write in his cheque book, first the date, then cash for the drawer's name, fifty thousand in figures and words, plus his signature. 'This will be yours when you deliver the negatives,' he muttered, without looking up.

'I was only wondering,' Ari said. 'Unfortunately these pictures and negatives can never be sold since they comprise part of the evidence concerning the disappearance and suspected murder of Rose September. As this does.' He took his tape recorder out of his inside jacket pocket and ostentatiously labelled the tape with the place and date.

'You see, Mr Palma, unlike last time, you can't buy your way out of this mess.' He put the tape and pictures back into his pocket. 'Mr Palma, I'm giving you the opportunity of making a clean breast of everything. If you don't, I shall eventually find the truth, but it may take a little longer. You can thwart me every step of the way, but I'll get there. I'm telling you that now. You see, I always do.'

Angelo rang the bell and Ramona entered at once. Presumably she had been listening at the door. She flashed Ari a look of pure hatred and he was amazed at his own reaction. *He felt afraid*. Icy shudders were running up and down his spine. His hands began to sweat, his mouth to dry. He couldn't remember when he was last so afraid. This was the stuff of his ancient nightmares.

He turned away from her quickly, but he knew she had seen, and for some reason she, too, looked startled and afraid.

'Listen to me, sir,' he said urgently. 'Evil is buried down

there in the dunes. I sense it. If I've learned anything since joining the police force it's this . . . evil contaminates and corrupts. There will be no peace in Silver Bay until the truth comes out. Truth and atonement bring their own catharsis and redemption. The bitterness has been festering for twenty-eight years, sir. It's time the truth came out.'

The two men, equally obstinate, hard-headed and perceptive, glared at each other. Then Ari turned swiftly, shot a last perplexed glance at Ramona and strode out.

The moment he had gone, Angelo staggered, clutched his heart and fell into his chair. Ramona called out and Rob came running into the room from an adjoining door. His face looked bleak as he saw his grandfather fighting for breath. Rob flung open the drawer, placed two pills on his grandfather's tongue and lifted the glass of water that was always nearby.

'Okay,' he said, when Angelo had recovered. 'I heard every word. If I'm going to help you, I have to know the truth. I'll fight to get you out of this, but for God's sake, trust me.'

'I'll tell you in my own time. Don't hassle me,' Angelo muttered. 'I have to think. Give me some more water, Rob. It was all so long ago. Leave me now. I want to be alone. That young lieutenant won't give up until he gets the truth, we can count on that. There's a lot of aggression in that young man, but he keeps it carefully hidden.'

'Damn it, Grandfather, I need to know what's going on.' Rob strode out slamming the door.

Angelo opened his safe and took out an old album and spent a long time poring over pictures of the past. There was Ramona when she was young. How lovely she had been. He remembered the first time he saw her. He'd thought he was dead when he'd opened his eyes and seen this lovely gypsy girl with long, jet-black hair and her laughing, slanting amber eyes. Her lips had been wine red, her complexion as flawless as a Castilian noblewoman's. He could see her now wearing a red skirt and green off-the-shoulder blouse. And Claire Durrell, how lovely she had been with her brown hair, her freckled smiling face and big green eyes, until she became too sad to stay, and Pippa du Toit, whom he had eventually loved so dearly.

He took hold of the picture of his beloved son Trevor, and gazed long and hard at it. 'I have to protect you and yours, my boy. That's what this is all about,' he whispered.

In the middle of the night, Angelo woke with a severe pain in his chest. He fumbled for his pills and took two. Waiting for the pain to go, he got up. It was dark outside for the heat had brought the clouds and the moon was quite obscured.

'*Three deaths, followed by your son's. He will die before he comes of age,*' Ramona had said at his son's christening. Of course, she had been right. She had the second sight, there was no doubt about that. Pippa had taken the words as a curse, but he'd known it was a prediction and he had feared the future. After Trevor's death, Ramona had forgiven him and no one could have been more devoted to their family than she.

He sighed. He would have to tell Rob everything. Well, almost everything, and perhaps now would be the best possible time. The pain had reminded him that he was not immortal. He had always delayed telling Rob about his parents, but he could not die and leave so much unsaid.

Where to begin? he wondered as he put on his dressing

gown, switched on the landing lights and walked along the passage to his grandson's room.

'Begin at the beginning,' he muttered. And that was? For him the real beginning was gazing up into Ramona's laughing amber eyes.

PART II

Silver Bay, July, 1941.

———— • ————

Chapter 28

—— ——

The waves were his enemies, advancing in formation, towering ten metres high, white-crested, foaming angels of death, smashing down tons of ice-cold water that lashed the rigging, battered the deck and pummelled the life out of him, before cascading over the side. Around him was a bubbling cauldron of white and yellow foam, and visibility was limited to the next towering monstrous wave. He was locked into a nightmare of sleeting rain, sea spray and hurricane winds. That the yacht had not yet foundered was a miracle, Angelo thought, as he fought to keep the bows head-on into the waves. He was shaking convulsively and his hands had been numb for a long time. The wind was exploding in his face, freezing him, bringing tears to his eyes so that he could not see, drenching him with salt spray. It seemed that he had fled one war only to rush headlong into another. Despite his massive strength, he was helpless against the wind. He had lashed himself to the wheel and he hoped to God he and the boat would outlive the hammering they were suffering.

The storm had blown up without warning forty-eight hours ago somewhere off the coast of South Africa, he assumed. He'd hardly had time to haul down the sails and stow them below. The engine had stalled a dozen times since then and each time he had kicked it back to life, but he was fast running out of fuel. When he was no longer able to steer, he would capsize and drown. He was a strong swimmer, but there was no sign of land in any direction.

'Mary, mother of Jesus, save me,' he prayed, but without much hope. He had stolen the boat and he had no illusions as to his status in the Virgin's eyes. He was a thief. Stealing out at dawn from Palmi harbour mere days after he received his call-up papers, he had sailed through the Straits of Gibraltar one moonless night, moving south and hugging the West African coast for the next few weeks, until he knew from the sun and the sea that he was close to the equator. He had lain becalmed for days, sweltering in the tropical sun, saving his fuel for emergencies. This was an emergency to dwarf all others, he reckoned.

It had been plain sailing for the past three months. He'd fished for his food, used his water sparingly, lost a third of his body weight and tanned to a dark brown. His black hair was long and curling over his neck, his beard grew over his face down his neck to meet the curly black hair on his chest. With every day that passed he thanked God he was that much farther away from Italy.

The storm was worsening. As the day passed to night, Angelo sized up the odds and doubted he would ever see the dawn. The gigantic waves were too close. Gallant though the boat was, she had no time to scale the slopes and the sea was breaking over her, smashing her to death. The wind was deafening, shrieking and whining and buffeting the boat in loud bangs and groans. Above this din he suddenly heard a louder crack. The mast had split in two and it was falling . . . He ducked and tried to lunge sideways, but the mast caught him above the ear and he slumped forward unconscious.

*   *   *

The first thing he noticed as he lay only half aware, was the absence of noise. No wind, no storm, just peace and quiet, or was he dead? Then he heard a gull cry. Opening his eyes cautiously, he looked up into a sky of azure blue without a sign of a cloud. He blinked in the glare and closed his eyes again.

When he moved he realised how much his head hurt. Putting up his hand and fumbling for the pain, he felt sticky wetness and opened his eyes again to see blood on his hand. Then he remembered the mast falling. What a miracle he and this valiant, strong boat had survived the storm, he thought with a surge of affection for it. 'Thank you,' he whispered to whoever was listening.

When he pushed himself to a sitting position, whimpering with pain, he realised that his thanks had been premature. They were about to founder and he would be dragged down. He sprang into action, unstrapping the sheet with difficulty, his fingers fumbling, panic dulling his mind. Eventually he wrenched himself free and lurched across the deck. She must be holed somewhere below decks. Could he patch it up and pump out the water?

A glance down the hatch showed the futility of hope. The life rafts had been swept away and even now the boat was keeling over. He looked around for anything that could double as a makeshift raft, but the wind had swept the deck bare.

Where the hell was he? Which way was land? Screwing his eyes up, he searched the horizon. A tremor of joy surged through him as he seemed to see the misty outline of a small ring of mountains almost obscured under a cloud in the distance. Was it real or was he hallucinating? The image was gone and he shivered with apprehension. Kicking off his boots and oilskins, he stuck one foot tentatively into the sea.

The water was almost freezing. How could it be so cold? Where the hell was he? This was Africa, wasn't it? How long could he survive in these icy temperatures?

The boat shuddered like a man with death convulsions and keeled over. At that moment Angelo dived clear into the crystal-clear, icy depths. He emerged spluttering and shouting: 'Oh! Oh! Jesus! The cold! Oh God, the cold!' The sound of his own deep bass voice seemed to reassure him.

He set off at a crawl, but soon his breath was rasping and his arms and legs felt as if they were strapped to lead weights. Shooting cramps tormented him. He changed to breaststroke and gloomily considered his chances of making land. The icy cold was sinking into his bones, numbing him to the very depths of his being. He knew he was in danger of lapsing into unconsciousness, so he switched back to the crawl. He felt a bump against his leg and gasped in panic. Sharks! Then another. Whipping around, he found himself surrounded by playful seals, bobbing and diving and treading water to watch him, whiskers twitching, bright eyes alight with friendly curiosity.

Searching the distant horizon again, he could see only a stretch of cloud which seemed to be lying on the water. Yet the seals were swimming away and he knew they must be moving towards an island, so he set off in the same direction, singing to himself as he kept his arms threshing rhythmically through the water in time to the music.

Ages later pain began to sink deeply into him, into his stomach, under his ribs and through the joints of his knees and shoulders. It was unbearable. He began to count in time to the music, remembering his favourite operas, his arms rising and falling. The pain was spreading outward to his fingertips, but Angelo ignored it, he was back home listening to the music on Papa's gramophone. Was it an hour, or two, or three? He had no way of telling, he had fallen into a trancelike state, mindless and unfeeling, as he churned his arms over and over.

Darkness fell and he began to feel very afraid. What if he was swimming in the wrong direction? Surely he should wait for daylight. But when he turned and floated on his back and tried to rest, the cold crept into his head. He was blacking out and he knew that he must swim or die, so he began again.

He was half unconscious when he thought he saw a beam of light over to his right, like a far-off pinprick stabbing his eye. He yelled and tried to jump up, treading water, but fell back and took in a mouthful of choking brine. Spluttering, he looked ahead, but there was only darkness, yet he stared longingly, refusing to give up hope. There it was again – a tiny pinprick of a star, perhaps from a lighthouse. It was real. Far ahead of him, was light, land, people – life!

He began to swim strongly towards it. An hour passed and then another, but Angelo was aware only of the agony of forcing his limbs to keep fighting. He felt faint and sick and desperately thirsty. The salt coated his face, encrusted his lips and seared his eyes. His stomach was churning from the salt water he had swallowed. Occasionally he vomited into the sea.

Then he heard the sound of *Nessun dorma* and he was back in Spoleto watching his father dusting the record with a cloth and carefully placing the needle on to it. '*No man will sleep! No man will sleep! You too, oh Princess, in your virginal room watch the stars trembling with love and hope.*'

Every night Papa had played excerpts from his favourite operas for an hour before he began work. Papa was so soft, so gentle, so kind and intellectual. He had a vivid image of his father crouched over the antique table, under the swaying lamp, checking the school essays, taking off his glasses to polish them with his handkerchief. His mother would lean over him, enveloping him in her long black hair, kissing the top of his head: 'You work too hard, my sweet,' she was always saying. 'Come to bed, it's late.' How she had loved him! They had been a tight-knit family, bonded by the villagers' contempt.

When Father was a teenager, *his* father had squandered the last of the family's fortune, except the vineyards and the mansion which was locked into a family trust. As soon as he was trained, Papa had begun work as a teacher, eventually becoming the headmaster of the local school. Their old mansion had been split up into apartments and rented out. Mama had taken to her role as landlady with an energy that was scarcely believable. Father had done his best to be a good teacher and warn his pupils of the evils of the Fascist regime. Mussolini took power in October, 1922, the same month and year that Angelo was born. By then half the boys had left the school because they didn't like to hear what Papa told them, but he never gave up. For eighteen years he had fought for what he believed in, democracy and dignity.

Angelo could picture him now, standing on the rostrum, quietly talking to a packed school hall about human rights and dignity. He who respected everyone, was a living example of his teaching. He had been so dignified and unafraid when local Fascists, led by the mayor, had marched into the hall and taken him away, but Angelo, sitting in the front row, had been scared enough for both of them. From then on, he had argued, bribed, threatened, pleaded and wept for his father's life.

The memory had been so real. It faded into the night sky. Suddenly he was alone, more alone than he had ever been. He felt anguished by the utter impossibility of ever reaching land.

As he lay floating, his head back in the water, waiting for the inevitable drifting into sleep from intense cold, he seemed to see the school courtyard. The crowd jeering, hurling abuse. His father blindfolded, his arms tied to the post behind him. He could hardly see the wavering black-bagged figure through his tears. His mother's body was pressed tightly against him, and she was shaking violently. When they saw his body jerk and heard the volley of shots, his mother screamed in agony, jerked as if she had been shot and fell to the ground unconscious.

She had married the mayor, his father's murderer, two years later.

Memories! He had to get away. He sprang forward in a fast crawl, fighting to live, fighting for new life, swimming harder and faster. He had fled the old. Europe was dead for him. He was *en route* to the new, leaving bitterness and age-old feuds, the ferocity of politics, the cruelty of people and the fickleness of women.

A day after his mother re-married, his call-up papers had been served. Was he to fight for those who had murdered his father? He had left his step-father's home that day and travelled to the nearby seaside town of Palmi, where he spent two days studying the yachts in the harbour. Eventually he made his choice. The boat had been left behind by some rich English tourists and it was used occasionally by the local harbour master.

Angelo passed into a strange state of being half unconscious. The pain was there, but it was far away. He woke to daylight and saw a sight he would never forget, a ring of glorious mountains, graceful and sloping, rose-tipped against the oyster-blue sky, enclosing a turquoise bay.

Land or heaven? He had never seen anything so lovely, but he was fading fast, lapsing into unconsciousness, hardly aware of what he was doing.

Dawn in Silver Bay. Ramona paced the strip of garden in front of her tiny shack. She felt strangely agitated, but she did not know why. In a sudden moment of decisiveness, she knotted her long black hair into a bun on her head, grabbed her sandals and ran down to the quayside.

Gideon, her young husband, was mending the communal fishing net on the beach. Later he would row it out to sea and it would hang there, traversing the bay, suspended from a necklace of buoys until sunset, when the village men would band together to haul it in by two ropes, one at each end of the beach. They would share out the harders, mackerel, maasbankers and the occasional small yellowtail and stumpnose. Everyone got something, however small. Gideon, the strongest and the best rower in the village, would bring home the finest fish.

'Get out the boat,' she commanded, breathless and agitated.

'I'm busy,' he grunted. 'The nets aren't ready yet. What is it with you?'

She ran down to the beach and began to drag the smallest dinghy down towards the sea.

'Hey,' Gideon yelled. 'What the hell?' He ran after her.

There was always a strange communication between them. He didn't have 'the sight', but some bond he had with his wife helped him to understand her. He would have argued if it weren't for those dark eyes looking so intently into his. Everyone knew she was a witch.

'Don't ask . . . I don't know . . . I don't know . . .' she

muttered. 'Only that there is not much time, so row, Gideon. Row as hard as you can.'

'Which way?'

'I don't know. There's something out there.'

He sighed and bent over the oars.

'I heard a call,' she was saying in her thrilling low voice. '"Help." He called for help. "Help me and I in turn will help you."' She looked over the sea shaking her head and smiled at him. 'There will be anguish and pain and death, but it is our destiny. Out there . . . there is our destiny . . . for me and for you . . .'

On and on she went, muttering, searching the sea, her body and her dark face shaking with the force of her passionate involvement with her strange vision. Gideon loved her to distraction. She was his sun and he revolved around her as her adoring moon. They spun in their private constellation, their lives complete in each other, and their endless quarrels came and went meaninglessly. Words and actions could never scratch the surface of their love that went down like an unplumbed well, passing through their dream minds, far beyond this life, to other forgotten lives. Beyond time and space. Or so she told him often enough and he believed her.

He rowed until his back was breaking and it felt as if his arms were tearing out of their sockets. By now the villagers had put out the nets without him and this annoyed Gideon. There was nothing at all to see except the seals and two jackass penguins that bobbed around them, and once they saw a shoal of dolphins further off towards Cape Point. He knew from the sun that it was past eleven and with the knowledge came a pang of hunger, and this made him angry.

'How can you be such a fool?' He spat the words at her,

but his anger was not directed at her, just at himself. He was not the man she thought him to be. He felt ashamed of his hunger and thirst and his aching limbs. Her voice soothed him.

'It is here. Just be still. Be quiet.' She cupped her mouth in her hands and called. 'Hallo! Who is it? Where are you? Is there anyone out there?'

Then they saw him not far off, his arms moving jerkily like a rusty old windmill in a gusty wind, a dark shape hardly moving forward, rocked by the sea, emitting strange groans, like some weird sea creature.

'What is it?'

'It's a man, you fool!'

'What is he doing here, so far out?'

'Shipwrecked, I suppose. I'll hold the oars, you drag him in.'

She leaned far out on the port side, balancing the boat, while Gideon dragged in the body starboard. As the man was hauled over the side, he vomited a spurt of sea water into the boat. She threw the stranger down and lay over him, warming him with her body.

'Row, Gideon!' she commanded. 'Row for his life. It's almost gone.' As she gazed down at the sleeping giant, she knew that this memory would stay with her forever. The overpowering beauty of him hit her like a blow. Even though he was unconscious she could sense the strength and the wilfulness. His face was wide, a broad brow plastered with jet black curls, black eyebrows that were startlingly straight, and long black lashes. His nose was short and straight with flaring nostrils above sensuous lips and a jutting, obstinate chin. She could not take her eyes away from his face, the overwhelming sexuality took her breath away. Her eyes lingered

over his thick, sinewy neck and his lithe and powerful body.

Then his face seemed to change as she stared at him,
wavering out of focus. A new face was staring up at her,
a young man, as wilful, as strong, yet strangely different,
part of her blood and part of his, their seed intermingled,
a godlike heir reared in luxury and power to operate a vast
empire. *His seed and hers.* She had been shown. This was
why she had been called out to save him. Here lay her
destiny.

The moment passed and she shuddered. It was always
like this. She could not feel his pulse, but she could not let
him die. Tearing off her blouse and skirt she pressed her
hot body on his, breathing her life into his lungs, willing
her life force into him, drawing power from the sky and
thrusting it into him.

Unbearable pain flooded into Angelo as his limbs came
to life. The pain became a searing agony in every nerve
end, every muscle, every sinew and bone. He groaned and
writhed and opened his eyes. Looking up, he saw a sight
which took his breath away and made him bite back his
screams. A face like an angel's, heart-shaped, with a creamy,
coffee skin, framed by jet-black cascading hair. Her brows
were straight and thick, her lips wine red, her teeth white
and even, and she was smiling as a mother might smile at
a child. He felt helplessly caught up in the power of her
strange black eyes, for they were like nothing he had seen in
his life, strangely translucent as if lit from behind and they
were beaming love at him. He felt safe in this reassuring
glow. He could trust her. He allowed himself to lapse back
into unconsciousness.

Chapter 29

————— —————

The castaway's body healed fast, for he was superbly strong. That was the easy part, Gideon thought, watching him hauling in the nets. 'Gideon's boy,' the villagers called him, for he seemed happy to spend his days trailing along behind him like a shadow, helping out whenever he could. His limbs had thickened and filled out, his skin glowed, his hair was long and unruly, and he looked so much like one of the coloureds that no one gave him a second glance.

They called him 'Boy' because he would not tell them his name. Or could not? Gideon wondered, watching him carefully. He was learning to speak as a child learned, picking up the locals' sing-song tone, and their rich, abusive, humorous expressions, without a trace of a foreign accent, but they knew he was foreign. His mind had hibernated, but would it ever emerge? Gideon had his doubts as he watched him trailing along behind, moving like a zombie. He reckoned Boy's brain was damaged from his near-drowning experience. He'd seen it before. He said so often enough, but Ramona's reply was always the same: 'Give him time. He needs time.'

The months passed and even Ramona began to wonder if her 'sight' had played tricks on her. All summer long, Boy stumbled over the beach, retrieving fish, collecting shells, and playing with local dogs and children.

On the third Wednesday in October, Gideon and his shadow spent the morning fishing. The catch was good, and Boy was sent along to the local trading store to sell the fish or exchange it for wine.

Approaching the shops, he passed a gang of Italian prisoners of war, who were digging a trench for new cables to be laid. He stood on the pavement listening to their foreign voices and he understood every word they said.

How was that possible? Who was he? How did he get here? Then he remembered his bitter experience in the storm and the swim that followed. After that the images fell like blows as his subconscious released its heavy load – a kaleidoscope of hurtful memories – and he fell forward on to the pavement, dragged himself up and staggered to the beach where he collapsed on the sand like any other drunken *skolly* [coloured lay-about], so no one gave him a second glance.

The sun reached its zenith and slowly sank towards the horizon, and Peggy Cohen, who ran a beachside café, noticed his sorry state and sent Jimmy, her black cleaner, to fetch him into her yard. She gazed at the *skolly*, her face a mixture of pity and contempt, while her daughter stood straddle-legged, finger in nose, staring at him, too.

'He's a drunk and you must keep away from drunks,' she lectured her daughter. Bending over Angelo, she shook his shoulder. 'You must go home. If you lie around the police will lock you up at sunset.' She brought him some coffee with plenty of sugar and gave him a pile of sandwiches left

over from the day's business. 'Eat! Then you'll feel better,'
she urged him.

The fish were stinking by the time Gideon found him
stumbling along the beach towards the fishermen's village.
'Come along, Boy,' Gideon said kindly. 'I should never
have left you.'

Angelo looked at Gideon as if seeing him for the first
time. His eyes, deepset under bushy brown brows, were
full of changing expressions, as if they mirrored his soul.
Scorn, humility, pride, servility, hostility – it was all there,
a strange mixture of intense contrasts, one minute soft
and compassionate and then changing like the wind into
tremendous ferocity. There was cruelty there, too, and
sometimes all these expressions at once. His forehead was
strangely narrow for such a big man, his head flattish, his
jaw and cheekbones wide and protruding. His nose, spread
halfway across his face, was flat, with huge nostrils from
which ginger hairs curled and coiled. His lips were full
and pouting and his head and most of his face were covered
with a strange mixture of brown and ginger curls, while his
moustache was a light ginger and it fell over the sides of
his mouth, giving him a sinister appearance.

Angelo frowned and wondered if he were lousy. He
probably was, he thought. Reaching the cottage, he walked
into his room and stared into the piece of cracked mirror
Ramona had put on the cupboard.

'*Mio Dio!*' he called out in a voice that was suddenly
authoritative and manly. He frowned as he scratched his
beard. 'Shit,' he said. 'What a fucking dirty sight.' Then
he remembered that he never swore, not even in English.
He would not speak Italian again, he decided, or he'd land
up digging trenches by the roadside.

'Hey, Gideon. Can you lend me a razor?' he called out.

Ramona and Gideon came running. Suddenly he was a stranger. Ramona hugged him shyly, while Gideon slapped him on the shoulder. 'What's the fuss about?' he asked. 'Lend me a razor, Gideon.'

'Shit, man, you'd be a fucking idiot to shave off that beard for then your fucking cheeks would match your fucking arse. White as only a bloody larny immigrant could be. Know what I mean, Boy?'

Angelo laughed. 'My name is Angelo. How long have I been here? What day is it?'

When they told him it was October 22, 1941, he remembered it was his birthday and he was nineteen.

Ramona, who needed no excuse for a party, made a huge pot of fish and tomato stew. They killed old Cocky, their rooster, and turned him into a spicy dish, with rice, pumpkin, peas and sweet potatoes cooked with cinnamon. Gideon bought a gallon of cheap red wine, raw and strong, and the neighbours and friends came along to join in the fun.

'Talk about feeding the five thousand,' Angelo pondered wonderingly. There was food in abundance, for everyone had brought something, and by midnight there had been four bad fights and a good deal of dancing. Several of the men had taken out their guitars and they were singing and dancing, their music wild and free and lovely, and the girls from around gathered by magic in their best full skirts that flowed and billowed, so by midnight most of the villagers were gathered around Ramona's house, singing and dancing and necking in the moonlight.

Angelo watched them, and he loved them all. They were simple and good and trusting and they loved to sing and dance. They sang, even when they spoke, Angelo thought.

When the first light of dawn slunk over the sand dunes, and most of their guests had vanished, although some were snoring in the garden, and Gideon was groaning and holding his head, Angelo took Ramona by one hand and Gideon by the other.

'Thank you, my friends,' he said. 'Thank you for saving my life and hiding me here and looking after me.'

Later, in the silence of his room, he swore a solemn oath to repay the villagers a hundredfold for all the kindness they had shown him.

But how?

For Angelo, the days that followed were full of anguish. He looked with sad eyes at his poverty-stricken friends, noting their harsh lives and lack of necessities. Most of them had never been to a dentist, and few had all their teeth, while those over forty had hardly any left. Although cheap medical attention was available at state hospitals, it was rudimentary. There were so many cripples from polio, TB was rife, and meningitis was a scourge that killed too many children.

Despite living next to the sea that teemed with crayfish, fish and shellfish, they were all half starved. They lived on fish caught by trekking their nets and the odd half-crowns from odd jobs scrounged around the small white community. When it was too rough to fish they hardly ate, but they kept their hunger at bay by smoking *dagga* which they grew illegally in the mountains. Perhaps that was why they were always happy, Angelo pondered, as he watched the lucky employed few drinking away their wages on a Friday night, and suffering hellish hangovers on Saturday morning. On the whole, they lived in the here and now and never spared a thought for tomorrow, like children in the Garden of Eden. Yet there was enough potential to give them all jobs and homes. All he needed was capital, but how to get hold of it was a real problem.

'What we need,' he told Gideon, 'is a fishing trawler.'

Gideon laughed heartily. 'Man, I think your brains got addled in salt water after all,' he said, slapping his thigh.

From then on, every Sunday, Angelo attended mass at the local Catholic church in the valley. Father Richard Mooney spoke with a strong Irish accent and from his sermons Angelo gathered he had no love of the English. He had to trust someone, he reasoned, and plucking up courage he sought out the priest in the presbytery on Wednesday evening. He was a tall, thin man with pinched features and startlingly blue eyes.

'What can I do for you, my son?' he asked softly.

'I need help, Father.'

'And your name is . . . ?'

'Angel.'

'That's a right holy name, my son,' he said, trying to suppress a smile. 'You're not a Catholic, are you?'

'Yes. Why else would I be here?'

'Strange!' He frowned and Angelo could see that the priest did not believe him.

'I don't know of any Catholics living round the harbour area,' he said, 'but that's easily remedied since it costs nothing to become a Catholic.'

'I'm not from these parts,' Angelo began warily.

'You look and you speak as if you are, my son.'

The priest was looking uneasy, so Angelo blurted out his story leaving nothing out: his father's lonely fight against the Fascists that culminated in his death. How he had fled Italy when his call-up papers came and the long and hazardous flight down the west coast of Africa that ended in near-disaster when his stolen boat was wrecked, and how Ramona and Gideon had rescued him. He said nothing about Ramona's second sight, reasoning that this could only land her in trouble with the church.

'You see, Father, I could never fight for a creed which destroyed my family, and which I believe to be evil,' he explained, his voice hoarse with emotion.

'And your real name is . . . ?'

After only a moment's hesitation he told him that, too. After all, he had to put his faith in someone.

'*Dominus vobiscum*,' the priest said quietly.

'*Et cum spiritu tuo*,' Angelo replied without a moment's hesitation.

'Now, Angelo, sit quietly there and let me think.'

The priest came from Dublin. His grandmother was half-Italian and he identified with this young man.

'We have to accept that if you gave yourself up to the authorities you would be imprisoned for the duration of the war. Assuming that some of the prisoners-of-war and internees are Fascists, they might treat you as a deserter. You might not survive the war years in a prisoner-of-war camp.' Father Mooney's eyes took on a strange, intense expression. 'You were guided here, my son,' he said. 'I see it as my solemn God-given duty to help you. As it happens I am in a position to supply you with Irish papers. I'll do the best I can. Meantime, lie low, stay where you are, come to confession regularly and see me in a month's time. I'll have the papers for you by then.'

True to the priest's word, Angelo's papers were handed

to him a month later. He became Angelo Morgan, whose father hailed from Dublin and whose mother was Afrikaans. Both had been killed in a car smash and their fictitious child had been supposedly reared in a private Catholic orphanage.

'Your parents are real people and you might take time off to put a few flowers on their grave from time to time, my son, seeing as how they've lent you their name for the duration of the war,' Father Mooney told him when he said goodbye.

Angelo tried hard to picture what the couple might have been like had they lived, as he knelt at the plain stone cross in the Catholic graveyard in Athlone. He placed his bouquet of wild agapanthus, ericas and rosemary amongst the glassed-in waxed flowers.

As Angelo Morgan, he was a free man and he could work wherever he liked. He was filled with energy as if to recoup his lost months. Gideon laughed at him when he signed on as deck hand on a whaling ship to gain some capital.

'That's what they all say,' he laughed. 'But you'll come back and blow the lot on women and booze. They all do.'

Gideon was wrong. Angelo returned from the ice four months later with the magnificent sum of five hundred pounds, with which he bought a strong, eighteen-foot ski boat with two good engines, crayfish pots and a trawler net.

'What's the good of catching crayfish? You won't be able to sell them,' Gideon argued. 'Silver Bay is full up with fish and lobsters.' He was right!

So Angelo borrowed the priest's bicycle on a permanent basis and began door-to-door fish deliveries, and the housewives of Silver Bay, charmed by his virile, handsome appearance, bought so much fish that the butcher started complaining. Soon Angelo was delivering fish to hotels and hospitals within a twenty-mile radius. He was so busy delivering, he had no time for fishing, so Gideon took the boat out with a friend, while Angelo spent his days peddling his wares.

'If only we had capital,' he moaned to Ramona one evening while she rubbed his aching muscles with soothing ointment. 'Then we could buy a van and a trawler and set up a canning plant, employ people. We could supply the troopships coming round the Cape,' he said excitedly as his dreams flourished. 'We're losing out because we can't get the fish to where it's needed before it rots. But we could freeze it,' he yelled excitedly, jumping up. 'Why didn't I think of that before? What would a second-hand freezer cost?'

More than he had, he found out the following morning.

The bank manager, English, near-pension, introverted and conservative, was embarrassed by Angelo's request.

'But, sir . . .' Angelo interrupted him after being snubbed for ten minutes, '. . . why not use my boat as security for the loan?'

'It's not even insured, you tell me. What if you founder? You have no security, Mr Morgan. Now if you'll excuse me.'

'You'll be sorry,' Angelo snarled. 'I'll own this town one day.' He stalked out in a fury. He had to have the capital, but how?

Nothing much happened in Silver Bay. In 1942 the valley was favoured by the English riding community who lived on smallholdings with stables spread up along the river, and the arty types who lived in pretty homes clustered around the bay. The mountains boasted a silver mine, and the valley a few dairy farms, there was a small harbour for fishing boats and a lumber mill. There was work to be had there for two pounds a week, but it would take a lifetime and then some to accumulate the capital he needed. Angelo was close to despair.

Then, one Sunday night, the valley was woken at 2 a.m. by church bells. A ship carrying food, livestock and twenty-six British Air Force boys had been driven onto the rocks at Oudebaai, a remote rocky beach situated at the base of the towering Bobbejaan mountain, surrounded by miles of slippery, bush-covered slopes. The ship was sinking fast and all able-bodied men were begged to help carry equipment and ropes down the mountainside. The only access was a circuitous gravel track girdling the mountain, which petered out just five hundred metres above the beach. The villagers lugged their gear to the overhanging ledge and considered the perilous descent through thick thorny scrub culminating in a slippery sheer granite face, down to the treacherous ice-cold sea.

Angelo and Gideon had seen the distress flares at 10 p.m. and fetched some of the fishermen to trek around the mountain track with them. There they watched the drama as Cape Town's tug was driven back time and again by heavy breakers smashing against the cliffs. At 2 a.m., a massive wave brought the helpless cargo boat starboard-on to the cliff, lifted it as if it were a matchbox and dumped it on a ledge with a thump that echoed round the mountains. There it stayed, up to its plumb line in the sea, perched precariously in boiling spirals of foam while the breakers crashed over the decks.

The Air Force men and the crew gathered in a small crowd on deck, hanging on to each other and the rails and waving frantically towards the lights shining above. Their cries for help were lost in the roar of the breaking surf. To abandon ship would be suicide for they would be smashed on the surrounding rocks. The sheep in their cages on the decks cried piteously for rescue.

By 3 a.m. most of the village had reached the mountain path above. Flares and torches and binoculars were trained upon the trapped men who seemed doomed. By now the sea rescue launch had arrived, but could not approach through the breaking surf.

It was then that a figure was seen scrambling down the sheer cliff face, a rope around his waist, with Gideon playing it out from above, and Ramona shining a light.

Who could it be? the whites wanted to know, for he seemed to be a skilled mountaineer. Suddenly he was washed off the face by a giant breaker. Next he was seen dangling over the rocks, feet flailing for a foothold, buffeted and drenched by the waves.

A sigh ran through the crowd as he swung like a pendulum until he reached the ship's bows. Suddenly he seemed to be catapulted through space to land on the deck. He fastened his rope to the ship's rail and waved up to his friends. More ropes followed fast and soon the entire crew were being roped and hoisted up the cliff. They arrived one by one, scared, bruised and bleeding, one of them with a broken arm. They were all suffering from shock and exposure, and they were taken to hospital in the back of a truck.

Angelo was left alone. He waved to Gideon to start his descent, pointing to the beach at the bottom of the cliff.

The storm was blowing itself out, Angelo reckoned, and the ship would last a few weeks before breaking up. The biggest danger lay in its slipping off its rocky perch. He let the sheep out of their smelly cages and waited for daylight.

Dawn came, but the storm showed no further signs of abating and the ship shifted scarily once or twice. When the sun rose there was a sudden lull. At last! Angelo heaved the sheep overboard and they began to circle around, scrabbling at the bows and calling piteously. Keeping one large male until last, he made a rope collar and leaped overboard with the sheep. The terrified creature tried to climb on to his back, but Angelo pushed it off and set out strongly for the nearest channel through the rocks, hauling the sheep behind him. As he had hoped, the rest followed. Gideon was waiting on the beach and the two of them managed to drive the little flock up the mountainside. Before noon they had sold them to a local farmer for one pound each, no questions asked.

Angelo felt bucked with the fifty pounds. It was their first down-payment on a freezer.

The following Sunday at church, Angelo learned that the village of Silver Bay had been given a citation from the British government for saving the men. The priest gave an impassioned talk, demanding that his congregation give generously to a special collection for the daring youth who had risked his life to board the ship.

Feeling guilty at their passive role, the well-heeled community of Silver Bay paid up generously. Pale and trembling with shock, Angelo was handed two hundred pounds by the priest. More than enough cash to buy a second-hand van and a freezer.

'We're in business,' he told the astonished Ramona and Gideon when he got back from church. 'This is the start of our fortune. From now on we're never going to look back.'

Chapter 30

——— ———

For ten dreary days the iron roof of Gideon's cottage had creaked and groaned under the hammering of rain and hailstones. It was a June Saturday night in the midst of a foul winter and Ramona was grumbling and drinking too much cheap wine. Angelo had learned that the locals did not like bad weather. They skulked in bed and tried to dodge work, but he was teaching them better ways. His workers had been supplied with rubber overalls, hats and gumboots, and they had no excuse for being late however dark the morning, but he had had no success with Ramona. The cold depressed her, although he did not understand why, but he'd noticed her nerves became frayed by wind and storms.

'I used to bless the fish harvest,' she said softly. She half turned towards Angelo and in the lamplight he noticed again what a lovely woman she was. Her eyes were lustrous, the whites shining like the cluster of pearls in her ears. Her skin shone smooth and soft, her black hair fell over her bare shoulders and only her mouth was downturned. Lately she wore a dark red lipstick which seemed to highlight her every mood, for her mouth was as expressive as her eyes. Every flicker of interest or humour, every disappointment showed in her mobile lips.

'You know something, Angelo,' she was saying. 'I used to watch the frenzied silver bodies leaping in the nets as they were dragged in and grieve for them. I used to try to guess the size of the catch, and I used to pray for them. I blessed each beautiful silver fish. I loved them. Yes, I did. They brought us life! A fish for old Jimmy to keep him going another week, and a feast for the starving Hendrickse family, more milk for Freda to feed her baby, and little Jamie would get a *bokkem* for his birthday. Do you remember . . . ?'

Her voice tailed off, and tears glittered in her eyes. Angelo tried to understand her, but failed.

'Now I hate the fish. What are they? Soulless fillets! Piles of stinking offal! Masses of scales that stick all over me! And I stink, too. Smell my hands! D'you smell the stink? I scrub and scrub, but I can never get rid of the stench of fish. And the noise . . . hammering boxes, the girls screeching and yelling at each other, the slippery floor, the hosing, the cold, human indifference to the death of something that once lived. Well, who can blame us, they aren't fish at all, just kilos of fillets.'

She tossed off her wine and poured herself another full glass. 'The priest used to come down evenings and bless the harvest and we used to bless the poor fish in our minds. Now I hate them.' She hiccuped and her mouth became more downturned and almost ugly.

'But you have a refrigerator,' he said making his gruff voice sound soothing, longing for her to acknowledge his worth. 'And so many new dresses and look how nice your hair looks. One of these days we'll have enough cash to buy you a better house with a proper roof,' he added, looking up with a wry grin. The corrugated-iron roof leaked and the noise was like a tin drum as the drips landed in their iron bucket. It was the irregularity of the noise that did the most damage to their nerves.

'Having nothing was all right,' she said philosophically. 'We were used to nothing, but "a little" is not enough.'

'That's my girl,' he said, slapping her bare shoulder and laughing at her. 'Of course it's not. We'll make more and more. You'll see.'

Perhaps supervising the fish-freezing plant was not the right niche for Ramona, Angelo thought. Obviously he should not have pushed her into it. He'd look around. Young Visset, a packer, was a bright lad. He could take over and that would open up a job for another villager.

Gideon came back from the bar soon afterwards. His eyes swept over Ramona and moved on.

'Why are you looking at me like that?' she said truculently, fingering her earrings.

Gideon was so tension-charged they could almost smell the aggression. His face, full of contrasts, changed like the wind, but tonight contempt was uppermost. His lips were curling into a sneer, nostrils quivering with suppressed temper, eyes hard as agates.

'You're drunk and you look ugly when you're drunk.' His soft, silky voice was a warning on its own.

'So do you. Look at you! But you look ugly when you're sober, too.'

'I'm a man. It's natural that I should want to get drunk sometimes.'

'And I'm a woman and it's natural that I should want to be fucked sometimes.'

Angelo retired to bed with a book. He sighed. Why had everything changed? He had wanted to make their lives wonderful, but somehow it had not worked out that way. Gideon had become impotent in the face of his wife's improved status. But why? After all, he was making money, too, and their cottage was much improved with electrical equipment, a new lino floor and a kitchen table.

Angelo tried not to listen to their cruel retorts, but he could not help wondering why the village had changed. So far there were only enough jobs to employ one quarter of the locals, so the rest were fighting mad. Brawls and slanging matches broke out all the time. But was jealousy the whole story? Or was it something else? They seemed to have lost the Garden of Eden.

By now Gideon was eating his supper, but it seemed from Ramona's biting remarks that he had his knife and fork the wrong way round, his nails were dirty, his collar was filthy, and he was stinking like a pig. A swift slap stemmed her flow of words, but moments later he heard a hoarse yell, followed by imaginative cursing. Ramona had got her own back somehow. She always did, but Gideon was always caught unaware. Angelo sighed.

Eventually the front door slammed and Gideon's footsteps could be heard stamping down the path to the cobbled road, while Ramona's voice hurled insults after him. Then, at last, there was peace and quiet. But not for long. His door opened and Ramona poked her head in. She looked dishevelled, her hair awry, her eyes swollen, lipstick smudged.

'I hate him,' she whispered.

'No you don't. You love him.'

'I used to love him, but now I see what a peasant he is.'

'He's a good person. I have a lot of respect for Gideon. There's not many like him.'

'He can't grow. Like those books you gave me on dinosaurs, he can't cope with all this.' She gestured towards the kitchen.

'These are just things, Ramona. It's nice to have them, but it's not as important as loving each other.'

'Don't preach to me, Angie,' she muttered. 'He's changed. I don't know that man any more.'

She stretched, and pushed her hands into her hair, throwing it over her shoulder while her body arched and those beautiful eyes of hers beamed a message which was unmistakable. 'You and I know that we have so much in common.'

'But he's your husband.'

Angelo's mind was racing, his hands sweating, but he kept very still, without changing his expression. He felt like a man who had gone unafraid into the night only to discover that he'd blundered into a bog. What if he walked quietly backwards? Would he escape?

'No. We never married. Why should we? We've been together since we were fifteen, but we never felt the need to marry.'

He knew he was sinking as he tried to explain: 'I love you like my sister. I love Gideon, too. Maybe it's been too much of a strain having me here. I should find another place to stay.'

'No!' She began to cry and refused to be comforted. Eventually he got up and poured them both a brandy, hoping that this would make her sleepy enough to go to bed. She was in a dangerous mood, petulant, tearful and longing to be loved. He tried to keep distaste from showing in his eyes. Angelo disliked excesses. Inside Ramona's head was a pack of wild dogs that she could not control: envy, guilt, anger . . . and so many strange mongrels. Alcohol seemed to let the beasts loose.

Ramona caught Angelo's reproving glance and felt slighted.

Damn him! She was obsessed with him. Gideon knew and he watched her day and night, but now he had gone out to get even more drunk.

Hurrying to her bedroom, she plunged her face in icy water, bathed her eyes and recklessly squandered the last of the perfume Angelo had bought her, dousing herself with it.

Striding back into Angelo's room, she saw only a pile of blankets. He was pretending to be asleep. The fool! She watched him slyly. How young he was at times. He was nervous, she could tell from his rapid blinking. Perhaps he'd never had a woman. Oh how she longed to be his first. Her belly had ached for days, her thighs were heavy and moist, every nerve in her body seemed to be shrieking with lust for this beautiful boy. He was so near and yet so unattainable and her need was becoming unbearable.

She leaned over him. Pulling back the blankets from his face she gazed hungrily at him. He was sweating, yet it was freezing. She longed to run her fingers through the tousled black hair on the pillow. How lovely he was with his full, pouting lips, his perfectly even, delicate profile. Unable to stop, she ran her finger down the sloping line of his cheeks and touched his thick black brows that almost met over his eyes. Broodingly, she clasped the brandy goblet to her breast and contemplated her dreams which lay dishevelled on the pillow. Not just dreams, either, but happy expectations. Sometimes she had glimpses into the future, a certain awareness came to her and she had never been wrong. She knew their seed would intermingle. Out of their mingled blood would come a man great enough to control a vast empire. Her strength and his compounded, his brains and her intuition, their seed joined together to form a god amongst men. This she knew, but the when and how were not clear at all.

Until Angelo had entered her life, the future had been hazardous and she had not thought about it, living only for the present. He had changed all that. He had lit her future with brilliant dreams as crazy and unexpected as a Guy Fawkes display.

Her sexual longing was too hot to bear. She pulled back the blankets and gazed hungrily at his body, never having known beauty until she saw Angie lying almost naked in their boat. Now he was thicker, stronger, and even more lovely.

He sat up abruptly, black brows blending, eyes flashing fury. 'What the hell d'you think you're doing? You're drunk.' He pulled the blankets back and disappeared under them, head and all.

'Angelo,' she murmured, flushed and breathless as she fumbled with her blouse. 'Make love to me.'

Angelo felt too shocked to speak. His mouth dried, his heart hammered in his chest and warning bells were ringing in his ears fit to deafen him. 'How can I?' he stammered eventually. 'You love Gideon,' adding staunchly, 'and so do I.'

She began to take off her blouse under his anguished eyes. Then her shimmering black skirt fell to the floor. The rest of her clothes followed. She was so matter-of-fact. Why was that? At that moment he felt that he hated her. She had pushed him into a corner. She was part of his own, new family, close as a sister. Closer! He tried to explain: 'We're family, Ramona. Don't spoil that. I love Gideon like my brother.'

She laughed. Her hand stretched out and grabbed his penis. He saw her scowl as she felt it flaccid in her hand. Fury was unleashed, but she recalled the slobbering hound.

'You're shy,' she hissed. She lay over him, black eyes glittering, and there was he, shivering like the inexperienced boy he was, trapped in her hypnotic glare.

He sat up abruptly and fended her off. She grabbed again, reaching for the tip of his penis, squeezing until he gasped.

'Hey. Come on, Ramona. Let a guy have some peace. You can't turn me on by force, you know that.'

She sighed and stood up, unashamed of her nakedness. He watched her, mourning for their lost innocence, sensing the crumbling of his dreams. They could never recover what they had had. How could he explain that she had never turned him on and even if she did the result would be the same. He would never succumb. He had no sexual taste for other men's wives, nor darker flesh. The truth was, he hankered after creamy, Nordic complexions. As for a future wife, he wanted someone as aloof as she was dignified. A haughty English blonde snob with freckles on her nose. Someone to bring up his children properly and run the mansion and the estates he would eventually possess. Her pedigree must match his own. The Palmas could trace their noble roots back to the tenth century. All this he had planned for the far distant future. In the meantime, casual sex was restricted to anaemic-looking blondes who lived as far away from Silver Bay as he could reach in two hours driving. The brief blissful sexual release he achieved was physical, not emotional, and lately the coupling made him feel lonely, so he tried not to succumb too often.

Ramona was standing over him like a vengeful valkyrie, rubbing her nipples and her cleft in a vain effort to turn him on. Sighing . . .

'You're very beautiful,' he said to placate her. Then, in a moment of demented inspiration, he said: 'I've never had a woman. I don't know how. Please go away.'

She pounced. Wrapping her ruby red lips around his flaccid member she wooed him to astonishing heights. While he half-heartedly protested, she smothered him with her breasts and straddled him. Moments later she was gyrating her hips wilder than any belly dancer, until they both erupted in a paroxysm of groans. Angelo came to his senses fast, knocked her aside and jumped up, hurling himself into his clothes.

'You raped me! I'm moving out, Ramona. We're family. That's the strongest bond there is. Tell you what. I'll buy a business you can run. We'll go half shares and be partners. Would you like that? Now just forget tonight ever happened, and don't you ever try that again.'

She wouldn't stop crying and she wouldn't get dressed. He decided to leave her alone in the hope that she would pull herself together. When he walked out of his room, he found Gideon half drunk, his hand clasping the neck of an empty brandy bottle, lying on his back on the new rug by the fire.

'Had enough for one night, have you?' he asked, slurring his words.

'Nothing's been going on, Gideon. Nothing ever has.'

He looked up and nodded. 'Then tell me, why is she naked?'

'She felt upset. I think she's drunk. Tomorrow she won't remember.'

'Remember what?'

'Remember the argument. I swear to you, Gideon. It's nothing. I'm moving out of here.'

Gideon followed him out and down the road, so Angelo

sat on a bench and waited for him to catch up. How strange Gideon looked. His knife was clenched in his hand, his face was running with sweat, his hair was damp and plastered to his head, his moustache dripped with spittle and his eyes glittered with humiliation.

'Kill me if you want to, but don't look at me like that, Gideon. We're brothers, aren't we?'

Gideon collapsed beside him, his face bitter and crumpled. He looked as if he were crying but there were no tears in his eyes. 'I've killed many men,' he began in a growl. 'Killing means nothing to me any more. But I can't kill you. What's worse than you fucking my wife? I ask myself that. Do you know the answer?'

'No,' Angelo lied.

'I think you do.' Gideon sighed and walked back towards the house, leaving Angelo to curse himself.

'Oh God! What went wrong? I wanted to make them happy. But I will, I swear I will.'

Angelo stayed for a while, wondering where he was going to sleep. He heard a scream and then another. He was still wondering whether or not to interfere when Gideon's figure materialised out of the darkness.

'Come in, Angie. Let's get to bed,' he called.

Chapter 31

——— ———

The beach shack café had always puzzled Angelo. The owner, Peggy Cohen, seemed to neglect every opportunity the site offered, providing snacks only. Even the marvellous views were boarded up so that the barnlike room looked out on to the beach car park. When a *For Sale* was nailed on to the door he went along to investigate.

'I'm Angelo Morgan,' he said, holding out his hand.

Peggy Cohen knew very well who this imposing young man was because she saw him at church each Sunday. She had even thrust a couple of pounds into the collection box after the boat incident, partly to reward him for his bravery, but mainly because he was so damned sexy. Just look at him lounging in the doorway, a cigarette dangling from his lips, his large brown eyes missing nothing. He gave her a strangely intimate glance, one eyebrow raised, lips curling into a smile. He could go a long way with that smile, she reckoned, but behind his sexiness, and the wild, untamed energy, she sensed his cold reasoning and insatiable hunger. It was a little scary.

She'd heard he was doing well with his freezing plant so why would he want this awful place? The tourist season lasted for only three months each year. For the rest of the time she hardly managed to pay old Jimmy who cleaned up, let alone her own small salary. Her husband was fighting up North and she had never worked before she married. She was failing to cope and having to turn to her parents for help to support her three children. She'd put up the *For Sale* sign without much hope of anyone inquiring, yet Morgan seemed interested enough. Did he have any cash? she wondered. He looked shabby. Everyone in the village was talking about the Irishman who lived with the coloureds and spoke like them, too, and looked like a Greek god who'd come back to earth. No one knew where he came from, but most people suspected he was a coloured trying for white with forged papers. Socially speaking he was untouchable, but he seemed to be ambitious.

Angelo was aware of her scrutiny and her doubts as he examined the café. He reckoned he could make it work. The interior could seat a hundred, if it were properly arranged. Ugh! he thought, as he looked at the tubular steel tables, bare-boarded floor, iron roof and plain wooden counter with a few sad cakes under fly netting. He shuddered. He'd rather go hungry than eat here.

His fertile mind was soon imagining fishnets hiding the ceiling, and various seaside paraphernalia hanging around the walls. I'll call it 'Sands' he thought. While the front faced the beach, the back faced the quayside, so they could partition part of the space and sell fish and chips to fishermen and factory workers.

Another idea came to him: Ramona was a good cook, so why not specialise in traditional Malay dishes? He loved the spicy mutton and fish dishes she prepared. That would get the locals here, too. A bloke with a guitar would go down well. His ideas were coming fast and furious and he was getting excited.

'D'you like cooking?' he asked Peggy.

'I hate it.'

'It shows, but I have someone else in mind. So what can you do?'

Peggy hesitated. Why should she explain herself to this stranger? 'I never worked before I was married. I suppose I was too busy going to parties,' she admitted, 'and giving them. Oh, for the good old days.'

'Great! We'll start a catering division and you'll handle that side of the business.'

Peggy caught her breath and wondered whether to throw him out, but how could she? He was twice Jim's size.

'Take down the sign. It's sold, well, half of it's sold. We'll be equal partners.' He held out his hand.

Peggy was in a quandary. After a two-year separation from her husband, Vernon, she was frustrated and lonely, but the force of her longing to touch this black-haired hunk of flesh astonished her. Guilt washed through her as she thought of Vernon risking his life somewhere up there. She bit her lip, feeling wretched.

'I don't want to be your bloody partner. I don't want half of this bloody restaurant. I don't want to see people eating again as long as I live. I hate people, particularly when they eat. I want to get out.'

'So why did you start this place?' He felt sorry for her, she was so obviously unhappy.

'My husband bought it. I was always against it, but now . . .' She broke off and sighed. 'I'd like to see anyone raise three kids on army pay.'

'Tell you what. I'll take a half share now and in a few months' time, if you still want out, I'll buy your share at the going price. Okay?'

'Certainly not, but just as a matter of interest, have you got any cash for your half?'

'I'll pay out of my share of the profits. You need me, Peggy Cohen. Without me you'll founder.'

'Oh, get out of here,' she said irritably, turning her back on him.

'Here's my card,' he said. 'You call me when you're ready to talk.'

Peggy's business foundered, as he had predicted, and there were no offers. How sad she looked at church each Sunday. Angelo badly wanted to help her, but on his terms . . . so he waited.

Lately, he and Gideon worked all hours delivering fish in their two vans, but it was becoming clear to both of them that there weren't enough hours in the day for them to complete the work. They needed another two vans and four drivers. Nowadays, there were few laughs and too many arguments. Angelo knew that behind the griping was the trauma of him with Ramona and that this hurt would never be banished.

When Angelo went cap in hand to the bank manager the following Saturday morning, his greeting was two degrees above freezing, for a change.

'You run your account well, Mr Morgan,' the dry old banker said. 'Turnover is soaring, but what guarantee can you give the bank?'

'I don't suppose I'll ever have security, sir,' Angelo said. 'I can do better with my cash than investing in your bank. That's for fools, if you'll excuse me saying so, sir, I aim for larger returns than you pay. Right now I need two more vans and a larger freezing plant. I haven't got the cash for any of this, but I'll pay off over twelve months.'

The bank manager studied him thoughtfully. 'What exactly are your long-term aims?' he asked as he got up and closed the door. 'Let's hear some of your ideas, Morgan.'

Angelo tried to outline his dreams while the old man sat nodding shrewdly.

'By the way, Peggy Cohen is a client of ours, and a friend. I'd like to see her get on her feet, what with her husband in the armed forces and three small children to rear. I have a proposition to put to you.'

Angelo came home to find Gideon sprawled on the floor drunk. He was furious. He'd wanted to tell him the great news. The bank would back them all the way, just as long as they stuck to their forecasts, paid interest on due date, and kept assets well ahead of debts. They had the vans and they had half of Peggy's restaurant, too. He wasn't quite sure how Peggy would react to the news.

Angelo waited for the morning to tackle his partner, but Gideon forestalled him.

'I hate business, Angie,' his eyes were soft and lustrous, glimmering close to tears, his lips trembled, making his moustache quiver and the spittle on the ginger hairs glistened in the light. There was a smell of stale wine, tobacco and sweat all about him and Angelo sensed his moral disintegration. His guilt surged.

'You think everyone's ambitious like you,' Gideon said. 'That's not so, Angie. You think nothing of joy. You don't even know what joy's all about. I want to be free of your world. All these things . . .' he gestured around. 'They haven't brought me happiness. I don't suppose Ramona is happy either, not like she used to be. We've lost what we had. I'm not saying it's your fault, Angie, but you brought your world here to us, and ours fled. I like fishing and I love the sea. I used to be happy, now I dread each morning. Sometimes I even dread coming home. Leave me alone. I want to sit on the beach and light my pipe, and later row out the trekking nets. I don't understand you, and Ramona's become a stranger to me. I have to get back to the sea.'

'Hold it man, hold it,' Angelo said. A surge of bile was making him feel sick. 'What about our plans, a job for everyone, houses, a school in the village? You're not leaving. I won't let you. Okay, so I was wrong to push you into jobs you have no taste for, but you can't leave the company. You've been great, Gideon.'

Angelo sat on the floor thinking hard. If Gideon and Ramona weren't going to share in his coming wealth then what was the point of it all? He had wanted to create a village where he was loved and cherished. He had never forgotten his childhood days as a pariah in Spoleto. He never would. Here he would create his own perfect environment, but Gideon had to love him, had to fit in, had to be happy. 'You're going back to school, man.'

'School!' Gideon groaned. 'You're not hearing what I'm saying.'

'Trust me, Gideon. You're going to a maritime school for skippers and by the time you graduate we'll have our first trawler for you to skipper. I swear it!'

Gideon crawled under the blankets and remained there groaning.

It would not be long before Gideon gave in, Angelo reckoned. He could see Ramona was determined. It would take a tougher man than Gideon to stand up to her, but it dawned on him that he should have moved out of their cottage long ago, and would have, if it weren't for their pleading.

Peggy Cohen was sitting in her restaurant crouched over a cup of coffee, contemplating suicide. She had just come back from the bank where the manager had informed her of her new status. She'd been sold to Angelo Morgan. Well, that was what it amounted to, she told herself. The bank had sold fifty-one per cent of her café to him and they were holding the rest in trust until she paid off her personal overdraft. She couldn't even walk out without finding the cash to pay half the debts. She was hooked, sold into slavery, she might as well be branded and fettered. Humiliation kept her shivering and shuddering, fear had dried her lips and moistened her palms, and bitterness filled her mouth. Oh God! How can they do this to me? A quick call to her lawyer had convinced her that they could and they had.

When Angelo sauntered in, she was ready for him.

'Listen, you bastard. I didn't make the bloody war. I've always been rich and I'm not trained to do anything useful. I've landed up in this mess through no fault of my own. You can stuff this bloody café right up your arse for all I care. I'm not working for you, or with you, or any other bloody thing. As far as I'm concerned, you're far beneath my dignity.'

Angelo stopped short in the doorway and sighed. Just look at her! She had a defiant, bruised look about her that reminded him of a whore. Now he saw for the first time that she was not a true blonde for the black roots showed all too clearly. Her hands were a mess, her clothes shabby and she simply didn't fit into the image of the new 'Sands' he had so clearly fixed in his mind. Did she think he wanted to hang on to her? As far as he was concerned she was just another item on the debit column. She'd have to smarten up. He'd have to talk to her.

'How about making us coffee?' he said.

'That's it! The final bloody straw! If you think I'm

going to wait on you, you've got another think coming. I despise you.'

'You were kinder last time,' he said.

'Last time?' she frowned.

Lately she had lost her looks, he thought watching her. Her English complexion had become rough and patchy, and her hair hung lank and lustreless, but her features were good. Her blue eyes, though haggard-looking, were large and well shaped, but she was looking older than she should. She needed tender loving care and he decided to take a chance with her.

'I arrived here not knowing who I was, or where I came from. I was lost. Then, one day, I heard some prisoners speaking Italian and it all came back to me. I just about collapsed on the dunes, but you took me in and made me coffee and gave me sandwiches. Otherwise I might have been arrested. I might be digging trenches right now. That's one of the reasons why I'm here. I have to pay you back.'

She looked at him long and hard and then she said: 'Good God.' She fumbled in her bag, took out her compact and began to dab her face with a piece of dirty cotton wool which she had ground into the powder.

'Sometimes soldiers come home on leave,' he said. 'Is this how you want your husband to see you?'

'Missing in action,' she whispered. 'I was informed last week.'

She stared stonily at him and he sensed that she had walled herself up from the grief. Watching her, his anger seeped away and compassion flared and with it a sense of guilt, for he had run away from the war.

He locked the door and put the 'Closed' sign on it, but Peggy stood up and grabbed her bag, ready for flight.

'Don't go, Peggy.'

'Mrs Cohen to you,' she snapped.

'Mrs Cohen. Sit down.' He caught hold of her wrist and pulled her back, forcing her down into the chair. 'You're free to leave whenever you like, but first, please, listen to me. You're not the only person who's lost everything, and I'm not Angelo Morgan . . .'

As his story poured out, he sensed her interest and then her reluctant comradeship.

'Why did you tell me that?' she asked irritably. 'Can't you see you've given me a way out? I can have you interned.'

'If two people are going to get on together, they have to have equal power. We're both fighting for our futures and that of our kids and this restaurant is one of the tools we're going to use. Remember that. I may ask you to make the bloody coffee,' he said, imitating her accent, 'but you can have me locked up, interned and eventually deported. I might even lose my life in the process. Now. We're in this thing together and I've signed for all debts, so I'm doubly at risk. How about taking a stand for once in your life and creating your own destiny, instead of expecting it to be dished up on a silver plate? How about working for your kids' future? How about turning this failure into a success story? How about it, Mrs Cohen?'

'Peggy to you,' she said, and smiled. She began to laugh. At first it was a low chuckle, which became hysterical giggles, turning to a flood of tears. Clutching Angelo she sobbed out her fears for her husband, who was Jewish, and the terrible long waiting, and her loneliness and fears.

'You can lean on me, Peggy.'

'You!' She laughed scornfully. 'You're just a kid. How old are you? Twenty?' She burst into tears again.

'I have so many dreams for this place,' he said, when she had pulled herself together. 'What do you think . . . ?'

'Okay, Angelo,' she said, when he had outlined his plans. 'I'll give it a go. I'm going to work my fingers to the bones.'

He had the impression she was going to surprise herself.

Chapter 32

It was Sunday, November 8, 1942, four months after the launch of Sands, and they had just made it out of the red, which included the cost of renovations. Angelo reckoned they were sitting on a gold mine and he had told the girls as much.

It was two hours before opening and they had gathered early to celebrate with a champagne breakfast. Ramona was talking to her two cooks, while Angelo sprawled at a table waiting for his coffee and pretending to read. The sunlight was brilliantly reflected on the whitewashed ceiling and the reflected glow heightened the pallor of her skin so that she looked like a beautiful golden statue. Ramona sensed his interest. She was talking animatedly in a newly acquired deep voice, and fingering the pearl earrings and pendant he had given her last Christmas. Her gown was of ivory silk, with rows of frills, like the petals of a rose, and her fragrance was sweet like roses, too, and he looked at her with a sense of pride. She was like a beautiful work of art found in a junk shop and lovingly restored. She seemed to have recovered from her lust for him and lately she treated him like a younger brother.

She was planning to enlarge the packing department and talking to a quiet woman about joining the team.

The woman, whom Angelo knew, had no illusions about teamwork. Ramona was a stern boss who ran the plant like a sweated labour workshop. She was getting that way with the restaurant, too. Angelo made up his mind to talk to her about it, but he put it off, knowing that he didn't really have the guts to confront Ramona.

He could never work out why Ramona disliked Peggy, other than the fact that she was blonde, tall and stately-looking. Peggy hardly seemed to notice Ramona's existence, referring to her as 'what's-her-name?' or 'the cook-lady'. The two kept their distance, wary as two lionesses.

They had converted one of the built-on rooms into an office for Peggy and she ran the catering division, but she restricted her efforts to marketing and meeting people, leaving the cooking strictly to Ramona. Despite Peggy's superior ways, Ramona was delighted with her quarter-share of profits. The restaurant had become the latest Cape fad, and fish and chips did a roaring trade out back.

Someone switched on the music and then Peggy appeared, carrying a tray with champagne and orange juice. 'Here we are! Come and get it.'

The cork popped, the wine frothed and bubbled over, Peggy poured it into the glasses and moments later they were toasting each other and laughing. Even old Jim began to thaw, giving them a rendering of the Welly-boots dance learned in his gold mining days, whacking his thighs and boots as he leaped around the restaurant.

But why wasn't Peggy drinking? She sat stiff-backed and formal, looking a little lost.

'Come on, Peggy, join in,' Angelo urged her.

'I don't drink,' she whispered. 'Don't worry about me. I'm fine.'

'Surely one little drop wouldn't hurt?'

'Maybe not.' She looked at him hesitantly, took a glass and sipped it. Moments later her eyes were sparkling and her cheeks were flushed as she gulped down the rest of the glass and took another. Four glasses later, she was on the table dancing the can-can and doing it well, he thought, regretting the fact that he had pushed her into drinking. By the time breakfast was served, Peggy was slurring her words.

'You see,' she said, hanging around his neck and gazing up at him with cocker-spaniel devotion. 'I can't drink, so I never do. Now that I'm well and truly sloshed I have a few things to tell you. Number one, thank you! Number two, I won't be able to work today and you'll have to take over. There are things to be delivered. All the details are up there, and the cook-lady knows about it.' She pointed her thumb towards her office and giggled. 'Number three, I love you.' Then she collapsed.

Oh shit! Not again! Besides, this was his day off and he'd planned to climb another local peak. Instead, he took Peggy home.

'Live with me, Angie,' she begged. 'What d'you do for sex nowadays? I suffer, really I do, but Vernon's in a prisoner-of-war camp, I've just heard, and God knows when I'll see him again. Life is so bloody terrible sometimes. Oh, Angie! I can't remember what Vernon looks like any more and I've fallen in love with you. You need me. Yes, you do. You talk like a coloured, a *gammat*, and as for living with them, well, there's not a home in Silver Bay would so much as give you a cup of tea. I can introduce you to all the people who matter. The people you're going to need. I can do so much for you. Move in. Why don't you?'

'And Vernon?' he asked gently. Were all women only survivors at heart? he wondered, trying to keep his mind from his mother's perfidy. Must they always go for the best nest-builder, and to hell with scruples and loyalty? Were women really human?

'Peggy, listen to me,' he said urgently. 'We'll talk about this when you're sober. Have a good sleep and don't worry about anything. See you tomorrow.' Then he fled.

An hour later Angelo set off in the van with the first delivery of snacks, feeling sad to lose his day off. Exploring the local mountains was his Sunday passion. Well, it would just have to wait until next week.

It was a wonderful morning, the air crisp and sparkling and the sky a hazy blue, but the wind had dropped and it would be hot later. Gulls and cormorants were diving into the sea after a shoal of anchovies, pretty yellow birds called white-eyes were hovering over summer flowers that grew around in brilliant patches of fragrant blooms, and there was an air of contentment and plenty all around. Angelo felt happy to be alive. This was his home now and he loved the country with a deep passion.

He'd got his foot on the first slippery rung of the ladder, and he knew he was going to win through. Sands was not his only success. The fish-freezing plant had been considerably enlarged since its first installation. It was situated right inside the fishing harbour, near the quayside, so the trawlers were able to put in, off-load and sell him their catch within the hour. Then the fish were cleaned, scaled, boxed and frozen. They employed fifty female packers and they were selling the fish as fast as he could box it. Troop ships, and all manner of cargo boats, were thronging Cape Town's harbour, providing a huge, growing market which included local military and Air Force bases, hospitals and hotels.

Yet each new triumph brought only a glimmer of satisfaction, for it was swamped by his burning need to own more, much more. He was so impatient – a man with a driving mission, not all of which was centred upon himself. He felt a need to offer employment to every adult living in the fishing village, and he thought of this as his secret project. He visualised the settlement as it could be, with pretty painted houses all the way up the mountainside, a local school, a church, a mosque, a community centre, clinic and park. He'd even drawn his dream village, although no one, not even Ramona, had seen his plans. Only when the fisherfolk of Silver Bay slept snug in their own homes, with jobs and security, would he feel that he had in any way paid back the debt he owed them. Pushing the fishermen to success was like pushing a steamroller up a steep hill, he thought, but he'd do it. They would all climb out of the mind-dulling poverty that ruined their lives.

He was driving uphill through the valley now, admiring the pine-clad mountain slopes. One day, the eastern slopes would be covered in vines, and somewhere around he would pick a good spot and reproduce his family's Spoleto mansion. He would sit up there in splendour with his beautiful willowy blonde wife and dutiful children and he would gloat over the valley which would be his. He longed to own land, more and more land, but that was an ambition that would have to wait. Meantime, life was good. He began to sing an Italian song. Strange, he thought. He hadn't felt like singing for years.

Steyn du Toit, Peggy had told him, was a successful

builder turned miner. Apart from his various buildings
and businesses, he had valuable mining operations in South
West Africa. He also owned the west half of the valley.
The du Toits' home was perched high on the slopes of the
western mountain range. It was beautiful country, thickly
covered in *fynbos* [indigenous wild herbs and flowering
shrubs], but when the sun moved from its zenith and
sank towards the west, the valley slopes were plunged into
shade. So the delicate, intensely beautiful silverleaf trees,
that grew nowhere else in the world, flourished there. To
Angelo, land was measured in terms of its ability to produce
good grapes and the du Toits' was next to useless. Old man
du Toit seemed to think the same way, for half the valley
had been fenced off to provide a private game park for
steenbok, grysbok, dassies and lynxes.

Angelo drove carefully up the long driveway, trying to
protect the snacks. He hoped like hell that Peggy would
recover in time to supervise the final product, which was
to be finished off in the du Toits' kitchen. If not, Ramona
would have to take over.

Where was the front door? The driveway meandered
in a circular route, past a single-storey glass and steel
monstrosity which, he presumed, was their house. He
parked, frowning, and looked around. There must be an
entrance somewhere.

Then he heard a horse neigh and sounds of hammering.
Closer he could smell burning. Not far away a blacksmith
was hard at work and presumably he would know which
way to go. He walked into the stables, following the sound
and stopped short in surprise. Long, delicate white arms
were hammering the shoe on to the horse. A girl? A tangle
of Titian hair hid her face.

He moved forward and the horse took fright and reared

up, flinging the girl against the wall of the shed. The shoe fell, sparks flew and the horse panicked. Angelo caught hold of its bridle.

'*Eih! Eih! Piano . . . piano . . . Fermati! Eih . . .!*'

Rubbing his hands down the mare's neck he coaxed it back to calmness.

Then he looked round at the girl. She was sitting on a bench rubbing her shins. She wasn't pretty, he thought, and she looked strong, but to his mind, girls should not be blacksmiths. He felt sorry for her as he gazed into her green and slanting eyes.

'I'm really sorry I startled the horse. I hope you're not hurt. Are you?'

'No, I'm not hurt,' she said. 'Anyway, I was stupid.'

'No! You weren't. But . . . isn't this a man's job?'

She pulled a face at him.

'I'm serious,' he protested. 'This work will ruin your skin and your hands and that's a fact. Sooner or later you'll get kicked, perhaps in the face, and you have such pretty eyes. It's important for girls to look good. You'll do yourself an injury,' he said, speaking in the sing-song accent of the local coloureds. 'If you're desperate I can find you a job.'

'You're behind the times. Girls are doing everything nowadays.'

He picked up her hand, examined it. 'Strong fingers,' he said, 'but dirty. I hope it pays you well?'

She smiled. She seemed to find him very amusing.

'Beautiful,' he said, stroking the mare's long, silky neck. 'I've heard they're a pretty rich family. I wonder if they appreciate just what a little beauty they have here.' The horse nuzzled him.

She stopped smiling. 'I think they do.'

'I hope I never get so rich I can't appreciate things. I've heard he has a battleaxe for a daughter.'

'Yes that's true, but who told you?'

'My partner. I'm the caterer for tonight's do, but I can't find the front door. I was looking for someone when I frightened the mare.'

She nodded and studied him coolly, but there was only a frank, open smile and eyes that beamed kindliness. Something about his face put her at ease. He was young and aggressively handsome, in a rugged sort of way, and his dark eyes gleamed with humour. She wondered about his coloured accent. Everyone knew about the Irishman who lived down with the coloureds and pretended to be white and everyone was snubbing him, but he had been speaking Italian. Perhaps he was an escaped prisoner of war. She liked the way he smiled, for then his face broadened and the lines on his cheeks set into dimples.

He said: 'My name's Angelo. What's yours?'

'Pippa. I work here.' She shook his hand manfully.

'I guess I'd better get going. Where's the front door?'

'They put up a conservatory that hides the door, causing no end of problems. Silly really. Perhaps you should drive round to the kitchen.'

'D'you work full time here?'

'They have a lot of horses.'

'Yeah, I guess they do. Listen, would you do me a favour. Delivering cakes and setting them out is not my line. My caterer is sick. Would you put them on the plates, make them look pretty?'

'Why on earth should I?'

'Just to help a friend. Come on! Girls are better at that sort of thing. I'll take you to dinner in return.'

He reached down to pull her to her feet, but she sat

hunched up on the ground, her tangle of dark red curls
falling over her eyes.

She sighed. 'Ask me again when I've stood up,' she
said.

She had a problem, Angelo could see that. He was six
foot two inches tall and she was only a fraction shorter. She
was like a beanpole, thin, straggly and too broad-shouldered
for a girl, but she had a kind face and she looked clever. He
liked clever women. 'Nice to look you in the eyes,' he said,
putting a brave face on it. 'Usually I only see the tops of
girls' heads. How about it?'

'You're on. Listen. I have to go to the birthday party
tonight, but I don't have a partner. The truth is, I never
have a partner. If I help you now . . .'

'It's a deal,' he interrupted her, 'but it's a bit larny for
me. I'm not accepted round these parts. I must warn you
that if I come with you, I might disgrace you.'

'So they won't invite me again. Who cares? Please . . .'

'Okay. What'll everyone be wearing?'

'Black tie. If you haven't got one, there's a place in town
hires them. I'll give you the address. It's a lot of trouble for
you, isn't it? Perhaps I shouldn't have asked.'

'A deal's a deal,' he said. 'I need your help.'

He parked and they carried in the trays of snacks. The
kitchen staff were giggling and fooling around at the sight
of a blacksmith helping out in the kitchen, but he made her
scrub her hands carefully and inspected them before they
began. She made a good job of putting cakes out on the
plates he'd brought and she even made them look pretty.

'The job offer stands, if you ever get sick of hammering,'
he said. 'Where shall I pick you up?'

'Here,' she said. 'Please come early. Six-thirty would
be fine.'

He wasn't quite sure exactly when it was he realised who she was. Perhaps it was the peremptory way she called the cook to lock the snacks in the pantry, or her fierce words when the kitchen maid dropped a plate on the floor, or perhaps her amused expression when he offered her the job.

'Well, you've had your little joke at my expense,' he said when they'd finished. 'Have a good party, Pippa du Toit.'

'No, no, wait. You're coming.'

'Of course I'm not.'

He was unprepared for the swift punch in the stomach that caught him unaware. For a moment he could hardly breathe. 'Jesus! That hurt!'

'I despise men who go back on their word. I did all that work.' She was almost crying with temper.

'If you want me so much I'll come. But why should someone like you want a partner like me? From what I hear, half the bigwigs in the country will be flying down. D'you want to be seen with a coloured lout from the village?'

'Are you embarrassed to be seen with the local battleaxe?'

'Oh God! I'm sorry, Pippa. But it's not true. If you want me to come, the rules will have to change a bit. You'll be my blacksmith for the evening. Okay?'

'Of course,' she whispered, standing close to him. 'Don't be late.'

Why did he kiss her? he wondered afterwards. Perhaps because she was so damned bossy. That was his first big mistake. He felt her melting away under his lips, the fierce sullen pride of her crumpling at his touch. She was all sighs, grasping his neck too hard, clashing her teeth against his and pulling him fiercely against her. Had she never been kissed before? What had he got himself into? he wondered.

Chapter 33

———— ————

Angelo was late. He'd promised to arrive at six, but it was nearly nine when he drove up the driveway to Pippa's front door. For the first time in his life he was nervous. He'd never worn a dress suit before and he reckoned he looked like a waiter. He had said nothing about Pippa's invitation to Ramona and Peggy. Why should he? After all, he was just another guy at the party.

He knew how the girls operated. Peggy would be dressed up to the nines, keeping an eye on the guests and the supply of food, while Ramona took charge of the kitchen side, but she'd be looking pretty good, too. They'd hired a few more cooks, several experienced waiters and a dozen kitchen hands. There should not be any problems.

He arrived to find everyone running around in a state of high tension. Ramona was looking fabulous and so was Peggy, but they were having to keep the food warm because the hostess was missing.

'Heavens! What are you doing here?' Peggy looked startled, but pleased. 'Thank goodness! I could do with some help.'

'Sorry, Peggy. You'll have to cope. I'm off-duty,' he said while she gaped at him.

Peggy introduced him to Pippa's father. He was very tall

and thin and he curved over at the top like a plant that had outgrown its strength. His pale skin had been turned into gravel by the fierce South African sun, and he looked tired and intolerant. Angelo could see where Pippa got her features from, and hers were only slightly more feminine than his, unluckily for her.

'My daughter is unexpectedly delayed,' Steyn du Toit said. Then he caught sight of the box Angelo was carrying. 'That wasn't necessary, Mr Morgan, but the gifts are on the sideboard. My daughter will open them tomorrow. It was too kind of you.'

'I'll give mine to Pippa myself. Where is she? She should be here,' Angelo asked, wondering why Peggy turned pale and tried to catch his eye.

'She's feeling indisposed. Too sick to join us. We may have to go ahead without her.'

'That doesn't sound like Pippa. She was fine this morning when she invited me. Mind if I have a few words with her?'

Her old man scowled at him. 'I'm afraid that's out of the question. You say she invited you – as a guest?' he asked suspiciously.

'Yeah. You see, I thought she was the blacksmith. I made her help me with the catering, so I promised to come tonight in return for her help – if you see what I mean. She said something silly about me being her partner.' His voice tailed off in the face of her father's obvious disapproval.

'Come this way.' Steyn walked stiffly ahead of Angelo, clearly furious, but not knowing quite how to cope with the situation. They hurried along a huge curved passage, passing plants and flowers and now he realised that the house was built in the shape of a large tyre surrounding an inner garden of pool, lawns, shrubs and a fountain with coloured lights hidden away in the centre. Absurd, ostentatious and ugly, Angelo decided. They reached a door and paused there. 'Philippa, the guests are waiting,' her father called anxiously.

'Go away.' When Angelo heard her muffled voice he wondered if she was crying.

'Hey, Pippa,' he shouted. 'You're ruining the food. Everyone's waiting to eat. Don't do this to me.'

The door was flung open and she came out like a whirlwind, all punches and sobs and silly things women did and said. He caught a few words: 'cruel, late, a beast,' before her lips were thrust on his. He had to fight to keep his balance.

'Hey there.' He caught hold of her hands. 'Not so fast. You'll get kissed later, but only if you behave yourself. Have you seen what you look like?' Her face was swollen, her eyes red, her make-up smudged. 'What is it with you?'

'You didn't come. You promised.'

'I'm here, aren't I? But, Pippa, I'm just the caterer, Mick Morgan from the village. You can't fall for me. What's got into you? I'm going downstairs. Hurry up. You're ruining everything.'

'Why are you late?'

'I was in two minds about coming.'

'You promised.'

'That's why I'm here. I have a feeling this is a terrible mistake.'

'I'm sorry, sir,' he apologised to her father. 'I thought she was the blacksmith.' He heard her giggling in the background.

'Wait. Wait for me. I won't take long,' her voice sang, suddenly happy.

The old man shot him a look of utmost contempt and

stamped off. After a moment's hesitation, Angelo decided to follow him.

Five minutes later the band struck up with a waltz as Pippa walked into the room. She looked so awkward, stooping because of her height, wearing flat shoes that didn't match her billowing violet dress, her hair all over the place, face still swollen, but she was smiling and she'd reapplied her make-up and that was something to be thankful for, he thought.

Her eyes swept the room anxiously. 'Hello, everyone,' she said, looking shamefaced, as if she were standing trial for murder. She was a regular nut, he thought with a sigh. Poor Pippa. He'd have to help her get some confidence and then he'd fade out of her life. She fancied herself in love with him, but that was only because he was the first man to treat her normally. Besides, he was probably the only man she knew who was as tall as she was.

She hurried awkwardly towards him and hung on to his arm, which brought a buzz of conversation. He could hardly blame them for sniggering.

'You want to dance? Can you?'

'I took lessons,' she said, 'but I hate it.'

'Well, I love dancing, so you'll have to get to like it because we're going to go dancing a lot.' Suddenly the sun seemed to have come out. She was all beams and happy smiles as he pulled her to the dance floor.

'You mean that?'

'Sure! Now hold your head up straight, shoulders back, and stop falling over your feet or I'll stand on your toes. This is a waltz. One two three . . . okay?'

'Okay,' she whispered.

She wasn't so bad. At first he had to hold her pretty tightly to manoeuvre her around, but he got the hang of pushing her and after a while she relaxed and began to follow him.

'One waltz and then we eat. You've been holding up the works,' he said.

'No, you have.'

'I didn't quite understand how you needed me,' he said suddenly sensing the truth.

'I want to know,' she began, 'exactly why Angelo Morgan, the coloured fisherman, who's trying to pretend he's Irish and white, when everyone knows he's not, speaks perfect Italian to my horse in a sudden emergency.'

'I'd hoped like hell you weren't listening,' he said.

'Well, I was.' She tightened her grip around his neck.

'Don't do that, Pippa. Behave like a lady, can't you? I don't like public displays of affection. Okay? We'll be alone later.'

'Promise?'

'Promise.'

She was as subtle as a carthorse. Had she never heard of playing hard to get? Who'd brought her up? He began to tell her of his childhood, and his beloved father, and the vineyards he missed, and how he longed to try planting vines in the valley one day.

When they sat down for dinner, Angelo found himself sitting between Pippa and her father. The old man didn't look too pleased about it either, but Pippa seemed used to having her own way. Angelo was starting to feel annoyed. He could sense the amusement at his presence there and his face burned with shame.

Then he heard one of her bitchy friends bend over her and whisper: 'Did you have to search the fishing boats to find someone as tall as you, Pippa?'

Pippa deserved something better than the pseudo-Irish

caterer she'd stupidly fallen in love with, Angelo thought, watching her father in a sweat of embarrassment trying to look happy about his daughter's choice.

Angelo decided that silence would be his best bet. He endured the sly grins and nods stoically and ate sparingly.

The party was a huge success. Somewhere around midnight, Angelo heard the sound of singing. It was the fishermen's banjo band loping up in their fancy gear of cream and yellow frills, ribbons flying, satin shimmering as skinny buttocks writhed and wiggled, while they sang old coloured and Malay folk songs. Everyone went outside thankfully, for it was stiflingly hot in the house. Most of the singers clapped him on the shoulder, giving him toothless, grateful smiles as they fell all over the place. They had all drunk too much.

Then they left, their pockets full of cash. The sound of their voices came in snatches, carried by the hot berg wind.

Angelo leaned back on a bench near the rose garden listening to the night sounds, watching the moon move across the sky towards the craggy peaks. It was so peaceful. But then came the sound of someone playing the piano quite beautifully. Making his way back to the vast living room, he saw Pippa sitting at the grand piano. When she saw him she stopped.

'Don't stop.' Leaning over the piano, he rifled through the pile of music. 'Here, can you play this?'

She began the old Italian love lyric he remembered so well, and after a while Angelo began to sing, hesitantly at first, sensing and tasting and loving the beautiful Italian language he had missed so much. He was not singing for Pippa, but for all the beautiful women he had ever known and for his dream, the beautiful blonde goddess whom he'd find one day and marry.

From then on, Pippa haunted him. She made surprise visits to the beach café, examined the fish-freezing plant, invited him to anything she thought might interest him, from opera to dog shows. She made no secret of the fact that she loved him.

'She's sure got the hots for you,' Gideon told him. 'Marry her and you'll be very wealthy. You'll be able to turn your back on us.'

'I'd never do that, Gideon. Quite honestly she's not my type, although I'm fond of her. As for their wealth – I want to make my own. We're good friends. That's all.'

And they were. Over the next few weeks he taught her the rudiments of mountaineering and they explored the granite peaks, climbing down in the late afternoon to swim in the ice-cold Atlantic. He taught her to dance, and sometimes they rode along the beachfront and up through the lagoon.

More often than not he ate dinner at her house, but he always left before midnight. He was careful never to go further than kissing. He'd always known that giving a girl false hope was the cruellest thing you could do.

Pippa cornered her father over Easter when he was at home for a few days from his mines.

'He's sort of remote,' she said.

'Who?'

'Angelo, of course. Okay, so he's kissed me a few times, but he really seems to try to avoid me, or rather to avoid any intimacy.'

'If he's not interested in you then he must be peculiar. Is that it? You know, Pippa, the only thing I regret about being wealthy is your getting so spoiled. You have this thing about cash, you think no one can resist it. Well, I'm telling you, Angelo can.'

'He's the only man I've ever met who treats me normally. Besides, he's taller than I and he's so strong. He can even carry me.'

'You've been mixing with sissies – more's the pity.'

'Oh, Father,' Pippa grumbled. 'Try to be more encouraging. After all, I am your only daughter and if you want an heir it's got to be from Angelo.' She smiled sadly. 'I must admit it's a bit unusual. I mean, most men are falling over themselves to get their hands on our wealth. They treat me like a necessary nuisance that goes with it. With Angelo it's the other way round.'

'And that's why you want him?'

'It's one of the many reasons. I proposed and he turned me down. Can you believe that?'

'Yes, I can. I've been checking on him. Difficult with the war, but through some London genealogists I learned that he comes from an ancient family. His story about his grandfather losing their fortune is more or less correct. The depression finished them off, although the trust covering the mansion and the vineyards is still in operation. Not that it makes much difference. People put too much store by lineage. A man's what he makes of himself and that young Angelo seems to know what he's doing. You've been making a fool of yourself, Pippa. You can't buy him and you can't force him and quite honestly I don't think he wants to marry you.'

'Make him,' she said. She flung her arms around her father. 'I never wanted anything so much in all my life.

Surely you can make him. You've always been able to get your own way.'

'I could try, but I don't hold out much hope. I don't think he's for sale.'

Angelo was startled when Pippa's father invited him to lunch at the Cape Town Club in the Gardens. He introduced him to the other members and treated him like one of the establishment, which he was not, at least not yet. Angelo realised that he was being shown a world which he could have if he wished.

'Good trout this,' Steyn said. 'I have a log cabin up at Franschhoek. It's a beautiful place surrounded by mountains, plenty of wildlife and a lovely dam. I stocked it myself. How about coming up one weekend with me? We'll bring Pippa along if you like. Are you in love with my daughter, Angelo?' he asked out of the blue.

'No, sir. But I'm very fond of her. We're good friends. She's a gutsy girl. Unusual, and a good rider, too.'

'Good rider! My God! She's the South African dressage champion.'

'In that case, she's modest, too. She never let on.'

'Talented pianist.'

'That's true enough.'

'Good swimmer. She'll make a fine wife one of these days.'

'Sir, I am very well aware of Pippa's excellent qualities. I admire her tremendously. I'm proud to be her friend.'

'But you don't want to marry her?'

Angelo flushed and looked down at his plate.

'Of course she's my only heir. I wanted a son, but my wife died and I never felt like remarrying. I guess I brought her up as a bit of a tomboy. We used to go prospecting together.

She was a good companion even when she was a teenager. She should have been a geologist. She has a talent for it.'

By now Angelo's face was so burning hot, he felt he would explode. 'Sir, please. I have to do things my way. I know Pippa loves me, but I'm waiting for her to get over it. She's only twenty and she will forget me in time. It will be years before I can afford to marry. Meantime, for a girl of her position she's amazingly lacking in self-confidence. I've been trying to persuade her to like herself more.'

'It comes from those years spent out in the bush. She doesn't feel feminine,' Steyn said gloomily. 'You know, my boy, I've always thought those oriental arranged marriages work out better than love matches.'

'I agree, sir, but in this case, it would not be a sensibly arranged marriage, it would be your giving in to your daughter's whims, as you always do. She's spoiled, sir, and you are responsible. You've always given her whatever she wants and now she wants me. Believe me, sir, you'd do better to buy her another horse, or she might get hurt.'

'I apologise. Of course, you are right. I was trying to buy you, but with a cool six million pounds, give or take the odd shilling, in the form of transferred assets. Think about it.'

'No, sir.'

'Well, then. Let's have a liqueur and plan our fishing holiday.'

Later, Angelo was always to feel that Steyn had set him up, for he left the mountain chalet after the first night, claiming a business disaster needed his urgent attention, and he and Pippa were left alone in the mountains.

On the third night, Angelo succumbed to Pippa's sensuality. There was a bad storm and she came creeping into his bed, claiming to be afraid, which he did not believe, but the feel of her lovely breasts and her long silky legs was too much for him. They made passionate love. Having crossed the bridge there was little point in holding back, he reckoned, so they spent the rest of the holiday in bed, taking turns to fetch snacks.

Two months later, Pippa informed him that she was pregnant and begged him to marry her. After some soul-searching, Angelo agreed. What else could he do? he reasoned. He kept his private anguish to himself and firmly put aside all thoughts of blonde Venuses. He married her in the Catholic church under his own name, and in the register office under his assumed name on the same day.

The wedding party was even bigger than her birthday party had been and once again Peggy took over the catering. By the time the two of them returned from the town office, the guests were assembled, armed with confetti and rose petals.

Half the village had turned up and as the day turned to dusk, the fisherfolk guzzled a seemingly endless supply of alcoholic punch. By nightfall some of them were too drunk to stand, and they fell around the tables, knocking over chairs, insulting guests and yelling at each other. Gideon became tearful, mourning the loss of his friend. He took his banjo and sang tunelessly of lost friendship and the evils of women in general.

For the first time, Angelo saw another side of Pippa.

'Clear that coloured riffraff out of my home,' she raged. Her face was twisted with fury and she looked ugly and cruel. 'Don't ever invite them here again.'

The following morning they left for their honeymoon. It was wartime and they had to settle for Rhodesia and the Victoria Falls. Pippa had morning sickness, but she regained her health in the mid-morning and demanded more and more lovemaking.

When he returned, Angelo was ten pounds lighter, but the first down payment of the dowry was in his newly opened bank account. He bought a well-equipped trawler with it, which they named the *Philippa*, and Gideon, who was now qualified, became the skipper. For Angelo, there was no joy in realising his most impossible dream at last. Worse was to come, for when Steyn du Toit informed Angelo about their holdings, he was amazed to discover how wealthy they were.

Angelo tried to put a brave face on his plight. Pippa was clever, determined, hard-headed and rich. She would always work to get her own way, and she'd succeed, he sensed. As for him, he thought sadly, if he worked for a lifetime, he might never make as much with his head as he'd made with his prick. Nevertheless, he vowed he would double and treble the du Toits' holdings. There was no way he was going to be a pampered gigolo for the rest of his life.

Chapter 34

The nursing home was sterile and efficient and the nurses seemed devoid of human feelings, more like robots, Angelo thought, hating them. How could they smile and chat to each other while Pippa was suffering? He and Steyn were tense and uncommunicative. Apart from a couple of breaks for coffee they had been waiting for fourteen hours. At first Angelo had sat beside Pippa, wiping her face with a damp cloth, but finally he couldn't stand her pain and he went outside to wait.

A nurse popped her head outside the door. 'No change as yet,' she said cheerfully. 'Why don't you go home, Mr Morgan? We'll call you later.'

'At least she knows my name,' Angelo grumbled. 'I'd have thought she'd call out a number. This place is like a penitentiary and Pippa's in the torture chamber. Why is it taking so damn long?' He jumped up and began pacing the narrow passage outside the ward.

'Take it easy . . . for God's sake sit down,' Steyn snarled.

'There must be better ways of giving birth. Poor, poor Pippa. D'you remember what you said to me long before we married? You asked me if I loved her and I said "no". You said . . .'

'Love grows with time if you are well matched, which is why I believe in arranged marriages.'

'Yes, that's it, of course, you were right.'

He buried his head in his hands and tried not to think of Pippa's suffering. He could not banish the image of her lying there as white as death, groaning with pain and breaking out in a cold sweat. Another hour seemed to pass before the nurse reappeared.

'The head's showing. It won't be long.' That damned bright smile. He wanted to hit her. He crossed himself and said a silent prayer. Steyn stubbed out his cigarette, stood up and went off to the loo. He didn't look so hot himself, Angelo noticed.

Twenty minutes later they heard the first wails and soon afterwards they were called in. 'You have a lovely bouncing boy,' the doctor said.

Pippa looked shocked and exhausted, but she was smiling gently from the pillows. 'He's lovely,' she said. 'So lovely. It's like a miracle.'

Angelo caught her hands in his. He needed to be loved. 'You did all the work and I feel exhausted,' he said smiling at her. 'I love you.'

She didn't look at him. She was staring towards the doctor anxiously. 'Please give my baby to me,' she said. 'I want to hold him.'

Angelo wondered how this frail-looking lump of pink gristle could ever grow into something worthwhile. Yet when they allowed him to hold Trevor in his arms, he knew beyond any shadow of doubt that this was what his life was all about. Here lay his future, his destiny, his reason for living.

'I'm doubly blessed,' he whispered, fighting back his tears.

The nurse was getting agitated. She shooed the men out. 'Mrs Morgan needs to sleep and so does little Trevor,' she said.

'Let's have a drink,' Steyn said. 'We deserve it.'

They were both dishevelled and unshaven. Steyn was wearing old khaki trousers and shirt, and Angelo a pair of flannels, for the pains had started badly and unexpectedly at 6 a.m. that morning, and since then neither of them had wanted to leave the hospital.

'Come with me,' Angelo said. 'I know a place where we'll be welcome.'

He drove Steyn to the fishing harbour, to the fishermen's bar that hung poised on the first granite ridge overlooking the harbour.

'Are you sure?' Steyn hung around outside looking both uneasy and superior until Angelo wondered if he'd made a mistake.

'No, please . . . come . . . They are my friends,' he said.

They pushed their way into the throng of shabby figures talking animatedly in a smog of cigarette and *dagga* fumes, and the smell of cheap wine. It was the usual crowd and Angelo knew them all, some of them worked for him. Gideon was in his niche by the window overlooking the harbour, which was a place where he loved to get drunk. Six of his crew were drinking with him. Besides the locals, there were several Ovambos from South West Africa.

'Hey, Gideon! I'm a father,' Angelo yelled. 'It's a boy.'

Gideon let out a roar of approval. Everyone was cheering and laughing and applauding. Happiness, Angelo had learned, was never far away for them. It smouldered inside them like a dormant volcano, waiting to erupt at any time. The two men ordered drinks all round time and again and then they were thrust out of the pub and up the hill to

Ramona's cottage. She was strangely quiet. Angelo noticed for the first time that she was pregnant, too.

Angelo remembered his first year with them. He, too, had found pleasure in simple pastimes, but his life had changed and moments of joy were few and far between. What have they got that I haven't got? he wondered, listening to their laughter, watching them burst into spontaneous song, and loving them.

Pippa and the baby came home five days later and the house on the hill became crammed with toys, nurses, friends calling, and from time to time the doctor came. It was a woman's world. Sometimes Angelo would tiptoe into the bedroom Pippa was sleeping in for the time being, but she was always feeding Trevor. She had a problem with too much milk, her breasts were overflowing and knotting into painful lumps. At night before he retired he would watch her sleeping, her rosy lips parted, a glimpse of pearl gleaming between them. Her neck was long and graceful, her skin freckled and her red hair wild and tangled over the pillow and he would long to wake her and make love to her. Sometimes he loved her so much tears would come into his eyes. She was like a drug and his dependence was growing. He had everything a man could wish for, but he wanted his wife back. He needed physical love, but she had only one interest in her life right now and that was Trevor.

Angelo tried to get his wife's attention in the small periods between bathing, feeding, changing, and rocking his rival, whom he also loved. He was like a dog, grateful for the crumbs, but there were precious few of those. Had she ever needed him? Was he just the pet stallion who had given her what she wanted – a baby? What did she need him for? Her eyes answered his question – nothing!

'Hi, Pippa, remember me,' he said gaily.

'Sh!' she said, holding one finger over her lips.

He bent over the baby and reached out to stroke his cheek. The monster let out a wail of rage fit to burst the ear drums, his face screwed up in fury.

'You woke him,' Pippa said, equally furious.

'Oh hell,' he muttered and went out slamming the door.

The guest list had been drawn up for the christening party and the church service. His secretary kindly showed him the list, since no one else had bothered to ask for his approval. He was annoyed to see that none of his coloured friends had been invited. He did not know how to tackle Pippa, but he knew he must. He found her rocking the monster to sleep.

'Darling,' he said uneasily. 'You forgot my friends from the village.'

'If you call those drunken *skollies* your friends, more fool you. I won't have them in my house. You know what happened at our wedding. It was a disgusting exhibition of over-indulgence. Never again!'

'You can't punish them all because one or two became rowdy.'

'I'm not punishing anyone. I'm simply pleasing myself.'

'What about pleasing me? I work with them, I employ them, I have to invite them. I *want* to invite them.'

'No.' She bent over her child.

'Pippa, listen to me.' He began to massage her neck and her shoulders as she bent over the baby. She had always loved that. 'I must invite them.'

She shook off his hand. 'If you do, I won't attend and neither will Trevor. Silly sort of christening without the baby, don't you think? Stand them drinks in the pub down by the harbour. All they want are the drinks.'

'You couldn't be more wrong. And, Pippa, I insist.'

'No! That's my final word on the subject.' She turned and stared at him and he was taken aback by her coldness. She had never looked at him so remotely. He felt a twinge of fear. Now that he loved her so much he was terrified of losing her. 'I will not have coloured guests in my house. It's not done, and I won't allow it, and Father agrees with me. Why can't you see things his way? After all, it's his house.'

Angelo went outside to think. It was not his home, true. So it was time to move. He decided to buy some land and build his own home for his family. He felt emasculated by his father-in-law's power. What good was a man if he wasn't master of his own home? When was it she had sensed his dependence? By falling in love with his wife he had lost the upper hand. And she, who had always been anxious to please him, had been quick to spot her advantage. He decided to compromise and throw a party for the village folk at Sands. He did, with the help of Ramona and Peggy, but hardly anyone came. He sensed Ramona had had something to do with that.

The day of the christening dawned, and Angelo felt saddened by the whole affair. It was afternoon by the time they returned from the ceremony. The house was like a flower show, the garden full of trestle tables decorated with hibiscus flowers, and piled high with food and bowls of fruit punches. A team of hired waiters with trays of champagne and wine were threading their way through hundreds of chattering guests.

Trevor had at last recovered from being splashed with holy water, handled by strangers, and generally inconvenienced, and was sleeping in his sumptuous crib, while the guests filed by on tiptoe, oohing and aahing and placing their gifts reverently on the table beside him. Angelo glanced surreptitiously at his watch. Four o'clock! It was almost over, thank God.

Then he heard the sound he had been dreading: a distant snatch of song, dozens of banjos played in unison, marching feet. He moved to the window and glanced down over the valley. A cloud of dust was snaking along the gravel road and he could see glimpses of bright colours moving under the trees. Soon he could plainly hear their voices singing.

He turned and frowned at Pippa. 'They are coming. Listen. D'you hear them singing? Even though you would not invite them, they are coming. If you are rude to any of them, I swear I'll leave this house at once.'

She turned pale, bit her lip, and then quickly turned back to the guest who was bending over the child, but he saw two tears rolling down her cheeks. There was no pity in him, only annoyance at her arrogance, and anger with himself for being so weak.

The moving phalanx of singing people was reaching the bottom gate and moving through the gardens. Headed by Ramona, with Gideon trailing behind, they mounted the steps and strode in to the du Toits' immense sitting room.

The guests fell into an uneasy silence. Ramona was dressed in billowing yellow satin robes, perhaps to hide her advanced pregnancy, while her followers, who had left their work in the packing plants and boats, were wearing overalls and gumboots, but each one was carrying a gift and Angelo wanted to cry with shame.

'You didn't invite us,' Ramona said, standing close to him, 'but here we are and we've brought presents. What's happened to you, Angelo? She bosses you.'

'You're right! I feel ashamed. Look, Ramona, it's difficult here, but you will always be my friend.'

He looked into her eyes and saw that she was longing for acceptance, but pride, anger and love were mingled there, too. Only Ramona could reveal so many emotions at one time in those glowing eyes of hers. She stepped forward and thrust her present on the table.

'May I look?' she asked, gesturing towards the queue.

Angelo strode angrily to the crib. Ignoring Pippa's cry of 'No, leave him', he picked up Trevor. 'My son,' he said.

Ramona stared and turned pale. Her eyes took on a strange, trance-like expression, as if seeing inwardly. Oh God! he thought. She's going into a trance. Here, of all places.

'Death,' she muttered in a hoarse whisper. 'He brings sorrow – to you and to me. Three deaths before his. He will die before he comes of age. Others will follow.' She placed her hands protectively over her stomach.

As Pippa screamed and grabbed her baby, the priest stepped forward and held up his crucifix. 'In the name of Jesus . . .' he began.

Angelo caught hold of Ramona's arm and pushed her outside. 'Get out and take your evil curses with you!'

She was crying softly and wiping her cheeks with the back of her hand. Sadness shone in her eyes, and compassion was there, too. 'No, not a curse. Never!' she whispered. 'Just the *sight*. Oh God! I saw it all. Our fates indelibly entwined, our sorrows shared. I should have left you to drown. I would have if I had only known.'

'Go!' He pushed her down the steps and heard shouts and jeers from the villagers. There was a surge towards her, but Ramona held up her hands and they fell into sullen silence.

'We have brought our gifts. Angelo thanks you all. Now we are going home.' Hostile faces, boots and white coats surged past, hands outstretched plucked at cakes, sweets and glasses of wine. Plates crashed, pies and cakes were stamped under feet, but Angelo was too distressed to care.

Angelo crumpled into a chair. He wanted to scream until the roof flew off with the force of his anger and his denial. Lies! All lies! But deep inside a small sad voice reminded him that Ramona had never been wrong.

They were gone. The sound of their singing was faint on the wind. Pippa was crying and Steyn had his arms around her.

'Don't you ever let them come here again,' she said, her eyes wild with fury.

He placated her as best he could and promised to do whatever she wanted. In her way, Pippa could be as intimidating as Ramona.

'They'll not come here again,' he said, 'but I'll never turn my back on them. They saved my life and I'll do whatever I can for them. They'll always be my friends and I'll see them in their homes. She meant no harm. She has no control over these fits of hers. It's nonsense! Forget about it.'

But Angelo knew that he could never forget.

Chapter 35

After the débâcle of the christening, Pippa hated the villagers. She held Angelo personally responsible for Ramona's uninvited appearance and she urged her husband to sell out his interests in the fishing harbour and concentrate on building up her father's mines and properties, but Angelo would not.

Daily they faced each other over a chasm of divided loyalties. He wanted her to move out of Steyn's house. He even bought a mansion on the sunny side of the valley, the eastern, white side, which was sheltered from the wind, and from where the views were exceptional, but Pippa refused to move, so eventually Angelo sold it.

There was hardly anything about him that suited Pippa after the birth of their child, Angelo sensed. He was happy-go-lucky about the money he made, having no talent for enjoying wealth, only a need to create things – people, businesses, homes, factories, but at least he never complained about his wife's excessive spending. The more she spent, the more he made.

As the war progressed Angelo made a fortune, for there was a huge demand for packaged, exportable protein. He again extended the fish-freezing plant and a canning factory followed. A year later he was able to start building his third factory.

His share of the profits was spent on his two passions, wine and people. He bought several fine vineyards and wineries in Paarl and Franschhoek, employing foremen to run the farms and he was lucky to find an expert wine blender trained in France.

True to his early promises, Angelo set himself the task of providing jobs and facilities for everyone in the fishing village. The mood was good. Coloured artisans mixed freely with whites, Silver Bay was in the forefront of integration.

On Angelo's birthday, in October 1944, he drank too much wine and made amorous advances towards his wife. It was just over a year since Trevor had been born and he and Pippa had not made love since the birth. Her coolness stunned him into anger and later, in bed, he reached out and roughly pulled her on to her back and clambered over her.

'I don't feel like making love,' she said icily.

'I do,' he grunted.

He pushed her legs apart with his knees. Pinning her arms on to the pillow, he lunged into her. She did not become aroused, submitting but not participating, although he tried to woo her for a long time, holding back, caressing her, stroking her, kissing her neck, nuzzling her hair – all the little tricks that used to turn her on. Eventually he came, but it was a poor imitation of the real thing.

'What's happened to us, Pippa?' he asked sadly.

'It's your obstinacy,' she said. 'Your peasant ways. You shame me by flaunting your coloured friends. I can't believe you would do this to me. I cannot love you if you won't live like a civilised person.'

'Oh, Pippa,' he said sadly. 'Which of us is civilised?

There's a name for women who use sex for their own ends.'

Pippa began to cry. Somehow the sound of women's tears weakened Angelo to such an extent he just wanted to run away. Perhaps it was the memory of his mother's tears the night before his father was shot, he reasoned, or later, the night before she married his murderer. Whatever the reason, he knew he was beaten. Tears unnerved him. He would never take Pippa against her will again.

Trevor grew into a sweet, sensitive, clever child, but now there was a new family war-zone, as he fought Pippa over their son's upbringing. Deep in Angelo's heart was his fear of Fascism and all totalitarian creeds. To Angelo, there were two sorts of people in the world, those who believed in the rights of the individual and those who simply survived by pushing down the weak. *It's nothing to do with us*, was a phrase that made him feel sick. He was determined that his son would learn his values, which he, in turn, had learned from his beloved father. In the mornings, he would take Trevor down to the fishing village and leave him in the care of his packers, while he attended to business, and they would spoil the child and play with him for hours.

He knew that his liberal views infuriated Pippa. He still drank with the coloureds in their bar over at the harbour, he often went to Ramona's house for dinner and he took her children out with Trevor on his launch.

'I will not have my child associating with dirty fishing people,' she screamed one day. 'I'll leave you if you try to make me.'

'For my part, I won't have my child grow up a Fascist,' he told her angrily. Little Trevor watched and listened, his eyes wide with shock, his mouth down-turned with misery.

Pippa sighed, sensing that she would never be able to change him, and she deliberately began to stifle her sexual feelings for this beautiful but wilful maverick she had married. He was flouting their social code and their values.

In mid-1945, when Europe rejoiced at the war's end, Angelo predicted that waves of European immigrants would bring much-needed skills and labour to South Africa. He frequented the Ritz Hotel, where the immigrants were housed, finding welders, carpenters, draughtsmen and technicians. The profits were flowing, Silver Bay was expanding, and there was cash for everyone. Soon he increased the fishing fleet to eight trawlers and a fishmeal plant was built. Employment opportunities abounded, bringing new coloured families to the area and before long neat little cottages were spread up the mountainside.

When Trevor was four he began to wet his bed. A visit to a children's specialist revealed that his parents' many fights were upsetting him. So Pippa established another bedroom for Angelo on the south side of their house. 'So that you can see your beloved village,' she said spitefully, 'and keep out of my hair.'

Six months later, Angelo donated a large sum to the church to establish a multiracial, preschool kindergarten. When the project was finalised, Trevor and Ramona's twins, Bill and Frikkie, were the first three pupils to attend. Pippa and Angelo had a final, wounding fight, and then retired to their separate suites. They met occasionally for meals.

A year later, another large donation from Angelo's factories founded a private church school for all races. Angelo was fast seeing at least a part of his dream come true. Silver Bay was the perfect village where he was feted and admired and the people were content and well off.

But Angelo was beginning to fear the future. He read the signs and he remembered his father's warning. 'The human race is one family and all kinds of caste systems are evil, whatever they are called, and however well they are disguised.'

Forty-six years after its defeat in the South African War, Afrikaner nationalism triumphed on May 28, 1948, when the National Party (known as the Nats) was voted into power on its promise to preserve white power and the Afrikaner culture. The instrument to be used to put this policy into practice was *apartheid*. A patchwork of 'home-lands' would become the basis of separate 'national states'.

Trying to make the plan work required nationwide social engineering and mass movement of various pockets of the population. Indian and coloured activists formed defiance groups, but they were ruthlessly put down in waves of arrests.

By the end of the decade the country was well into a police state. During the fifties, crippling new laws were promulgated to bind the social strategy, blacks were finger-printed and numbered and issued with reference books. The coloured people were removed from the voters' roll, and separate schools and a university were established. By the end of the decade *Apartness* was successfully established.

The nightmare first entered Silver Bay and the nearby city suburbs with the erection of numerous '*Whites Only*' signs, on the toilets, restaurants, cinemas, opera houses, dance halls, bars, hotels, public spaces and benches. Par-ticularly hurtful were the whites-only buses, children's playparks and beaches.

Faced with this humiliation, the coloured people turned away from the whites. They began to feel second-class, pariahs, worthless. Lack of self-pride led to more drunkenness, crime and sexual violence within the families. No one really cared as long as this rot was restricted to coloured areas. With the lack of policing in non-white areas, criminal gangs took over and the inhabitants went in fear of their lives.

The English liberals of Silver Bay resisted albeit half-heartedly, so policemen from the Transvaal, with right-wing loyalties, were transferred to the Cape. They had no sympathy with English 'kafir-lovers' and they made it their vocation to clean up this cesspit of English racial immorality.

Behind closed doors, Silver Bay's inhabitants swopped experiences. Herman Parker, a banker, was arrested for immorality while driving home his wife's babysitter. From now on, the community decided, wives must accompany their husbands when transporting maids. Maids without work permits were dragged out of their rooms before dawn, imprisoned until their trials, fined heavily, and bundled off to the Homelands. Peggy was fined for allowing a non-white to sit at a table to drink his cream soda. The Brians, who were away on holiday, returned to find their dogs had starved because their maid and gardener had been unexpectedly deported. Mrs Thompson's blind gardener, Patrick, whom she'd kept for philanthropic reasons for donkey's years, was arrested, beaten up and sent away. A policeman arrested Tanya Lockyer for swimming naked in her pool behind high walls. The policeman had climbed a tall tree, carrying his binoculars, and Tanya received a hefty fine for public indecency. Little Maisie Primrose, aged two, was seen naked on the beach and her mother fined in court.

It wasn't long before most signs of white rebellion were quelled. As for the coloureds, the stigma of being second-class was settling deep into their psyche. They felt inferior and were pathetically grateful for any kindness.

Father Mooney spoke out fearlessly from his pulpit, but wherever he went he was watched and followed by plain-clothes detectives. Every Sunday, two detectives sat in the back row of the Catholic church making shorthand notes of his sermons.

Angelo had always coveted the eastern slopes of the valley, for they were sunny and gently sloping and he sensed they would make good vineyards. Many of them were owned by coloured people who had held the deeds for three generations or more. But then came a team of government officials who informed the luckless owners that they were unlawfully living in a white area and they must move to the coloured village. Their cottages and smallholdings were to be auctioned by agents appointed by the State, acting on behalf of the owners.

Despite their liberal leanings, many of the residents of Silver Bay attended the auction in the hope of rich pickings. Angelo went along, too. For the past few weeks he had been wrestling with his conscience, on the one hand not wishing to profit from government policy and the coloureds' misfortune, on the other, longing to own this land which he had been trying to buy for years.

Despite his avowed intention of keeping away, he could not resist going along. It was just as he had expected, beautiful neglected sunny slopes, the odd donkey still grazing around, since their owners had nowhere to take them, chickens strutting in the sun, the former owners in a sad, isolated group, watching the proceedings with hostile eyes. Somehow bitterness and grief could not compete with the sunny nature of the area, the oak trees full of twittering birds, the streams gurgling down the hillside, the beautiful clear morning, all this seemed to make the black-clad, dark-faced mourning group totally incongruous amongst all the loveliness.

The auctioneer was selling the first two smallholdings separately, and bidding opened briskly at four hundred pounds, but slackened off at six hundred pounds.

Angelo could pick out the determined buyers, for he knew most of them. The Bronsons, the Jouberts, both property developers. In no time the bidding reached eight hundred pounds. Then he heard Peggy Cohen's clear voice call: 'Nine hundred pounds.'

'A thousand!' Angelo blurted out. He simply could not resist. At that moment the urge to own these beautiful slopes outweighed all other considerations. There was a sudden hush. If Angelo wanted the land, there was little point in bidding against him. Everyone knew that. Each time a piece of land came under the hammer, he had to call out, had to own it. By noon he had acquired the entire parcel of smallholdings for a song.

He walked back to his car with mixed feelings, part satisfaction, part guilt at his own weakness. A coloured woman stepped forward and shook her fist. 'Judas,' she jeered. She spat at him and her spittle landed on Angelo's arm. He took out a handkerchief and wiped it off. Now they were all shouting at him. Well, he could see their point. He ignored them and walked slowly back to his car.

The following morning a mysterious fire broke out at his fishmeal factory. Angelo called the police and the insurance company, and the damage was soon repaired. From then on he engaged a full-time security service.

Without his coloured friends, Angelo became bitterly lonely. In his home he was a pariah, where even Trevor, who had reached the age of twelve, seemed to side with his mother; in his village he was a traitor where no one would pass the time of day with him; in his factories he was the boss, and 'yes sir' and 'no sir' was the extent of any conversation. *So be it*, Angelo thought bitterly. He began to lose all faith in human nature as he became introverted and deeply hurt.

Chapter 36

It was the beginning of September, 1955, springtime, but the most dangerous season for the Cape fishermen, for then the sou'easterly gales begin. Rushing up from the Antarctic, icy winds whip the freezing sea into a fury of exploding surf and 100-foot high waves.

Twenty-five miles south-west of Silver Bay, Gideon had missed the gale warning, for they had run into a massive shoal of kingklip and it had been all hands on deck to unload their magnificent harvest of fish. All his life Gideon had fished in sight of land, using the mountains as his weather guide, for the towering clouds gave ample warning of a coming gale, but this time he had lost sight of them.

It was 6 p.m. when the first blast smashed into the trawler, tearing down the radio aerial, slamming hatches, and showering the men with sea spray. It had been a hard knock and Gideon was a worried man as he altered course and steered towards harbour at full speed. The next ten minutes were calm, a false calm, as he knew from bitter experience.

The second blast brought the full force of the gale and from then on there was no letting up. Gideon shuddered and changed course to run into the wind and he watched with mounting unease as daylight waned and darkness came. When the wind from the south-east switched freakishly to a south-wester, Gideon's heart sank. It was not for nothing that the fishing folk called the sou'wester a black sou'easter, for it brought hurricane winds and pelting rain. He suspected they were in a hurricane track, but he hoped it would not last longer than a few hours.

All that evening, the wind mounted with a ferocity that was awesome. By 9 p.m. the *Philippa* was dragging both her anchors. They were forced to heave them in and face into the teeth of a Force 10 storm and a wild and savage sea. The trawler rose to take most of the big waves, but she took some across her decks with maximum damage. Miles from the nearest haven, Gideon could do little more than accept the punishment. By midnight the *Philippa* was being swept clean on her decks, spray was breaking high above her mastheads, and the trawling gear was badly damaged. Black water was falling on to the decks to a depth of six feet. The stanchions of her rails were smashed, the trawler winch had been broken and swept away, the nets were lost and her starboard lifeboat was shattered in its chocks. Her hatches began to break under the monotonous impact of the waves, and soon the holds were flooded.

By now the crew were besieged in their quarters, and dared not open a hatch or port. Gideon and his mate were in their safety harnesses.

By 2 a.m. the trawler had taken such a battering that Gideon ordered the mate to send out distress signals. The emergency weather reports were sounding increasingly ominous and the distress frequency was crackling with calls from other fleets. They could hardly hear the radio above the high-pitched scream of the wind and the sonorous thunder of the breaking seas. The *Philippa* was barely able to hold her own.

Then, at 3 a.m., a thick mist and heavy rain came lashing round the trawler. Visibility was down to four metres and there was still no answer to Gideon's signals. He was aware that they were badly off course, but he had no way of telling, for rain and fog hampered navigation.

A sudden freak wave tossed the trawler broadside, tearing her belly out as she was flung across a reef of rocks. In that split second, Gideon realised exactly where he was and he knew he was as good as dead. As the trawler heeled over, icy seas flooded her engine room. The lights flickered once and went out. Within five minutes she was flooded in every compartment and her doom was sealed. Now she was breaking up fast under the merciless assault of heavy waves on sharp reefs.

Gideon fought his way out of the wheelhouse. The lifeboats were swept away and the crew were wearing life jackets and clutching each other, but a wave lifted them clean off the deck and into the surf. A gargantuan column of white spray broke across the bows and the boat keeled over.

Gideon fell into the foaming water. The icy temperature sent him into shock and he was only dimly aware of being smashed against rocks and dragged down by the undertow.

'I killed him,' Angelo muttered when his trawler's wreckage was located four days later. He had a vivid image of Gideon as he had once been, wearing his tattered trousers and buttonless shirt tied in a knot at his waist, rowing out the trek nets and grinning happily. 'What have I done?' he sobbed. 'He was never meant to be a skipper. My blind ambition cost him his life.'

Peggy was overworking and close to cracking up, anyone

could see that, Angelo thought. Sands had been her only interest in life since she learned that her husband had died in a prison camp towards the end of the war. Lately, she'd been creating havoc with Ramona by interfering in the kitchen, complaining about the quality of the catering, blaming her for lost orders, shouting at the waitresses and making everyone's life a burden.

Angelo took time off to hear her complaints. 'Now you've told me all the trivial things, tell me the important problems,' he said, when she finally paused for breath.

'Such as?'

'How's your love life?' Lately she had been living with an unemployed British immigrant.

'Null and void,' she said angrily. 'I threw out lover-boy. He thought that this place was going to keep him in luxury for the rest of his bloody life.' She sighed. 'Next time I'll be more careful, but getting rid of him wasn't easy. It was horrible! But look here, Angelo, I'm not just making trouble for the sake of it. Ramona's a changed person. She's not the same woman you used to know.'

'Well, what do you expect?' he said angrily. He raised his hands. 'I give in. I don't want to fight. It's just that she can't get over Gideon's tragic death and we must pull together to help her.'

Suddenly Peggy burst into tears and crumpled into a chair. Watching her, Angelo wondered what he'd said to provoke this outburst. He crouched beside her and put his arms around her.

'What have I said? What's the matter? Come on, I'll take you home. Crying isn't good for morale. The staff will think we're going bust.'

She laughed through her tears. Back in her cottage he looked around with interest. It had changed so much since they went into partnership. Good paintings, Persian carpets, antique furniture and all modern conveniences had transformed the cottage, and the garden looked cared for with a swimming pool beside a rockery.

'Coffee?' she asked.

'What about a Scotch – or whatever you have.'

He followed her into the kitchen and saw her tears splashing around. 'Hey there,' he said, grabbing a cloth to wipe her eyes.

'Don't stick that dirty cloth in my face,' she grumbled.

He threw it into the sink.

'I'm sorry,' she sobbed. 'It's not easy to throw out someone you love. I had to do it, because he didn't love me. I caught him in bed with someone else, right here in my home. Can't you see that my loss is every bit as bad as Ramona's, but she gets all the sympathy? I walk out at night and see all those lighted windows, with families inside, tucked up together, safe and content, and there's me who can't get a man, not a decent man. I don't know why that is. What's wrong with me, Angelo?'

He tried to comfort her as best he could.

'You know, Peggy, you're not the only one who's lonely. One can be lonely even when married. Even if it looks good, a wife and kid and all the trimmings, it can still be hell.'

'You?'

'Yes, I suppose so. I don't usually talk about it.'

'I don't know why I'm being such a fool,' she sobbed. 'After all, it's been a long time. So why now? Why do I choose this moment to crack up?'

'You're not cracking up, Peggy,' he said. 'You're just in need of a little love. As I am. Pippa and I haven't made love for years. She doesn't need a husband. She has a son and a father and that seems to be enough for her.'

'You two should move out of Steyn's house.'

'Yes, I aim to do that one of these days, but so far she's resisted all my efforts. They're away together right now. They flew up to South West. You know he has umpteen-dozen mining camps up there and they wanted to inspect some new concessions. In a way, Pippa is quite mannish, but where her son's concerned she's a lioness. Nothing and no one touches that boy.'

Watching her, Angelo thought how wonderful it would be to just let go and make love to someone other than one's wedded spouse. Could he trust her? She needed love and so did he. He truly loved Pippa, but he felt abandoned and unwanted, although he was confident that with time and patience Pippa would learn to love him again.

As he bent down and brushed his lips over Peggy's bare shoulder, he became suffused with desire for the first time in months. He felt his body awaken. It was not just an urge for sex, but a resumption of life, a need to hold, to touch, to enjoy beauty again – to be hungry.

'Ooh,' she said. 'I love being stroked. I wish you'd never stop.'

'I'm in no hurry,' he whispered. 'I have nothing else to do, but to stroke you.' He lovingly stroked her back and then they went into her bedroom and she undressed. He stroked her beautiful, firm breasts and the white soft flesh around her thighs. He kissed her body, and her nipples hardened and she groaned softly.

Watching her, he felt confused. Conflicting emotions struggled to gain precedence. He desperately wanted some physical love, but part of him wanted to be faithful to Pippa. Peggy moved, groaning, opened her eyes. 'Don't stop,' she said.

Instinct took over. As he thrust into her, a moment of

guilt struck him. He felt he would be punished for his lapse in his vows, but then desire took over and he came, in a magnificent release of pent-up emotions and physical frustration.

Later, when he returned home, he found the police waiting. The sergeant asked him to come into his study. Then he suggested they sit down. Angelo was feeling thoroughly alarmed as he waited impatiently for the sergeant to come to the point.

'Sir, I have extremely bad news for you. The light aircraft, which your father-in-law, Steyn du Toit, was piloting over the Namib, crashed into the moonscape area, killing everyone on board.'

'Who was on board?' he managed to whisper.

'Your wife Philippa and her father and a geologist called . . .'

'Where is my son?' Angelo asked, interrupting him. 'Pippa would never have travelled without him.'

'Evidently she did. Your son was slightly sick and she left him in the care of the hotel manager's wife, a friend of hers.'

Angelo crumpled into his chair, his head in his hands, and remained there, shaking.

'Is there anything at all we can do for you?' the policeman asked.

'No,' he said.

There was nothing anyone could do for him ever again. As he flew to SWA to fetch his son, he knew that he would grieve alone for many years.

Ramona mourned Gideon more than she would have thought possible. It was not that she had loved him so much, but that he was as much a part of her as her right arm. She could not cope without him. She was left to fend for herself and her three children in an increasingly hostile world. Change was all about her, Ramona sensed. Bad changes! Everything was becoming cruel and senseless. She was no longer allowed to sit in a 'white' restaurant to order even a cool drink. Beach toilets were for whites only. Even the beach was for whites only, except one tiny patch next to the harbour. The buses were for whites only. Non-white buses were few and far between and overcrowded with rowdy black labourers.

Deprived of Gideon's moral support, Ramona began to crumple and draw into herself. Even Angelo had changed. Had the new white élitist philosophy got to him, too?

The fishing harbour was becoming overcrowded as more coloured people were deprived of their cottages in white areas, some having owned them for three generations. They were being crammed into the only coloured area in Silver Bay, which was the tiny settlement above the fishing harbour. She couldn't blame Angelo, it was government policy, but so many of the newcomers were not working for his many companies and in the face of general overcrowding the apartments became dirty and stinking, the roads were thronged with children and refuse lay around. There was never any peace in the village. She longed to get away from it all, but where could she go? Only servants could live in white areas.

A month after Gideon's death, a government official came snooping around Sands to investigate claims that the business was partly owned by a non-white. This broke several laws, including the Separate Amenities Act, he told Ramona sternly. He explained to her that she wasn't even allowed to eat or drink in her own restaurant. She could sit down at the table, he said, but as soon as even a glass of water was placed in front of her, she would be breaking the law.

Beaten and cowed, Ramona acknowledged defeat.

Angelo spent days arguing with her. He wanted to issue shares so that she could retain ownership of her quarter share legally, while being employed as the cook.

'I don't have the guts to fight,' she told Angelo. 'Can you ever understand what I feel like nowadays? I'll tell you!' Suddenly she was shouting, the tears running down her cheeks. 'I feel like some lousy dog, a pariah, an untouchable, a leper. I feel I should ring a bell as I walk along the street, so that normal folk, like the local plumber or the electrician, who are too good to sit on the same bus as me, can move away. I feel lower than a slug. I wish I were dead. Besides,' she went on, 'you can be sure Peggy had a hand in this. How else would they have found out? She's wanted my share of Sands for a long time. I won't fight her. I don't want to work with her ever again.'

'If you're right I'll make sure she pays through the nose for our half share,' Angelo promised her. She was right, and when Peggy confessed, Angelo lost another friend.

Guilt-stricken, Angelo tried to think of some way to compensate Ramona.

'Just let me be your housekeeper,' she begged. 'It's the only way I'll get to have peace and space. I want to live in a pretty cottage in your grounds and do my job well and get away from all this. I never want to walk the streets of Silver Bay again. I hate it. I feel so . . . so loathsome. I'll be a good housekeeper. I know I will. Besides, you need me to bring up Trevor.'

'Oh, my dear . . . please . . . you don't have to sell yourself to me, Ramona dear. You're far too good for the job, but

I can see the advantages for you and for me. I shall build you a beautiful cottage and you will design it.'

That week she took her little daughter, Rose, who was ten, to a mixed Catholic private school in Bechuanaland, where they had never heard of apartheid. Bill was sent to the Christian Brothers integrated school and his twin brother, Frikkie, who was retarded, was sent to her relatives who were farm workers in Malmesbury.

She still had the 'sight', she knew. They might take her self-respect, but they could not take that away from her.

Her seed and Angelo's seed combined. She had seen that prophecy and she knew it would come true, but not through her body. She was old now, and wrinkled before her time, but there was Rose who was showing promise of great beauty. She would be brought up as a white girl, taught to speak properly, and she must get a good education. So Ramona packed up her cottage and cried bitterly as her children left home. On the first day of the following month, October, she started her duties as Angelo's housekeeper.

From then on, Angelo's world was his son, Trevor. He rode, swam and played tennis with him, took him mountaineering, helped him with homework and taught him the rudiments of business.

A few years later, when Trevor was sent to Fettes College, in Edinburgh, to complete his schooling and gain entrance to a British university, Angelo found himself completely alone.

Chapter 37

——— ———

Trevor Palma stared through the porthole in the first-class section of the SAA airliner, longing to see the mountains far below, but there was only the flat, brown vista of the Karoo desert with the occasional straight road cutting through the drab landscape. Back in London, when he was homesick, he had longed for his father and home, but overwhelmingly it was the mountains and the sun that he missed the most during his six years in exile: two years in boarding school, three at the London School of Economics and one year working at a leading commodity broker in the city. At least he'd been able to fly back each holiday.

He grinned happily as the air hostess brought another Scotch on the rocks. He was glad to be back. A new life awaited him. London had been a fantastic happening for Trevor. Coming from a small town, he had thrown himself into the swinging sixties, enjoying all it could offer in free love, pop art, twist and bop, meditation and even a little marijuana from time to time. Lately he'd grown a beard and his light brown hair hung on his shoulders. He'd taken to wearing floral shirts and a band round his forehead, but he drew the line at earrings and tattoos. He hadn't fooled anyone, and he sensed that. Something about his cool, green analytical eyes, and his long bony face, made everyone take him very seriously, which was a pity he often thought. He was very much a career man and he looked it. He couldn't wait to take over Father's empire.

They were descending over the Franschhoek mountain peaks. He looked down, revelling in the sight. He had forgotten about the sheer space and size of Africa, thousands of square miles of desert, miles of mountain ranges, long, silver-white beaches, huge farms, vast dams. A lump came into his throat, he was so happy. He flashed a smile at the air hostess and she smiled back conspiratorially. Home at last, her smile said.

Angelo was waiting impatiently at the airport, but his son was first off the plane. He flung his arms round him and did not notice the curious, admiring glances of the women in the crowd. Father and son were both tall, attractive and distinguished-looking men. Now in his early forties Angelo looked in the prime of life; there was no grey in his curly black hair, his figure was trim and muscular. He was a fanatic about keeping fit, jogging daily, taking long swims in the bay and climbing the local mountain peaks at weekends. His face was lined, his skin tanned almost black, and except for his eyes, he almost fit the part of a happy, successful man. Only his eyes were hauntingly sad.

Angelo stepped back and gave a brief critical appraisal of Trevor's hippie hairstyle and beard, the beaded necklace and the floral shirt. He smiled to himself. He'd been visiting Trevor regularly, talking to his lecturers and tutors, and he felt that he knew his son rather better than most fathers. He welcomed his business acumen, his ambition and determination. Add to that his breeding and Trevor was altogether special, Angelo thought fondly. Let him enjoy his brief hippie excursion. Hadn't he just brought off a brilliant coup while working in London? He'd bought

up a defunct fishmeal plant in the Argentine for next to
nothing. He was scarcely out of college, but already he'd
made them international. Well, that's why I sent him over,
Angelo thought to himself. It was a sacrifice. I missed him,
but he's back now with a hell of a lot of knowledge packed
away under that unruly hippie hairdo. Let him enjoy it
while he can. He'll only be young once.

Despite the funny clothes, he's a chip off the old block, the
chauffeur decided after listening to their conversation all
the way home. They talked exclusively about money . . . the
price of fish and fishmeal and how the new South American
plant was working, and just how important fishmeal was
going to become as a worldwide basic foodstuff. And
then how Trevor had forced up the price of coffee by
withholding stocks in warehouses, and just how important
it was that they increase the frozen-food division and get a
monopoly on Mozambican langoustine and prawns. No one
seemed to notice that the spring blossom was out and the
oak trees in bud, and how delightful everything looked.

Before they'd even reached home they were going at each
other hammer and tongs, as they often did every holiday.
Trevor wanted to purchase a deep-sea fish-factory ship. He
knew of one going cheap in Japan, and it would only take a
million to refurbish it. The old man wasn't so sure.

'Father, listen to me. Why can't you understand that it's
foolish to be at the mercy of the shoals, for they're at the
mercy of the plankton. Why the hell should our profits
depend on the vagaries of plankton?'

Trevor was getting hot under the collar.

'With the deep-sea fish factory we can follow the shoals
right to the South American coastline if necessary. I've
done the costing. It works. I don't see how we can lose.'

'And the pilchards and anchovies?' Angelo asked. 'They'll be fished out in no time. Self-defeating in the long term.'

'Who cares about the long term? We can make money fast. The sea's teeming with pilchards, our problem is catching them within the limits of our trawlers. Well, how about it?'

'I'm still thinking,' Angelo said. 'You can't expect me to make up my mind just like that, but I'll look at those figures of yours.'

'Oh, for God's sake. If you don't hurry, the Japs will get in first.'

The chauffeur sighed. He'd like to be rich, but he'd hate to be so single-minded about money. Young Trevor was biting his lip with impatience.

Trevor spent the day at home with Angelo, swopping stories, relaxing and sitting out in the sun to get a tan. It took a few days to get acclimatised in the plant, so much had changed, but eventually he had time to look up old friends.

It was good to see Emanuel Fernandes again. They'd been at school together, but Emanuel had gone on to study art at Cape Town University and fallen head over heels in love with the model, Juliette, who had posed nude for them. She was half-French, half-Ethiopian. Trevor had never discovered why she had come to South Africa. She was tall, creamy-coloured and a little too strong, both in mind and features.

Everything about her seemed a little larger than life, her features, her eyes, hands, feet and mouth. She was always pushing her viewpoint home, never able to compromise. To his mind it ruined her sex-appeal, but Emanuel was crazy about her. She seemed to swamp his mild and over-sensitive friend. God knows how Emanuel really saw her, because he transposed everyone and everything he saw into modern cubist shapes and brilliant colours, which were eventually executed in stained glass.

His friend had bought Juliette a cottage in the fishing village and Trevor couldn't help admiring it. It looked vaguely Arabic with the thick stone walls painted salmon pink and scarlet poinsettia falling all over the place. Emanuel had become a Rastafarian which, Trevor discovered, gave him the moral licence to smoke as much pot as he liked. After the greetings were dispensed with, the two of them got down to the serious business of drinking red wine and smoking pot. Trevor took a couple of puffs only because he had to get back to the factory at 2 p.m. for a meeting.

'My dear friend,' Emanuel gushed after a couple of joints. 'Join us in a tree-planting ceremony. We shall have something of you when you're gone.'

'I'm not going anywhere. Not any more,' Trevor said laughing. Nevertheless, he joined them in flipping *dagga* seeds into the backyard under the poinsettia. 'I'm taking over the factories,' he told them happily. 'Father will devote himself to making wine, once I get the hang of things, that is. It's his long-standing ambition. He bought a winery in the Paarl area and he's all set to blend his own wine. Once upon a time, his family produced their own wine and he's never got over the longing to return to his roots.'

Drawing the smoke deep into his lungs he experienced a sense of completeness and satisfaction with his world. The long years of studying, the happy, carefree holiday in Greece last month with his best friend, Claire Durrell, the business coup he'd pulled off, his deep love and understanding of his father, his renewed sense of camaraderie with Emanuel, all this and the pretty house and the midday heat of the sun, and the views over the bay, had conspired together to make this perfect moment in time, right here and now, a moment of deep fulfilment. He drew deeply on the joint and again experienced a sense of union between himself and his world.

Nevertheless, at precisely seven minutes to two he stood up. 'Bye, guys! See you,' he said dreamily.

Dreamy or not, he had no intention of being late for the meeting.

As he drove down the road towards the harbour he thought he saw a vision. A girl passed, wearing a full red skirt and an off-the-shoulder white blouse, her black hair flowing over her shoulders, her feet pushed into white high-heeled sandals. She was long-legged and narrow-waisted, but it was her face that amazed him, for with her huge eyes, small straight nose, sloping cheek bones and generous full mouth, she was that very rare phenomenon, a totally perfect woman.

He laughed to himself. Obviously no one could be that beautiful. He was higher than he had realised. Had Emanuel mixed something with the *dagga*? But he wouldn't do that, surely? Perhaps he shouldn't smoke again, he thought cautiously.

Angelo was waiting for him. He sniffed around like a bloodhound and smiled grimly. 'Just watch it,' he said. 'It creeps up on you. Well, of course, you'd know that, being the smart guy you are.' He patted him awkwardly on the shoulder and Trevor stifled an urge to give a smart answer. Sometimes Father was so damned patronising.

He repressed the image of the girl he'd thought he'd seen and put his mind on the business in hand. Dreaminess, visions and joints were soon quite forgotten.

*   *   *

It was his third night home and he had arranged to take
Claire Durrell to the opera with Father. Watching the old
man gaze so sexily at Claire was almost funny. How old
was he now? He quickly calculated – 43. Strange that his
hair was still black as pitch. For an old man he was pretty
sexy, Trevor thought fondly.

Claire was close to the original Nordic blonde beauty
that he knew his Dad had always coveted. She was busty,
but slender, her perfectly shaped head could carry off
long straight blonde hair to perfection. Her green eyes
were unusually light in colour, and they looked at you
in a dreamy sort of way, so you got to thinking that she
fancied you. Her skin was creamy white, her limbs long and
supple, her profile perfect. Her family owned the farmlands
down a long line of mountainside on the north-eastern side
of the valley, which Father always claimed would make
the perfect vineyard. Was it the prospective vineyards or
Claire's Nordic genes that he wanted to secure for the
family? Trevor had never been sure, but it amused him
to see how the old man almost drooled over Claire. He and
her parents had been pushing their offspring into marriage
ever since Claire had reached puberty.

Trevor was extraordinarily fond of Claire, but marriage?
He had no desire to settle down until he was thirty at
least. He gazed at her as he waited for her to unwrap
the present he'd brought her. Then he winked. Her old
man swept Angelo into his bar for drinks. Trevor glanced
at his watch. 'Make it a quickie, please, Dad,' he said. 'We
can't be late.'

'Oh, Claire,' her flashy mother said, looking disappointed
as she hurried into the room with a swish of satin on
nylon stockings and enough perfume to imperil everyone's
oxygen intake.

'Such a dull dress, darling. I had hoped you'd wear your new Dior. It's so modern and daring.'

Claire laughed. 'The neckline's too low for the opera, Mother. Don't worry, Trevor's seen my cleavage. He knows exactly what I look like. After all, he's seen me in a bikini.'

She winked at him and he smothered a grin. They'd spent a week together on a Greek island where she'd bathed topless and sometimes bottomless, too, and they'd divided their nights between dancing and fucking in equal ratios. Neither of them was ready for marriage, but they colluded in humouring their parents. Whatever happened they'd both decided they'd be best buddies for life. She had been studying in London, too, but taking psychology and English.

Sitting in the old Alhambra, clutching a box of chocolates for Claire, he felt a surge of pleasure as the curtains opened. Moments later, he sat up with a jolt. The long black hair and the flowing red skirt of the opera star reminded him so forcibly of the girl he'd seen in the village that he spent the rest of the evening worrying whether or not she was real, missing the performance entirely.

When they left later, Angelo pointedly took a taxi to his club. 'You youngsters don't want me around,' he said.

Claire's parents had gone to bed, leaving them time to be alone together, so they obliged by making love on the settee. Trevor closed his eyes and thought about the black-haired beauty he'd seen. It was amazing how she'd turned him on. Probably the joint, he thought, but nevertheless he visualised her down to the last detail. To his horror, when his fantasy faded, he found he had come inside Claire.

'Oh Lord!' He sat up and gazed at her ruefully. 'Is it all right? Or is it a bad time? What on earth can we do?'

'I'm wearing a diaphragm,' she said. 'I guess it's okay.'

She looked worried, so he pinched her bare backside playfully. 'If your parents knew what a good lay you are, they'd stop trying to entice me. I simply can't resist you. Come on, lie still, I'll massage your back.'

She could never resist that. In no time she was dreamy and purring and forgetting about their small accident.

Chapter 38

———— ————

Each lunchtime Trevor hung around the street below Emanuel's cottage, hoping for another glimpse of the dark-haired girl he'd seen. Or imagined? Was she merely a drug-inspired hallucination? Could anyone be that beautiful? All the women he'd ever dreamed of were moulded into those exquisite features, and those lustrous dark eyes. The image of her seemed to hang around him. He could not help laughing at himself, but still he hung around, just in case.

'No – never again, at least not on a working day,' Trevor said the following lunchtime when Emanuel offered him a joint. 'Potent stuff! What exactly is it, apart from *dagga*, that is?'

'Nothing else, Trevor. I wouldn't do that to you. You should know that. What's got into you?'

'I walked out of here slap-bang into a hallucination. I saw – correction – I thought I saw a woman so perfect that Hollywood moguls would zoom in on chartered jets, artists would queue to paint her, and men would kill to possess her.'

'Hm!' Emanuel laughed. 'You seem smitten. Sounds like Rose September. But surely you know her? Her mother is your housekeeper and Rose works in your canning plant. She's really nice.'

'Nice? No, never. Can't be her. No one could call such a vision nice!'

'Okay, so I don't have a Thesaurus, but if it's Rose, watch out! She's got a rough, nasty Hungarian boyfriend, called Jânek Jözsef.'

Trevor toured their plants, hunting amongst the barrels of fish and offal and sacks of fishmeal, but there was no sign of the girl he had imagined, and in a way he was glad. How would one cope with such a woman? It was his secretary who mentioned the name Rose. He was nagging her for the typed figures he'd prepared on the costing of his proposed factory ship.

'I couldn't finish in time, so I gave them to Rose September. She worked late last night, but I haven't checked her typing yet.'

'I'll do it,' he said. Ten minutes later he called his secretary to send in Rose. Silly how his hand was shaking. He smiled at himself and lit a cigarette. Any moment now she'd be walking in and smashing his dreams.

There was a gentle tap. The door opened and his mirage walked in, but this time she was even lovelier. How was that possible? She wore no make-up that he could see, but her skin was velvety and so light. Her lips were wine red and they were full and perfectly shaped, incongruous in her delicate face with her tiny nose and shell-like ears and pointed chin, under a mass of wavy, fine black hair. But all this was trivial compared with her huge and lustrous eyes which glowed with warmth and humour and underlying sensuality. He almost groaned aloud. It was as if all his life had prepared him for this one moment of deep significance. He felt a strange sense of fatalism. It was as if they were inextricably joined to the present moment and each other.

Good God, he thought in shocked silence as he struggled to pull himself together. What's happening to me? Still he sat on in silent contemplation, drinking in all that loveliness.

'Are the figures all right? Is something wrong?'

Her voice was cultured. He had mentally prepared himself for the locals' sing-song accent, but she sounded so right. 'They're extremely well done. Congratulations.' Did one say that to a secretary? He was making a fool of himself. 'I hear you worked late on them. Thank you.'

When he noticed the ring glittering on her fourth finger he dropped the sheets on his desk. So she was serious about this damned Hungarian.

She smiled, a soft, tremulous, secret smile that lifted the corners of her mouth and made her eyes shine even more. Was she laughing at him? 'Then may I go now?'

'No! Rose . . . Is that your name, Rose September? Are you really Ramona's daughter? How is that possible?' Then he realised how rude he sounded, yet her skin was so light and her voice so different from their housekeeper's. 'I mean . . . all these years she's brought me up and I never met you,' he hurriedly corrected himself. 'Was she hiding you? We're practically siblings.' Perhaps that one was a mistake, but some of her shyness seemed to have gone.

'I've been in boarding school most of the time.'

'And holidays?'

Why was he asking all these difficult questions? Rose wondered and she frowned. He had put his finger on a sensitive place where it hurt. It was the holidays spent away from home, usually with schoolmistresses, that had wounded her so much. Last week, for the first time, she had plucked up courage to ask her mother why.

'You're so lovely, Rose,' Mother had said. 'I used to look like you. Look at me now! I didn't stand much of a chance of getting away from being – well, what we are – coloured people. My voice, my ways . . .' Her voice tailed off and for a while she was deep in thought. 'I have big dreams for you. I sent you away so that you would talk, think, act and feel white.' Mother had been wrong. Never for a moment had she felt white, nor forgotten the stigma of being coloured. What a waste of her childhood. She smiled bitterly. 'Mother had some strange notions. I think she was mistaken.'

'You must have been lonely. I suppose you felt rejected and bitter sometimes.'

What business was it of his? Her chin went up and she stared defiantly at him. He seemed to flinch, so she relaxed and smiled. Strange eyes, she thought. Caring eyes. Were they green, or blue? Somewhere in the middle, she decided. There was something very sensitive about him and he was on the defensive. Why was that? After all, he was the boss. He didn't seem very sure of himself. He was clever, no mistake about that. Everyone was talking about how brilliantly he'd done at university and how he was going to take over running the plant, but he seemed so sort of lost.

'Look, you've worked very hard, and done very well, and I ruined your evening, so I'd like to take you out for lunch – a business lunch, of course.'

She almost giggled. 'I have a boyfriend,' she said, 'but he won't mind a business lunch. He'll understand.'

'Lunch it is,' he said lightly. 'See you in the car park at twelve forty-five? Fine with you?' She flushed and nodded. She wanted to come, he could see that. Somehow he would have to get rid of the Hungarian. Did he work here? If so he'd get him transferred. She had to be his. As she walked out of the office he realised that nothing in his life had meant so much to him.

* * *

Over lunch Rose explained about her bookkeeping studies, which she had just completed, and her plans for the future. She repeated the students' girlish jokes about teachers at the 'tech', and said she was working as a typist-bookkeeper and moving up to the accounts department soon.

How naive she was. Her eyes glowed and sparkled, she giggled often after she had finished her first glass of wine, her breasts shimmered and moved against the fabric of her cheap nylon blouse, but he could imagine how tantalisingly lovely they were. Her neck was swanlike, it rippled when she threw back her head to laugh, which she did often. A little crucifix dangled provocatively just at her cleavage. Her fingers were strangely small and beautifully shaped. He longed to catch hold of her hand. He had never desired any woman so desperately. He knew he would kill for her, work for her, devote his life to her, but she had to be his.

What a child she was, oohing and aahing over the *crème brûlée*, getting tipsy and slurring her words.

'This is fun,' he said. 'I miss my friends in London. I'd be pleased if you'd have lunch with me often. We can try out the different restaurants. Sands has the most marvellous paella, and "Rodrigos" excels in its tapas. I know a place in Wellington where they make the best bobotie in the country. We could fly there for lunch and fly back again. Would you like that?' he asked, trying to coax her.

'I've never been in an aircraft,' she said wistfully.

'Tomorrow,' he promised. 'For lunch. If we're late I'll say you were taking dictation.'

She giggled. 'Why not? There's no harm in lunch,' she said. 'Jânek can't grumble at that.'

A bolt of jealousy tore through him, stunning him with

the force of its savagery. 'Where does he work, this boyfriend of yours?' He tried to sound casual.

'On the ships. Whatever job he can get. He loves the sea, you see.' She giggled again. 'That sounds odd. I sound funny. I think I drank too much.'

'Nonsense.'

'He's only been here for a year. He's from Hungary and he's doing manual labour while he learns English. He was a teacher,' she confided. 'He wants to teach again one day.'

His hand slid over hers. Her carefree, little-girl smile fled. She trembled and flushed, but left her hand in his. Now she was the seductress, smiling gently, the immortal woman, secure in her sexuality, tasting and learning about her power.

'I must tell you the truth.' His eyes were moody and brooding. 'Since I first saw you, I've thought of nothing else but you. I was coming out of Emanuel's house when I saw you walking through the village. I searched the whole damned plant for you, and there you were right under my nose. You are absolutely safe with me, Rose, but give me a chance. Give *us* a chance. Don't go and get married. Not right now.'

'When you look like that, you look a bit scary,' she said. Her other hand was playing nervously with her glass.

'I'm being too serious? Life is fun, isn't it? Tomorrow will be fun. Just you wait. We'll skim over the mountaintops and land right at the restaurant's door.'

She giggled again. 'How can I say no? I would love to fly. I don't mind about the lunch. Just the ride. That would be enough.'

When they arrived back at the plant she jumped out of the car and ran off as if she were afraid someone would see her. He watched her disappearing through the staff entrance and mourned the loss of her presence. Would she come tomorrow? Would she? The question obsessed him and he could think of nothing else all day. He fudged his meeting with the board and noticed Angelo giving him some hard looks. At 5.30 exactly his secretary called.

'That Rose September wants to see you. She won't say why.'

His heart sank. 'Send her in.' He felt sure she had come to cancel their date.

She looked so nervous. 'I've never flown before, so I don't know whether to dress smartly for the restaurant or wear slacks for climbing on to the plane.' What an agony over something so absurd. He laughed with relief.

'Wear whatever you like. I'll lift you up,' he promised. 'I know, wear that red skirt and white, off-the-shoulder blouse. The clothes I first saw you in. Would you do that for me? But bring a jacket.'

He stood up and walked towards her. Nearer, he could smell her perfume and the scent of her body which excited him. He was so much taller than she, looking down on her made him feel uneasy. He gently undid the tight ribbon which bound her hair into a pony tail. 'It's bad to pull your hair so tightly. You can damage the roots. So wear it loose, like this,' he said, letting it fall over her shoulders. 'Oh, Rose. I'd do anything for you,' he whispered. He bent down and kissed her cheek, pressing his lips against the firm warm skin, turning his back on ancient loyalties and ties.

Chapter 39

——— ———

'We're engaged, aren't we? Rosie, look at me.'

Rose was reluctant to look into his eyes, but eventually she felt compelled to look up at Jânek. The sight of him sent a wave of sickening guilt racing through her. Haggard eyes, unshaven cheeks! Clearly he was going through hell and she felt so wretched. Only four weeks ago he had thrilled her with his dark, wiry hair cut into a crew cut, flashing blue eyes and tanned, sinewy arms. He was so tall and good-looking and she had felt sure that she loved him.

Nervous hands, sulky mouth! Just look at him! Rose cringed and tried not to notice how much weight he had lost. How ill he looked. His eyes were bloodshot with deep shadows underneath. She could imagine his nights of grief, for she knew how much he loved her. She had never seen him like this before. For the first time she realised he was a dangerous and emotional man and she felt a twinge of fear.

He seemed to read her mind. 'Don't look at me like that, Rose, I love you. I would never harm you. I'd rather die than hurt the hairs of your head.'

She smiled faintly. Jânek had escaped from Hungary a year ago, but he was a clever man and he was learning English fast. His speech was full of whimsical mistakes and muddled metaphors and she loved him for it.

'Is it so easy to throw me away? Us? All our dreams? Don't you care about my feelings? You've been treating me like shit, but all I did was adore you. If you loved me, you'd think twice before you made such a fool of me,' he said, his voice deceptively quiet.

'How am I making a fool of you? It's not fair to say that. It's a job, that's all. A job's a job!' She twisted her ring nervously. Her finger felt swollen and the ring obtrusive and constricting.

'A job? Who're you kidding? Employers don't fly you to lunch at the most expensive hideaways. Look at your clothes. That dress! It cost a fortune. How long did you think you could pull the wool over my eyes?'

'I have a clothes allowance because he needs me at all these functions. Like yesterday. Trevor gave a talk at some club in town and I had to attend dinner and take notes of all the questions. He needs me.'

'Trevor? So he's not Mr Palma any more. If he's what you want, then I'll step out of your life, but, Rosie, dearest, make up your mind. You know he's after you. You can't take all this – all these clothes and lunches and God knows what else and pretend it's all in the line of business.'

'But it is. You don't understand. He's never made a pass at me,' she said. 'Never!' That was the truth, but not all the truth. It was the way he looked at her that gave him away. His eyes burned with fury if another man spoke to her. Because she was light-skinned, Trevor's companions assumed she was white simply because she was well-dressed and with him. And being accepted, the men seemed to crowd around her. Not one of those men would say good afternoon if they met her in the fish market, but somehow in these smart places and wearing these smart clothes, she fitted in. What did he want from her? She was still waiting to find out. All she knew was that the sun came out when Trevor entered the room. He had changed her life and put her on a pedestal and she loved it. She did not feel that she owed him anything, but in a way she loved him. He wanted her to belong to him, and the exciting world Trevor was offering beckoned like a lantern to a moth. It smoothed healing salve on the slights and humiliations of being a second-class citizen. She had always hated being forced to live in a coloured ghetto.

Being reared in a multiracial convent with white girls, smug in the superiority of their white skins, had damaged something deep inside her. So she had made a point of coming first in everything, studying nights in the bathroom where there was light, revelling in prize-giving. Hadn't she proved time and again that she was not second class? But still she suffered from the stigma of not belonging. If you weren't white you weren't anything.

Trevor had pushed home her acceptability with the force of his intellect, his wealth, his power and his obvious admiration of her. While she was with him, no harm could come to her. But what exactly was the cost of all this favour? She had absolutely no idea what Trevor wanted from her.

'You fool! You silly little fool! He's a sneaky bastard, I'll give you that. He's fattening you up for the kill. I don't like this. I don't trust him. Give up this trip to Mozambique. D'you hear me? If you go, it's over between us. There, now I've said it for you. You have the choice.'

She wouldn't give up this trip. She had dreamed of little else for weeks. Without thinking, she pulled hard at her ring and it came off her finger and tumbled across the floor. 'There's your ring, Jânek. The truth is, I don't know what I want. Can't you understand?'

He sped after the ring, picked it up and gazed at it before

putting it in his pocket. Then he looked up and smiled sadly. 'You can stew in your own gravy,' he said.

Stew in your own gravy! She almost burst into tears. At that moment she had such a strong yearning to run and comfort him, find the ring and thrust it back on. She did love him, she decided. She truly did, but this new world was too fascinating to abandon. 'I love you, Jânek,' she said. 'I'm sure it will work out. Just give me time.'

It was mid-summer, but there was a cold wind blowing. Beyond the car park Trevor could see a shoal of dolphins leaping in and out of the sea and diving through tall breakers. Then he noticed a tall, dishevelled man, who looked foreign, hanging around behind him.

'Oops! Here we go,' he murmured, examining his rival critically. The man was tall and appeared to be skinny, but Trevor, a trained boxer, knew he was tough and sinewy, a typical rough kid from a bad neighbourhood, with plenty of streetfighting behind him, his cheeks already deeply furrowed. His blue eyes, deepset in his long bony face, were bloodshot and he blinked rapidly all the time. Tension, Trevor guessed.

The man halted. 'I've been waiting for you,' he said.

Trevor was expecting a fight and he sized the other man up carefully. His opponent looked as if he would stop at nothing. He's been through the mill in Hungary and he doesn't mind pain, Trevor decided, realising that a quick knockout using his professional boxing skill was the best he could hope for. If he got badly mauled, so be it. Too bad if he got a hiding.

'What do you want? If you want a job, try personnel.'

'Fuck you, Palma. You know who I am, Rose's fiancé.'

His soft voice did not deceive Trevor. Here stood a dangerous man.

'I was told she'd broken off with you. Or so she said yesterday. Didn't you threaten her?'

'Threaten her?'

That seemed to knock him off-balance. Trevor glanced at his watch impatiently. 'What can I do for you, Mr . . . er . . . ?'

'I came to tell you something, Palma.' He peered at Trevor deceptively mildly, but Trevor saw the steel underneath the calm. 'I don't have a weapon with me today, but I do have the guts to kill you. I just want to let you know.'

Trevor's eyes shone with amusement. 'You're warning me of your intent to kill me? That's a punishable offence.'

'I don't want you to have any false ideas about Rosie. We're engaged, but we never made love. I respect her. She's a lovely girl.'

'She is,' Trevor agreed cautiously.

'What exactly are your feelings towards her?'

'None of your damned business. Now if you'll excuse me . . .'

'I want you to know that I intend to keep my eyes on her.'

'I must compliment you on coping with English idioms. Almost right,' Trevor said. What the hell was he doing standing on one leg swopping foolish remarks with this oaf? Perhaps I should just swipe him, sort of break the ice, he thought.

'I never fight,' Jânek said, as if reading his mind. 'I only kill. Believe me, Mr Palma, I shall kill you if you hurt my Rosie.'

'*Your* Rosie? Altogether wrong, old boy. You need to get up to date.' He was deliberately taunting him, longing for an excuse to hit him. A couple of good punches might see the back of him.

'I want Rosie to be happy. If you're the best man for her, then good luck to you. But if you harm her then . . .'

'Don't threaten me, or I'll have you deported. I can have you deported, I hope you realise that.'

'Do you love her?'

Somehow the very earnestness of this troubled Hungarian stopped him from being trite. 'Yes, I love her,' he said. 'I intend to marry her, but she doesn't know that yet. You see, she doesn't know me very well. I was hoping we could be friends first.'

The fool looked happy. Damn him! How could he be so unselfish? He'd lost out to superior cash, worldliness and power. Trevor felt sorry for him. 'She's so lovely, you see,' he found himself explaining. 'A rare jewel seldom seen.'

'She's also a person. Tell me, do you always buy your women, Mr Palma?'

Trevor felt annoyed with himself for confiding in this cretin. He grimaced. 'Only when they're so exquisite.'

'If you think you can corrupt her with your wealth and your worldliness, just remember I'll be waiting one night on a dark corner.' His face was deadly white and he was shaking badly.

Despite his intention to remain calm, Trevor was fast losing his temper. He dropped his case and took a step forward, lifting his fist to punch hard at a face to which he had taken an intense dislike. Jânek backed off.

'I told you, I never fight,' he said. 'Waste of time. Nothing's ever solved by fighting. Now killing, that's another matter.'

So much for hairy Hungarians, Trevor thought, as the tall figure loped off across the car park.

*   *   *

To Claire, Trevor's sudden invitation to lunch was a godsend. She had to talk to him, but she had felt unwilling to contact him first. For once in her life she was at a disadvantage. But why hadn't he called?

His reassuring smile went a long way to dispelling her tension when they met. 'It's good to see you again, Claire, you look well,' he said. Then he frowned. 'Well, maybe a bit pale. You should get some sun.

'We must have a slap-up meal to make up for the past three weeks I haven't seen you. What are you doing with yourself nowadays?'

They ate oysters, calamari, grilled crayfish and prawns in a superb mixed platter with ice-cold green Portuguese wine and garlic bread. What a feast! Claire tucked in, only too happy to take her mind off her problems for a brief respite. She was pregnant, she feared. She had made an appointment with her doctor, but he had said it was too early to tell. Nevertheless, she had missed her period and she was usually so regular. First thing in the morning she felt sick, but it passed and later her appetite was gargantuan. All she wanted was Trevor's reassurance. Just to know that if the worst came to the worst he'd make an honest woman of her. Of course, neither of them wanted to marry so young, but what else could they do?

Claire was halfway through her meal, talking about the holiday they had had in Greece, remembering the good times and drowsy from the wine, when Trevor picked up his glass.

'To you and me, Claire. We've had some great times together. We're the closest of friends, wouldn't you say that? I hope and believe we'll stay best friends forever.'

'Of course,' she said, her eyes glowing with trust and affection.

'But, Trevor . . .'

'I know it's not what our parents had planned, but we always intended to live our own lives. Claire, dearest, I've fallen in love and I want you to be the first to know. I hope to introduce Rose to you soon. I know you will love her. She's the most beautiful woman I've ever seen, excepting present company, of course.'

Claire tried to smile, but her face seemed to have frozen. Her ears were singing, her lips could hardly move. What could she say? How could she tell him now?

From then on, Claire's lunch was a nightmare as she talked too fast and too loud about nothing in particular and all the time she was thinking: so that's why I haven't seen him. Damn him! What the hell am I going to do? A wave of loneliness and humiliation swept through her, making her feel sick. She had never thought she would ever lose him. For the first time she realised that she had always loved him and that she was losing something infinitely precious.

Later, somehow, Trevor took her over-bright chatter for acquiescence. He put a hand over hers. 'Thanks, Claire,' he said.

Thanks for what? For being the biggest sucker in the world? She pulled her hand away too violently and knocked over her glass. It rolled and smashed on the floor. A few heads turned as she jumped to her feet and grabbed her bag.

She fled, but Trevor came running after her.

'Claire, darling, I never guessed you cared,' he bleated. 'Forgive me. If I'd known, I would have acted differently, but didn't we always say . . . I mean, we talked about it often enough.'

'Get lost, Trevor,' she said. She ran to her car and drove off, blinded by tears, but not as blind as that idiot, she thought, the silly fool. He was still waving from the middle of the car park. Why couldn't he have guessed? What would her parents say? 'Oh God help me,' she whispered.

Chapter 40

——— ———

Paradise Island was well named, Rose thought, lying on the hot sand, feeling it warm her belly and thighs, her face cushioned on her arms. It was dusk, but the soft wind was warm and the sand seemed to have trapped the sun's heat. Yet another perfect day was almost over. Only four left! She shivered, wishing she could stay forever. Her holiday with Trevor had been the happiest time of her life. Had she ever truly known happiness before? she wondered.

'I could sleep the night here,' she murmured.

'Let's! I'll get them to send down supper.' Trevor was half asleep, too, as he sprawled on the sand, his deep voice muffled in his towel. He sat up, stretched and groaned. 'I'm sunburnt. What d'you fancy, fish, fish or fish?'

'Fish,' she giggled.

She lay in the sand thinking about their fabulous trip. She had never dreamed people lived like this. They had flown to Mozambique in the company's private aircraft, and been met there by the hotel's driver who took them on a tour of Lourenço Marques, before returning to the Polana Hotel. Total luxury awaited them there with a suite of two bedrooms and a huge lounge and balcony overlooking the esplanade and the sea. They were treated like visiting royalty, nothing was too much trouble.

Each morning the Portuguese traders and fishing fleet owners, pompous and fat, with flashing teeth and rings, had arrived to ply their wares to Trevor, who treated them to late champagne breakfasts before unravelling their costs, and adjusting their prices. His mind was as sharp as a razor, she discovered, and he was tough and decisive. His calculations were finished while they were still comparing costs and profit ratios and bemoaning the hard bargains he made. The deals were struck, signed and witnessed on the spot.

After that they explored Lourenço Marques, eating peri-peri chicken in picturesque cafés, returning for the afternoon siesta before swimming in the pool. Nights had been spent exploring the cobbled downtown dock area, where beautiful women sang fado, and dark-skinned whores lingered in alleyways. Four days later they had taken a launch to Paradise Island and from then on she had almost lost track of time as they swam and slept in the sun and swam again, dined on prawns, langoustines, lobster and spicy fish, and drank too much ice-cold Portuguese wine. How could she ever return to normal life after this? she wondered.

The food arrived in picnic hampers and Trevor spread the cloth and filled her plate with shellfish, avocados and tomatoes set on a bed of spicy rice. She sat up abruptly, trying to throw off a surge of depression that had penetrated her defences. She sipped her dry, ice-cold wine and felt it surging into her bloodstream, making her toes tingle.

'I feel so useless,' she blurted out. 'I've done nothing for days. I'm just a cricket watching the ant work. When winter comes I'll die.'

His eyes mocked her. 'What would you like to do? Your wish is my command, oh mistress.'

You're never serious. What's going on? Why are we so close and yet so far apart? she longed to ask. If only she could understand him. Her questions were tormenting her, but she bit them back and hung on to her composure, but two more glasses of wine loosened her tongue. 'What do you want of me?' She blurted out her most secret question and then stopped, her mouth slightly open, a look of horror in her eyes. 'It was the wine talking,' she said. 'I'm drunk. Forget it.'

'The answer to your question,' he said, speaking slowly and deliberately, 'is that I'm hoping you will love me.'

'And then?'

'And then I shall woo you, and make passionate love to you, and eventually marry you.'

She flushed and sipped her wine, watching him broodingly over the glass. It was his wealth that stood between them. Lately guilt had been added to her muddled emotions. Mother intended that she should marry Trevor. She flushed when she remembered her mother's last-minute advice. 'Come back engaged or pregnant – the one's as good as the other.' Would making love bring them closer? She loved him, but a part of her rebelled against belonging. How could she explain this? Why be scared? she asked herself. But she could not stop trembling. She reached behind her back and unfasted the clip so that her floral bra top fell down and her breasts sagged slightly to their normal pear shape, but tonight her nipples were swollen and big. She could feel her cheeks flushing as she clasped her glass at breast level obscuring his view.

One eyebrow lifted, his lips curled into an uncertain smile. 'Just like that,' he said. 'This time you took me by surprise. You see, Rose, you are so vulnerable, but you have this one weapon, you are utterly beautiful. By far the

most beautiful woman I've ever seen. I crave beauty. I long
for you to be mine. I want you to be there every morning
when I wake, and at night when I sleep, so that I can look
at you. This is wrong. Underneath all that beauty is a real
woman. I have to find you, Rose, I have to get to know you.
Hence this trip. I could never be like a small boy that pulls
the petals off a rose and abandons it.'

Rose trembled, for a part of her realised that he would be
this small boy and her petals would fall. But she had to hang
on to this wonderful new world she had seen so briefly.

'Make love to me. I want us to be close. You see, I am
so lonely.'

Why did he sit there watching her, his cynical smile
hovering. He seemed to see right through her.

She flushed. Bending over she grabbed a crayfish and bit
into it, but the garlic butter ran down her chin and neck and
trickled along her right breast right to the tip of her nipple.
Oh, how embarrassing! She grabbed a paper napkin, but
Trevor caught her hand. He pushed his mouth over her
nipple and sucked and then licked the butter away. 'Hm!
The most delicious young lady, but even better garnished
in garlic sauce,' he said.

Swords of painful pleasure were assaulting her everywhere, in her breasts, her belly and her groin. She could not
cope with such an excess of strange new feelings. Dropping
the lobster, she clenched her fists and screwed up her eyes.
Oh God. Is this what it's like? Help me. Do something.

Her skin was salty to taste, he found, as he ran his lips
over her body. She moaned gently. How fragile she looked.
She was too lovely to be human, yet he sensed an acquisitive
nature under all this abundance of loveliness. He should
have stuck to his intention to find the real girl and discover
what sort of person she was. It was not too late.

Why was he hesitating? Rose wondered. She longed for the closeness that would bind them. 'Oh, oh,' she sighed. 'Oh, Trevor. Please.'

She lay back on the sand and moments later heard him whisper: 'So be it, Rose.'

He made love tenderly, wooing her gently, sending her to heights of pleasure she had never known existed. Later when she lay on his shoulder, complete and satisfied, and filled with a pleasant, fulfilled drowsiness, she whispered: 'I never dreamed it could be like that, so beautiful, so meaningful. Surely we could never be closer than we are now. I feel bonded, don't you?'

The wind rustled the palm leaves, the waves splashed gently on the sand, a sea bird called and from far off came the strains of romantic music, but from Trevor there was no reply.

Angelo Palma had taken to bird watching, the villagers said, or hiking, or maybe he just liked walking his Rhodesian ridgeback dog. Afternoons and evenings he drove to one of the many viewing sites, parked, and set off along a mountain track, returning at dusk.

It was autumn. Proteas stained the slopes pink, yellow and orange, wild flowering beans climbed amongst the shrubs and the veld was full of the scent of wild rosemary, aloes and lilies. Hundreds of varieties of bright daisies flowered amongst the grass, and sunbirds darted from proteas to bottlebrush, and hopped into the sweet pea trees.

Angelo kept his motives to himself. He didn't want some smart-arsed estate agent buying up the land he favoured. At last he had found the place for which he had searched for months. It was strangely situated in no-man's land, halfway between the coloured and the white areas. Strictly speaking it was a nature reserve, as all the mountain slopes were, but he felt sure he could obtain the land by one means or another. There were hundreds of varieties of wild flowers, the most beautiful and massive proteas, and the birds were so numerous your head reverberated with their song.

More important, to Angelo, was the view. It was the only place in Silver Bay from where he could see his new fishing trawlers, his yacht anchored in the marina, his vineyards, the du Toits' land and home, which he and Trevor would soon be leaving, the canning and freezing factories and the entire curved valley. He could see the broad river snaking its way down the valley, through the flat farmlands and cutting through the village, spreading to a delta in the marshy swamps, half of which he owned, and where Steyn du Toit had once built a beach cottage for seaside holidays. On his left were massive sand dunes, blown up from the beach by thousands of years of wind, to spread right over the mountain neck and down to Oudebaai below. For a while he had considered building his manor right on top of the ridge, but a few minutes in a howling sandstorm soon changed his mind.

This plateau on the mountainside was the perfect site. He sat down and gazed over the valley, admiring the panoramic vistas, imagining himself in his own study, just about three floors above the rock he sat on. It was perfect. His arms came out in goose pimples as he considered his massive architectural dream. He would reproduce his old Spoleto home in exact detail. Already architects had been sent over to study the villa where his mother still lived. One day that, too, would be his, and he would sell it, for he would never return to Europe. This was his home.

After a while his thoughts turned to Trevor. How disappointing children could be. The entire village was gossiping about his son's very public affair with Ramona's daughter. If he favoured darker flesh, why the hell must he involve both the family and the business? God knew the boy had done brilliantly at university. He seemed to have some sort of a genius intelligence, yet commonsense was entirely lacking.

He would have to speak to him, but he hated to quarrel because his son had been away for so long. Perhaps that was the problem. Overseas there were different views about racialism. Here the authorities were frenziedly keeping the races apart and God help those who fell foul of the law. If Trevor were caught in a compromising situation with his girl, six months hard labour and cuts would be the minimum penalty. Yes, he must point out the facts of life to Trevor, he decided, and for once he must be really firm. He felt heavy with sadness about the coming confrontation as he made his way back to his car.

The discussion, which took place on the balcony where they were eating dinner, became a heated fight within minutes.

'I don't understand you, Trevor.' Angelo realised he was shouting and made an effort to calm down. 'If you can't consider your own safety, what about hers? They'll put her inside for years and when she comes out, if she comes out, you won't recognise her. Is that what you want?'

Trevor turned pale. 'I don't have to stay here. I can earn my living anywhere. I've proved that much at least.'

The fool! Angelo felt he'd explode with pent-up anger. He wanted to punch him, and he nearly did. He'd always been a good boy, seldom needing disciplining, and now he'd gone overboard for some coloured girl. Angelo had not seen Rose for many years, but he had heard she looked like Ramona once did.

At that moment it seemed that all the cash he had pumped into the boy was quite wasted. Was there no gratitude for what he had done? 'If you walk out on me and all that I've built up, I'll remarry and disinherit you,' he said. The boy flinched as if he'd been struck. Those green eyes took on a mulish expression he remembered so well from Pippa. 'Do as you feel best. It's your fortune,' the boy said.

Damn him! Perhaps he would, too.

Angelo was slightly ashamed of his own lack of self-discipline, for he had fallen madly in love with Anne Marais from across the valley, and lately his feelings had developed into a haunting need. She was the blonde he had always coveted. Her father, who had died a year back, had once been the lighthouse keeper, until it became defunct when they set up a better beacon on the mountain towering over the bay. Anne had received a good education and become a teacher at the local school. There was no denying her beauty, but she was sixteen years younger than he and this worried him. Did the years matter? he wondered. He was as fit as he could be. They were close friends, but he had hesitated in proposing. After all, he had Trevor to consider, too.

I've always put him first, but he hasn't once thought of what this liaison of his would do to me. Was he bewitched? He had always been obsessed with running the factories and estates. Suddenly all their dreams and hopes were to be thrown aside because of a woman. It didn't make sense.

'Listen, I love you, Father,' Trevor said, his eyes filling with tears. 'I always shall, but I love her too. You can't expect to live my life for me. Of course I can make my own way in the world. I've had a marvellous education, thanks to you, but this is my life, and in a way Rose is part of my life, too.'

Unable to control himself, Angelo leaped up. Knocking his chair over, he flung open the door. Ramona jumped back. Had she been listening?

'Oh, hello,' he grunted. He hurried outside and collapsed on the chair by the pool, taking great gulping gasps of fresh air. Since he'd dismantled the conservatory, they had a lovely view over the valley to the sea.

He soon began to feel better and his problems less ominous. The boy would grow out of this silly infatuation. He began to think about Anne. He knew she was wondering why he held back. Part of the reason was their age difference. Yet he could still jog five miles and climb the mountains without difficulty, he could put in a sixteen-hour work day and still play squash at night, beating most of the younger men, so what more could she want? Perhaps he should make love to her. He knew that she wanted him to, she clung to him, hung on to his kisses, sat close beside him in steamy petting sessions, wore lowcut dresses – he knew all the signs. He'd held back for only one reason – Trevor. She would be bound to want children and how would Trevor cope with sharing his inheritance?

'Miss Marais just called,' Ramona said, approaching from the shadows. 'She rang off. She asked you to go over . . . something important. She said it was urgent.'

Strange! She was so formal, her many invitations offered days in advance. Perhaps something was wrong.

When he drove to her little hillside cottage on the other side of the bay, he saw that the house was in darkness and the gate shut. He rang, but there was no answer.

Various emergencies flitted through his mind. Perhaps she'd been burgled and locked herself in somewhere. After ringing once more, he grabbed his torch from the car, climbed over the tall, wrought-iron fence and crept up the driveway. Then he heard a strange noise, something like a groan. He began to sprint towards the sound which was coming from the summer house overlooking the fish pond. 'Oh God, let her be all right,' he prayed. He suddenly realised how much he loved her.

There was that groan again and it raised the hairs on his arm. What would he find? There was a long iron pole lying near the door and he grabbed that. Smashing the door open with his foot he charged in, stick in hand, sending the powerful torch beam around the room.

'Anne, darling, where are you?' he yelled.

Oh God! A swift glance took it all in. Mike Russell, the out-of-work journalist whom he'd met twice and detested, was wearing a pair of black socks with suspenders and that was all. He looked like some slimy creature that had crawled out of the sea. Anne was entirely naked. He had a brief vision of her open mouth and startled eyes. Then he switched off his torch.

'Forgive me,' he growled. 'I got a message that you wanted to see me urgently. When I saw the house was in darkness, I thought you might have been burgled. I heard the groans . . .'

His voice broke off into a deep sob.

'Goodbye, Anne.'

'No . . . no . . . Oh God! Oh, Angelo, I'm sorry . . .'

The last thing he heard were her sobs.

Chapter 41

——— ———

Angelo sat in his car gazing ahead blankly, all his senses revolting at his vision of white flesh and the stench of another man's semen. She'd said she loved him. What a bitch! He would never forget her shocked, wide eyes. One thing was sure, she hadn't called him. Had Ramona set him up? And why? To warn him? If so, she had done him a favour.

He started his car and drove slowly through the streets, not caring where he was going, but knowing he could not stay there, and he could not face Ramona's eyes either. Not yet! What a fool he'd been! He wanted to cry, but he could not. His hurt was almost unbearable. She was a whore and as such not worth a moment's pain, he told himself. He refused to suffer like this. To hell with her. With a massive effort he forced his mind away from Anne forever. Letting go was painful, but ten minutes later he had himself back under control.

Poor Claire! For the first time he wondered if she were suffering over Trevor's affair with Rose. He decided to have a drink with Claire's father and find out how the land lay between their two offspring.

The first thing he noticed when he was shown into their hideous pink living room he so despised, was the air of tension and unhappiness. Tessa, Claire's mother, who was always so overdressed, looked bedraggled. She nodded coldly without really looking at him, her pale grey eyes glittering behind diamanté spectacles. Harold, his nose redder and shinier than usual, his bald head gleaming to match, shook his pendulous jowls and looked embarrassed. 'You must excuse Tessa. She's upset, but it's silly of her to hold you responsible.'

'For what?'

'Claire's pregnant. Perhaps you hadn't heard. She's been very ill. Terrible business. She cut her wrists, but we found her in time.' He shuddered. 'We went out to the ballet, she was supposed to come, too, but she made some excuse to stay home. When we got back we found her lying on the bathroom floor, white as a sheet, blood everywhere, and she was having convulsions. Jesus! I tell you, Angelo, I wouldn't like to live through that night again. We called the ambulance and the police and the doctor. He said he couldn't do a thing because it was a job for casualty. Half an hour later we were still waiting for the ambulance. Tessa began to perform, so the doctor made a bed in the police van and gave them permission to take her to casualty. Thank God we returned in time. The doctor said she wasn't all that badly hurt, it was more of a plea for help than a serious attempt to kill herself. I don't understand them. I tell you, she was having convulsions. Horrible. I thought I'd lost my little girl.'

To Angelo's horror, Harold began to sob. He patted his shoulder awkwardly. There was a faint smell of ether around, which always bothered Angelo, and the family's depression seemed to hang in the air like a bad smell.

'Does Trevor know?'

'She won't let us tell him. She'll never forgive me for telling you.'

'Sometimes we have to take a stand, Harold. This is one of those times. They think they're grown-up, but they're behaving foolishly . . . both of them. I'm so sorry. What else can I say? I'll speak to Trevor and of course they must marry at once.'

'It's not so easy,' Harold said gloomily. 'Come and have a drink.' Harold took his arm and pulled him towards the bar. 'Let's drown our sorrows.' He'd been doing too much of that by the look of things, Angelo thought, as he allowed himself to be pushed into the newly converted annexe, which presumably was Tessa's concept of a man's bar. He shuddered at the toby jugs and brass ornaments, tossed off his neat Scotch and left as soon as he could.

Harold followed him to the door. 'Honestly, Angelo, you think that when they've reached twenty your troubles will be over, but it seems they're just beginning. How could she cheapen herself so badly? I thought she was a virgin, but there's ways and means of preventing these things. I mean, she has a degree. She's not a fool. How could she do this to us?'

'I blame Trevor. We'd all assumed they'd marry soon and I expect Claire did, too. I'll speak to him. He must come to his senses. Don't worry. I shall force him to marry her.'

'Yes, thanks, Angelo. No one wants a shotgun marriage, but what choice do we have? She said something else, too. It seems that she discovered that she loved Trevor and went to lunch with him to tell him she was pregnant, but he spent all lunchtime talking about this Rose and how he wants to marry her. I'm sorry for you, too, my friend. We bring them up decently and this is all the thanks we get.'

*   *   *

Trevor was feeling bruised and misunderstood after a terrible fight with his father and now he was racing over to Claire. 'For God's sake,' he muttered several times. He certainly wasn't going to be branded with the names Angelo had dug up from some bad Victorian novel.

He found Claire sitting in the sun reading a book. Most of her face was hidden by huge sunglasses, a floppy hat and a scarf over it. Both of her hands and arms were bandaged and she was having trouble turning the page. He picked up the book and put it aside. Crouching in front of her, he held both her bandaged hands.

'Both of them? Why both?' he asked.

'I wanted to be doubly sure.' She laughed harshly.

'Oh, Claire! Dearest Claire. I'm so sorry. But how could it happen? How could it be possible?'

'The night we went to the opera, I suppose. That's the last time we made love.' She took off her sunglasses and he could see how pale she was, and how the deep shadows under her eyes almost disfigured her face.

'But that wasn't long ago. Are you sure?'

'I'm six weeks overdue and the pregnancy test came up positive.' She tried to smother a sob and it turned into a hiccup.

'Dearest Claire. But even if I'd known, we were never engaged, we never spoke about marriage. I have promised to marry Rose,' he blurted out after a long and painful silence. 'I love her very dearly. I can't let her down.'

'And me? Damn you, Trevor!' She began to cry softly.

Trevor stood up and paced up and down, feeling trapped. 'But, Claire, you never loved me. You always said you didn't. I mean, we've been going out on and off for the past four years and we've often laughed at our parents' plans for us.'

'I only realised when . . . I mean afterwards . . . Oh hell! What a terrible mess.'

'I don't believe that you love me at all. You've just got some sort of a personality change because you're pregnant. You're broody, that's all it is. Let's go to London, Claire. We'll go together, find the best specialist, arrange for an abortion and then go on holiday. By the time we return, it will all have blown over and no one will ever know.'

'If that's what you want, then I accept,' she said.

He frowned at her hopeless tone of voice and her bleak eyes. Poor little thing. But there was Rose to consider and his promises to her. 'I feel a heel, Claire, both to you and to Rose. The truth is, I feel guilty towards both of you. Let's get this over and done with as soon as we can.'

It was starting to sleet in London, but the discreet rooms of the Harley Street specialist were warm and bright with out-of-season flowers. Trevor waited impatiently while Claire was being examined. He was worried about Claire and tense with misery at what had to be done, but there was no alternative open to them.

He and Claire had not been able to leave at once. First they had to wait for her to recover, for she had lost so much blood, and by then it was time for the annual fishmeal conference, held in South America this year, where he was giving a marketing talk. So a month had been lost. Last week they had flown to Paris and done a few shows and spent a few days trying to brighten their lives before tackling this awful thing, which they both tried not to refer to.

His mind switched back to Rose. Before leaving home, he had bought her the best diamond and sapphire engagement ring he could find at short notice. He had visited her in the Septembers' little house overlooking the harbour, and the rest of the family had tactfully cleared off, leaving them the tiny sitting room.

'Which would you like first, the good news or the bad news?' he had oafishly said and only moments later thought how crass it was to assume that his proposal was a godsend. So he had quickly altered his good news to tell her about the huge contract he'd been offered for their fishmeal, the bad news was his overseas trip, and at the end of it he had produced the ring.

Something about his manner had been wrong, for she had frowned. 'Marry me, Rose. We'll have to go abroad for the ceremony and apply for permission to live here, but it might take a while, so in the meantime let's get engaged.'

He reckoned that could go in the *Guinness Book of Records* as the worst-ever proposal. She had put on the ring and told her mother, who had called in the neighbours, which had been awful. Why was Rose so different from the rest of them? Was it because of her smart boarding school? They had escaped from the noisy crew and walked to the company park and sat there watching the children on the swings.

'I have something very important to tell you, darling,' she had said, 'but the news must keep until you return. Hurry back. I'll miss you so much.'

He could still picture her beautiful, glittering amber eyes, so soft, so full of humour and compassion, clever eyes, wise eyes. To Trevor she was like Eve, all women rolled into one. He was counting the days impatiently until he returned.

He was startled out of his daydreams when the nurse answered her intercom, stood up and told him the specialist wanted to see him. Trevor quivered with distaste. This was not part of the bargain. He was merely the driver in this little exercise.

The doctor was overweight and looked like a butcher and Trevor squirmed slightly on Claire's behalf. He stood up, thrust his hands into the pockets of his white overall, and assumed a patronising air. 'Young man, our plans don't always work out as we might wish,' he began without any preamble. 'If they did, I expect the human race would have become extinct long ago. This young baby intends to be born, it seems. You can't blame your Claire. She was wearing a diaphragm with cream, and she made a point of never having sex on those days when she thought she could be impregnated, but Nature has all sorts of tricks to combat man's feeble attempts to foil her. The point is, it's too late for an abortion. Claire is not strong, far from it, and her life would be at risk. Besides, the baby is well formed by this stage. Just look here!' He switched on a light and lit up a panel in the wall and they were treated to a series of slides on the development of the foetus. Trevor began to feel like a murderer and very nauseous.

'Fate has played a role and you must make the best of it. Claire tells me that you are engaged to someone else. Well, you must have felt strongly about this young lady to impregnate her in the first place. You've been friends for years, your parents wish you to marry. Do the right thing, young man, or you'll live to regret it. Even in the sixties the slur of being an unmarried mother is very unpleasant.'

Trevor was so dazed he hardly knew how he got out of there.

'This is all I can offer, Claire,' he said wearily in the taxi. 'I will marry you now if you agree to stay on here in England, or France, or any damn place you like. I'll buy you a house and supply you with plenty of cash. Thank God money isn't a problem. You must understand that I have other plans for my future. In a nutshell, I still love

Rose. After the child is born we'll divorce. I'll work out acceptable terms of settlement and then I must be free and you must promise me not to return to South Africa until we are divorced.'

Looking at Trevor, Claire knew that she had lost something infinitely precious and dear to her. Why had it taken her so long to realise how much she loved him? She didn't even have a photograph, but she felt that the image of his clever, caring face with his slanting green eyes, his frizzy, light-brown hair, his long and bony face, would be imprinted in her mind forever. Would she ever see him again?

She agreed tearfully to his terms and they were married the following morning. Trevor transferred a large capital sum from his South American holdings and engaged a lawyer to look after the legal and financial details. He left the following day.

On the plane home, Trevor hit on a plan which he thought might work. He would apply for Rose's reclassification as a white. He was pretty sure that this could be achieved with a little bribery, but it would take time, maybe years, and time was what he needed the most. The application would meander through a morass of red tape. She would need letters from her doctor stating that she looked white, testimonials from school friends stating that she had always associated with whites, and so on . . . The demands were endless and it would give him a chance to divorce Claire after the birth of their child.

Meantime, he would get his lawyer to draw up a legal document similar to a marriage contract. Ramona would have to be satisfied with that. He would find a quiet house, hidden from view, and Rose and he would live together without any interference from the outside world.

Oh how he longed to be with her. He could not wait to reach Cape Town.

It was raining, which was all wrong for March. Trevor, followed by his grumbling architect, was tramping through the marshes, taking a circuitous route around the old lagoonside house. Trevor was throwing instructions over his shoulder, but the architect kept losing his footing and swearing softly as he slipped in the mud. Trevor's eyes were shining, his face glowed and he was oblivious to the rain as he visualised a lodge-type home with a thatched roof, and a huge double bedroom overlooking willow trees trailing their fronds into the lagoon under an azure sky.

'White paint, black beams, Tudorlike . . . you get me?' he snapped. 'All the trimmings, rambling roses, that sort of thing. Knock down all the ground-floor walls, make one huge living room, chintzy furniture, antique tables, oh yes, and an antique writing desk in one corner. D'you get me?'

He listed his demands, cajoling, bullying, bribing, threatening.

'Hold it, Trevor,' the architect moaned. 'Just come here. Stand here! Now take a long hard look at this place. What d'you see? A broken-down shack. Right! So be reasonable. As for willow trees and bougainvilleas trailing through the windows – maybe in twenty years time . . .'

'Dig some up and move them. Hire a crane. Get the best horticulturalists in town. I haven't got twenty years and neither have you. Twenty days is more like it. Get two building teams and work them round the clock.'

'Impossible,' the architect snapped.

'Do it,' Trevor insisted.

Would she come here? Would she live with him as his

wife, hidden away amongst rushes and reeds and thick glades of mimosa and milkwoods, sheltered from prying eyes? Would she? Trevor felt he would die if she said no. But he couldn't shake off a premonition of doom. He had been tossed headfirst into a world of lying and deceit and this bothered him. He had no talent for it. The best thing he could do was play a waiting game and hope to hang on to Rose until he was safely divorced. Nothing else mattered. He was obsessed with Rose.

A month later he took Rose to see the house. She fell in love with 'Willow Lodge' as soon as she set eyes on it. The two wandered through half-finished grounds and gardens, sharing dreams and necking like two lovebirds. Trevor felt he would burst with happiness.

Chapter 42

In her Kentish garden, Claire was pulling out weeds. Strange that the weeds were familiar to her, yet the birds and some of the flowers were completely different, she thought. English birds sang so much more sweetly than the birds at home, and the spring flowers were lovely, but at that moment she would have given anything to see the brilliant flash of a sunbird, or the darting yellow white-eyes, or a sugarbird trailing its kitelike tail. Oh for the call of a *piet-my-vrou*, or the haunting warble of a rock dove.

She stabbed at the weeds' roots in temper. The truth was she was homesick and lonely, and very angry. How had she got into this mess? She often toyed with the idea of begging her parents to stay with her. They knew nothing of her bargain with Trevor. She had simply written to say that she had left him and preferred to live overseas until her baby was born. How could she tell them the truth?

It was six weeks since Trevor had flown home and she missed him so much. His lawyer had helped her to find the right house, settled all bills, and each month he sent her a generous allowance, but right now she needed love more than she needed cash.

She sighed and stood up. As she did so she felt a strange stirring of life inside her. It was a new feeling, rather like butterfly wings fluttering in the depths of her womb. For a full four seconds she stood entranced.

At that moment Claire's baby became real to her for the first time. She pictured him as a miniature version of Trevor, for she knew he was a boy. She walked inside and sat down gently, hands pressed upon her thickening belly, thinking deeply of her present sterile life and her son's future. She realised that she had been wrong to agree to Trevor's harsh and unnatural terms. She had no right to deprive her child of his father. She had accepted a bargain which was bitterly harmful to him.

From then on her baby became a real being, a separate person, someone she must love and protect. As the days passed she realised that she must break the promise Trevor had forced on her.

She felt amazed by the strength of her new resolve. Claire had never fought for anything in her life, being satisfied with whatever fate sent her way, but now she had someone more important than herself to fend for, and she would give her life if need be for his rights. He had the right to a father, a proper home and family, his own country, a place in the sun.

The following day, she put the house in her lawyer's hands and booked a passage home.

It was a lovely, late-summer day in April and Claire experienced a sense of deep joy as she looked around. To feel the warmth, to see the mountains, to experience the space, to breathe the crisp, sparkling seaside air was like heaven.

No one expected her, so she retrieved her luggage and took a taxi. Should she go home to her parents? No, she reasoned. She would go straight to Trevor's home and demand that the family accept her and her son.

The moment she saw Angelo she realised she had a formidable ally. He grabbed her, swung her round, hugged her and, one arm round her, drew her inside. 'Dearest, dearest Claire. Where have you been hiding? I've been longing to see you. And my grandson, how's he doing?'

'He's here, safe and sound. I often feel him moving, Mr Palma.'

'Papa, Papa, please, Claire.'

'Having Trevor's son has given me so much courage,' she told him. 'I have broken my promise to Trevor. I want to tell you about it. Perhaps you can advise me. I've been so lonely.'

Her story poured out and without meaning to she found herself sobbing on Angelo's shoulder.

'We'll have to be clever,' he said eventually. 'And we'll have to be strong. Can you be strong?'

She nodded. 'For my child I can do anything.'

'So we'll enter the world of fantasy, my dear, and we'll wait for the storm to erupt around us.'

Three days later Trevor was checking the mail when the receptionist brought in the newspaper with his coffee. He scanned the business pages casually, but suddenly his attention was riveted on a picture. 'Good God, it's Claire,' he muttered.

He skimmed through the caption: 'One of the distinguished VIPs aboard the new British luxury liner which docked today was society hostess Mrs Claire Palma, who returned to South Africa from Britain by ship for health reasons. Mrs Palma, who is expecting a baby, said that she had been resting in a clinic for some weeks. "It's great to have her back," her father-in-law, Mr Angelo Palma, said.'

Ten minutes later, Trevor stormed into his home and came face to face with Ramona. 'Where are they?' he snapped.

The hatred in her eyes was awesome as she gestured to the office.

'I can explain,' he muttered. 'I will see you later.'

'White people don't explain to their housekeepers,' she said. Her eyes had gone curiously blank. She looked weird, he thought. Dismissing her from his mind, he rushed into the living room.

Ramona watched him slam the door shut and then walked swiftly to it. Peering through the keyhole, she listened carefully.

'Damn you, Claire. We had a bargain. I kept my side of it. I've always been honest with you. I never denied that I love Rose, I married you to give your baby a name.'

'Our baby, Trevor,' Claire said so softly Ramona could hardly hear.

Trevor was shouting with frustration. 'We had a deal. You promised.'

'Pull yourself together.' Angelo's voice was as hard as a diamond edge. 'We are Catholics and I won't allow you to divorce Claire and neither will she. You will never marry Rose, I promise you that. It is *this* marriage that will endure, not your silly fling with a half-caste girl. Forget your mistress, buy her off your back. You have to think of your son now. I'm leaving you two alone. You've never been a cruel man, Trevor. Look at her! Can't you see what you've done to her? Now sort something out.'

Outside the door, Ramona cursed Angelo. 'I should have left you to drown at sea, you two-faced, perfidious monster,' she whispered. She hurried outside, too tense to endure another word.

'How could you do this to me, Claire?' Trevor asked softly. 'I gave you everything you asked for. What more do you want?'

She looked up, sad and forlorn, but with a new determination in her eyes, which he could not mistake. 'I'm here for him. I'm here because you are his father, this is his home, and Papa is his grandfather.' She spread her hands protectively over her belly. 'I love you, but I love him more. I would kill for him.'

Despite his anger, Trevor was filled with compassion. She was like a timid cat which turns into a leopard when her young are threatened. What courage had it taken to come back all alone, to fight for her son? The poor little thing. Clearly she was not well. Just look at her, with her thin pale face, the deep shadows under her eyes, and her hair so lank and dull. He had a sudden strange feeling that they were all playing out their predestined roles in a tragedy from which they could not escape. They were all victims. He crouched beside her and took her hands into his. 'Poor, dear Claire. I meant you no harm. I understand you and I forgive you. The truth is, I admire you for your guts. We must work something out – for all of us.'

He took her hands into his and kissed them gently. 'Be patient with me, Claire. I love Rose very dearly, but looking at you now, I realise that I love you, too, and I have made you suffer. I'm sorry, Claire.'

She leaned back slightly, took his hand and placed it over her stomach. 'Feel!' she said. 'Feel here. Your son is moving. He kicks like crazy.'

Trevor felt her stomach gently. It felt like a bird

fluttering under the palm of his hand. 'He moved,' he whispered. 'What have we done? I know I'm going to love him, so help me God.'

Despite his compassion for Claire, his love for Rose was stronger. Trevor packed the remainder of his clothes, cameras, fishing gear, sports equipment and, with all the rest of his personal paraphernalia, he moved into 'Willow Lodge'. Two days later he returned and spent the evening with Claire, but drove off at 11 p.m. He remained at 'Willow Lodge' for the next ten days, but good manners were inbred in Trevor and when he learned that Angelo and Claire were holding a dinner party he returned to be there at Claire's side.

'What the hell am I doing?' he whispered. 'How the hell did I get into this mess?'

Around 10 p.m. he moved to the bar and began to drink neat Scotch steadily. He needed a break from the incredible guilt that dogged his days and nights. When he was with Rose he felt guilty about Angelo and Claire, and when he moved home, he felt guilty about Rose. The tension was getting him down. He passed out at 2 a.m. and woke at eight the next morning to find himself in Claire's bed. She was wearing a blue negligée and she looked quite lovely. He gently laid his head on her belly.

'I'm sure I can hear his heart beating.' He pulled up her nightdress and examined her thickening waist. 'Pregnancy suits you,' he muttered. Despite his intentions, desire surged and she was so desperate for love. He must love both of them, he decided and the thought was strangely comforting.

They made love, gently and confidently, like two close friends, loving the act and each other.

*   *   *

Rose had endured the worst evening and night of her life. For the first time she realised that she wasn't within screaming distance of anyone. She must have a burglar alarm. Finally she barricaded herself into her bedroom and read for most of the night, tortured by her jealousy of Trevor with Claire.

'You look a sight,' Ramona told her daughter when she arrived the following morning. 'We were fools. It's my fault more than yours. Stop crying, for goodness' sake. He's feeling guilty. You must get a date for the divorce. Force him, before it's too late. And make him pay. This house must be in your name. Make him tie up a large capital sum. The more he pays the more valuable you become to him.'

She looked at her daughter with mounting desperation and some bewilderment. She had the second sight and she had never been wrong. *Their seed intermingled, a godlike heir reared in the Palma household – part Angelo's and partly her genes, too.* She'd been shown. How could she be wrong?

Rose tried to stop crying. She sensed that Trevor loved her desperately, but his upbringing and his kindness could not allow him to leave his friend and ex-lover in the lurch. She could not believe that he loved Claire, nor Claire's coming child. She would wait. Things would come right. She would not listen to her mother.

Trevor smelled strongly of liquor when he returned to Rose the following evening. He looked desperate. His eyes were bloodshot, his skin had a greyish tinge. He went straight to the bar and poured himself a drink.

'I don't want to hurt you, Rose,' he muttered. 'You know that I love you, but Claire goes back a long way. She's been my closest friend almost ever since I can remember. We flew over to Britain for an abortion, but it was too late.

I'm sorry I didn't tell you the truth. I was too afraid of losing you.'

This was the third time he had told her his pathetic story. She turned her back on him and stared out of the window at the lagoon which was calm and full of peace. If she could only fall into its depths and be a part of that peace and not have Ramona instructing her and Trevor begging her, and Jânek skulking around the grounds.

'I married her, Rose. I did the honourable thing, but they want more . . . much more.'

Rose sensed that he was lying and turned and stared coldly at him.

'Don't look at me like that.'

'Like what?'

'Like you think I'm lying. All right, I am lying. Oh God, I love you both. I swear to God I love you both desperately, but I love you more.'

'But she is in your home. She has all the security. What do I have?' Now she could see hope dawning in his eyes.

'What do you want? This is our home, isn't it?'

'It should be in my name. That is what I want. I need to feel secure. When you go back to her, I lie awake and wonder what will happen to me.'

She knew she had made a mistake. Why had she listened to her mother? Trevor gave a deep, shuddering sigh and smiled. Now he was on strong ground and his guilt was seeping away. He understood about buying things. He knew how to pay his financial debts. He would set about buying her. Instinctively she knew this, but she could not take back the words.

She was right. The following morning his lawyer telephoned and asked Rose to be at his office at 10 a.m. sharp. Apart from the allowance she received, a large capital sum would be transferred to her name, so she would always have security. The deeds of the house would be transferred to her in the form of shares, since she was not allowed to own property in that area. The land, of course, belonged to the family trust.

In some strange way, the settlement seemed to put their relationship into a well-worn groove. Trevor visited her daily, but never stayed the night. She had become an expensive whore, she sensed.

From then on, shame and bitterness vied with loneliness and a sense of rejection. She was too ashamed to show her face at home in the village. Nowadays he never took her anywhere. He was ashamed of her. All her dreams had crashed. She had nothing left to hope for and she was filled with despair. Weekends were the worst, for he stayed home with his family, and she paced the garden and stared at the dark waters of the lagoon, wondering whether to throw herself in. The time passed agonisingly slowly, but Monday morning would bring Trevor, with a gift. It was always something valuable and they would make love ever more hastily. Then he left for work.

She had to win him back, but how? Sex was her only weapon. She bought outrageous underwear, and she wooed him with her body and her sex, learning to bring him to the height of lust and fulfilment no matter how tired he was. He visited her in the early morning before work, and again at lunchtime. He swore he was not making love to Claire. How could he? He was always quite spent by the time he left 'Willow Lodge'. Claire was enduring a bad pregnancy and hardly noticed if he were there or not, he confided.

To offset her loneliness, Trevor agreed that Rose should share her cottage with a friend. Juliette was happy to move in. Although she was now married to Emanuel, she felt like getting away from him sometimes, she said. From then on, Emanuel was there all the time and he brought his friends and they sat around the lagoon smoking *dagga* and singing. They, in turn, brought their girlfriends along, and every night turned into a party. 'Willow Lodge' echoed with laughter. The dance music blared into the night. A late-summer heatwave warmed the waters of the lagoon, so they enjoyed nude bathing in the moonlight, dancing around a *braai*, and smoking *dagga* while they gulped down gallons of homemade fruit punch, and shared fondues sitting around the embers.

Juliette's sister, Esme, a masseuse, wanted to join them and Rose was so unhappy she agreed, so the girl moved in, scattering shoes, clothes and books around. What difference did it make? The house looked like a slum nowadays and Rose was so unhappy she didn't care. She could endure anything, just as long as she wasn't left alone.

Soon every night the strains of dance music stole across the dunes, cars came and went, the bottlestore delivered daily.

Trevor's love was no longer so intense. She was losing him and this thought made her frantic. She bought more clothes, spent more of her allowance at the beauty parlour and hairdresser, spent hours on her make-up before he arrived.

Trevor was sitting next to Rose by the lagoon, holding her hand, watching the 'goons' . . . his name for the assortment of wealthy young men who fawned over Rose's friends. They were blatantly ignoring the law, and turning his home into a regular nightclub. Or was it a whorehouse? he wondered grudgingly.

He tried to come to grips with his feelings. His obsessional love was still there. If she found another man he would kill her, but if he found Claire with another man, he'd probably have a drink with her and remain her friend. Rose belonged to him, he owned her, she was like a lovely work of art that he had purchased, and lately she had enough curves to look like a Rubens' model, but still he lusted after her all the time. Claire was his friend and there was a strong bond of loyalty based on class, a long-standing friendship and their coming child.

On the whole, everything had worked out pretty well, he thought, all things considered, and he had settled into a pretty good routine. He visited Rose before breakfast, and again at lunchtime, lying in the sun with her and swimming in the lagoon. He left work at five, spent a couple of hours in the gym or sauna, or tennis courts, had dinner at eight and spent the evening with Claire and his father. Sometimes, like tonight, he returned around eleven to join the party. He had the best of both worlds and he had no intention of changing his lifestyle if he could help it. Hidden amongst the willows and milkwoods, this hideaway provided the offbeat amusement to satisfy his Bohemian side.

'Hey, you lazy sod, come and swim,' Emanuel called. 'You were far away – planning some new business coup, I bet. Greedy bastard! Don't you own enough?' He dived into the lagoon.

'Let's swim,' Trevor said to Rose. He took her hand and pulled her to her feet. 'Come on! You don't need a swimsuit.'

Watching her walk naked in public excited him. This marvellous perfection was all his. The heady thrill of ownership raced through him like alcohol in the bloodstream, intoxicating him. Taking her hand, he walked naked down to the lagoon.

A sudden flash alarmed him. 'What the hell was that?' he muttered. It seemed to come from one of the many rushy islands, haunt of birds and water rats. Calling to Emanuel he set off at a fast crawl. Pausing in the middle, he thought he heard the swish of a paddle, but there was no sign of anyone around. He sighed with relief as he pushed through the reeds, but looking down saw a discarded flashbulb lying there. Feeling thoroughly alarmed, he swam back to the shore.

Chapter 43

——— —

Across the lagoon, Mike Russell pulled the canoe into the Marais' shed, locked it, and cut across the fields to Anne's lighthouse, where he was camping out for free until he landed a job. He was broke and becoming desperate, particularly since Anne was getting restless for she wanted to be married. A year back he had given notice to his editor, and used his savings for a year's sabbatical in order to write a book, which had just been turned down by the tenth publisher. He couldn't understand this, since some of the paperbacks he saw in the shops were trash. To cap his disaster, he couldn't regain his job on the newspaper. So he was freelancing, but after a year out of touch, he had no leads or contacts and he was desperate for a break.

Lately, strains of dance music, shouts and laughter came drifting across the lagoon to the lighthouse. He knew that the fabulously wealthy Palmas owned the land on the other side of the lagoon, and some days ago he had crept down to the water's edge to investigate. What he saw sent the adrenaline surging through his body. He had sprinted back for his camera. Twenty minutes later, he took six marvellous shots.

The following day, when he developed them, he yelled with excitement. Here was the break he'd been praying for. Silver Bay's rich young men were cavorting naked with local dusky maidens. It would make delicious copy, local front page headlines, or better still he'd try for the scandalous back page of the national Sunday newspaper. This lot would all get six months hard labour and cuts. Serve them right! Mike didn't hesitate for a moment. But he needed more shots and better close-ups.

So he had hung around, night after night, getting the odd shot here and there, but he had not been able to get the close-ups he needed, until he discovered Anne's canoe. Tonight he'd scored a bullseye, he reckoned.

Silver Bay's very own blue lagoon, he wrote as soon as he reached his pad. *Sex, sin and smoking pot in the sand dunes as the rich and spoiled young white men take their pick of the village's prettiest coloured girls.*

'Fee, fi, fo, fum,' he sang happily as he dried the pictures in his home-made darkroom. 'I'll make a killing and then some . . .' He paused, startled. 'But I could get more if I kept mum,' he muttered. Now where the hell had that thought come from? Angelo Palma would pay a fortune to keep these pictures out of the newspaper. Wasn't his daughter-in-law pregnant? And here was his beloved Trevor, cavorting naked with some dusky woman, dancing nude by the fire, humping her in the dunes, swimming naked in the lagoon. It was all there.

He sat down with shock. He could probably demand half a million. What would Angelo pay to keep his son and heir out of prison? Shaking with excitement, Mike Russell picked up the telephone receiver.

Ramona was unlocking the door to her cottage when she heard a noise in the bushes. She swung round, but a powerful torch beam blinded her and a dark figure lurched towards her.

Relief set in when she saw that it was only Jânek. He looked defeated, she noticed without pity. His eyes were red from weeping, his shoulders sagging, his whole demeanour was that of a beaten dog.

As he approached, a sudden psychic jolt left her shivering. It was like two currents meeting, fusing, flaring and as quickly over. An invisible flash lit up her world and in that brief non-moment of time the knowledge of so many unknowns became known. Her own death, for instance. Yes, she thought with sudden acceptance. Here stood death. So many deaths, but who else . . . ? She flinched and bit back her cry.

'I won't hurt you.'

'Not yet.'

'You and your crazy second sight. Why don't you face reality for a change?'

I'm facing you, aren't I? she thought. She stood squarely in his path, bracing herself, her body shaking with the passion of her revelation, dark eyes blazing.

Jânek halted and looked puzzled as she stood her ground.

'I've been waiting for you.'

That was obvious. She watched him carefully and saw that his pale blue eyes were blinking too rapidly.

'Look,' he said. 'I'm unarmed. You've got nothing to be afraid of. I swear it. I have to talk to you. Please, go inside.' He put his hands on his head. 'Search me. You'll see.'

Ramona turned, opened the door and switched on the light. Her hand hovered near the panic alarm button Angelo had installed. Not now, not yet, her inner voice told her.

She held back the door and he walked in and stopped still

in the middle of the floor, gazing round hesitantly. Ramona was aware of the reason for his late visit. She took off her shawl and threw it over the nearest chair.

'Now, talk,' she said. 'And be quick. What do you want?'

'I want to know if Rose is happy. You see, she won't see me.'

She shrugged and he crumpled on the settee. He was too sad to be lied to. At the same time, why should she confide in him? Rose was not for him. She had fought long and hard with her daughter when she first announced her engagement to this . . . this foreigner. Yes, he was foreign to them in every sense of the word. He didn't belong in their world. Maybe she had fallen for his looks. He was tall and wiry, not powerful-looking, but possessing a steely strength. His hair was black, his eyes blue, his skin fresh and ruddy and in the days when he and Rose were together, he'd exuded joy like a seal exudes oil. Perhaps that was his charm. Now joy had fled, leaving only bitterness.

'You have a nice place here,' Jânek said, waving his hand. 'You're doing all right. Is Rose a part of the deal? You serve with your labour, Rose with her cunt. You have this cottage and a pension. And what's in it for her? Jewels, perhaps? Don't tell me about "Willow Lodge". It's on their land and therefore not worth the paper it's written on. If she must be a whore . . .' he spat out the hateful word, 'then let her get something out of it. God knows she's beautiful enough. I must know if she's happy.'

She watched him cautiously. Impossible not to feel sorry for him, he was so obviously beaten. He has nothing left to lose, she thought, so he is dangerous.

'D'you want some wine? I have some opened.'

He nodded, looking surprised. She went to the sideboard and poured out two large tumblers and handed one to him.

'So carry on,' she said. 'Get it off your chest.'

'I want you to get her away from him. Or else . . .' he broke off and shuddered. 'I must know . . . Has he set her up properly? I mean, is he looking after her? Even if he is, what about respectability, a real home with a real husband, children, the whole bit? Doesn't her happiness count for anything?'

Ramona gulped down her wine and poured another. 'You don't understand.' She leaned against the wall, gazing at the ceiling and her eyes took on a strange, trancelike look, as if she were looking inwards. 'I always knew our seed would be entwined, his and mine. But then I wondered. When Rose grew up to be the image of me I knew there was a second chance. I groomed her, reared her, educated her in a white convent . . .'

'She's always been your tool,' he whispered. 'You never loved her. You used her.'

She dropped her eyes and began to tremble. 'I'm always right . . . He will still marry her,' she said. 'It was foretold to me long ago. Her child will run the Palmas' empire.'

'Your evil predictions make me sick. Satan's words come pouring out of your lips like obscene oaths, and as for your eyes, they see only evil.'

She began to feel afraid again. Was he cracking up? Or had he always been a little mad?

'I don't want you to think that you're forgiven,' he said. 'I want you to know you're on the line. If anything happens to her I shall kill you. You are the arch manipulator of all this. Now tell me, is she happy?'

'Happy? What is happiness? You're a fool to give it

a second thought. Get out of here or I'll sound the alarm.'

He walked off into the night and she watched him leave with a sense of fear. She sensed that he was about to topple over the edge of sanity.

Chapter 44

_____ _____

It was 9 p.m. when a curt summons from Angelo brought Trevor rushing up from 'Willow Lodge'. Father had never sounded so angry, nor so anxious. 'Get here as fast as you can,' he'd said.

There was a thick sea mist rolling in from the south-west. It was drifting up over the dunes and the lagoon, blotting out vision. Rose was apprehensive. 'I feel sick. There's something horrible out there,' she whispered.

Sometimes she was just like her ignorant old mother and this infuriated Trevor. 'It's just a mist,' he snapped. 'Don't be so damned superstitious. Sometimes you act like the villagers.' As he started his car, remorse gripped him. She didn't deserve that taunt. He rushed back and wrapped his arms around her. 'I'll be back in no time,' he said. 'Why don't you go to bed? Read a book. I'll be back before you fall asleep.'

Angelo was standing in his study gazing over the bay, trying to gain control of himself. In his initial blind fury he had considered disowning the boy, sending him out of the country, or leaving Silver Bay for good. After a day's reflection he had realised that his son was in a difficult situation. There was no honorable way out for him. All he could do was appeal to his sense of logic.

He tried to force himself to look calm. But Trevor knew at once that something was very wrong. His father looked shattered and for the first time he showed his age. He was on the very edge of losing control. What the hell had gone wrong? He stilled a shudder of unease.

'I've just had a visitor,' Angelo's said. 'Michael Russell, Anne Marais' lover, paid me an unexpected visit.'

Trevor had a sudden recall of Mike Russell at the yacht club party last month. He spent the evening draped around the bar, his blond hair glistening in the light, blue eyes alight with amusement as he pulled everyone to pieces. He had a tremendous sense of humour, but always at someone else's expense.

Angelo flung a package on the desk. 'I had to pay him two hundred thousand rands. He wouldn't take a penny less. He wanted a million, but I played for time. I've got a week's grace, I said I couldn't raise the cash at short notice, so we'll have to act fast. This will set him up for life. The bastard! But I'll get him back eventually.

'Go on! Take a look.' There were tears rolling down his cheeks and that, more than anything, unnerved Trevor.

He picked up the photographs, and fell into a pit of shame. There were eight shots of him humping Rose in the dunes. Sweet Jesus! What did they look like? Then there were the shots of them swimming naked and some of them were naked when they danced around the fire. There was Emanuel with Julie. Shit! He'd have to warn them. And Jack Bronson with Julie's sister. 'Oh God,' he groaned. Why weren't we more careful? He shook himself and dropped the rest of the pictures on to the desk.

He slowly realised that Angelo was talking. 'Look at that.' Angelo pointed out of the window. 'It always amazes me.'

Trevor stood beside him. Around them was a sea of

white, gleaming like a snowfield in the moonlight. The sea, beaches, fields, roads, houses and sand dunes were all lost under the thickly rolling fog. Above them the mountain peaks reared up like islands and the night sky was crystal clear.

'It will creep up over here soon and we won't see a damn thing. Listen! That boat's lost its bearings by the sound of things. They'll land up wrecked if they aren't careful.'

They could hear a ship's siren which seemed to be coming from too close into the bay.

'Sometimes I think our family is like that, Trevor. We're drifting in the fog with no direction, no idea how to get out of the mess we're in, moving towards disaster.'

'I'm so sorry, Father,' he said. 'So truly sorry. I never meant this to happen. I never meant to harm anyone, ever, and least of all you.'

'Am I asking so much, Trevor? I want peace in my home. I want my son back. He's all I have and I love him. I want my daughter-in-law to smile with joy occasionally. I want my grandson to grow up in the security of a proper home, with a united father and mother who love him.

'I've worked hard for the family, my boy. It wasn't always easy, as you can guess. I've risked my life many times to get here, right here, where we stand now, particularly in the early days. I did it to get back what the Palmas once had, not so much for me, but for my children, and their children. I deserve to succeed because I slogged my guts out for you . . . Now put your house in order, Trevor. I'm ordering you to do this thing and I'm begging you, too. Do your duty, my boy. That's how the Palmas have always operated. In the long run that's where happiness lies.'

'Please . . . Destroy the pictures! Claire might . . . or Ramona . . . God forbid . . .' Trevor whispered.

'Naturally! But the bastard has the negatives. He's threatened to put them in every newspaper, and of course there's the police . . .'

He stood up and walked stiffly to the cabinet and poured two neat whiskies. 'Here,' he said, pushing one towards his son.

'In a way I blame myself. Maybe I was wrong to send you overseas for so many years. You don't understand the feelings, nor the laws here. Sex across the colour bar is a dreaded crime because it destroys the roots of the Afrikaner culture – their dream of *apartheid*. That's why the punishments are always so severe. It threatens their future security, you see. You would get cuts and years of hard labour. My money wouldn't be able to buy you out of it. Nor her.'

He began to write a list of names. 'I recognise some of them. You must tell me who's left out. I'll have to call all the parents together so we can work out how to get you fools out of the country, at once. I'm not paying a million to that bastard, because it wouldn't end there. He'd be milking me for life.'

'Oh, Father,' Trevor whispered, the lump in his throat unbearably painful. 'Please believe how sorry I am. I'm sorry for everything – for you, for Claire, for Rose. But I won't leave Rose. I'll take her away, at once. What a fucking mess.'

'What about Claire? How could you do this to her? And then there's your coming child. Claire's not strong. This could kill her.'

Trevor shrugged helplessly. 'If I do the right thing by her, what about Rose? I must think. Right now I'm panicking. I have to get out of here.' He turned in the doorway. 'You did the right thing, Father. Thanks! A week is long enough. I don't know what the hell to do right now, but I promise I will by morning. The truth is, I love them both, but I'll make a plan. You have my word.'

Trevor fled out into the mist, feeling grateful for its disguise. He felt exposed and cheap. Those awful pictures seemed to shed a new and scathing light on his sexual obsession for Rose. Leaving his car, he walked down the valley road towards the sea, then turned and meandered along the beach road not caring where he was going, just needing time to think. What the hell was he going to do? Surely his son deserved a father? He could not imagine his own boyhood without Angelo. Where exactly did his duty lie? What was right and what was wrong?

He walked on rapidly, realising that he was nearing the harbour. The mist was thickening, making haloes of eerie white around the harbour lights. It was cold. He shivered and quickened his pace. Strange, but he could not shake off a feeling of vulnerability, a strange sense of being exposed. He stopped suddenly, listening carefully. Someone was following on rubber-soled shoes and they were not more than a few yards away. He heard the crunch of a stone dislodged and then a short skid from a misplaced step. He looked over his shoulder, but could see no one. The night was full of drifting white shapes and darker shadows, but none that seemed to have a living form.

He jogged forward and stopped by a street light. Now he knew for sure that he was being followed. It could be any coloured skolly gang, but it sounded as if it was only one person. He would have to try to defend himself. He fingered his gun, feeling depressed as he backed against the lamppost.

His pursuer was running towards him. A figure loomed

up, only feet away and lunged forward, swift as a cobra, ripping his knife up into his ribs. There was a sharp, stabbing pain that took his breath away. 'Jânek!' he mouthed.

Trevor pulled out his gun. Fumbling for the trigger he fired at the retreating black shape. He thought he'd hit him. Then he screamed out into the night for help. Strange how the pain had gone. Perhaps he wasn't badly hurt. He tried to run forward. He badly wanted to fire again, but he was afraid he might hit an innocent person. It was getting so dark. Even the mist was darkening and his body seemed to be turning to stone. Nothing worked. He tried to call out, but his lips would not move. He was vaguely aware of shouts and a whistle blowing and then his world disintegrated.

As one awful day followed the next, Angelo wondered if he had turned into an automaton. Robotlike, he coped with the police and the funeral parlour. He went to the morgue to identify his son's body, and he endured the terrible visit of the female undertaker who wanted to discuss the relative merits of coffins and brass handles. He paid Ramona a large sum to get Rose out of the country, but he refused to see her. When he saw her swaying and sobbing at the graveside, he turned away.

He coped with Claire and her nervous breakdown, and sent her to the best clinic in the country. Then he called a meeting of the parents of the young men and women who could be identified in the pictures and he assisted them financially to get their children overseas fast.

But where were his tears for his only son? They seemed to have fled. When Ramona told him she was leaving his home forever, he did not even feel a fleeting sense of loss. He had walled up his emotions. There was no pain, nor joy in his life. He would never love again, he knew. Never again. From now on he was inviolate. He expected nothing. He did his duty and ran his many businesses to the best of his ability.

When Mike Russell arrived, cocky and swaggering for the balance of the cash, Angelo threatened to charge him with blackmail, but he didn't want his son's memory dirtied and Russell sensed this. They were both at a stalemate and Russell left, swearing at him.

Later, robotlike again, he fought to keep his grandchild by his side. The tiny baby was born in the clinic and brought home by a trained nurse, who agreed to stay on for a few months. He seldom looked at the baby, but he made sure Rob had the best possible care.

He had to be tough again when Claire left the clinic, for she refused to live in his home, despite his pleas. She was going away with her parents, she told him, and she wanted her child back. Her efforts to regain custody of her two-month-old baby were futile. He was prepared to prove that she was mentally unstable and he could ruin her parents with a long drawn-out legal battle, he told her. He would stop at nothing to keep his grandchild. It was back to the clinic for Claire as she had another breakdown. She would never dare to try again, he sensed, for now she had a history of mental disorders, although they didn't last long.

He was surprised when lawyers contacted him and told him that she had set up a trust fund with all that she owned and would eventually inherit, which would go to her child when he came of age. More fool her, Angelo thought. He had more than enough cash for his grandchild. He wanted to tell her this, but Claire had left the country.

He had always felt guilty about the way he had treated Claire. He looked up at Rob expecting censure, but Rob was staring at him with the strangest expression in his eyes. What was it?

'I never wanted to deprive you of your mother,' he told Rob, looking up, haggard and old. 'I never wanted Claire to leave. I loved her. Perhaps I should have told her this, but my feelings had all drained away.'

The old man looked tired, Rob thought. He glanced at his watch and saw that it was nearly 3 a.m. It had been a long and emotionally draining ordeal for Angelo, who never talked much nowadays. But Rob knew that he couldn't let him off the hook yet. He had not explained about the skull in the dunes, nor why he had bulldozed 'Willow Lodge' to the ground to hide the evidence.

'But that police lieutenant was questioning you about a skull which had been buried in the dunes. If I'm to help you, I have to know.'

Angelo sighed, as if facing an ordeal. He stood up, holding his back. 'Old age is making me stiff,' he said. He began to pace the bedroom, pushing his fingers through his white hair. He had to clear his throat a couple of times. Rob fetched him some water from the bathroom.

'Rose came back later. She said she didn't care if she went to prison or not. She moved into "Willow Lodge", which she claimed was hers, and she had the deeds to prove it, but of course it was on our land. She sent a message that she had to see me, that I must come down to the house. I decided to do that, but I must tell you that it went against the grain. You see I blamed her for your father's death and for the break-up of his relationship with your mother.

'It was summer, but pouring with rain, I remember. The place was like a morgue, although Ramona had kept it clean, but the sadness and loneliness seemed to hang around like a bad smell. She'd brought her elder brother, Bill, along with her for moral support. In a way that was lucky for me.

'She had her demands ready and, quite honestly, she wanted more than I could give. Much more! I refused point blank. Then, suddenly, she went berserk. She began to scream at me, calling me every sort of a blackguard she could lay her tongue to. She flung herself at me, kicking and punching and scratching my face with her nails. She was beside herself.

'I pushed her hard away from me and she sort of staggered, lost her balance and next minute she toppled over the banisters, breaking her neck in the fall. Oh God! You can probably imagine how terrible it was.'

He sighed and crumpled on the bed, pushing his hands hard over his face and up through his hair. Then he shook his head as if to shake off the unwanted memories. Watching him, Rob thought how vulnerable he was. And all these years he'd thought he was hard, but he wasn't. He was just a man who had bottled up all his emotions because he couldn't stand the pain.

'You see, Rob,' he said, blinking fondly up at his grandson. 'To give Rose what she wanted would have prejudiced your rights. I couldn't do that to you. I had to protect you.

'Bill September and I buried her out the back of the house. We took turns in digging an eight-foot trench. I said a service of sorts and neither of us shed any tears. I promised Bill to replace the deeds of "Willow Lodge" with enough cash for him to build a smart house and own the land, too. Plus his own fully equipped fishing trawler. He seemed satisfied with the deal. He said he could bring his mother round to his way of thinking. I suppose he must have succeeded because they told everyone that Rose had gone overseas. From then on they became quite rich.'

'Wouldn't it have been better to have told the police the truth?' Rob asked gently.

'I thought of that, but too many other matters might have come out, not just for me, but for everyone.'

'So why is Ramona our housekeeper? I don't get that.'

'That's the strange part of it. A month later she came to see me. She said that our fates had been intertwined by our double loss. She said she would like her job back because she wanted to bring you up properly. She said a hired nurse could never replace a mother's love and that I needed her. She was right, of course. She forgave me for Rose's death and that meant a great deal to me. She brought you up well. No one could have been more devoted. Well, that's it! Now you know everything.'

'Including your anger when I wanted to marry Kate.'

'I hated her father. If it weren't for him, Trevor might still have been alive. I never wanted you to marry her because I knew I'd ruin him eventually, and that this would make trouble for you in your marriage. I'm sorry, Rob, but the bastard deserved all he got.'

'Grandpa, look at me! Do you swear that that's the truth, the whole truth, and nothing but the truth?'

'As near to it as makes no difference,' Angelo said.

'I'm going to get a good criminal lawyer. I don't believe the police have a case against you. They can't do a damned thing. Bill September knows it was an accident.'

'If you say so,' Angelo said.

'And this Hungarian who killed my father – what happened to him?'

'He was shot through the leg by Trevor and caught by the police. He stood trial and was sentenced to death, but he appealed and his sentence was changed to life. He served twenty years and he was deported at the end of his sentence.'

'You look exhausted and no wonder. Come on, Grandpa,' Rob said. 'Back to bed. I'm going to make you a hot toddy. I'll bring it up to you.' He put his arm around the old man. 'Life hasn't been easy for you, has it? You deserved better. It's not fair.'

'I have you,' Angelo said. 'You've made up for most of the rest of it. I love you, my boy.'

'I love you, too,' Rob whispered.

PART III

Chapter 45

——— ——

Ari had sat cramped up in a small cane chair, amongst potted plants and bric-à-brac for the past four hours, but he felt no discomfort, he had no concept of time, for he was totally engrossed in Bill's story. It was a warm summer evening. Now that the squatters had been burned out, the Septembers were able to open their sliding glass doors. Ari could hear the waves splashing on the sand, and see the moon, a lustrous arc, descend towards her shimmering reflection. A lovely night! Hannah, faded and sad, came in carrying a second round of coffee and biscuits and Ari gulped his gratefully.

True to her word, Hannah had pressurised Bill to tell Ari all that he knew, but the information had come grudgingly, extracted with pressure. There was more where that came from, Ari reckoned. He decided to try again.

'Okay, let's recap. Let's go back to when Rose returned from Mozambique. When was that, now, December 1964?'

Bill nodded.

'Exactly seven months after Jânek Jözsef was arrested for killing Trevor?'

'He should have been hanged,' Hannah cut in on them bitterly. 'He served his twenty years and then he was deported. People like him are not fit to walk the earth.

Trevor was a real gentleman. The nicest man you're ever likely to come across.'

Ari waited, crunching a biscuit, letting her have her say, then he turned back to Bill.

'Why the seven-month lapse between Trevor's death and Rose contacting Angelo, which led to her death?' Ari asked.

'I don't know.' Bill was becoming increasingly resentful.

'And why did Angelo Palma raze "Willow Lodge" to the ground?'

'How many times must we go through all this? Because she said it was hers, which it was. He didn't want any claims on that house. After all, it was built on his land, no doubt about that, and she'd been running a regular whorehouse there.'

Ari had a strong suspicion that Bill was holding back. He watched him carefully, noting his strong face and hard eyes. There were beads of perspiration on his brow, and one of his eyes had developed a tic, so he wasn't quite as calm as he tried to make out. Ari decided to keep pushing.

'So,' he said, flipping back the pages of his notebook. 'Angelo arrived at ten-thirty p.m., and listened to Rose's demands. He refused to pay her more money than she had, namely the deeds to "Willow Lodge" and a small private income set up by Trevor, plus the fairly large capital sum of thirty thousand pounds. They argued, Rose lost her temper and lunged at him, losing her balance and plunging to her death. Correct?'

'You've said it,' Bill said, mopping his brow and shifting uncomfortably in his chair.

'Why didn't you two call the police? It was a clearcut case of accidental death, wasn't it? You were a witness to this.'

'He didn't want the bad publicity. He was afraid people might not believe us.'

'Why wouldn't they?' Ari paused, reached out to take another biscuit and then thought better of it.

'I'll tell you what I think happened. Angelo lost his temper, blaming Rose for the death of his son. They fought and he flung her over the balcony, breaking her neck. Then he bribed you to keep your mouth shut. The trawler and your house are worth close on half a million, aren't they? Is that worth being an accessory to murder?'

Behind him, he heard Hannah gasp. He turned and saw her shocked eyes as she collapsed on to the settee.

'They're worth that now, perhaps, but not then,' Bill grumbled.

Ari was reminded of the children's party game of hunt-the-thimble. He had been getting warm, but he was moving away from the pressure area, so he was cold. Watching Bill was a dead give-away. He looked pretty relaxed right now. Strange that the massive bribe was not the area that troubled Bill. But there was something that scared him. Ari decided to try one last time.

'You did all right, Bill, didn't you? A house in the village, which eventually enabled you to buy this home, a fully equipped trawler, plus ten thousand pounds deposited in Ramona's account the next morning. What was that for? To pay her for her daughter's death? Was she satisfied with this compensation? Is that what a daughter's worth?'

Bill jumped up angrily, his eyes looked wild, his cheeks had turned grey. Ari knew he was in the hot zone again. It was Ramona's anger that frightened Bill. *He was covering up for his mother, or perhaps he had helped her?* What had they done? And why? For money, or for revenge?

'How did Ramona get even with Angelo Palma, Mr September? Do you know?'

'Haven't you caused enough trouble?' Bill shouted. 'What's it all about? What gives you the right to ask all these questions? Rose was dead and buried years ago. What about my daughter, Mandy? Why the hell don't you get on with finding her?' he roared.

'That's why I'm here,' Ari replied quietly.

Bill shot him a look of contempt and rushed out, slamming the door.

Watching Hannah made Ari feel guilty. Unable to cope with the trauma of her horrid imaginings, she was wasting away. Her skin was sallow, her eyes ringed with dark shadows, her lips were dry and colourless and she was full of nervous gestures. She seemed on the point of cracking up.

'Will all this talking really help?'

'Of course!' He tried to look confident.

'I don't understand why I must suffer like this, and still try to keep up appearances, dressing, combing my hair, talking to you as if everything was normal, when *she*'s out there somewhere, maybe she's dying, or sick, or being beaten or raped . . . Oh God! Why Mandy? Why did he take my little Mandy?'

'We're trying our best.' He sounded pathetic, he realised. He flushed, but Hannah did not seem to notice.

'I want to ask you something: where's God? Where's the helping hand I always thought would be there? I feel so alone. I want to lie down and howl like a dog, but how will that help my Mandy?'

'The best way to help her is to try to think of anything you might have overlooked. Anything strange about her boyfriends, any new friends, had she mentioned anyone hanging around?'

'I think of nothing else,' she said. She sighed. All the world's woes seemed to echo in her sigh.

'Mrs September . . .' Ari peered anxiously at her. 'In your heart of hearts, do you believe that your daughter is still alive?'

'Yes.' She said this without hesitating.

'I've found that mothers are invariably right. You see, there is some sixth sense between you and her, or that's what I believe. I've seldom known a mother's intuition to fail.'

'Thank you,' she said. 'She's somewhere . . . I know she's scared, and alone, but she's somewhere out there and she's alive.'

'You must keep believing that she'll be sitting here quite soon. Visualise it, believe it, thank God for sending her back to you, pretend that your prayers have been answered. It works.'

'I'll try. So God help me, I'll try.'

Ari was glad to leave, he felt so inadequate. He went on to the Bronsons and found them on their stoep, still on sundowners, although it was almost midnight. Gill rushed off, to make some snacks, she said, but he guessed she'd be tarting herself up, which gave him a good ten minutes.

'Here's the rent.' He put an envelope on the bar.

'I feel guilty taking the cash, old boy. You haven't slept here for two weeks. Are you sure you want the room?'

Jack's blue eyes were gleaming with malicious humour and his face, swollen like a ripe red pumpkin from Scotch, was cracking into a broad grin.

'I get home late and leave early, so you don't see me.'

Jack burst into loud guffaws.

'I have some photographs here. I'd like you to identify the people. D'you mind?'

'Surely not, my boy. Local, are they?' His joviality vanished as the pictures were spread in front of him. His face became purplish, his forehead gathered moisture, and soon several drops were trickling down his jowls. He took out his handkerchief to wipe them away.

'I wish I could get a hard on like that nowadays,' he said, trying to hide his shock with a joke. 'Wow! Those were the days, eh! If Gill saw this she'd die of envy. Perhaps it would be better if she didn't see them, old boy. If I identify everyone, will you promise not to show these snaps round the village?'

Ari promised, and Bronson identified several highly respectable local professionals, including the dentist. He only knew the girls by their first names, but Ari knew which females had gone overseas on the Palmas' many bursary awards, and he reckoned these girls had been the lucky winners.

'Put them away, Ari, and sit down. Have a drink.' He got up, poured a neat Scotch and thrust it towards him. 'You're so young,' Bronson said. 'How can someone like you possibly understand the sixties? In a way, we were at war here, English youth against the Nats and their "solution" to the racial problem. Sex was only a part of it. It was a delicious way to cock a snoot at the government and their bully boys. What a lark! But then we were threatened with exposure and only too grateful to be bailed out by Angelo. Of course, his son had the most to lose. Then Trevor was suddenly murdered, but you know all that.'

Ari leaned back in the rocking chair and closed his eyes. All at once he was laughing. How many hours of sleep had he missed? How much of his precious time off had he spent in the newspaper library? How many days questioning villagers? He had suspected that they were jointly and severally concealing an ancient crime and he had been right, but what did it boil down to? A multiracial whorehouse! Ludicrous – in today's times. But then it was a different matter. Half the village's rich young men and the prettier coloured girls would have been arrested, tried and imprisoned. But those laws belonged in a museum now, so why wasn't everyone having a good laugh about it? What else were they concealing? And why? Perhaps out of loyalty to Angelo Palma, who had helped most of them at one time or another. *Did they think that he had murdered Rose?* Was that it?

Jack looked over his shoulder and frowned. 'Here comes Gill. Keep these out of sight, old boy. Mum's the word! Okay?'

'Sure.' He pushed the photographs into the envelope. 'By the way, did you ever see Mike Russell around the lagoon?'

'Good God, no. He was courting Anne Marais, Kate's mother. Regular social climbers, they were. She used to paint and he wrote, but they were always on the bones of their uppers until he finished his book. He made enough cash from it to buy a diamond mine in Namaqualand, although it wasn't published in this country. Banned, he told me. From then on he never looked back, until recently that is.'

He should have looked back, Ari reasoned, then he might have remembered the Roman who was stalking him.

It was time to explain to Kate the significance of the photographs she had given him two days ago. She had the right to know and he'd better get it over and done with, he decided. Ari had been longing to see Kate all day, but it was past midnight. Would she be sleeping? As he drove down the winding steep road, he was staring towards the lighthouse. Despite the light shining from the top floor Ari felt bad about arriving so late. What would she think of him?

Five minutes later, he was in no doubt about his welcome. Kate flung herself into his arms. She looked like a schoolgirl, scrubbed and shiny clean, smelling of toothpaste and wearing a plain, white cotton nightdress.

'Darling, darling, darling,' she cooed. 'I've been missing you.'

This went a long way towards calming his tormented doubts about her feelings for him.

'Have you eaten?' she asked.

'No, but don't bother.'

'What would you like?'

'Anything, as long as it's no trouble.'

'Ham sandwiches with mustard and cucumber?'

'Sounds great.'

'And a beer?'

'No, it's too late. Do you love me, Katie?'

'What about tea?'

'Not unless you have rooibos. Kate, answer me.'

'Be patient with me. I still love Rob. Oh, by the way, he's proceeding with the divorce. I got a letter today.'

'Hm! And how do you feel about it?'

'Oh, I don't care. Bits of paper don't control my emotions,' she said vaguely. 'My big problem is that I still love him. I feel married to him. I have the feeling that I always will. Now, milk and sugar?'

'Heck, Katie, what sort of questions are these? A guy likes to feel his girl remembers these things.'

'Isn't it different with rooibos?' She frowned. 'I bought it specially for you today, so quit moaning.'

Ari felt guilty. He'd been meaning to sneak some provisions into the kitchen. He knew she was short.

'How's the work going?'

'Hah!' Stretching out both arms, she stood on tiptoe and then solemnly raised her hands towards the sky. 'I'm a rocket! Just watch me. *Home and Garden* magazine has featured Melissa's house. And the newspapers are doing articles, and suddenly I'm famous. Melissa's having a big do to "launch" me. I've had offers for two big contracts this week alone. Can you believe it?'

'Quite frankly, yes. I seem to remember telling you to have more courage because you're good.'

She twirled around and jumped as the kettle let off its shrill whistle.

'*There is a tide in the affairs of men* . . .' she began waltzing around with the teapot, '*which taken at the flood* . . . Hah! Just you watch me, Ari St John.'

Why did he feel peeved? he wondered. Wasn't that a little beneath his dignity? At the same time, would a successful interior decorator marry an almost penniless policeman? She looked so happy. Tonight was not the best time to tell her about her father.

Then she stunned him by saying: 'Just where are those photographs you took? D'you remember? The ones that came out of that old trunk.'

'Oh, Katie, to be honest I came to tell you about them, but I don't want to spoil your news. Another day will do.'

'You might as well get it off your chest, I won't sleep if you don't tell me. I can see it's important.' She was chopping bread and slapping on ham and butter as if born to it.

'Kate, the photographs you gave me were of Trevor Palma, Rob's late father.'

'Good God, naked in the sticks with a lovely siren.'

'With Rose September actually.'

'Oh my!' She turned, looking serious.

'Someone photographed the goings-on at the old beach house and blackmailed Angelo. This person was paid enough to set him up with a mine in Namaqualand, but Angelo never forgot. He waited for years to get his own back.'

Kate sighed as her happy mood fled.

'I wish I'd left this for another time,' he said uneasily.

'What's the difference?' She was trying to be brave. 'I had to know. If it weren't my father, I'd probably say: "good for Angelo".'

He winced as he watched her stabbing the ham. 'Mind your fingers,' he said.

She ignored him. 'You know, Ari, there's no law says you have to love your father. I used to love my mother so much, but after she died I felt shunned. I never knew why that was. I always tried to please Father, but never succeeded. I felt wretched because he didn't love me and I didn't love him. Now I feel just a little bit less guilty. Perhaps he really is unlovable and unloving. Perhaps it wasn't all my fault. Strangely enough, the news has made me feel lighter. It's as if something heavy fell off my shoulders.'

'I didn't want to spoil our evening. I just felt that you had to understand Angelo's motivation.'

'Will you stay tonight, Ari?' Kate said so briskly that she might have been proposing a business deal. 'I don't want to be alone. I need your shoulder to lie on.'

'Take your pick, Kate,' he said, rippling his biceps on one side and then the other.

'You clown.' She laughed thinking: sometimes I love you. D'you know that? Sometimes I wonder how I could cope without you.

She said: 'How long can you hope to stay at Silver Bay? You've been here four months or more. Aren't you due to be sent back? And what about Mandy? Will anyone ever find her? What do you think?'

Her questions plunged him into gloom. 'Yes, I'm due to return in six weeks' time. Yes, I will find Mandy. Does that answer all your questions? Furthermore, if the worst came to the worst, I could leave the Force, but you didn't ask me that, did you?'

She looked up, feeling startled at his tone of voice.

Oh dear. Sometimes you remind me of Rob, she thought. I wonder if we would ever have got together if it weren't that you're so often like him, especially now that you are sulking.

He sensed that this was not the night for sex. Kate was spent and troubled and she clung to him and fell asleep quite quickly. Later, as she lay sleeping on his shoulder, Ari wondered about the future. How could his love feel so right if it were just a passing affair? The thought of losing her was almost more than he could bear. He began to plan his future. He would have to leave the police. He hardly made a living wage for one person, let alone two.

On the other side of the valley, Rob Palma lay awake, tormented by visions of Kate and Ari in bed together. He was suffering bitterly.

All his life he had been nervous of trusting anyone, knowing that people could only be bought, but with Kate he had been blinded by love. He was a fool, he knew that now. How she must laugh at him. The whole village was laughing at him.

The problem was, he could not stop loving her and it hurt so much. Since the day he had fallen for her, he had worried himself half to death for fear of her infidelity. Now she had done the very thing he had dreaded and feared the most. She had cheapened something that was very precious and made a fool of him in front of the entire community and his grandfather.

She was a bitch, a cruel and vicious woman, and she was a fool, too, for she had fucked her way out of the moneyed classes. Without beauticians and hairdressers, she'd get old before her time. She was always in the sun, tanning her skin to leather. He knew, because he watched her through his powerful binoculars. One of these days she'd come crying, but he certainly would not take her back.

He was amazed she had lasted so long on her own. She had been so spoiled and so proud. He had tried his damnedest to get that police lieutenant removed, but Gerber didn't seem to have the power. The villagers were saying that the policeman was his *doppelgänger*, and they were predicting all kinds of doom for him. To hell with the lot of them. It was Kate who was moving towards disaster, not him.

Unless he killed her lover. This thought came to him often, as he lay in his lonely bed. He would keep his grief at bay by plotting exactly how it could be done. In the morning, on his way to work, he would laugh at his silly nightly imaginings, but all the same, he had three foolproof schemes that would rid the world and him of Lieutenant Ari St John forever.

Chapter 46

———   ———

Ari arrived at his office before 6 a.m., in order to check the computer and get out without being hassled, but he was not early enough. Ian Frost, nicknamed 'Frosty Face' by Willis Gous, was already there. He cornered Ari, blocking the doorway, one hand on the wall, the other carrying his carton of coffee. Short of pushing him back, Ari was trapped, which was something he hated.

If I had an office with two doors, I could simply nod and leave, he thought. He began to plan how he could change places with Smit and Gous, who shared this luxurious arrangement down the passage.

Frost came from a Public Relations background. He owned a small share of the local branch of a multi-national PRO agency, which had recently been appointed publicity agents for the Nationalist Party. His specific job was to persuade coloured voters that the authorities cared for each and every one of them. The hope was that they would vote for the Nats in the coming first multi-national election. Frost had been given an honorary status of 'major', while he poked around the Cape police stations looking for any- and everything that could be used to project this kindly, 'big daddy' image. He had organised several media appearances for Ari. Next week, together with the Septembers, Ari was supposed to make a national appeal to Mandy's kidnappers. He shuddered when he thought about it.

Ari hated Frost. He hated his paunchy stomach, his red hands, the way he tilted his head back to stare down his pointed nose, while his grey eyes glittered with a false air of bonhomie. He hated the way Frost demanded attention, and used his honorary position to force home his absurd ideas. He was a creepy bastard. Ari had avoided Frost as much as he could, but yesterday, his Colonel had called from Pretoria to rap Ari over the knuckles for his lack of co-operation. Evidently Frost had complained to the Minister.

Right now his grey eyes were crinkled up and his white capped teeth shone in a grimace. Was that supposed to be a smile? Ari shuddered. 'Well done, my boy,' Frost said generously.

'I'm very busy, if you'll excuse me,' Ari replied coldly.

'You must learn to take credit, where credit is due. That was a very good ploy yesterday.'

He was so damned patronising. Ari could feel his temper rising. 'What the hell are you talking about?'

'Why . . . ? Digging up the sand dunes. What else? Very visible! Very rewarding! We had journalists from two local newspapers and the Sunday national paper, plus TV coverage. Not bad, if you consider I knew nothing about it until you got started.' His eyes revealed his triumph. 'Now, if you'd let me know beforehand I could have really scored.'

'It wasn't for publicity,' Ari snarled. 'I was looking for something.'

'For Mandy, I hope.'

'D'you mean you hope she's dead and buried six foot under?' He shot a contemptuous glance towards Frost.

'I mean I hope you're leaving no stones unturned,' Frost said smoothly.

Nothing fazed that bastard. He was as thick-skinned as an elephant and twice as crafty.

'Look here, St John,' his voice purred with intimate undertones as he perched on the edge of Ari's desk. 'I've been doing a survey around the village. Most folks hereabouts are not sure who they'll vote for, but they're pliable. If we make a real case out of finding Mandy, that is, if you pull your finger out and get down to some action, we could gain their support.'

'Mr Frost,' Ari said, deliberately avoiding his honorary title, 'I am a policeman and my only concern is finding Mandy and arresting her kidnappers. You have another task. Now you can use whatever I do for your own ends, I can't stop you, but don't expect to manipulate me in order to provide media jaunts for no other purpose than catching votes. Let me tell you something, Frost. You are hindering me in my investigations and wasting my time. I, too, am prepared to take my gripes to the Minister. Just keep out of my hair, if you know what's good for you.'

'Sometimes I think you're deliberately obstructing me,' Frost said, gazing down at his coffee.

'So isn't it time for your next complaint to my superiors?' Ari asked quietly. If it wasn't for his honorary title, I'd punch the old windbag, I swear to God I would, he thought.

'Perhaps you don't care if the Nats get in or not, my boy. Well, that's your prerogative, but look at it this way. Part of my brief is to improve the image of the police. You guys have inherited the "baddie" image of the old-style Gestapo police, with their beatings and interrogations. You're the national scapegoats for apartheid. Did you know that there are more suicides amongst the police than any other sector? And more policemen get murdered than in any other sector? And more policemen go in fear of their lives and need psychiatric care than any other sector . . . ?'

He was getting into his stride. Ari sighed and examined the window, but it was barred.

'I know about you, Lieutenant,' Frost said, smiling nastily. 'I've seen your file. You're one of them, aren't you? You killed a black suspect in Soweto. You're ripe for extinction. I'm trying to revolutionise the image of people like you. A thankless task, if ever there was one. Why don't you help me?'

'You're right,' Ari said, longing to throttle him. 'I can be dangerous. See what I mean? Now get off my back if you know what's good for you.'

Frost's mouth opened and shut like a goldfish, but no sound came. Ari escaped quickly, taking great gulps of the pure, unpolluted fresh air outside.

Ari was in a hurry. He had just picked up some disturbing news on the computer. Simon Ackerman, Mandy's one-time boyfriend, had shot himself. Ari drove straight to Hilda Ackerman's beachfront apartment. Willis was already there. 'Straightforward suicide,' he told Ari. 'The boy went into his room and shot himself right after a confrontation with his mother.'

'Where's the corpse?'

'Gone to the mortuary, but he was still alive when we arrived. He died while we were waiting for the ambulance.'

'Say anything?'

'Yes . . . He muttered "Mandy" several times. That's all. I'll show you where he did it.'

Simon's room was much the same as any other teenager's pad, but the scuba diving gear, cameras, tapes and binoculars and the large blood stain on the floor, brought a lump to Ari's throat. 'I've asked for a post-mortem to pick up his drug intake,' Willis said.

'And where is his mother?'

'Under sedation in her room. The doctor won't let anyone in, but I got hold of her before he arrived. She told me that she's been paying protection money to Sam Patel. He has a house somewhere nearby where the kids gather to smoke pot and listen to jazz. It's a sort of fashionable club for drop-out youths, but Sam puts the squeeze on all their parents, a novel protection racket. It seems they're paying through the nose to ensure that their offspring get only pure *dagga*, nothing added to it, no coke, no crack, no opium, nothing that will wipe them out, or get them more hooked than they already are.

'Jesus – Ari!' Willis burst out. He wiped his brow with his handkerchief. 'We had him booked for kidnapping and dealing in drugs, caught red-handed, what more do they want . . . ? That was on a Friday. He was out on the streets by Monday. Some clever dick of a lawyer got him out on bail and the trial's been put back a year because Patel's team of dirty lawyers want to examine every single piece of evidence the State has against him.'

Ari didn't answer. That was why he wanted out of the Force. As fast as he arrested criminals, they were back on the streets. He had known that Sam Patel was a free man. Known and expected it.

'So tell me about Hilda Ackerman,' he said.

'Evidently she showed her son how much she'd paid Patel over the last twelve months. She explained how he was upping the monthly price for his safety. She couldn't meet his demands so she was faced with selling her business. She told Simon that either he must agree to stop smoking *dagga* or she'd have him committed until he kicked the habit. He went upstairs and shot himself. Just like that! I sent the body for an autopsy, just to see if Patel kept his word. Maybe he was hooked on the hard stuff despite Patel's assurances. We'll see.'

Ari swore. 'I've just about had enough,' he said bitterly.

'Join the club! I don't know a guy in the Force who isn't looking for a new job.'

'Look, Willis. It's my day off. I wanted to see Hilda, but I'll wait for your report. See that I get it by tonight, please, with the autopsy findings, just as soon as they come in.' He clapped Willis on the shoulder and left.

Ari drove on to the beach. He wanted to witness this morning's radical move, after which, he reckoned, nothing would be the same again. He arrived just after ten, but like most matters of cataclysmic importance, the event was taking place without fanfare or trumpets. The officials might have been selling fish, Ari thought, feeling amused.

The squatters hung around in a muttering, suspicious group near the end of the beach. Ari had a sense of regret as he watched them. Eunice should have been there. What a triumph this would have been.

Some anxious-looking whites were clustered together in the car park. Three government officials were gesticulating as workmen erected a post with a board on it. The squatters surged closer as they hammered a map on to the board. History was being made, but there was a sense of unreality. A journalist and photographer from the morning newspaper stood around looking bored.

With the support of most of the white ratepayers, blacks

were to be sold their own plots freehold. After more than forty years of apartheid, the first blacks would move into an upmarket white area, as landowners. Silver Bay was taking a massive step forward into the new South Africa and showing the way to other communities. For the minimal price of two hundred rands, payable over a period of years, a family would receive a small piece of land on which they could erect any type of a dwelling they could afford. Water, electricity, sewerage, communal toilets and washrooms, drainage and a road had already been installed and paid for by Silver Bay's ratepayers. A community hall, a church and a clinic were in the process of being built.

No one knew quite how to begin. Some stands were better than others, being more sheltered and closer to the latrines. Some even had a view of the bay, but they were all going for the same price and no cash was being put down now.

'Okay, you lot, line up here,' an official called. 'You,' he said, pointing to an old man. 'What's your name?'

'Monges Mboya,' the old man muttered. White-haired and dignified, he was not going to show emotion at this unexpected turn of events. There was a catch in it somewhere. There always was. Mboya blinked at the map. He could not read, nor visualise abstractly, so he pushed his thumb firmly into the centre of the map.

'Number 237! That's your plot. Sign here. Don't forget your number.' He wrote the man's name into his book. 'You'll be getting your deed of sale certification one of these days. Next!'

The new landowner spat on the ground contemptuously, eyes flashing. He wasn't going to be fooled by empty promises.

'Hey there, friend,' Ari called softly in Xhosa. 'Let's go and see where your piece is.'

Still not believing it, Mboya climbed into the car and allowed Ari to drive him along the main road to the estate, which was situated in a former forestry reserve and lay midway between two exclusive housing areas.

They found Site 237 without difficulty. Two officials were hanging around waiting for the rush.

'This is yours, Mr Mboya,' Ari told him. 'There's a nice view from here and the latrines are over there. There's room for a small house and a vegetable garden. A tree would look good. What do you think?'

The old man spat again, his face showed his confusion, but hope was dawning in his eyes.

'This is the new South Africa,' Ari said. 'You've got rights, and with rights come duties and responsibilities. It's your responsibility to build a good home and look after this place.'

'My land?'

'Yes.'

The old man's eyes became dreamy and trancelike. He held up his clenched fist. 'I never thought I'd live to see this day, my boss,' he said solemnly. Slowly he turned a full circle, his hand held high. Then he straightened and flung out his arms, circling slowly. He laughed. 'Hah!' he called loudly. And then again: 'Hah!' His stumble became a whirl, his muttering took on melody as he lifted his head to the sky. 'Hah! Hah! Hah!' Loud, staccato yelps of triumph. Clapping his hands on his boots, he circled and leaped, time and again, strong as a young man, at one with joy and the morning.

Ari had volunteered to drive Kate to the hospital where

Tabson was having his final and most vital bone graft. He was feeling anxious as he picked her up. She made him coffee while he told her about Mr Mboya and the sites. 'You can pride yourself in the role you played, Kate. You forced them to act.'

'Oh, they would have done it anyway,' she murmured. 'It might have taken a little longer. That's all.'

Ari drove silently, obsessed with Hilda and her tragedy. He was wondering how to put Sam Patel and his evil ways inside once and for all.

Kate, too, was tense and anxious. Prior to the operation, the doctor had explained to both of them that the final outcome lay in the lap of the gods. Now came the time of reckoning, the culmination of weeks of pain for Tabson, and worry and expense for Kate. Ari had insisted on being part of the project, reckoning that she might need him. God knows, he badly needed to be needed, but so far she had resisted his offers of financial assistance.

After Kate's initial bout of fear she had become ferociously independent, refusing any kind of help. He wasn't allowed to offer a shoulder, lend money or fix things around the house. 'I can cope, thanks,' was her perpetual answer to his offers. He felt angry when he heard that. He had threatened to get a rubber stamp made and stamp the message over every damn thing that needed fixing in the lighthouse. Why couldn't she give a bit and learn to lean on him? It was amazing that she'd allowed him to drive her to the hospital.

Look at her now, white cheeks, haggard eyes, deep shadows smudging her cheeks. She looked as if she hadn't slept for a week. She was gazing ahead blankly, her mind fixed on her private fears, teeth biting her bottom lip, hands gripping each other. Couldn't she reach out to him once in a while? She hadn't spoken since they left the gardens. Sometimes she was so poised and lovely, but other times, like now, she folded into herself and became despondent, like a lost girl.

'What is it?' he asked. 'Tabson?'

She sighed. 'I'm scared. I've played at being God. I was so sure . . .' She broke off and shivered. 'It seemed enough to will his leg to get better, but what if something has gone wrong? The specialist warned me that he might never be completely cured. Or worse! There's always a chance of failure. Tabson believes so strongly that he'll be normal – like other boys. I don't think he could bear it if we failed.

'Maybe I've been too optimistic with him, but I wanted to give him something to hang on to through all these operations, all the pain and discomfort, all those weeks in a plaster cast. The poor kid!'

Poor kid! Ari thought in amazement. Tabson had fallen with his arse in the butter. He'd grown a foot higher with the high-protein extracts Kate was pumping into him. Intensive coaching from a retired teacher had got him up to standard to join his age-group in a private school, where he was booked to start just as soon as he was better. He was very bright, it seemed. Lately he even spoke like Kate.

No, it was Kate who deserved the sympathy, not Tabson, Ari reasoned. Either way, he knew she was in trouble, but he didn't want to tell her this. If the operation failed, the family would undoubtedly sue her. They would not lose the chance to make a fast buck. Maybe not so fast either, she'd be paying for life.

And if it were completely successful . . . ? Well, he'd rather not think of that. He understood that she needed Tabson, just as Tabson needed her. She wanted someone to depend on her, someone to provide her with the impetus to get out into the market place. Since the morning when she decided to go it alone, she had been ferociously efficient. She was taking typing and bookkeeping lessons prior to opening her own business. She was going to work from home to cut costs, but Melissa was prepared to back her with the working capital she needed.

'I'm broke, and I have to get working,' she had moaned to him last week. That was true enough. Her horse and most of her jewellery had been sold, which must have brought in a tidy sum, but Tabson was not short of toys, books or clothes and the fridge was stocked with food. Dopey ate the best dog food, and Frikkie was gaining weight. Besides, the operations must have used up much of her small nest egg. She was not frugal, he realised.

He had a sudden inspiration about helping her. 'I hope you haven't forgotten that we're going fifty-fifty on Tabson's medical bills. How much have we laid out so far?'

'But, Ari, we've discussed that *ad nauseum* and you agreed to quit nagging me. I'm paying.'

'How selfish of you. I rescued Tabson and I promised his grandmother to look after him. I think he's as much mine as yours, but you want all the credit for yourself.'

'Oh . . . what a horrible thing to say.'

'Sometimes the truth hurts.'

'Do you think I'm like that?'

'Yes,' he lied. 'And twice as stubborn.'

'It's just that it was my idea,' she said, less sure of herself now. 'I decided to do this thing, not you, so I must shoulder the costs. I seem to remember you telling me not to go ahead.'

'Only because it was such a risk. Let's face it, I was being negative.' He reached out and squeezed her hand. 'We're almost there. We'll know soon enough so cheer up. I want to repeat something that Tom told me last week. He's a bit of a mystic, maybe a bit unbalanced, who knows? He said, we create the quality of our auras by the way we conduct our lives. He said a good aura attracts good vibes, good things, luck perhaps – and vice-versa. Like attracts like. He told me that the best protection from evil and bad times is goodness. You're brimming over with it, so I guess Tabson will be all right. Please, Katie, don't deprive me of sharing in this.'

Kate glanced at Ari suspiciously. Was he just trying to help her out? Studying his profile told her nothing. No one could ever read Ari's mind. He was a strange, introverted guy who could be kind or ruthless, however the mood took him. In that way he was just like Rob, but Rob usually took a conscious decision to do what was right for him. Ari, on the other hand, saw himself as his brother's keeper. What made that vital difference? she wondered. Two men, so much alike, one ferociously saintlike, the other ferociously selfish. Was it just upbringing, or something deeper?

'Well, if you put it that way, how can I refuse?' she whispered. 'But tell me more about Tom. He told you all that? Tom, the legless fisherman? How amazing! You've made me feel more confident. D'you think there's a word of truth in it?'

'Yes,' Ari said. She glanced sidelong and studied his expression, but once again she had no idea if he were telling the truth or stringing her along. It was a nice concept, so she decided to adopt it as her own.

There was a brooding introversion about Ari that she didn't understand and his on-going obsession to punish the guilty was unusual in a man of his intellect. Without doubt, he was one of the cleverest men she'd ever met, as clever as Rob. But there was much more to Ari. He really cared for everyone.

He looked down suddenly and grinned. 'What do you say to a little fuck?' he said, trying to make her smile. It was his favourite corny joke.

She dismissed the usual reply: hello little fuck. 'Yes,' she said earnestly. 'As soon as possible. I need you, specially today. Whatever happens now, I want you to hold me and make love to me and tell me why you are like you are.'

'How's that?' he asked, turning towards her momentarily.

'Look out!' she shouted.

He righted the car. 'Sorry!'

'You almost put us in the ditch.'

'Sorry again. What do you mean – like I am?'

'Caring,' she said. 'Not to be confused with careful.'

He laughed and reached out to squeeze her knee. Moments later he was driving into the hospital car park.

Chapter 47

——— ———

Ari parked and followed Kate to the reception desk, feeling proud of the admiring glances she picked up, but when the receptionist sent them to the waiting room, the smell of ether and disinfectant made him feel depressed. Ari hated hospitals. Perhaps that was why he had been unwilling to let Tabson endure the pain and trauma. What if something had gone wrong? But Kate had been determined, sweeping away all opposition. Any minute now they'd know if she'd been right. Just look at her chewing her fingernails. She was scared to death, too.

'Hey, Kate, he'll be all right. Any improvement will be a big deal for Tabson . . .'

He'd sure said the wrong thing. She scowled, and turned her back on him.

Ari could be a fool sometimes, Kate thought. Just *any improvement* was not good enough. She'd been practising positive thinking for weeks, imagining Tabson kicking the soccer ball, jogging down the beach, walking tall and proud like any other boy. As for praying, she'd practically worn out her knees. He *had* to be normal. Nothing else was acceptable.

The theatre doors opened suddenly and the surgeon appeared wheeling out the unconscious boy. Something about his demeanour frightened her. He looked so serious, as if he were crying inside. Yes, he was. She could see that now. His eyes were wet with tears. Her heart lurched and her mouth dried.

'Mrs Palma . . . or rather, Kate, my dear . . .' He took both of her hands in his. She could only nod for her voice seemed to have fled.

'God smiled on us. In my most optimistic predictions I could not have imagined such a successful outcome. If the healing takes place as it should, Tabson's leg will be one hundred per cent normal. He tells me he wants to play soccer. Well, he will. Just make sure he follows instructions to the letter during the healing process. It's up to you now, my dear. I'll explain everything before he leaves hospital. If you believe in miracles, Kate, this is it. You can feel proud.'

Kate could not speak. She felt her face twisting up and the tears welling out of her eyes. She could only squeeze his hand and bite her lip. She couldn't even say 'thank you', her voice had fled, and then he was gone.

Later, in the recovery room, she bent over the sleeping boy and took his hand in hers. He opened his eyes and there was no question there . . . just blind faith . . . she had been so scared of letting him down.

'Your leg's going to be fine,' she whispered. 'Completely normal, just as long as you rest until the bone graft heals.'

He clutched her hand and fell asleep. She watched him pensively and broodingly. He was the first family she had ever had. He was her child, or her brother, someone who depended upon her, someone to fight for and work for, someone to love.

The nurse pushed Tabson towards the swing doors. 'There's no point in staying now, Mrs Palma. He'll be sleeping most of today. Come and see him tomorrow,' she said.

'Yes, thank you.'

Kate hurried out ahead of Ari, not wanting him to see her tears. She was so grateful. 'Thank you, God,' she muttered.

'Wow!' She said in the car. 'Wow!'

'A guy would be happy to share some of this triumph, Kate,' Ari said softly.

She stared at him in surprise. His cheeks were wet. He was so strange, so full of complications and contradictions. He was a really tough man. She'd heard so many rumours about him: how he'd risked his life to rescue Tabson and beaten Patel to a pulp.

'As a sign of a very special friendship I will allow you to pay half,' she said huskily, 'if you really want to. Or a quarter, or whatever you like up to a maximum of half.'

'Half,' he said, without turning his head. 'I feel privileged.' Was he laughing at her? He was a big tease.

Just look at him, smiling so smugly. He had a great profile, a delicate straight nose – a woman would love to have such a nose – features that were perfectly balanced, a heart-shaped, thin face with two deep grooves running from his nose to the side of his mouth, black curly hair, glistening with purple glints, sensuous lips and big brown eyes. Looking at him turned her on. But underneath that tough, sexy, happy-go-lucky exterior, was a deeply introverted man. He suffered deeply over his failures, she had learned, particularly over his inability to find Mandy and his lack of progress on the dunes' murders. Then there was that business of the disappearance of Rose. Everyone thought he was mad to worry about a twenty-eight-year-old murder, because there was a new murder every night in the squatter camp, but he wouldn't let up.

'Would you like to go out to lunch to celebrate our good news?' he asked.

'Let's stay home and celebrate,' she said. 'Or what about a compromise? Let's go out later for dinner. I really need some T.L.C. I didn't tell you, well really, it seemed insignificant compared with Tabson's operation, but I lost the court case against Rob. I heard this morning.'

'What court case?'

'*The* court case! The bird sanctuary! You know very well that I was trying to prevent Rob from developing the property and draining the swamps on his side of the lagoon. I lost! That's all there is to it.'

'I see.' Ari lapsed into silence, frowning as he drove. Kate still seemed to care for her hard-arsed husband. They were going home to make love, she had made that much clear, so why wouldn't she say that she loved him? Why wouldn't she be his? Was he just a convenient body? The fact that she was still married to Rob was like a thorn in his flesh, it kept on hurting. Even worse was the fact that she still cared. He knew he wanted to marry Kate. In his life he had not wanted anything so badly. There was something about her, not just her looks, or her courage, but the essence of her. It was as if a font of goodness was hidden inside her. He longed to be part of her and it. He loved her so much he wanted to touch her and hold her and make love to her all the time. The slightest look could turn him on, yet that wasn't enough. She had to be his.

'Any news of your divorce?' He tried to sound casual.

'Since yesterday, you mean? I told you Rob's divorcing me.'

He tried to pluck up courage to voice his disturbing thought: 'You still love him, don't you?'

'I really don't want to discuss Rob with you, Ari,' she said, putting her hand on his knee to show that there was no ill-feeling. But she was thinking: Yes, I do love him with all my heart, but maybe this feeling of love will go away. She had a feeling that Rob needed her, too. Even now, even though the divorce was going through, and despite all those flighty actresses and models he'd been taking out, she sensed that he needed her badly. She missed so much about him, for instance, his clever sense of humour, his fine, decisive mind. Hardly a day passed when she was not thinking of him, or remembering the early days of their marriage.

And Ari. How did she feel about him? She knew that he was falling for her and that worried her. He was enormously attractive. Just looking at him turned her on. He was so much like Rob, too. Perhaps that was what attracted her in the first place.

'Would you go back to Rob if he asked you to?' Ari asked out of the blue.

'He has asked me several times,' she answered, wishing he would stop trying to interfere.

'Why did you say no?'

'I can't live with Rob as a pauper. There's no future in a partnership where one person holds all the power. I have to stand on my own feet before I could dream of returning to Rob.'

'Returning to Rob? So that's what this is all about? And where do I come in? Just a body to keep you warm in bed while you make enough money to deserve Rob and his millions?'

'Oh dear,' she said. 'How did this happen? It sort of crept

up on us.' She closed her mouth firmly. A little late, she thought. The car stopped. They were home already. 'Out you get,' Ari said. 'Look here, Kate, I'm not interested in fucking someone else's wife. Make up your mind who you want, me or him. Maybe I'll see you later.'

'Oh, you beast! You knew how much I wanted you to stay. Typical, I must say. I should never have let down my defences. How could you spoil this lovely day?'

He caught hold of her hand. 'I can't bear it, Kate. Divorce him quickly and marry me. I'm not a robot. Don't tell me you might go back to Rob.'

'Then don't ask,' she snapped. 'You asked. The truth is, I don't know. Sometimes you sound like Rob. Why must I belong to someone? Why can't I be myself? Why is love so possessive? Does love give rights and special allowances? What's love all about anyway?' She broke off wondering if she were in love or in lust with Ari. 'What does it mean if you say you love someone? That you are theirs forever, tossed into a kind of body slavery, a total sacrifice of freedom?'

Oh boy! Now she'd done it. Ari was as sulky as a schoolboy. She got out of the car and he raced off, tyres squealing, dust flying. She felt as if a strange weight were pushing her down into the earth. But then she smelled fish *braaiing* and she wandered down the beach to where Frikkie was turning six fish on the grid.

'Ah, Frikkie, you caught yourself some fish.'

'For you, Missus Kate,' he said.

'But it's Thursday, your day off.'

'Missus Kate still eats on Thursday.' He looked up and gave her a toothless grin, his eyes dark with worry. 'How is he?'

'Wonderful,' she said, her good mood partly returning.

'Perfect. The operation was successful. We've all been very lucky.'

He beamed.

Frikkie knows the secret of love, she thought, watching him thoughtfully. He loves Tabson and me, but his love comes out of himself like a stream bubbling water. He expects nothing back. Perhaps he's the wise one, not the fool, after all.

Gous and Smit were on the way out, each had commandeered a patrol van with a couple of constables, when Ari arrived back at the station.

'Who are you after?'

'Patel's place. We're bringing in the kids.'

'Hang on while I park.'

Moments later they were speeding towards Patel's so-called 'Island Clubhouse', built on a ridge overlooking the ten-mile-long Kommetjie beach, which Hilda Ackerman had told them about.

Hidden in scrubby bush, concealed from both the road and the beach, was a well-worn footpath going down from the highway above. It was nothing more than a shack, Ari noted, the interior covered in old-style pop art against black painted walls. The roof was corrugated iron, disguised with reeds, the bar counter was of coconut husks. God knows where he'd got so many, Ari thought. It looked as if he had transported the entire building from some abandoned Indian Ocean island and reassembled it here. Tropical shells littered the tables and there were plenty of bamboo screens sheltering table nooks. A very necessary part of the decor, Ari reckoned, or newcomers might see what they would soon look like, he thought in disgust. The kids were unwashed and unshaven, smelling of sweat, *dagga* fumes and stale, cheap wine. Some of them were sniffing glue, their noses running with snot, their eyes gummed with sores. How much were their parents paying to keep them off the hard stuff?

The bartender ran off into the bush, but Albert Smit, a long-distance runner, soon marched him back.

'I'd like to burn this place down, but we need it for evidence,' Ari snarled. 'Leave two men to guard it. Detail a round-the-clock observation and pick up all the kids who call.'

The so-called manager, barman, and waitress – a skinny girl who looked as if she might have Aids – were locked in the vans with their twenty-five customers, and the entire screaming, dirty bunch were driven off to the cells.

'You coming along to pick up Patel?' Willis asked.

'What's the point? His lawyers will have him out in time for dinner. Leave him alone today.' He had something else in mind.

Ari turned away, not wanting Willis to see the fury in his eyes.

A call came in for Willis to get on up to the new squatter camp and Ari went along. Within a day, the camp had become a hive of activity. The concept of land ownership had brought about a metamorphosis in the alienated, dumped community. Men and women were attacking the ground with pickaxes, laying their foundations, cementing in the posts and hammering on corrugated iron. Women were plodding up the hot dusty road, piles of corrugated iron on their heads, their kids trailing behind, clutching nails and wire. The atmosphere was tense as the squatters defended their sites, while newcomers tried to oust them. The word had got around and the homeless from all around were trying their luck. It was like putting back the clock to the old gold rush days. Banished to the homelands for half a century, the people were hungry for a stake in the cities. They would kill for their land if necessary, and someone had.

The victim lay in a pool of blood near the perimeter fence. Ari gave Willis a hand to hoist the corpse into the back of the van. Taking down the details was a wasted effort, as usual. No one knew who he was. No one had heard or seen anything, they claimed, but someone must have loved him, Ari reasoned. Someone would talk eventually.

Sending Willis to the mortuary, Ari kept on with his questions and by sunset he had the story. Two men had claimed the same site and one had won. This was Africa where a man could be killed for a rand. Your own small clod of earth was a priceless fortune.

Temperatures were soaring at the local school hall, Ari discovered when he went looking for Kate. There was a ratepayers' meeting about the squatters and most of the locals were voicing their grievances. He could hear the shouts when he parked his car fifty metres off.

Kate and Melissa were sitting on the platform looking self-conscious as they tried to keep their knees tightly together and sit up straight. Kate looked wonderful in a blue dress, very high-heeled blue shoes and her hair swept up in a blue band. He winked at her and gestured with his hands to say that he was sorry he was late as he found an empty seat near the front. Tempers were boiling and Ari hoped the meeting wouldn't come to blows.

'I'd like to say something,' Meg's daughter, Irene, shouted in a loud voice from the back of the hall. Eventually the audience quieted enough for her to speak. 'I've been watching the car park where the black taxis and buses unload. Almost a hundred of them tumble out daily. They stand there looking lost and dismal. Sometimes they ask around the shops here for jobs or cardboard cartons. Then they walk down to the beach, or up the mountain, and quite a lot find their way to the new squatter area. Somehow they all fit in. I've heard there's hundreds more than we originally catered for a few days ago. We'll have to stop the influx or the camp will be unmanageable and the original squatters will suffer, too.'

'There's a deliberate campaign to send them here,' Melissa said firmly. 'We really can't blame them for our problem. The politicians promise them so much and then they're dumped on the pavements. They have no cash, no jobs, no shelter and no hope. No wonder they're so aggressive. They have nothing. Shouldn't we help them? The church minister across the way is collecting blankets and things, so if you have any old stuff . . . Well, I have a good deal of furniture I don't need, and pots and pans – that sort of thing. It would be nice to form an organisation. One afternoon a month wouldn't hurt anyone. I mean, we've all got stuff we don't use . . . it's a case of getting hold of it.' She broke off and leaned back.

There was an awkward silence. Then someone yelled 'Kafir-lover' from the audience.

'Don't feel sorry for those bastards,' Jack growled. 'They'd slit your throat as soon as look at you.'

Then Meg spoke up. 'I agree with Mrs Grant. It's true. There would be less housebreaking if they had more. You can put my name down,' she said to Melissa.

'What's the point? They'll break in anyway. They're starving . . .'

'There's a group of vagrants right behind my house on

the mountain,' Gill Bronson called out. 'They defecate in the bushes. My dogs rolls in the mess and then come into the house to roll on the carpet. We have to keep the dogs locked up. You can't believe the stench.'

'My kids are afraid to play on the beach . . .'

'My cat went missing. I'm sure they ate it . . .'

'You're all so smug,' Lynette, the dentist's wife, called out angrily. 'You've been so smart. The squatters are far away from your homes now. But what about me? I live in the Oaklands estate, right next to what used to be a lovely forestry reserve. We used to be up-market. Now we can't give away our houses. They've broken into my house four times. They only took food. I felt sorry for them, but I can't afford to feed them. Besides, the broken glass cost more than the food. So we've had to fence our property . . .' Lynette was almost in tears.

'That must have cost a packet . . .'

'Yeah!' Dave answered. 'Ten thousand rands. I had to take out a bond. Bloody hell . . .'

Jack Bronson stood up. 'I stand to lose a fortune with a new development I just bought right next to the forestry reserve,' he said quietly. Everyone knew that Jack had millions invested in a proposed shopping centre near the main road. 'I've always been liberal. This is the thanks I get for it. Are we going to do nothing while they cripple us financially? I'd like to get a group together to plan a campaign to send them somewhere else.'

'It's not just a financial problem,' Dave added. 'They fight amongst each other. Faction fighting has begun already. Soon they'll be robbing and mugging all over Silver Bay. If we don't send them packing we'll all be victimised. I'm with Jack.'

No one was sure if they wanted to be named, but Ari guessed several would be contacting Jack soon.

'Just because we're liberal, doesn't mean we want to kiss goodbye to our house values,' Lynette retorted.

'Or smell their stink . . .'

'Or have their blasted wood fires smoking up the atmosphere . . .'

'Their bloody dance music, Saturday nights go on all night. I nearly go nuts. How the hell can they afford a loudspeaker?'

'It's the shebeens. There's three of them . . .'

'They're always fighting. My mother had a petrol bomb chucked at her yesterday, it came right into the road, but fortunately it missed her car . . .'

The local vet stood up. 'Listen, the lagoon area is polluted with *Giardia*, a rare type of parasite that lives in the stomach, it's usually only found in Third World countries – now it's in Silver Bay. The squatters – of course. I've treated three infected dogs today. The point is, kids can catch it, too. Keep away from the river delta area.'

Silvia Jones, the estate agent, smiled ruefully as she stood up. 'I haven't sold a house for a month. Everyone's scared to come to Silver Bay. The market's absolutely dead.'

Emanuel spoke for the first time. 'They're taking the fishing jobs away from the coloureds. There'll be trouble over this. The coloureds won't stand for it.'

'It's like a science fiction horror movie . . .'

'Yeah! But we can't get out of it. Aliens have moved in and they plan to take over . . .'

'Over my dead body!'

'Hear-hear!' Pandemonium broke out. Everyone was shouting. Some of the young men in the back rows started to chant: 'Drive them out . . . drive them out . . .'

Kate stood up reluctantly. 'Listen,' she called out. 'Listen, please! Shut up, you lot at the back.' Eventually they did. 'This meeting has a purpose. It's to sort out those who want to help from those who want war. A number of us are willing to get together and help our newest ratepayers . . .'

'Fat lot they'll pay.'

A storm of applause greeted this remark.

'Nevertheless,' Kate went on. 'They are here forever and some of us feel that the best way to cope is to help them integrate with us. Here's a list of people to contact if you want to help, and remember, it's not just them you're helping, it's us. This meeting's closed.'

Kate could be a real toughie when she felt like it, Ari thought, admiring her as she ignored the hecklers and shouts of derision and calmly walked down the aisle handing out her leaflets.

Melissa's name was right at the top, he noticed wonderingly. Was this her new image, or did she care? And did it matter anyway? The fact was, they were doing something positive.

'Kate, I'm sorry,' he whispered. 'I'll make it up to you tomorrow. I have to work tonight.'

She turned briefly, a strange expression in her eyes, almost as if she were the guilty party.

Ari drove on to the harbour. He had to find Jean Graux. Luckily Jean was on the quayside, waiting for the ferryman.

'I've got to get that son of a bitch, Patel,' Ari said to Jean. He told him about the house and the kids he had seen and the foolish, desperate parents paying out protection money month after month, and Simon, who had died muttering Mandy's name. Did that mean something?

'It's not just revenge. I figure he might know something about Mandy. What if she's been there? What if he gave her something stronger? He might even have sold her?'

'Or buried her,' Jean said. 'Let's get that son of a bitch and make him talk.'

Chapter 48

——— ——

Long Beach seemed to stretch out forever, a broad silver band glistening in the moonlight. It was a cool night, but the three men hurrying along the sand were sweating. Two of them wore shorts and T-shirts and they were bare-footed. The other man looked out of place in his silver-grey mohair suit, shiny leather brogues, already ruined, tie askew.

When the police car had unexpectedly driven up a cul-de-sac leading to the deserted end of the beach, and Sam Patel had realised that he was not being charged at the police station, he had struggled and screamed enough to wake the small community sleeping in their beach bungalows nearby. Ari had silenced him with a hard chop on the jaw. Now all they could hear was his panting breath as he stumbled behind them at the end of a rope. His eyes flickered left and right desperately, but there were only quicksands on either side. He knew the score.

Glancing sidelong, Ari noted that Jean was enjoying himself. After twenty years as an African mercenary, torture must be routine to him, Ari thought with a flicker of distaste. What sort of a life must he have led? He claimed to be in his early fifties, but he was strong and superbly fit. His skin was burned as dark as an Indian and his bushy black eyebrows contrasted oddly with his white crew cut hair. His eyes were strangely luminous, great glowing brown orbs. Right now they were sparkling with fun.

There was a high sea running with huge breakers crashing on to the shore. They dragged Sam along the sand towards the boathouse, twisted the rope under his crotch and over both shoulders until he was securely harnessed. Tying the rope to the side of the boat, they pushed off into the surf. Both men jumped in as the engine turned and the boat shot forward. Sam gave a brief, high-pitched scream of terror. Then the rope jerked, and he was tossed high into the air. For a few seconds he was spread-eagled, pulled like a kite, jacket billowing, then he fell out of sight under foaming waves.

'Okay . . . stop!' Ari yelled two minutes later when they were clear of the breakers.

Jean kept going. 'Chicken,' he called, grinning over his shoulder.

'No . . . stop!' Ari dived for the controls, but Jean pulled back the throttle and the engine cut. Moments later they were rising and falling over the heavy swell.

The rope was almost immovable. Ari feared Sam had been taken by a shark and he was dragging in the shark as well. Or was his body caught on rocks? 'The rope's snarled,' he called, panic rising. A dark shape appeared nearby, spluttered and then sank.

'He's alive,' Jean grunted.

Ari bent over the stern and hauled the rope clear. 'Okay, pull!' Sam's body broke surface again in a shower of glittering drops as they hauled him into the boat.

Moments later, he was groaning and gagging over the bows. He pretended to lapse back into unconsciousness. Jean caught him round the hips and pushed. 'He's a goner. We left him too long. Chuck him back.'

'No!' The high-pitched protest ended in a sob.

'That was just for starters,' Jean told him, prodding his fat belly with his toe. 'You'll see just how imaginative we can be if you don't talk.'

'We'll wait,' Ari said. 'Is this a good place?'

'As good as any, if he talks. If not . . .' He jerked his thumb over his shoulder. 'The sharks feed on seals right over there by the island. Packs, sometimes, but he can talk here, if he wants to. Okay, Sam, let's hear what you can tell us.'

Except for Sam's rasping gasps and hiccuping sobs there was silence.

Jean started the powerful engine and within seconds they had gathered enough speed to plane over the surface of the water, hitting the wave crests with a series of bumps. Sam groaned as he lay face-down on the deck. He crawled to the side and tried to drag himself up, but years of easy-living had made him gross and weak. Eventually he dragged his head and shoulders on to a pile of fishing nets and hung on.

As they crossed the wide bay, the eastern sky turned from grey to turquoise and then the first rosy beams pierced the sky above the mountain range. By the time they reached the island, the sun was rising and the sea was a deep shade of turquoise, the waves white-crested. A crowd of inquisitive seals came bobbing around the boat as they tossed Sam overboard.

'I can't swim,' he cried despairingly. His arms and legs flayed the surface. The seals plucked up courage to dive under him, knocking him. He panicked and sunk under, surfaced screaming, and sank again.

Ari jerked the rope and Sam came floundering close enough to the side to hang on. He tried to pull himself in, but he was nowhere near strong enough.

'Help . . . Sharks . . .' he gasped. His eyes were rolling up, and he seemed on the point of collapse.

'Yeah. Plenty this morning,' Jean said.

Ari sat back and looked the other way, wishing this was over and done with, trying not to hear Sam's voice as he ran through the usual chorus of pleading, begging, bribing, threatening, but always lying. Ari had heard it all many times.

Eventually Sam's strength ran out and he quieted, and stopped trying to haul himself into the boat, which he'd learned was an impossibility, and hung on, saving his strength.

'Peace at last,' Jean said.

'Huh! Where's the sharks this morning?'

'Wait,' Jean said.

Twenty minutes later there was a sudden surge of seals towards the island. 'See that? That means the sharks are coming in for breakfast.' He winked, but Sam began to sob.

Soon he was begging for his life. 'Save me. I'm a Christian. A good Christian. I run a legitimate business. I have nothing to tell you, nothing. What's all this about? You want to see me eaten alive? Is this how you get your kicks? What have I ever done to you? You guys don't earn a lot. I can pay you . . . plenty . . . name your price.'

'Shut up,' Jean said. He filled a bucket with water and poured it over Sam's face, the man choked, his one hand lost its grip and he fought to get it back on the bow.

'If you can't tell us what we want to hear, save your breath,' Ari growled. 'Where's Mandy September?'

Sam began to sob. 'I never saw her. In my life . . . I swear to God. I've never set eyes on her. Never even heard of her until she was kidnapped.' Another bucket of water set him spluttering and choking, but this time he hung on.

Ari saw a shark's fin skimming past. Sharks were rare hereabouts and he knew he was lucky. He bent over the side, and hauled on the rope, pulling Sam half out of the water, so he could twist him round.

'Take a look,' he growled. 'There's the first. They can smell your fat guts and they're coming after you. Why did you have Tom set alight? Why did you want him dead?'

'Not me. I swear to God.'

Ari lowered him slowly back.

'Bastards, bastards, pull me out . . .' He was sobbing, spluttering and screaming with rage.

'You don't need your feet to talk with,' Ari said, playing out the rope.

Arms whirling like a windmill, Sam reached the bows and hung on desperately as Ari emptied another bucket over him.

'Tom talked!' Sam sobbed when he stopped choking. 'He's an informer – your man. You know that. That's why!'

'Tom never talked,' Ari said. 'So what exactly were you afraid he might tell me?'

A sudden swell cut across the bows, rocking the boat. A shark's fin cut past at ferocious speed, circling the boat. A jolt of fear surged through Ari bringing bile to his throat. He looked down into Sam's frantic eyes.

'He's got the smell of you all right. Talk fast!'

'Tom knew . . .'

'Knew what?'

'Fuck you, man,' he yelled.

'It's coming in . . .'

Sam saw the fin and screamed. 'He knew I set light to the squatter camp,' he gabbled.

'You!' Ari was too shocked to move as his theories collapsed around him. It was Jean who jerked hard at the rope hauling Sam half over the bows. He kicked like an upended turtle. Excited by the flailing legs, or the smell of fear, the shark bumped against the side of the boat, knocking it hard, and then again.

'Jesus!' Ari peered over the side at the dark shape twisting and turning and the powerful tail churning the water. Then he realised what Jean had done.

Ari caught Sam by the shoulders, propelled him round and ducked his head down until his nose was near the water. 'He's hungry,' he said.

Glancing back, he saw Jean lowering a second sack of offal. This guy knew his business. Sam had pushed himself back into the boat and he was screaming, high-pitched and mindless.

'One bite can cut a man in half,' Jean said gravely.

'Okay, over you go . . .'

Sam gripped Ari's shoulder and hung on hard. His voice was calmer now. 'I'll tell you whatever you want to know. I never intended anyone should die,' he muttered. 'I burned out the shebeen because they were undercutting my prices in the village. I swear to God, I never intended to kill anyone. Why should I? They're customers, aren't they, but they were buying their booze at the wrong place.'

'You own that bar up on the ridge?'

'All of them,' Sam gasped. 'I own three bars in the village.'

'So four people died because someone undercut your prices? Am I hearing you right?'

'I told you,' he blustered. 'I didn't intend they should die. I wanted to destroy Boysie's outfit. He had no right . . .'

You had no right, Ari was thinking. He remembered

Eunice and her shattered, black corpse. The farmer from the Ciskei. The old man and his child. But the death penalty was expected to be abolished and Sam would probably be out in a matter of months. He might never stand trial. He longed to kill the bastard.

'Tell us where Mandy is,' he growled, pushing him towards the side.

Sam was fighting for breath, shocked almost out of his mind, as he stared down at the massive, frenzied shark. 'I never saw Mandy. Never in my life,' he sobbed. 'I could lie, but how could I lead you to her? I don't know where she is. I can't tell you what I don't know.'

He lapsed into a deep depression, moody and sullen. Then he passed out, but Jean revived him with cold water.

'How do you know Mandy wasn't one of those kids in your so-called dirty clubhouse?'

'I make it my business to know. I get their names and addresses. That's how I get to their parents.'

'And if they don't want to tell you?'

'They never want to tell, but there's their car number plates, and sometimes I have them followed home. It's easy. They're only kids.' His voice had lapsed to a whisper. He was going off into shock, hardly aware of what he was saying.

Ari listened bemused. He was staggered by the unexpected information, but Jean carried on.

'How much do the parents pay you?'

'Depends, I go for one-third of their incomes.'

'And if they won't pay?'

He shrugged. 'I give the kids what they want. I'm a businessman, that's all. I supply people's needs. If those snotty kids want crack or coke, or mandrax, I sell it to them.

That's what business is all about.' He closed his eyes, head slumping against the bows, his body racked in shudders that were fast becoming convulsions.

'He's had it,' Jean said. 'We could bring him round with brandy, but I reckon he's told the truth. You've enough to book him for murder, extortion, dealing in drugs. Will that do?'

'Jean, thanks,' Ari said.

'I'd like to kill him for you, because I don't think you're the killing type. At least, not as a rule,' he said. 'But I think you'll need him back in the station. I've taped the conversation, if you can call it that.'

He unravelled the rope and threw the last sack of offal over the side. 'Have it all, Jaws, you deserve it,' he called down.

'D'you think he'll live?' Ari asked, prodding the unconscious man with his toe.

'He will. But I wouldn't say much for your chances if his boys catch you alone one night. Watch out, Ari.'

'That's the story of my life,' Ari said.

By 10 a.m. Sam had been formally charged and was in the cells. Ari would put in an urgent plea that no bail be awarded, but he didn't think he'd win, not nowadays. Appeasement was the name of the game. He sighed, put a coin in the coffee machine and sat at his desk sipping the muddy brew. He felt depressed. Five months in the Cape and he was no nearer to finding Mandy. He had been so sure that there was a link between the kidnapping, the dunes murder and Rose's murder, but he'd been wrong.

He sat doodling with his pen. There had been no ransom demands, no clues, no idea why she'd been kidnapped. A new thought occurred to him. Was someone punishing her because she resembled Rose so closely? Who had hated Rose the most?

Claire? Jânek? Either of them might be able to add to his meagre knowledge of Rose's death. He was still convinced that this was linked to Mandy's kidnapping. Jânek would never get back into South Africa, but Claire might be easy to trace. He picked up the telephone.

His hunches had seldom been wrong. Besides, he had no other avenue to explore and only one month left here, so what did he have to lose?

Chapter 49

— —

Ari was impressed by the entrance to the game lodge, a long avenue bordered with brilliant flowering shrubs, sloping emerald lawns, fountains, a croquet lawn, and then the graceful hotel reminiscent of colonial days. He had flown to Durban, hired a car and driven north up the coastal road, cutting through lush tropical greenery and sugar plantations, towards Mtubatuba, where Claire Gardner ran a small, exclusive hotel situated near the gates of Umfolozi Game Park. Here her visitors could enjoy the best of both worlds: untamed nature in daylight hours, and total luxury from sundown to sunset, or so the travel agent had told him.

He parked, picked up his overnight bag and walked into the white-tiled foyer under thatch, and stood staring longingly at several brilliantly executed wildlife paintings. On the rare occasions when he yearned for wealth, it was to possess something beautiful.

'You're not supposed to do that,' a charming voice came from behind the counter.

He looked round in surprise, and realised why he had not noticed the woman. She was so calm and still. A swift glance drank in all of her, her fading blonde hair cut in a fashionable short bob, her Grecian profile with a straight, short nose to match, and her lovely green eyes, observant and wise. She had dressed to match her eyes in a green floral dress, and tiny emerald earrings. Her skin was smooth and unblemished and she was still beautiful, although she was in her late forties.

'What am I not supposed to do?' he asked, walking towards her.

'Carry your suitcase. Relax! Everything is done for you here. That's what this place is all about – pampering.'

'And who pampers you?' he asked. Was she Claire? he wondered. Instinctively he knew that she was. He began to feel sorry for Rob Palma. To be deprived of such a mother was a rare loss. Would a woman like her, with eyes that shone with compassion and humour and a mouth that was smiling so delightfully, abandon her child?

'I pamper myself,' she said and laughed.

He signed in, explaining that he was there for one night only and paid in advance.

'Are you here on business?' she asked, glancing at the Cape Town address in her register.

'Yes. I'm a policeman.'

'Good heavens!' She looked amused rather than shocked. 'Who, or what, are you after?'

'I think you, but I'm not sure. Are you Claire Gardner, formerly Palma?'

'You've worked that out for yourself, haven't you?' A tiny frown appeared on her smooth, broad brow. 'Why? What is it? Is anything wrong?' All at once she looked frightened as a new thought occurred to her. 'Is my son all right?'

'Yes. The family are fine.'

She let out her breath audibly. 'Is it something scary?'

'Not unless talking about the past distresses you. I'm investigating a recent kidnapping and I need information about events that occurred around twenty-eight years ago. Maybe you can help me.'

She glanced down, but not before he had seen the pain that flitted across her face. Deep grooves lined her forehead and fleetingly she looked her age. 'Then I guess it can keep a while. There's a shower and a Jacuzzi in your room. You'll find your bar is well stocked. I'll send up some ice. Would you like to dine with me, say at eight?'

'Thank you.'

'Tonight we have a *braai* in the garden. The weather's perfect in the evening at this time of the year. Dress smart-casual, please. Oh yes, and we have evening safaris here, ten until two a.m. There's quite a lot to see on our own territory: hippos, rhinos, warthogs, antbears, all the buck. Would you like to go?'

'I'll stick to the hotel, thanks. I was brought up in the wilds: Kenya, Zaïre, Zimbabwe. When I go into the bush I like to do it at length and alone.'

'Oh, one of those, are you?' She gave him a secret, knowing smile and turned back to her bookkeeping. Was she really forty-nine? When she smiled, she looked like a girl. He felt drawn to her, as he hung around, noticing the delicate subtle perfume that mingled with the scent of honeysuckle in a vase on her desk.

The porter beckoned and reluctantly he followed him to his room. Flinging open the shutters, Ari gasped with pleasure at the view over the small, private game park: green hills and gentle valleys stretched away to the horizon and were lost in purple mists. Two water buck were grazing on the lawn right under his window and further off he could see three men trying to chase a family of warthogs off the golf course. A scent of the river wafted up, mingled with the smell of damp grass and the heady perfume of tobacco flowers growing in clumps along the wall. There was a sense of peace and timelessness. Ari felt that this was a moment of deep significance; it was almost as if his inner-self was trying to tell him something.

By eight-fifteen, Ari was sitting at the edge of the lawn, at a table laid for dinner, watching the cook flicking the chops around with a deft hand. The trestle tables beside the *braai* were filled with salads and decorated with hibiscus flowers. Frogs were croaking down in the river and he could hear hippos snorting somewhere nearby.

Claire came across the lawn, stopping to chat to guests and he heard their happy laughter. She was slightly plump, he noticed, and it suited her. She had changed into a dress of green silk with little white daisies on it. Her hair was pushed back with a band and she wore a necklace of emeralds that shone in the light from the flares. He wondered where her husband was, or if she still had one.

He decided to ask when they had greeted each other and sat down. 'Where is Mr Gardner?'

'Is that an official question?' A wary look had come into her eyes. Perhaps she was the target of local, unmarried males.

'No.'

'Well, let's skip that one and get on to the official questions,' she said gently.

'I'm sorry if I offended you. It's a big place to run on your own.'

'Yes, it is, and I'm not offended. He died some years back and I decided not to remarry. I loved him and I hate talking about it.' She smiled self-consciously and shrugged her shoulders. 'It's self-service tonight. Let's go for it.' She was determined to be cheerful and remote and Ari tried to play along. He kept off the subject of his investigation during dinner, and instead told her of the game parks he knew further north. They began to discuss the problems of culling and protection in general.

'You seem to know a great deal about running a game farm,' she said after a while. 'I could do with someone like you around the place.'

'For me it was a toss-up, game farming or the police.' He smiled ruefully. 'I'm beginning to think that both ideas were wrong.' He told her about his adoptive parents and how they had tried to push him into an academic career. 'I'm thinking of continuing my studies in criminology.'

It was only much later that he decided to bring up the subject of his visit. 'I'm sorry that I have to rake up painful memories,' Ari said, when they had finished dessert and were still lingering over the wine. 'I'm investigating the kidnapping of Bill September's daughter, Mandy. This, and other crimes, seem to me to link back to the death of Rose September.'

'I didn't know that she had died!' Claire interrupted him. 'I was told she'd emigrated.'

'That was the story spread around, but it wasn't true. Let me tell you what I've found out so far . . .'

His story lasted through coffees and liqueurs. Finally they moved to a bench on the front lawn overlooking the river.

'So what more could I possibly tell you?' she asked, gazing dreamily down to the river. 'You seem to know everything.'

'I don't understand why Rose waited for seven months before returning to demand more money from Angelo Palma.'

'But didn't you know . . . ? Rose waited until her baby was born.'

Ari gasped and sat up. 'Baby? She was pregnant?'

'Oh yes!' Claire sighed. 'That was the problem, we were *both* pregnant. You see, Lieutenant, Trevor and I were getting closer. He was crazy about his coming son. I thought I was winning through, but all the time I was losing. Neither I nor Trevor knew that Rose was pregnant.' Ari noticed that she was looking haggard and he wished he could stop upsetting her.

'I always thought that Rose's strategy was masterminded by Ramona,' she went on. 'She was a lovely girl in an eastern sort of way, but she never seemed over-bright to me. She would never have had the guts to do the things she did on her own. She played a waiting game and gave birth in Mozambique. When she came back she telephoned Angelo and told him she wanted her baby recognised as co-heir to the Palma fortune and she wanted Angelo to legally adopt him. Angelo refused. Later he told me that they fought and that she had lost out, and then emigrated.' She shuddered. 'Do you think that he murdered her? He's capable of doing that.'

'I don't know.'

'You see,' Claire turned and, flushing, she placed one hand on his arm. 'I wasn't there at the time. After Trevor was killed I had a nervous breakdown – or that's what they called it. To me, it just seemed that I was too miserable to move or to eat or to listen to people. I just wanted to die. I had to remain in the sanitorium for a while. My baby was taken back to the Palmas by a nurse, who stayed on to look after him. Nowadays I find it difficult to remember how sad I was. I blame myself for losing my baby.

'I returned from the clinic when Rob was two months

old. I told Angelo that I was leaving and taking Rob with me. This was about two weeks after Rose and he had quarrelled.' She took a deep breath and sipped her liqueur. 'Do you want to hear all this?'

'Yes, please.'

'I began packing up my baby's clothes, but Angelo called in his lawyers and they obtained a court order preventing me from taking Rob. They managed to prove that I was mentally impaired and in no condition to look after my child. It was horrible!' She shivered and rubbed her arms vigorously. 'I had another breakdown, nothing serious, just an attack of nerves really, but that gave Angelo all the ammunition he wanted.

'While I was back in the clinic, Angelo had himself appointed Rob's legal guardian. He came to see me and told me that if I tried to take Rob he would disinherit him and take Rose's baby in his place. That was how I learned about her child.

'I said I'd take Rob anyway, just as soon as I was better, but my parents and their lawyer pointed out that I could never win, not with my medical record, against Angelo and his money and his coven of lawyers. Angelo told me that my parents would be ruined by the legal battles he would create. He promised that Rob would get the best of everything, so I left him there. I should have stayed, but I couldn't bear the memories, nor that horrible house.

'D'you know, Ari . . . I can call you Ari, can't I? I went back one day and saw Rob. There was no bond, no rapport, nothing. That was a bitter moment.'

Ari saw the tears trickling down her cheeks, and put one hand over hers. 'Mrs Gardner . . .'

'Claire.'

'Claire, you have no need to reproach yourself.'

'Oh, yes, I have, Ari.' She wiped her cheeks with the back of her hand. 'Any woman who has parted with her child will understand how treacherous I feel. I ran away and left him, when he needed me, but I just couldn't stay.

'Then there was Angelo. I'd always thought he was the kindest man in the world until he showed his teeth. He was intent on convincing the court that I was incapable of looking after my child. What sort of a man would do that? He was never quite the same after his wife died, my parents told me. He put all his future hopes into his dynasty. He had been obsessed with Trevor and he transferred all this love and devotion to Rob. He had such dreams.' She turned to him and gave him a wistful smile.

'So finally I put all my inheritance into a trust for my baby, everything I owned. When I die, this farm will be his, too. I hope that he will realise that I love him, even though I left him. You know, Ari, it took me years to get over all this. Finding out that Rose had also had a child was the final straw.'

A hippo snorted and she stood up and leaned over the fence, looking down to the water. She was a lovely, but sad woman, Ari thought, watching her. He longed to comfort her, but how could he?

'How is Rob? Is he happy?' she turned and smiled softly at him. 'What's his wife like?'

Ari did his best to reassure her, feeling guilty when he described Kate to her.

'Is there anything else you want to know?' she asked, turning and putting her hand on his shoulder.

'That about covers everything,' he said.

'Then I'll say goodbye,' she whispered. She left, but Ari had the strangest feeling that he would see her again very soon.

Later that night, he found himself thinking about Claire's lovely, but sad eyes. Finally he gave up trying to sleep and switched on the light. He poured himself a Scotch and picked up a brochure on the game farm, conveniently placed beside his bed.

Beware: Visitors are reminded that the wild animals in this park are very dangerous. Please do not approach them, he read.

'And take even more care when you leave,' he added for his own benefit.

Chapter 50

———— ————

Ari was sitting beside a helpful young woman who was checking birth registrations on the computer at the Home Affairs Office. Her skin was white and flawless, and above the neckline of her floral dress he could see the plump mounds of her breasts. Her breasts bounced and her red hair shimmered and shook and she excited him with each movement she made, while her green eyes shone with invitation.

'Here we are,' she said. She bent forward to peer at the screen, and Ari achieved a marvellous vantage point above her, so he could see her lacy pink bra and her nipples almost protruding over the inadequate garment.

'Anton Palma September, born Lourenço Marques, Mozambique, December 18, 1964. Mother: Rose September, unmarried,' she called excitedly. 'She registered her baby at the South African consulate there, in order to have his name put in her passport to bring him back to South Africa.'

'That's it! You've done it!' He caught hold of her hand and squeezed it hard. 'Now check deaths.'

She groaned laughingly.

There was no entry there, but there were other possibilities: adoption, emigration, change of name, and Ari wanted them all checked out. The young woman did not complain, but eventually he had to give up and reluctantly tear himself away from all that luscious flesh.

Driving back, he pondered on the fate of Rose's baby. Why had no one mentioned Anton? Did he die? If so, where was the death certificate? Had he been murdered? He would have been twenty-eight now. There was always the possibility that Palma had sent the child overseas. Strange that Ramona had never mentioned him. Nor Bill? Obviously they were covering up something, but what?

He found Ramona in the laundry, scolding the ironing woman who, she said, had ruined the shirts. The moment she saw him her face darkened, her black eyes shimmered with malevolence, and her mouth tightened to a taut line. Age had not been kind to Ramona. There was no gentleness to offset the harshness of the deep lines and grooves in her eroded skin. She looked like a mad old witch with her grey hair hanging round her shoulders. Could she ever have been lovely like Mandy? People said so, but it was hard to imagine.

As usual, the sight of Ramona brought out his aggression. She was the stuff of ancient nightmares.

Steeling himself, he said: 'Mrs September, I have a few questions to ask you concerning the kidnapping of Mandy September . . .'

'You're wasting your time,' she said, sneering at him. 'Do you think I would kidnap my own granddaughter?'

The ironing woman looked relieved to be let off the hook.

'And concerning the whereabouts of your grandson, Rose's son, Anton Palma September,' Ari went on, unperturbed.

She bowed her head, but not before he'd seen the fear there. 'Go!' She muttered to the servant. 'Scrub the back steps. I'll do this.'

Grabbing the water bottle, she turned her back on him and sprayed the shirts. He guessed she was playing for time to regain her composure.

'Why was Anton September killed, Ramona? You know, don't you? Was it the only way you could avenge yourself on his father, Trevor? Yet he was your flesh and blood, too. Didn't that count for anything? Or did Angelo Palma force you to kill the child? Was that the deal, Ramona? Get rid of Trevor's bastard child and thereby eliminate all claims to the Palma fortune, in return for the substantial payments, plus a house, a trawler and a pension made to you?'

She remained bent over the ironing board, pressing the steaming iron on to the shirt, while he waited, hating the smell of steaming damp laundry. When she looked up, she was smiling.

'Rose never had a child,' she said.

'Obviously you aren't aware that the child's birth was registered at the South African consulate in Lourenço Marques. Rose had to do this to bring the child home.'

'Ridiculous! There are no records left from pre-revolution days.'

'You're being foolish and wasting time, Ramona. The Home Office has all the details on computer. The consulate records were evacuated.'

Ramona crumpled on to the laundry basket, wiping her forehead with the pressing cloth. 'It was so long ago,' she whispered. 'I hardly remember. What could I do? The child was a nuisance. I was working. Rose was dead and no one wanted to look after the baby. I certainly couldn't, so I took it to relatives of mine. My brother brought him up as his own child . . .'

This was a massive anti-climax. Ari let out his breath like a pricked balloon. 'But why send him away?' he stammered. 'Why did no one mention him?'

'Who remembers a baby from so long ago? There are too many babies around the village. I didn't want to be saddled with her bastard. Angelo didn't want him hanging around here for obvious reasons.'

'Do you know where Mandy is?' he asked, out of the blue.

'If I knew, I'd be there to fetch her home,' she said, shrugging at his foolishness. To his surprise she wiped her eyes with the hem of her apron. So she did have feelings after all.

'I want the address of your relatives where you left Rose's baby. I'll check out your story.'

She began to swear under her breath. Ari had the impression she was putting a curse on him. Stupid old hag with her superstitious rigmarole, yet he felt uneasy.

It took days before Ari forced the farmer's name out of Ramona and traced her family to a wheat farm called Smitsplaas, tucked amongst the beautiful mountain range behind Malmesbury. The farmer's wife listened to his story and pointed towards the whitewashed huts. Carrying a bottle of brandy wrapped in tissue paper, Ari walked five hundred yards past a kraal to the cluster of square brick houses behind a grove of trees, where the farm labourers lived.

Ramona had grown up on this farm and her brother, Piet, still drove the tractor. He lived with various women who came and left, leaving their children behind, Ramona had told him. Piet's latest love, he saw now, was an old, battered-looking drunk with Hottentot features which showed in her eroded parchment skin, her slit eyes and flat face. Here was the height of deprivation and the squalor was absolute, the stench unbelievable, a mixture of tobacco, wood smoke, paraffin and unwashed bodies. The curious children, barefoot and scabby, thronged around him like midges at dusk.

'You say you're a policeman,' Piet was watching him cautiously. 'So where's your uniform?'

Ari flicked out his ID, but the old man could not read.

'Ag, man! He's from the police. It says so here,' one of the boys called out.

'I didn't steal her eggs,' the old man whined. 'There's rooicats and snakes here, but the missus doesn't understand these things. City bred!' He spat on the ground.

Ari put his bottle on the box that served as a table and offered the old man some of it. Piet seemed to be speechless for a while. He kept staring at his mug and smacking his lips while mumbling through toothless gums, about the gods favouring him. Eventually he knocked it back in one gulp.

As soon as Ari sat down, he began to itch all over. He couldn't wait to get home and fumigate his clothes and hair. He'd have to fumigate the car, too, he thought gloomily.

'Listen, Piet,' Ari began. 'Twenty-eight years ago, your sister, Ramona, brought her daughter's baby back here and left him with you. I've come to see the boy, Anton. Is he here?'

'You're wasting your time,' he muttered. 'Dozens of children are brought back here adding to our burden. Twenty-eight years ago? You must be joking.'

Piet was staring meaningfully at the bottle until Ari poured another generous tot. This time Piet sniffed at it, and rolled it round his palate like a connoisseur, an expression of pure heaven on his face.

They talked about the crops and the difficulties of farming in general until Piet had drunk two or three tots. Then Ari stood up and retrieved his bottle. 'I must be off . . . sorry you can't help me.'

'Sit down, sit down,' the old man said, pushing the chair towards him with his foot. 'Jog my memory. What did he look like? Maybe I could remember something.'

Ari obliged again.

'You're a real friend,' Piet said. 'Not like her. Ramona was always a pain in the arse, even when she was young. She couldn't get off this place soon enough . . . hated it! As for that child. Skinny little baby he was, and so light-skinned. Her Rose had been up to no good with a white man. Perhaps that's why Rose didn't want him. I told her to pay for the child's keep, but she said he wasn't worth paying for. I remember her words: "Let him die, no one wants him." But he survived.

'We had him for two years. He was always sick, always crying – more trouble than he was worth. The other kids bullied him because he was so white.'

Ari leaned back, closed his eyes and forced himself to relax. The old man was lost in his drunken reverie. Something relevant might emerge.

'God knows how he managed to survive. He caught everything – measles, mumps, whooping cough, pneumonia. The old missus who died later always called the doctor if our children were ill, so he survived. Ramona wasn't none too pleased about that. He fell in the dam one day, but somehow he got out. Then the other kids flung him in a hole and buried him. They came running to tell us he was dead, so we went to look for him, but he'd disappeared. We reckoned that was the last we'd see of him, but the next day he came stumbling into the hut, covered in scratches and mud, snivelling his head off. The kids said he came crawling out of a porcupine's burrow. I called Ramona and told her to take him away. The devil looks after its own. There was something odd about that child.'

'How old was the boy when she took him away?' Ari stood up, anxious to get out of the place.

'Just over two, maybe two and a half. I don't remember.'

'This is yours,' Ari said, giving him the rest of the bottle. 'I don't know if I'll be back.'

Ari walked over the veld feeling oppressed and disgusted. He only felt better when he was racing back along the motorway to Cape Town.

By 6 p.m. he had showered off the dust of the journey and his disgust of the old man and his filthy, verminous shack, doused his hair in a generous portion of delousing shampoo and thrown his clothes into the washing machine. Despite this, he still felt contaminated as he drove down to Kate's place. So he swam in the cold sea, diving through breakers, surging through the waves in a fast crawl, driving himself until his muscles ached and his skin tingled. Then he swam slowly back.

He arrived to find Frikkie crouched on a rock beside the door. There was blood on his collar, his cheeks were scratched, but washed clean, one eye was swollen and the bruises were showing. He'd had a beating. Ari put one hand on his shoulder. 'What happened to you, man? Someone's given you a thrashing.'

Frikkie stared at his feet, immobilised and catatonic in his distress. Ari felt his arm and his shoulder. He was rigid, each muscle clenched, his eyes gazing sightlessly at the lighthouse door. There was no sign of movement or recognition as Kate rushed out carrying a first aid kit.

'It's one step forward and two steps back with Frikkie, I'm afraid.' She began to dab surgical spirits on to his scratched cheeks. 'He was getting along fine,' she said as she smeared ointment on Frikkie's cheeks. Ari was touched by her gentleness.

'Who did this to you, Frikkie? Who beat you?' she asked. There was no sign that he heard her. 'Amazing that he managed to get here,' Kate said.

'When?'

'Just now. I came out half an hour ago and here he was.'

'When did he go missing?'

'Well, he didn't. He went off after work yesterday. He was fine then. I saw him last at about five.'

'Has he been like this before?'

'Yes.' She looked up, frowning at him. 'That time after the fire on the dunes. He was burned, remember? And once before . . . The village boys can be very cruel. When they call him a *bobbejaan* he gets fighting mad.'

'He needs medical attention.'

She frowned. 'Once, in the old days . . .'

She always referred to her former marriage as 'the old days'. The *good* old days or the *bad* old days? Ari longed to know, but didn't want to provoke another fight by asking. Instead he scowled at her, but she didn't notice.

'. . . Ramona and he had a quarrel and he got like this, so we called an ambulance, but the mental hospital discharged him. They said they were short of beds and he would never improve, and that anyway he was harmless. They gave him a tranquilliser.'

'Have you any tranquillisers?'

'No, but I have a bottle of brandy.'

'Let's give him some food first.'

'I made some soup,' she said flicking him a brief, uncertain smile.

Minutes later Kate was bent over Frikkie watching him spoon soup into his mouth. It smelled delicious and Ari realised how hungry he was. 'It's not too hot, is it?'

'No. It's fine. Actually, I made it for supper – a huge pot full, with pumpkin and parsnips – all the things you like.'

'Mmm! My favourite.'

'I know.' She smiled up at him and he grinned back, feeling his doubts and pessimism falling away.

Frikkie's mind was still in shock, but his body reacted to the taste of Kate's soup and came shuddering back to life after he had swallowed the first mouthfuls. Soon he was able to hold the spoon. The brandy set him choking and coughing. Moments later Frikkie became distressed, rolling his eyes and shaking badly. He stood up, flopped back, and gaped at his legs that could not hold him. He would have tumbled off the rock, but Kate steadied him. Kate stared questioningly at Ari.

Frikkie peered up with his baffled eyes, clenching his big fists. His lips began to move, slowly framing the words that Ari strained to hear.

'Who . . . hit . . . you . . . Frikkie?'

'Ramona,' came the whisper that was half a sigh. 'She hit me . . . with a stick. She wanted to kill me . . . but she was wrong.' He evaded their questions by retreating into himself again.

Gradually, under Kate's persistence, Frikkie's eyes came to life again and his body straightened slowly in obedience.

'Missus . . . Missus . . . she says I took the money and cheated her.'

'What money, Frikkie?' Kate's voice was so gentle, but so compelling.

'The money Angelo gave her to kill the child. I did what they wanted. I took it out in the trekking boat and I threw it over the side,' he said urgently. 'I swear I did. I told her the truth.'

'Fetch a pencil and paper, Kate,' Ari said quietly, but she shrugged him off angrily.

Ari got up and went to get the pad from beside the telephone and a pen that was lying there.

'Which baby did you have to kill, Frikkie?' Ari asked.

'Don't answer him,' Kate said urgently, shaking Frikkie's shoulder.

'Kate!' Ari snarled in sudden fury. 'There's more to this than Frikkie's liberty. There's Mandy, for starters. Don't interfere.'

There was a puzzled silence as Kate froze and Frikkie's face turned slowly from one to the other. Kate's expression troubled Ari. Her eyes were telling him to go to hell.

'You can tell us, Frikkie,' Ari urged him, ignoring Kate.

The old man began muttering, moving his head, bunching the muscles of his strong scraggy neck, his massive brow frowning, his black eyes recessed, almost out of sight but gleaming there under his tousled black fringe of hair and jutting brows.

'Frikkie,' Ari said sternly. 'Tell me what you had to do.'

'Drown the child.'

'No,' Kate shouted. 'You have no right.' She wanted to put her hand over Frikkie's mouth, but Ari hung on to her as Frikkie stumblingly incriminated himself, telling them in stops and starts and muddled words how he had rowed out the nets in the predawn darkness, with the toddler hidden under them, so he could toss the child overboard with the nets.

'Enough!' Kate said fiercely. She broke away from Ari and ran to the lighthouse. 'He needs a lawyer. I demand that you stop. You made me make him drunk. Damn you, Ari!'

Anger surged. Why did she think she had the monopoly on compassion? Was she the only one who loved Frikkie?

'Trust me, Kate.'

'You?' she said, scornfully, alienating him.

'I advise you to keep your sympathy for the innocent,' Ari warned her, losing his temper and saying things he did not mean.

'He is innocent, because he doesn't understand right from wrong. He wouldn't harm a fly.'

'Only a baby.'

Kate gasped. 'You are a bastard, aren't you? A really big bastard. You tricked me into making him talk. I hate your world and I despise you.'

'Why?' His sharp incisive voice cut through her self-reproaches as he searched for words to hurt her back. 'Because I don't make money? Because I try to pro-tect the victims and punish the criminals? Because I'm detaining someone who just might have murdered a baby? Or because I'm removing one of the lesser moons who revolve around Kate's magnificent sun and bask in her indulgence?'

She rushed inside, slamming the door behind her and Ari sat down on a stone, feeling sad. He couldn't arrest Frikkie on his drunken ramblings. At this stage he had not made up his mind that murder had been committed, but he had to admit it was looking likely.

He helped Frikkie to his bed and returned to sit alone on the dunes, worrying about the case. Would Angelo want Rose's baby dead? Maybe! Clearly he would want to avoid future claims on the estate. But would Ramona kill her own grandchild? Possibly! Ari had already investigated three cases of mothers killing their own children. Ramona was only the grandmother and she had been paid well to keep the child off Angelo's back. But murder?

Ari was relieved when Kate came out carrying two beers and a plate of sandwiches. 'I don't want to fight with you, Ari,' she said with a warm smile. 'I just don't agree with the way you were handling Frikkie. Let's be friends.' That was Kate for you. Quick to anger and quick to make friends. She never held a grudge. That was one of the many things he loved about her.

Chapter 51

The room was lit by spotlights that brought out the glow of the rose panelling, the yellow-wood ceiling and the long polished oak desk where Rob was still working. In front of him was a calculator, a small pad and a sharp pencil. That was all he ever needed. Everything else was carried in his head.

Rob heard a tap on his office door. He frowned and called: 'Come in.' Glancing at his watch he was surprised to see that it was past 10 p.m. He had been engrossed in his calculations. This was an area in which he felt both secure in himself and happy – a world apart. Financial manoeuvring, wheeling and dealing, marketing, planning strategy, all these were both a joy and a comfort to him. Even Kate's treachery could not spoil this world. He wrote down the latest figure, switched off the calculator and glanced up. Ramona was looking furious and he knew why.

'It's so late,' he grumbled.

'I saw your light. I wanted to speak to you privately.'

'Sit down.' He stood up and turned to the window, trying to compose his answer to her anticipated plea. From here he could see the whole sweep of the valley, the broad river, the swampy river delta, and the lighthouse which nowadays blazed with light until Kate went to sleep.

Tonight she was still awake. Was she reading? Or having sex with her lover?

Turning away with a shudder, he watched the lights of his trawlers swaying from side to side in the gentle swell. All twelve of them were in harbour being fitted with advanced fish-finding equipment. Finding economically viable shoals was become increasingly difficult. There were too many trawlers and too few pilchards. This was one reason why he had decided to cut out the middle man and process only the fish that were caught by his own fleet. The notices had been sent out to the seven freelance skipper-owners, including the Septembers, last week. They would be ruined, he knew this, but he had to do what made economic sense. He had chosen an opportune time to axe them when Angelo was visiting his vineyards. Grandfather was sentimental and would try to protect the Septembers, and perhaps the others, too.

'What is it, Ramona?' he asked casually, moving back to his chair.

'I have a story to tell you,' she said, her black eyes watching him intently. 'Twenty-eight years ago . . .'

'Oh for God's sake . . .' he fumed. 'Come on, Ramona, it's late. I have to finish this work. Do we have to go back twenty-eight years for you to beef about the new fishing arrangement? I can't help you, I'm sorry. It's plain economics. I know what you want and the answer is no,' he said flatly, cutting in on her anticipated rhetoric.

Damn! He had lost his temper. He had intended to talk about the problem of competing in international markets. Well, he still could.

'Listen to me . . .' Her voice swelled out powerfully, like a priest at the start of his oratory: 'Twenty-eight years ago, when I put you, my grandson, Anton September, into Rob

Palma's cradle, it was not so you could ruin us. It was to give you a fortune. You have that fortune, but I will never allow you to ruin Bill. I have guarded and protected you for all these years. But not for this!' Her voice rose to a crescendo as she leaned over the desk. 'Oh, no. Never for this!'

'You've gone mad,' he gasped. He wanted to get up and strike her, but he was rooted to the chair, unable to move. He seemed to be far apart from this crazy nightmare, watching the drama, but disbelieving all of it. Absurd! Insane! She was towering over him, eyes blazing, fists clenched. Was she crazy? He hung on to that comforting possibility. Perhaps she really had lost her mind.

'I drowned the real heir, so you are quite safe.' She left, shutting the door quietly behind her.

Rob glanced at his watch out of habit, picked up his calculator and tried to continue where he had left off, despite the loud buzzing sound in his ears. Now where was he? If he could knock off ten per cent . . .

Oh God! He wiped his forehead, noticing that he was damp with sweat. He felt cold and hot at the same time. Obviously she was lying. Crazy old fool! She would say anything to help her son. Anything! She was fiercely protective of her family. *Hadn't she gone to extraordinary lengths to help her grandson? Him? Oh God!*

What had Angelo said? He tried to remember his exact words: *'That's the strange part of it. She said she would like her job back because she wanted to bring you up properly. She forgave me for Rose's death and that meant a great deal to me.'*

Ramona had never forgiven anyone in her life. Revenge was more her style, and she had exacted a merciless revenge. Earlier, Angelo had said: *'To give Rose what she wanted would have prejudiced your rights . . . I had to protect you.'*

From whom? From Rose's son and his half-claim to the estate? But he had got it all – Ramona had seen to that.

No! Never! This was nonsense. He desperately wanted to wipe the whole silly scene out of his head. What a load of crap! He stood up and began pacing his office, trying to think.

He had to repress an urge to race after her and batter the truth out of her. *Or, better still, batter her to death?* God damn it! She had no right . . . no right to tell such downright wicked lies. What was she after – blackmail? Could it be true? No! But why had she always protected him so loyally? No mother could have been better than she. Had Rose given birth? Could he wake up his grandfather and confide in him? But Angelo had banished Rose's coloured bastard from any recognition, in order to protect Claire's baby. 'Well, Grandfather,' he muttered. 'You have nursed a cuckoo in your nest.' He was the one Angelo had feared so much, and with good reason for Rob knew himself to be formidable. Unbeatable! Perhaps Angelo was psychic, too. That was funny. He laughed harshly, but even to himself it sounded like a howl.

He was an interloper and if Angelo found out he would be disinherited and banished from the family. All this, he thought looking round, belonged to someone else. He stood up and peered into the gilt-framed antique mirror Kate had hung over the sideboard. Ramona's black eyes peered back at him. Why had no one noticed? He longed to destroy Ramona for what she had done to him. But what was the alternative? Where would he be now?

Unable to bear his tormenting thoughts, Rob raced out of his office, down the stairs to the front door. He noticed the security guards watching him curiously as he ran across the front lawn.

He found Ramona in her kitchen. Flinging himself at her, he gripped her arms, shaking the life out of her as panic engulfed him. He was drowning in it, fighting for his breath. His heart was about to explode. If he destroyed her would he destroy the evidence? Would her damned secret be buried with her?

'Who knows . . . ? Who knows besides you?' he roared.

'I know, and you know. Frikkie, too.'

'And who else?'

'Be quiet,' she hissed. 'People will hear you. I haven't kept this secret for twenty-eight years for you to blab it out.'

'But why? Why?'

She shook his hands off her arm and backed to a safer distance. 'This home is your rightful place,' she said, scowling at him. 'You have the blood to be here. It was foretold to me long ago. His blood and mine . . . a man who would control a vast fortune. You!'

'Damn you, Ramona! I made my own fortune long before I took over theirs.' Now why had he said *theirs*? Was he going to believe this old hag and her lies?

'You had a sixth sense for business. Admit it! You always knew which way to go, always made the right choices . . . even as a boy.'

She was smiling now, sitting in her chair, rocking backwards and forwards, eyes gazing tenderly at him. What if he killed her now? Then he remembered the security guards. He collapsed heavily on the kitchen chair.

'Where do you think you got your intuition? From me,' she was muttering. 'You always knew the right thing to do. Admit it. My intuition, his brains.'

'*His* brains? *Angelo*'s brains?' he queried.

'You are Trevor's son, too.'

'Jesus!' He had forgotten that connection. The thought was like a reprieve from the death cell. Rose and Trevor had had a child. It made sense. He buried his face in his hands, trying to think. The thought uppermost was that Angelo was still his grandfather. He was still a Palma. At that moment nothing else in the world counted.

'Surely Grandfather must have expected some claim from Rose's son? What did you tell him?'

'That you drowned.'

'And he believed you?'

'Why not? Claire's child drowned.' She handed him a brandy which he tossed down.

'You killed it?' he asked, aghast.

'Never you mind!'

'So what do you want from me? You'll find I'm a difficult man to cross.' He laughed harshly.

'Don't worry,' she said softly. Her hand rested lightly on his shoulder. He felt insulted, *but she was his grandmother*.

'Nothing has changed. The deed was done for its own sake. I wanted my offspring to become rich, powerful and white. I was successful. Look at you! Marry again, Rob. Have children. I'll never mention this matter again. Just don't try to ruin your own kith and kin – now that you know who you are. There's your proof, if you still need it. Angelo would never have done what you were planning to do. That's my side of you coming out.' She bent over him, grasped his face in her hands, and kissed him. That, more than anything else, convinced him.

A deep shudder ran through him. Every part of him seemed to be in deep, physical revolt. He heard a sound like a groan, and realised it was himself. He stood up, grabbed a vase from the table and hurled it to the floor. 'No,' he roared. 'No, no, no.'

He came to his senses later to realise that he was alone. He had been lying across Ramona's table, punching the wood, and his hands were bleeding and bruised. 'Ramona,' he yelled, but she was gone.

He shouldn't be here. As he stumbled outside, he saw the gardener, standing in his shirt, wide-eyed as he brandished a stick.

'It's all right,' Rob said curtly. In the hall, the night security men stared curiously at him. Let them stare. No one knew. Only he and Ramona. But hadn't she said Frikkie knew, too?

Back in his office, he locked the door, poured himself a drink, and began to pace the floor. He'd solved enough business problems in his life. Problems were opportunities for correction. How many times had he drummed that into the timid minds of his various managers?

He took out his notebook and wrote: Problem: *identify threat*. Solution: *eliminate threat*.

He sat deep in thought for a while. For some years Rob had paid a yearly retainer for the services of an industrial spy, who went under the glorified title of a freelance research economist. This was a bit out of his normal line, but the man was topnotch. He thought nothing of burgling the premises of his opposition if Rob needed their figures. Right now he had to know more about the real heir. Was he really dead?

He picked up his receiver and dialled the spy's home number. 'We have to meet now,' he said curtly. 'There's an all-night bar at the Waterfront called Joe's. See you there at midnight.'

He was beginning to feel better. He had diagnosed the problem, but he needed more facts. Then he could execute the solution.

*   *   *

Ari awoke before dawn to the sound of the telephone ringing. In the darkness he fumbled for the lightswitch, but heard Kate pick up the receiver. 'It's for you. It's Willis,' she said sleepily.

As Ari took the receiver, Kate switched on the light, blinked at him and pulled her pillow over her face. Ari knew it was bad news. Why else would Willis contact him here? He was on duty tonight, Ari remembered.

'Another death,' Willis said. 'I thought you'd want to know about it. I'm going up to the Palmas' place now. Ramona's been murdered. See you there.'

Frikkie? he wondered as he dressed rapidly. 'Kate,' he said, shaking her. 'Ramona has been murdered and I suspect Frikkie. Do not let him into the lighthouse. Do you promise?'

'You are unbelievably stupid at times,' she muttered.

Ari raced downstairs and rushed first to Frikkie's room, but there was no sign of him and clearly his bed had not been slept in.

As he drove to the Palmas' he was pondering Frikkie's drunken statement. Had Ramona really paid Frikkie to kill her own grandson? Would she do this, even for a trawler, a house and a great deal of cash? If so, she had paid the price. He arrived, parked and followed the sound of voices and the bright lights shining amongst the trees. The photographers had not yet arrived and two police constables were guarding the corpse.

As Ari parked his car near the cottage, Willis came to meet him. 'No one's touched anything,' Willis said. 'The security guard heard nothing suspicious, but he noticed that the light was on late, and this was unusual, so around four-thirty he came to investigate.

'I'm beginning to think you're right about a link between

the killings and the kidnapping,' Willis said. 'What's it all about?'

About Rose, I suppose, Ari thought without answering. Someone wants to pay them all back for what they did to Rose. But why now? Why not then?

Ramona's eyes lay some distance from her body. They had been torn out of her head and left there on the grass. How pitiable her corpse looked. How helpless and frail she had been. Yet she had always seemed so strong. She was wearing a nightdress and gown. Presumably someone had called after she had gone to sleep, but why had she let them in without raising an alarm? Someone must have had a legitimate reason for coming to her house in the night. Frikkie perhaps?

As he studied the corpse, Ari began to shake with anger. However many murders he investigated, he could never lose this sense of outrage. He had an inborn need to punish the guilty and protect the weak. Without her fearsome eyes, she was nothing. Just a haggard old woman with white hair, dampened by the grass, thin and old before her time, with blood all over her mutilated face. Her body lay limp and discarded. Who had feared her eyes so much he put them out? Frikkie, he thought again.

The security guard enjoyed his moment of drama. He spun out the story of how he had walked over and stumbled on the corpse. Much earlier he had heard her fighting with Frikkie. 'She was screaming fit to bust and he was bellowing like a castrated bull. Later she and Master Rob had been going at each other hammer and tongs in the study. Mr Palma ran after her and followed her back here. They fought for an hour, then he came back to the house, packed and left. He was as white as a sheet when he rushed off in his car,' the guard said.

When the corpse had been photographed and removed, Ari searched the ground with a powerful torch, trying to re-create the scene in his mind. He walked into the cottage, noting the cleanness, the smell of polish and the flowers and cushions and pictures. He could smell coffee. It was warm in the coffee filter, and it smelled quite fresh. For whom had she made coffee? Not for Frikkie surely? Ramona would not waste good coffee on her idiot son. He was shunned because he was the *bobbejaan*, and Ramona was a proud woman. Would she make coffee for Rob Palma, when they were fighting? It didn't make sense.

Why had she let the intruder in at night? he wondered as he searched her cottage. She must have had a reason. Was it possible that he had mentioned Mandy? It was only a hunch, but it seemed to fit. Glancing at the wall he noticed a space in the pegboard which was covered in snapshots. He studied the pictures intently for they provided a kaleidoscope of Ramona's life. There was one of her and Angelo and another woman standing outside a beach shack with 'Sands' written above the door. Good heavens, he thought, looking more closely. She was well dressed and groomed around the time when her children were young. She looked rich and well-to-do and happy. He had never seen Ramona look happy. How lovely she had been when she was young. Each picture was stuck to the board with a drawing pin and right at the top was an empty space. Strange!

Ari went outside and examined the earth, pushing through hydrangeas. Some of them were broken and there were footprints. He called the boys over to take the prints and he went back to his car.

Ari was deep in thought as he drove back to his office. Someone had hated Ramona enough to put out her eyes.

She had died horribly. Why? Because of her rumoured second-sight? Who hated her enough to do this? So far he had two suspects: Rob Palma and Frikkie.

It was nine o'clock by the time he reached his desk where he called the office of his superior, Colonel Greg du Plessis.

'Sir, I want permission to bring in additional forces to comb the mountains around Silver Bay. I have another murder here. Yes, they are connected. It's the girl's aunt. Yes, sir, a regular vendetta. I have three suspects for the kidnapping and I believe that Mandy might be hidden in the caves on the nearby mountain slopes. There has to be a connection between the crimes, you see, and the kidnapper is within striking distance of the rest of the locals, and able to come and go as he likes. The mountains provide perfect cover.

'There's another matter, sir. In 1967, Rose September's baby of two and a half years disappeared. I have a sworn statement from a man who is mentally retarded that he drowned the child on Angelo Palma's instructions. Palma is a big fish around these parts, but I'm aiming to pull him in for questioning.'

'Thank goodness you're showing some action at last, Ari. I was beginning to think you were cracking up. Use all the men you like. As I told you earlier, it's important for us to be seen to be searching right now. The election's looming closer. By the way, this Angelo Palma is white I assume?'

'Yes, sir.'

'And the baby in question is coloured? As you can see, I've been keeping abreast of your reports.'

'Yes, sir.'

'Well, that might be worth a few more votes. Go ahead, Ari. You're in charge down there. Just one thing. Are you going to find this Mandy?'

'Yes, sir,' he said, after only a moment's hesitation.

But whether or not she'll be alive is another matter, he thought sadly, but he kept that to himself.

Chapter 52

⸺⸺ ⸺⸺

At dawn, the following morning, Kate was woken for the second time by Willis who had come to take Frikkie away.

'I can't believe that Ari would send you,' Kate fumed. 'What is he? A mouse? Or is he a man? Who cares anyway? He's made a terrible mistake.'

'Off the record, Ari doesn't believe that Frikkie killed Ramona or Rose's child, but there are too many witnesses to his fight with Ramona to let him remain at liberty. I'm detaining him for questioning,' Willis said.

'How will poor Frikkie cope with prison?' she said anxiously.

'Ari's sending him to the mental ward of the military hospital in Wynberg. He'll get treatment and he'll be questioned by a qualified psychiatrist. Please don't worry yourself further.'

'It's all very well to say that, but even if he is all right, how am I to cope without him?' she grumbled. 'I'm going to get him a lawyer. You tell Ari that. You guys can't be allowed to steamroller people like Frikkie.'

'Do you believe that, Kate?' Ari asked, coming silently up from the beach. 'Is that what you think of me?' She flushed and went inside, but Ari followed her.

'Kate, I promise you that Frikkie will be released within

the week if he's innocent. Give a guy a break, Kate. I have a job to do.'

She relented and made him coffee, but still she felt sad for Frikkie, knowing how he would hate to be shut away from nature. Heavens! Was it only six o'clock? It seemed like mid-morning. She might as well make Tabson's breakfast, she thought.

It was March 15, late summer, but the cranes and geese were leaving early this year; it would be a cold winter. Tabson woke and ate his breakfast and went outside to scatter mealies and watch his goose trying to fly. It ran and jumped, and tried to take off, flapping urgently, but soon tired. Its mate had been swooping down for days, urging the goose to go with her. She was circling high above, and honking urgently, longing to leave.

Watching through the kitchen window, Kate saw Tabson bite his lip, and stare down at his leg. He looked forlorn as he picked up his bag and limped off to school. In some strange way, he identified his crippled leg with the goose's wing, Kate knew. It had been an anxious time as they waited for the day when the plaster would be removed, but the day had come at last and tomorrow they would know just how successful the three operations had been.

She sighed and tried to suppress her anxiety. She ought to be working, she knew, for she had three large commissions, and she was excited about them, but today she was too tense to work. She decided to take the morning off and walk round the lagoon and see if the fynbos showed signs of recuperating.

It was dry and the water level was low, but shrubs and grass were sprouting out of the former shack sites. However brief and destructive human habitation had been, the debris had enriched the sandy soil. Even the burned port jacksons were sprouting more thickly. In a year or two the fire will be forgotten, she thought wonderingly.

Wandering around the edge of the lagoon, she heard knocking and caught sight of workmen's orange overalls flashing through the green. Rob never gives up, she thought trying to stem her disappointment. He just couldn't wait to get in there with his damned condominium. But why were they building so near to the border? He could build right up to the water's edge if he wanted to, she reminded herself bitterly, since she had lost the court case. Moving closer, she realised that the men were digging on her side of the property. Anger surged as she ran towards them.

'What on earth . . . ?' she muttered, stopping short and frowning.

There was a ramp built into the lagoon, half on Rob's and half on her side of the shore, and the prefabricated sides of a large wooden shed were lying nearby. Presumably they were going to erect it over the lagoon.

'I think you've misjudged your position,' she said icily. 'You are trespassing on my property.'

The workmen dropped their tools and stood eyeing her uneasily. One of them went to fetch their supervisor who came hurrying towards her looking like a student in his khaki shorts and shirt with his bright-eyed enthusiasm and mop of ginger hair.

'Mrs Palma, I presume,' he said, extending his hand to shake hers. 'I was so hoping you'd drop by. This is an exciting project and I feel honoured to be right in on the start of it. The sanctuary will serve as an example to anyone who owns wetlands and it will save so many endangered species.'

She gasped. 'Who are you?' she asked. 'What's going on?'

'John Hemmings, from the Avian Demography Unit of Cape Town University, ma'am. I have the honour to be planning this bird sanctuary.'

Kate bit her lip and hung on to her composure, but her eyes were pricking and there was a lump in her throat that threatened to choke her. Her knees felt wobbly so she sat on a tree stump. 'Tell me about your plans,' she whispered.

'I'd be glad of your moral support and your ideas, Mrs Palma. You see, your husband said that he'd leave it entirely to us.' Hemmings laughed nervously. 'Only one condition – it has to be called the Kate Palma Bird Sanctuary.'

Like an obituary, she thought. A monument to dead love and long-forgotten hopes. She glanced at Hemmings and saw the tension in his eyes. Perhaps he was afraid she would want to interfere.

'It's a big project and naturally I'm nervous, but confident that the best place for the bird viewing site is here. I'm sure you'll agree with me. You see, visitors will have easy access from the road and they will walk along corridors that are entirely enclosed in wire netting. Tunnels really, perhaps with thatch on top. The birds won't see them, and even more important, the public won't be able to do much damage – human nature being what it is. From here there'll be a magnificent view right up the lagoon. Your husband is donating some powerful viewing equipment, but of course you know that. I heard today that the Ornithological Institute intends to use this sanctuary to reintroduce some nearly extinct species. They have four pairs of red-chested fluff-tailed species. Did you know that you have several African marsh harriers here? They're very rare.' He was so excited. Then he broke off and frowned.

'What is it? Have I upset you?' he asked, peering intently at her.

'The wind makes my eyes water.'

'I see.' He didn't comment on the windless morning.

'When did Mr Palma give you the go-ahead? He forgot to mention this to me.'

'The day after he won the court case. He decided he was wrong and you were right, Mrs Palma. You've been battling for this for a long time, haven't you? He told us the whole story. Congratulations!' He grinned broadly. 'Your husband felt so bad about winning that he set up a million rand trust fund to manage the sanctuary. Those are the sort of guilt trips we need. This will be a world showcase, I shouldn't be surprised,' he went on happily. 'There's at least two pairs of painted snipes here. Seldom seen nowadays, but I spotted them up in the reeds.'

He babbled on happily while Kate tried to control her desire to burst into tears. Why now, Rob? Why not then? Why did you have to put us through all that agony? Oh, Rob. What a strange, obstinate, hard-headed man you are. It's too late for us now. There's too much to reproach each other for. Besides, our divorce is almost finalised.

She hurried back to the lighthouse to telephone Rob, but he was uncontactable, 'somewhere in the interior of the Namib desert,' his secretary said.

It was a momentous day for Kate. When Tabson came home from school, she took him to see the viewing site and they wandered around the lagoon, noting how the shrubs and wild flowers were resprouting, and collecting more debris. It will take years to pick up all of it, she thought, but maybe that young Hemmings will send in a team to clean up.

Returning at dusk they found their goose had gone. Tabson burst into tears. Kate fretted and tried not to look worried as they searched for an hour, but eventually gave up. She had bought a cake and they sat outside on the sand dune overlooking the sea to eat it. Tabson kept on calling, unwilling to give up.

'If I find someone ate him, I'll kill them. I'm telling you that now,' he said, his bottom lip trembling.

'Eat your cake. It's chocolate – your favourite. I'm sure he's around,' Kate lied. Tabson munched his cake without much enthusiasm. Then he leaped up.

'Missus Kate,' Tabson's excited voice cut into her dreams. 'Look up . . . Look!' He was jumping up and down, waving and yelling, pointing towards a drift of clouds coming in from the sea. At first she could see nothing, but then she thought she saw two large birds circling overhead, but they were so high. They were soaring, circling, swooping in the warm evening air thermals.

'Could it be?' Her heart hammering, she ran off to fetch some mealies and she scattered them round the lighthouse, calling to the goose as she always did.

Out of the mist, one of the birds rocketed down, zooming earthwards at an impossible speed, like a falling rock. Just above the lighthouse, he braked with his wings and landed with a thump on the domed roof.

'Come down then,' she coaxed him, and he swooped in a broad circle around them, landing heavily. He began to peck at the mealies as greedily as he always did, just as if nothing had changed.

'Oh, Tabson! He made it! We did it!' Kate caught hold of the boy and hugged him, whirling him round. There was another thud as the female landed, legs splayed, eyes watching them nervously, head turning this way and that way. She snatched a few mealies and retreated to a nearby tree where she perched, calling and grumbling.

Their goose ate every last mealie and then soared off from

a running jump. Moments later the two circled the lighthouse honking noisily and flapped off towards the swamps.

'Next year they'll be so safe,' Kate said, thinking of Rob and his incredible gesture.

It was early afternoon, but the curtains were drawn and it was quite dark in the ward. A nurse was sitting in the shadows in the corner of the room. She stood up when Ari and Willis walked in.

'No visitors,' she said. 'Doctor's orders. Evidently this man is under arrest.'

'That's all right, nurse.' Willis showed her his badge and smiled. His blue eyes and broad grin softened the hardest females, Ari had noticed.

She gave him a girlish smile. 'Can I take a short break? Would you hang on here until I return?'

'Go ahead,' Willis said.

The light wasn't strong enough for Ari to see Frikkie's expression, but his skin looked greyish and his eyes kept moving from the window to the door, like a wild creature penned up and ever-watchful, waiting its chance to make a break for freedom. Lying on the white quilt, his hands looked huge and they were clutching each other, and the sound of his breathing was harsh. He was pathetically out of place indoors. Was he the man he was looking for? Somehow Ari didn't think so.

'Hello, Frikkie,' Ari said as cheerfully as he could. He bent over him and clapped him on the shoulder.

'I'd like to go now,' Frikkie said. 'Missus Kate will be needing me. Who's watering the vegetables and feeding the goose?'

'The goose flew away with its mate yesterday, Frikkie. It's been back for mealies a couple of times.'

Frikkie's eyes brightened momentarily and he smiled. One of the hospital staff had given Frikkie a crew cut and he looked exposed without his tangled mass of black hair hanging over his forehead. His eyes were very expressive, Ari realised. He'd never seen them properly before. He looked afraid and so vulnerable. What sort of a life had he lived, shunned by his family and his peers and without friends? No wonder he clung to all wild creatures. Could that be a motive for kidnapping a young and beautiful girl? Ari wondered. But no! Frikkie couldn't drive, Frikkie didn't have a passport and he had no possibility of getting into Botswana. But still there was the baby he claimed to have drowned and he was a prime suspect for the murder of Ramona. He even had a motive – revenge for the way she had beaten him.

Seconds later, Dr George Fink hurried in. He was short and slight, with a mop of frizzy black hair and eyes glowing with humour and intelligence. 'Sorry I'm late, Lieutenant,' he said. 'I was called to another hospital.'

Ari introduced Fink to Willis.

'I've tried to shake him, but he clings to his story of drowning the baby as if it's his life raft,' Fink said thoughtfully, rocking on the balls of his feet, his hands in his pockets. 'Of course, it's quite the reverse, but I'm working on a new technique of hypnosis. He doesn't respond to the normal methods of putting him in a trance. I think I'm getting a breakthrough, but it might take a few days.'

Ari listened as Fink questioned and cross-questioned Frikkie, but he stuck doggedly to his story that he had drowned the child to please Ramona, who in turn had been pressurised by Angelo Palma.

Fink got on to the murder of Ramona. It took a while before it sank in that she was dead. Then Frikkie began to sob bitterly like a small child. He can't be that good an actor, Ari thought, watching him incredulously. He's innocent. I'm wasting my time here.

Leaving Willis to take Frikkie's statement, Ari left.

Not far away, Kate was sitting in the orthopaedic hospital with the doctor and Tabson. It was the first time Kate had seen Tabson lose his courage. He had sat so still while the plaster was being removed, his fists clenched, his eyes tightly shut and now he would not open them. The nurse was rubbing his leg clean with surgical spirits. 'Come on, Tabson. You can look now,' she urged him, but the boy was rigid with fear.

The doctor took off his glasses and wiped them. He was smiling softly as he turned to Kate, his blue eyes blinking myopically. He looked tired, she thought.

'The leg will be stiff for a while,' he explained. 'That's why he must do his exercises twice a day without fail, just as I showed you.

'You can stand up, young man,' he said, turning to Tabson.

Tabson remained immobile, too scared even to open his eyes.

'It's fine. Everything is all right. You can look,' Kate whispered, bending over the boy.

He peered up at her. His eyes were full of anguish and there was so much longing there. Kate knew that he was too scared to hope.

'It's all right. As good as the goose's wing. I promise you.'

Tabson tore his eyes from her face reluctantly and gazed hesitantly around the room. He shuddered, then he looked down and remained huddled over his knees.

'The leg looks thinner now, but don't worry about that,' the doctor explained. 'Exercises will build up the muscles. Try it out! Go on!'

Tabson seemed unwilling to stand. First he wiggled his toes and they worked. Next he examined his leg carefully, saying nothing, running his fingers over the scars, smoothing his skin. Then he hung on to Kate's hand to pull himself to his feet.

She helped him up. 'You don't need help, Tabson. You can do it on your own,' she said, removing her hand.

He took three faltering steps across the room, hands outstretched to balance himself. And another three, faster this time. Next, he put his hands into his pocket and began to jog around, whistling nonchalantly. He sauntered across the room, rocking from his heels to the ball of his foot, and back on to his heels. Puzzled and more hopeful, he bent his legs, stretched and jumped.

His face split into the broadest grin she'd seen. 'Wow, Missus Kate,' he said. 'It's a miracle, just like you said it would be. It's as if it never was. Like I was never a cripple. Like a bad dream that's gone.'

His excitement was feeding on itself, mounting and taking hold of him. All at once he was racing round the ward, arms outstretched as play aeroplane wings, lips pursed as he hummed the drone of an engine. He zoomed out of the ward and they heard him racing along the passage, clattering down the stairs and moments later he was whirling around the lawn below, circling and swooping, wild with joy.

'He's always been so solemn,' Kate said wonderingly.

'He has a whole lot of playing to catch up with, Kate. And another thing, you'll find he'll be accident prone for a month or two. Remember, he must do these exercises every morning and night. That's essential!'

Kate nodded happily, shook hands and went off to collect Tabson.

After the jam scones, which had been wolfed down at great speed, because Tabson was in a hurry, they drove on to the bicycle store. Now came Tabson's reward for being brave through the pain and discomfort of his three operations. The promised prize was a mountain bike. It was costly, but Tabson deserved it, Kate decided. Anyway, she had so many orders nowadays, she could stop worrying about money.

The proprietor lent her a rack to hold the bike on the boot of her car, and they drove home, with Tabson on his knees on the back seat, too scared to take his eyes off the precious bike in case it disappeared.

Kate parked in the carport Frikkie had made amongst the trees. The car had barely stopped before Tabson leaped out, took his bicycle and jumped on it. Moments later he was wobbling along the gravel track, towards the lighthouse. Kate lingered, wanting the moment to last. The day was so precious. She felt that she would remember it forever, but moments later, Tabson came running back, wheeling his bike, his face pale, and his eyes full of fear.

'Missus Kate, Missus Kate! You must help me. Don't let them take me, Missus Kate!' He looked frantic with fear. She had never seen him like this before.

'Who, Tabson?'

'My folks are here.' He burst into noisy tears.

Kate felt as if she'd been kicked in the stomach. A hard swift shaft of pain spun through her, and suddenly she was short of breath.

Surely not? How could they know? Why today of all days? She began to run towards the lighthouse. She must call Ari.

But Ari was already there. He was standing with a small solemn group at the lighthouse door. There was Boysie from the squatter camp and a man and woman she had never seen before. The woman was massive, almost six feet tall, with broad shoulders and she was vastly overweight. She wore a frilled floral dress which made her look larger than life. Her husband was huge, too. A tall, lean, intent man with rimless glasses and a Mao-style tunic worn over jeans. Kate unlocked the door and they all trooped inside.

'We have come to fetch our son,' the woman said firmly. She beckoned to Tabson, but he hid behind Kate, hanging on to her skirt like a small child.

'My son has been away for too long,' the man said. 'He is getting to talk and act and think like white people.'

'So is that so terrible?' She hung on to Tabson's hand. She could feel him shaking.

'I love you, Missus Kate,' he muttered, his voice hoarse with sadness.

Kate turned to Ari. 'Help me,' she said, too shocked to think.

'They came to fetch me, of all people, to force you to hand over their son. They are taking him back to the Homelands. There's nothing you can do, Kate. I have explained all that you have done for Tabson, but they knew that. They've been keeping an eye on the situation through Boysie here, who is a distant cousin, and they knew today was the day the plaster would be removed.'

'Ask them if I can adopt Tabson,' she asked desperately.

Ari spoke in Xhosa to the father, but he replied in English, talking to Kate.

'Tabson is my only son and I want him back. He must help with the cows.'

The woman was becoming angry, blaming her husband for the delay.

'They think you are trying to kidnap their son,' Ari said. 'They are angry with you.'

She felt shocked and furious. 'They didn't give a damn when he was crippled,' she flung at them.

'But now he is not a cripple and he is *my* son,' the woman said in remarkably good English.

'You let him go as slave labour. You had no right. He nearly died.'

'He has to go, Kate. I've already checked with child welfare and a lawyer. There's nothing you can do to stop this. It was predictable and I was going to warn you, but I didn't think it would be this quick.'

Tabson was crying silently, the tears coursing down his cheeks, as Kate helped him to pack his possessions.

Fifteen minutes later Tabson was bidding a tearful farewell to Dopey. 'Say goodbye to the goose,' he sobbed. The small procession left the lighthouse. First the father, carrying a box of toys and books, then the mother with the suitcase on her head, her hips swinging from side to side under her voluminous skirt, and lastly Tabson, his bicycle balanced on his head. This hurt more than his tears – this sudden return to tribal custom was like a slap in the face.

She ran after him and squeezed his arm. 'Tabson, listen to me, you'll be older soon. Then you can come back. Meantime, ride your damn bicycle, or push it,' she muttered, hoarse and furious.

Tabson was locked into his own misery, quite lost to her.

'*Bunjalo ke ubomi* – that's how life goes,' he said. He had already retreated from her world into the sullen fatalism of his race and his bicycle remained on his head.

It had all been so quick. 'I can't believe it's happened,' Kate blurted out, when she had hurried back to the lighthouse. Dopey put his large head on her lap and whined as if he understood, and that made it worse. She burst into tears and nothing Ari could say would comfort her.

'They didn't even say thank you,' she sobbed. Perhaps they were right, she thought. She hadn't asked them, or even let them know. She had a terrible feeling that she would never see Tabson again.

Chapter 53

———— ————

As the first rosy glow of dawn lit the horizon, a Cape canary trilled loud and clear. Then a chorus of birdsong vibrated from the bushes around them. It was late March, the beginning of autumn, and as the sky lightened Ari saw that the sea was covered with thick white fog which was drifting round the base of the mountains. It would clear in an hour, he knew.

Gerber and Ari and two more officers were standing in a huddled group under some bushes near the start of the mountain track. Their vehicles had been well hidden under the port jackson trees. They were poised for action, but two units had not yet arrived and their lateness was prejudicing the success of the operation.

So far Ari had thirty men and dogs moving along the track to encircle the mountain. Another twenty would arrive soon. Ari was checking the time anxiously when they heard a vehicle approaching. A police car came into sight, skidding badly, and became stuck in a patch of loose sand. Ari tried to keep his temper down as Ian Frost emerged.

'How the hell did you get on to this?' he asked.

Gerber went a trace redder. 'Just leave it,' he snapped at Ari. He sent two constables to rescue the car and park it off the track.

Then they caught the sound of aircraft engines. At first it was distant, but soon it was clear that helicopters were approaching, hugging the coast and moving towards them from the north.

'God damn it,' Ari exploded. 'What the hell . . . ? Who . . . ? We were relying on stealth. Now we're finished.'

The unmistakable drone of helicopters moved towards them, louder and louder still until, in a swoop of malign intensity, two military aircraft broke through the mist to hover over them.

'You son of a bitch,' he shouted at Frost. 'Who gave you the right to interfere? If I'd wanted helicopters now, I would have called them.' Gerber put one finger on his lips to motion caution, but Ari was too furious to care.

'That's enough, Lieutenant,' Gerber said.

'It's finished,' Ari grunted. He shrugged and turned away, his face set into a scowl. 'I never liked that fucker and I like him less now. He'd better look out. One dark night when there's no one around . . .' he muttered to Gerber. His eyes were glittering with suppressed anger as he shot a quick glance at the PRO.

'Shut up,' Gerber repeated. 'That's an order. Where the hell are the other units?'

'Late! Listen here! Are these guys going to hover over us, just to show the kidnapper exactly where we are, and what's going on? Who's in charge here? I thought it was me. It's not, that's clear enough. In fact, I quit.'

At that moment another police vehicle laboured up the rough track. Fifteen more constables spilled out of the back wearing camouflage overalls and carrying automatic rifles. A major in battle fatigue, complete with headphones, hand-held radio set, and a couple of attendants, one of whom was carrying a portable chair, and the other a large trestle table, approached.

Ari wanted to throw up. 'Sir,' he said. 'With all due respect to your rank, this is my operation. I planned it and I wanted speed and silence. Now you are late and you've made enough noise with these helicopters to frighten away our quarry before the men are fully positioned.'

'Why aren't they in position?' he blustered.

'Some of them are, but some of the cordon has only just arrived – with you, sir, and there's another unit still to come.'

The major frowned. 'And you are?'

'Lieutenant Ari St John, sir.'

'Then let's get on with it, shall we? Search now, argue later. Okay? What's your plan?'

'We're throwing a cordon around that circular mountain there,' he pointed to the track that led off southwards, 'like a girdle around the middle of a fat lady. There's no escape downwards, no harbours, just very treacherous currents and razor-sharp rocks and heavy surf. Upwards leads to the mountain peak, but over on the south side of the mountain, our target could escape through dense vegetation to reach the back of the fishing village. The cordon above the village is not yet in place, and the helicopters will have warned our quarry, so they could still escape that way. Men are on the way there. We had planned to be in position within fifteen minutes, sir, but we need to complete the girdle with more men.'

'I see your point, St John. Get my men into the cordon with all speed. Quite honestly the first I heard of this operation was a telephone call from Major Frost late last night. I'll get the helicopters to guard the bush above the village.'

'Thank you, sir.'

'Look here, St John, off the record, is this for real? What makes you think they're here at all? After all, this girl, Mandy, disappeared in Botswana. I thought we were on a general mopping operation with strong political undertones.'

'I think we are now, sir. But I had reason to believe that the kidnapper is operating from a local base, hence this search. You could hide an army in the dense brush around here. There's several abandoned block houses and gun sites hidden away, relics of World War II, and hundreds of caves above the track. It's believed that satanists hang around there. Then there's a few abandoned fishermen's shacks around the shoreline.'

'Have you got an ordinance map?'

'Yes, sir. Here, sir. Every structure is clearly marked and numbered.' He spread his map over the major's table.

'Here comes your last unit by the sound of things. Get the cordon in place, Lieutenant.'

Ari gritted his teeth and made the best of a bad job as he directed the men around the mountain, trying to ignore the butterflies in his stomach. Was Mandy here? If so, what would the kidnapper do to her when he heard the sounds of a search? Would he kill her and hide her body, or attempt to flee with her?

The volume of sound was intense, dogs barking, the drone of the helicopters, and then came a new threat, the excited chattering of the village folk thronging up across the dunes behind three wobbling four-wheel drive vehicles, one with cameras already in action. The media had arrived! Naturally, since Frost was there. Ari was appalled by the size of the crowd. 'A bloody circus,' he muttered to no one in particular.

*　　*　　*

Jânek had hardly slept at all when the sound of the helicopters woke him. He forced his eyelids apart, but after a few moments of incredulity, he leaped into action. Racing up the stone steps he jumped on to the blockhouse roof. His heart jolted and his mouth dried as he saw two helicopters moving along the coast, heading up towards the south side of the peak. Grabbing his binoculars he examined the surrounding bush. Above him, on the circular track, groups of police were taking up search positions. He looked around. The sky was turning pale grey, while rose streaks were piercing the eastern horizon. It would be daylight within minutes. Too late to escape.

He ran down to the old ammunition store, shining his torch in his haste. Rose was sitting in the middle of the wire netting cage shielding her eyes as the light blinded her. 'Get dressed,' he shouted, throwing her clothes at her.

Locking the door, he ran back outside and frantically threw petrol around the bush. Seconds later it was blazing, giving out a thick black pall of smoke. This might get them across the track, but he would have to carry Rose. One thought haunted him. Had they found his truck? He had hidden it in a grove of dense trees and bush near the road beyond the dunes.

Rose began to cry as the daylight hit her face on. She was like a little blind mole, holding one hand over her eyes, whimpering and choking on the smoke. He shook her arm. 'Run with me. Run, or I'll kill you,' he said.

She stumbled, fell forward, and lay there, inert, as if unconscious. He bent over her, turning her, and as he did she struck upwards with a sharp stone she had concealed under her body, a swift hard knock near his eyes. He shook his head, scattering drops of blood.

Jânek felt himself falling into a daze, his eyes going in

and out of focus. 'Bitch!' He punched her hard on the side of her face, hoisted her over his shoulder and began to move uphill, stopping to listen every few minutes. From the sounds of the dogs, it seemed that the trackers were moving down towards the sea, but then he realised his mistake as he heard shouts and realised that more groups were searching both above and below the track. There was a light north-easterly breeze and the fire was spreading rapidly. He would try to keep on the west side of it, stay hidden in the smoke and run across the track. Then he would encircle the mountain, just above the cordon, keeping to the thick scrub bush, until he reached the slopes above the village. The only danger was the wide open stony patch above his truck. He'd deal with that when he got there.

Pulling strength from his anger, Jânek pushed himself to a standing position with Mandy slung over his shoulder. Visibility was almost nil as the clouds of smoke swirled around him. His eyes were burning, his mouth felt choked and he knew he might get caught up in the blaze. Already he could feel waves of heat coming from the inferno of blazing bushes. He had no time, for he could hear the helicopters circling the mountain and the fire would not last forever.

He began to run uphill, taking long strides, forcing his body to move faster and faster. Rose stirred and groaned and fell back into unconsciousness. The sounds of the fire were everywhere, roaring, hissing and crackling around them, but he knew they had a chance, so he kept running.

'Rose,' he called. 'Are you all right?' He had knocked her out, but she might be pretending again. He was angry with her, but he loved her. He would guard her with his life, but she must be obedient. She had disobeyed him once before and the resulting chaos had ruined both of them for years.

*   *   *

Ari wasn't sure how the fire started. It might have been from a cigarette carelessly thrown by one of the onlookers, or a deliberate attempt to make an escape route through the smoke. The natural *fynbos* had long since succumbed to the curse of the imported Australian rooikrantz and port jackson trees. With their oil-saturated leaves and bark the trees exploded in a blaze of sparks and fire. The helicopters were blinded on the south side of the mountain, but the pilots tried their best.

By the time Ari and his group reached the scorched and ragged edge of the blaze on the other side of the mountain range, the pressure of heat had become unbearable and breathing was difficult. Sweat poured out of them all. Now the helicopters were backing off away from the smoke. Then, out of the blaze trickled a sorry column of swaying, wine-soaked bergies, carrying their pitiful possessions and a wailing baby. Compassion stirred as Ari watched them. Humble and degenerate, each a clone of the other, they lived in the caves and begged for cash to buy wine and food, being unemployed and unemployable.

He was startled into action as a shot zipped against a rock behind him. Simultaneously the report blasted his ears. Suddenly they sprawled behind cover. The shots seemed to be coming from a nearby cave. Ari flung a teargas bomb inside and seconds later his men charged. Two youngsters were guarding a cache of drugs, mainly mandrax by the look of things. Shouting and struggling, they were handcuffed and secured. Ari called for reinforcements to transport the prisoners and drugs back to base.

For two more hours, the cordon of men beat their way through the bush. Hanging on to their excited dogs they fought their way down slippery steep slopes in thick smoke, moving towards the sea, while Ari and a small group patrolled the road above. Around eleven there was a radio call from Willis.

'I saw movement in a hut on the causeway, but the tide's coming in. It'll be cut off soon.'

'Are you sure?'

'Someone's there. I saw movement at the window.'

'Get over there, but be quick – three of you and dogs – and be careful.'

'Okay!' Ari waited, while the minutes passed agonisingly slowly.

'Oh God,' he heard. 'They're insane.'

'What is it?'

'Cats strung up, an altar, bones, looks like a baby's skeleton, too. Dried blood all over the place, and live pigeons and chickens in cages, bones, and some weirdo in black crouched in the corner wailing. I think she's female.'

'Bring her in, Willis. Let the birds go, but don't touch anything else. I'm sending a team down right now. If there's no sign of Mandy, get back into line as soon as the team pitches. Be careful. If the tide gets up, wait. It's too dangerous to swim I've been told.'

'Stay here? I'd rather drown. Jesus . . .'

The morning wore on with dust and smoke, the wind changed direction frequently, one constable broke his arm, and Willis stood on a cobra that bit him. He had to be rushed to emergency. The fire blazed on and the smoke made searching hazardous.

Jânek was finished. He had carried or dragged the half-unconscious girl halfway across the mountain. He was burned, his throat was sore from breathing smoke, and he was racked with pain. Here on the south side of the mountain there was no fire, but the helicopters flew round and about, up and down, for they knew this was his only escape route. As Jânek flogged himself to keep moving, he gasped for air and tried to ignore the pain in his back and legs. Slack-kneed and wobbly, Jânek watched the helicopters progress through a blur of sweat-soaked eyes, cursing at his exhaustion which was hampering his escape.

At last Jânek staggered in sight of his vehicle. Only one last dash across open ground. Panting and exhausted he kept crawling forward, dragging the unconscious girl behind him, until he was within fifty yards of his truck. Now for it!

He examined Rose carefully. She lay still with her eyes closed. It hadn't been easy for her, the poor little thing. Look at her, scratched and bleeding and covered in soot. He hoisted her over his shoulder, fireman fashion, and moved towards the open ground. Moments later he was charging, head down, over the veld. He was almost there. Then he tripped headlong over a stone and he and Rose fell heavily.

Rose lay still. Very still. 'Oh God! What have I done to you? Oh, my little Rose,' he crooned, rocking her in his arms. 'It's all right, Rose. We've reached the truck. We're safe.'

She came to life in an explosion of screaming, kicking, biting, clawing fury. Beating him off, she ran, but slipped on the loose soil and fell again, yelling loud enough to be heard miles off.

'Help me! Help!'

He hit her hard, again and again until she lay still. Blood was trickling out of the corner of her mouth. He gathered her into his arms and rocked her. 'I'm sorry, Rose. I'm sorry. You made me do it,' he sobbed as he dumped her in the truck and raced off down the mountain track towards the fishing harbour.

There was a road block ahead, but it was open to let a TV truck pass through. The place was swarming with journalists and the police would not be able to fire in safety. He accelerated and shot forward, knocking the barrier down as he heard shouts and screams. He would have to get rid of the truck, he knew, but he had been careful. The truck was not registered in his name.

When they found the abandoned blockhouse, and the miserable evidence of Mandy's incarceration in the underground ammunition depot, Ari began to curse. He was tired, hungry and filthy, and the whole project had failed. The kidnapper had escaped, taking Mandy with him. Searching carefully he found strands of hair, a shoe lace, a hair clip, ear studs and a button carefully buried and he guessed that Mandy had done this in case anyone ever found her awful prison. Leaving guards and fingerprint experts hard at work, Ari searched the surrounding area. He saw the tracks, the stone with blood on it, the broken bush where the kidnapper had dragged his victim uphill.

If it weren't for the warning given to his quarry by the sound of the helicopters he would have rescued Mandy. The thought was driving him nearly crazy with fury. He longed to get his hands round Frost's throat. It took an hour to withdraw the men and move out, but Ari let Gerber get on with it.

When, much later, he returned to the station, tired, dishevelled and utterly dejected, he walked into the charge office to find an impromptu press conference taking place.

'We are pulling out all stops to find Mandy September,'

Ian Frost was saying. 'If she's out there, we'll get her.' He was talking crap as usual. This time he wasn't giving anything away because no one was telling him anything.

Ari put in a call to the department of prisons, then he called his superior in Pretoria.

'The fingerprint department is putting the prints we found on computer now. I want an immediate check against those of Jânek József, sentenced to twenty years in 1964 for the murder of Trevor Palma. I wouldn't normally bother you, sir, but I need this as of now.'

Ari waited until the conference was over and called Frost into his office. Lashing out with his right fist he caught the man across the cheek bone, knocking him backwards against the bookcase, drawing blood.

'That's for losing Mandy,' he said. 'If you want to make anything of this, I'll tell the nation exactly how you fucked up. I'm leaving the force anyway and I don't give a damn. Now keep off my back, or next time I'll put out your light. You got me? I don't want to see you around my investigations.'

He locked his door, put his head in his hands, and tried to think. Who had kidnapped Mandy? Jânek József was his guess and he would soon know if Jânek had returned to Silver Bay under a false identity, bent on revenge for all those who had hurt his beloved Rose. But why kill Ramona? Because she had encouraged her daughter's liaison with Trevor? Had he blamed her for his broken engagement? Was Trevor only the first in a long line of planned reprisals? Was it possible that twenty years in prison had in no way dampened his fury, nor his longing for revenge? Was it he who had thrown the fire bombs into the hold of Bill's trawler? And why? Did he think that Bill and Angelo murdered Rose?

At the same time, Ari argued, Rob was a strong alternative suspect for the murder of Ramona and then, of course, there was Frikkie. What a bloody mess. He sighed. This morning had been a bloody disaster from beginning to end. But at least he knew that Mandy was alive, or had been very recently. So where had she been taken? He stood up and fetched some coffee. Then he sat at his desk doodling to keep tension at bay while he waited.

Ari felt a failure. He had been sent to Silver Bay to find the girl, and instead he had uncovered just about everything else. What other secrets would the town reveal? And where had Mandy been taken? If he were right, then both Bill and Angelo were in danger. He would have to warn them.

He spent the rest of the morning waiting for the department of prisons to send József's fingerprints and photographs.

At ten the report arrived from the doctor at the morgue: Ramona had been killed by strangulation and her eyes had been put out prior to death. She had put up a brave fight, but she had been gagged, although the gags had been removed after her death. Ari shuddered, thinking of Mandy at the mercy of this monster.

It was noon when the telephone rang. Ari picked up the receiver. It was Colonel du Plessis. 'Ari, I have to hand it to you, the results of your fingerprint comparison have come in. The kidnapper is none other than Jânek József, born 1942, in Hungary. Emigrated to South Africa in '58. In 1964 he was sentenced to twenty years hard labour for the murder of Trevor Palma. He served his full sentence and was deported to Hungary in '84.'

'So Jânek is back,' Ari said. 'And he has embarked on a vendetta for the death of his Rose.'

'Details are coming down to you – shots, prints, et cetera.

Now listen to me, Lieutenant, keep your hands off our PRO man. He's got a job to do, just as you have, different motives, different targets, and if you get your lines crossed just ease up a bit. He's put in a complaint that you attacked him, but I've filed it in the shredder. I won't get away with that twice.'

'I probably would have rescued Mandy if it weren't for him. He loused up my plan by calling in helicopters and the media.'

'Keep going, Ari. You'll get him. I have the greatest faith in you.'

Ari sighed as he replaced the receiver. Lately he had very little faith in himself.

Chapter 54

——— ———

Ari drove to the Palmas' house in the afternoon, his stomach fluttering with butterflies, his jaw clamped in stern determination. The compulsion to unravel this tangled web of lies and murder had become an obsession with him. After three weeks of nagging and waiting, he had received permission to open a murder docket for Anton September, who went missing twenty-six years ago at the age of two. He could move at last.

He drove up the long, winding leafy avenue, admiring the oleanders and brilliant bougainvilleas and wondering what it must be like to be so wealthy. He parked, walked up the stone steps and rang the bell, but there was no manservant to open the door. Ramona's death seemed to have sent the household into shock. He rang the bell three times before a maid appeared.

'I've come to see Mr Angelo Palma,' Ari said, showing his badge.

'Wait here,' she said, pointing to an antique bench near the door. She returned shortly afterwards and led him to Angelo's office.

'Shut the door,' Angelo said in his deep, booming voice. 'The staff have gone to pieces. Ramona used to run this place like a military camp. Now . . .' He raised his hands gesturing the utter incompetence of everyone around.

Angelo was looking pretty fit, Ari thought, watching him. He was a man Ari had learned to admire and he felt a deep sympathy for him.

'You are Mr Angelo Palma . . .' He began his routine, noting Palma's shocked expression. Angelo bent over and slid open his desk drawer. Ari tensed and waited, wondering if he would pull a gun on him. When he retrieved a bottle of pills, Ari reached out fast and grabbed them.

'What are these, sir?'

'Heart pills. Good God! What did you think? This is pretty bad, isn't it?'

'Sir, I am detaining you for questioning concerning the murder of Anton September, aged two years, who disappeared during March, 1967.'

'You have a murder docket?' he asked incredulously.

'Yes, sir.'

'You're a very thorough and determined young man, aren't you, St John? Well, I admire you, but you're making a silly mistake this time, my boy.'

'Sir, I must ask you to accompany me to the police station. Where is your grandson?'

'I don't know exactly. Somewhere in the Namib. Why? Are you going to arrest him, too?' He smiled to himself.

'He could pack some clothes and things and look after your affairs.'

'I'll get bail, I assume.'

'No, sir. At least, I don't think so, because of the circumstances. The truth is, I hope to be able to hold you until I have found and arrested Jânek József. I believe that you are next on his list to be killed. Well, it's just my theory, sir.'

'Jânek? Good God! You think he's back here? I'd kill him myself if I knew where he was. He killed my son, Trevor, but of course, you know that.'

'Yes, sir.'

'And what makes you think . . .'

'Sir . . . with respect . . . I'll be asking the questions,' Ari said.

'Aren't you a little scared of arresting someone of my prominence? I like you, Lieutenant, and I want you to know that I did not murder Rose's son or anyone else. At least, not directly.'

'I know that, sir. You paid Ramona, to persuade Frikkie to throw the child overboard out at sea.'

Angelo frowned. 'Is that what he said?'

'These sort of questions will be dealt with down at the station, where we can take a statement from you.'

'Very well.'

Angelo stood up, rang the bell and sent the maid to fetch his coat and pack an overnight bag. 'Call my grandson. Leave a message at his headquarters,' he told her. He picked up his bottle of pills. 'I'm at risk without these damn things,' he said.

'By the way,' Angelo asked in the car. 'Why exactly are you detaining Frikkie? He's quite harmless, you know. A little simple-minded, that's all. I'd been meaning to come and see you about Frikkie, but I asked Gerber about him and he told me that Frikkie is getting treatment from a top psychiatrist.'

'Not really treatment, sir. Frikkie was brain damaged at birth. There's nothing anyone can do. He was the second born of Ramona's twins. Lack of oxygen, I suppose. It was common then. Frikkie is being questioned under hypnosis about the drowning of Rose's baby.'

'And he led you to believe that I . . . ?'

'Sir, please. We're almost there.'

Ten minutes later, Angelo was sitting in Ari's office, a Dictaphone on, and Willis, his foot bandaged, looking both unhappy and embarrassed was sitting in the corner by the door.

'Now, sir, this is going to be long and distressing. Would you like coffee? Or a sandwich? If you need anything please ask.'

'I'd like a glass of water,' Angelo said. So far he seemed amused rather than worried.

Let's see how you feel after the first hour, Ari thought sadly.

'Okay, sir, now please remember that Jânek József is out there somewhere on a reprisal mission. Is there anything at all you can remember about him that might help us to identify him?'

Angelo sipped his water and gazed blankly at the wall. 'I don't remember ever seeing him until afterwards,' he said. 'He was tall and scraggy, dark hair, blue eyes, but you know all this. At the trial he said next to nothing, but when he was convicted, he sang a song in Hungarian. He had a fine tenor voice. I was surprised. Sorry I can't help you there.'

'Okay, let's get going. I have a theory which I wish to discuss with you. Perhaps we can shed some light on the problem.'

'Another problem?' Angelo asked, smiling slightly. 'Surely you should be working on Mandy's kidnapping and Ramona's murder?'

'Bear with me, please, sir. I believe it's all interconnected. Go back in your mind to 1964 when Rob was born. It was a very terrible time for you, sir. Trevor had been dead for seven months. József was awaiting trial. Rose came to you with her baby and asked you for more money. Tell me what happened.'

Angelo looked around the room. 'It's hot. No air conditioning. Mind if I take off my jacket?' He looked very calm and collected as he draped his coat over the back of the chair, but his eyes were glittering with regret.

'My hands are not clean, but it's not quite as you may suspect,' he began. 'I killed Rose and Ramona, but with my cruelty, not with my hands. At my age, you want to wipe the slate clean. Past sins have a habit of coming back to mock you, and ruin your sleep.'

Ari leaned back and closed his eyes, listening intently to the story of ancient loves and hatreds. It seemed to him that Angelo had long since tried himself and imposed a life sentence of self-contempt and isolation.

'I'll remember that night as long as I live,' he went on. 'Rose thrust her baby at me – it was crying loudly – and she said: "Here is your grandchild. You must accept him as a Palma, for Trevor's sake. Bring him up as your grandchild, your joint heir, because that is his right."

'I refused point blank. I offered her a generous income, but she wasn't interested. She wanted her child's position to be legalised. We argued, for a long time. If it hadn't been for Claire's baby I might have accepted him.'

He looked up and Ari saw the anguish in his eyes. 'I failed as my father's son,' Angelo said softly. 'Despite his teaching, and I must never forget that he gave his life for what he believed, I had become contaminated by racism. The truth is, I didn't want a coloured heir.

'I remember she stood leaning against the balustrade and she said: "Accept my son as your joint heir or I will throw myself down."

'I said, "No. Don't be a fool. I'm offering you a way out."

'"If I were dead you would take him into your home where he belongs," she said. Suddenly she smiled. It was almost as if she had only just thought of that and found the idea comforting. Before I could stop her, she threw herself backwards.'

He shuddered and buried his face in his hands. For a while no one spoke. Ari watched Palma carefully. He was not lying, he could swear to that.

'I've always known that I killed her. You see, she thought that if she were out of the way . . . poor, misguided girl.'

'We'll have a short break. Stay here,' Ari told Willis.

He went outside and poured three coffees from the machine and carried them back. 'Not very good coffee, sir. Some days we can hardly recognise whether it's coffee or tea, but the sugar will do you good.' He sat sipping his until he felt that Angelo had recovered.

'So you and Bill buried Rose and you paid him to keep quiet about her suicide and her baby.'

'Yes.'

'You were afraid of the scandal if the reason for her suicide came out.'

'Yes. How could I put that added burden on to Claire? She did not know that Rose was pregnant.'

'But you told her later.'

Angelo looked up startled. Then his eyes glowed with unshed tears. 'You've seen Claire!' It wasn't a question.

'Yes.'

'How is she?'

'She's lovely. Serene, secure, I think, but sad. She said: "Angelo frightened me. I saw the other side of him. I never knew it existed."'

Angelo sat hunched over his desk, his head in his hands. At last he looked up. 'Lieutenant, try to understand, I had lost everyone who had ever meant anything to me. Then my son Trevor was taken from me. I coped in the only way I know how. I walled up my emotions. I became a machine.'

'Let's get back to that night,' Ari said briskly. 'What happened to the baby while you were burying Rose?'

'Good God! Do you think I buried . . .' He looked up shocked and terrified.

'No. I have proof that Anton was alive at two.'

'I see.' He shook his head like a bull shaking off flies.

'Did you hold the baby?'

'No! I can't . . . I like children, but I can't cope with babies. They're more for women.'

'Let's go on to Claire. She was in a clinic, but she came home and tried to take her baby away.'

'That's correct.'

'And you prevented her from doing this?'

'Yes,' he said softly. There was a long silence. Then he said: 'I felt guilty and, well . . . evil, but I could not let that child go. It was all I had left of my son.'

All she had, too, Ari thought. 'So you were involved in the business of bringing up the baby?'

'Not at that stage. Good heavens. It was a tiny infant. I had nurses. Later, Ramona took over.'

'Weren't you surprised when Ramona came back and forgave you for the death of Rose?'

'Yes,' he admitted. 'I never realised that she was so mercenary. She drove a hard bargain. I must admit I thought less of her for putting a price on her daughter's life.'

'Was she usually so forgiving?'

'God no. Not her.'

'Vengeance was more her line, wasn't it?'

'Just what are you getting at, Lieutenant?'

'How often did you see Rob?'

'For God's sake! Does it matter? A baby's a baby. He was well looked after. I started to take a hand in rearing my grandchild when he reached the toddling stage. What can a man do with a little baby?'

'Bear with me,' Ari said 'Frikkie said that Ramona had given instructions that he should throw the baby into the sea. He was paid two hundred rands to do this, on the instructions of you, because you didn't want Rose's bastard around. Would Ramona kill her own grandchild?'

'Not her! That's why your arrest is so absurd.'

'I believe that she exacted her own fitting vengeance,' Ari said. 'My theory is that Ramona had planned that you should accept her grandson, whether you wanted to or not. When she asked you for her job back it was to guard Rose's child and bring him up. You destroyed her Rose, so she destroyed your legal grandson by giving him to Frikkie to throw into the sea. It makes sense to me. What do you think? There must be a reason why she decided to rear Rob. There must be a reason why she told Frikkie to drown a toddler. Is it likely that she might have swopped the infants? Answer me this, Mr Palma – does it make sense to you? Did Ramona have the opportunity to exchange the babies?'

Angelo stood up and lurched forward. Moments later he was gasping for air.

'Call a doctor,' Ari told Willis. He fumbled in Palma's pocket for his pills, found them and put one on his tongue. Minutes later, Angelo, lying flat on his back on the carpet, seemed to be recovering.

'It's only a theory,' Ari said. 'I'm not saying it's so.'

Angelo's face showed his fears. He was shaking visibly.

His lips were blue, his face white, and his eyes were haggard.

'Help me up,' he said. 'I want to sit in the chair. Help me! If, God forbid, this were true, then what happened to Claire's son?' he asked in a hoarse whisper.

'I don't know, sir. All I know is that there were two babies, much of an age, both from the same father, both with similar features. One was brought up by you and the other was put on a farm until he was two. He was teased by the other children because he was so white-skinned. Then they forced Ramona to take him away, so she told Frikkie to drown him. She remained in your house to look after the other baby. You must work out which one you think is which.'

'Oh my God!' Angelo crouched forward in his chair, his arms were flung across the desk, his face buried in his arms.

'When's the doctor coming?' Ari whispered urgently to Willis.

'Any moment now.' When Angelo looked up, his face mirrored his doubts: his lips were twisted, his eyes were a mute appeal.

'Didn't you ever want to know what happened to Rose's baby? After all, he was also Trevor's son.'

'Yes, I did,' Angelo whispered. 'As the months went by I regretted my actions. I asked Ramona to send me photographs of the boy from time to time.'

'What did she say?'

'She said she would. But then, when Rob was about two and a half years old, she said that her grandson had drowned in a farm dam. I was very upset.'

'Yes,' Ari said softly. 'Now, Mr Palma. To change the subject. Did you know that Rob had tried to cancel the arrangement whereby you purchase the fish from privately owned fishing trawlers?'

'No. I don't believe that he did.'

'Well, last month he did. You were visiting the vineyard at Paarl when he sent out the notices. Here's one of them. I got this from a friend in the harbour. At the time, Bill September was in a frenzy. He laid off his crew and they got together to claim compensation. Would you say Rob was the sort of man who gave in to blackmail or threats?'

'You must be kidding,' Angelo said, with a proud chuckle, but the smile fled and his eyes became bleak again.

'Ramona came to see Rob late at night. The two had an explosive fight. Strange that! The boss and the housekeeper. Ramona left your grandson's office, but shortly afterwards Rob ran to Ramona's cottage and they continued the fight. After a while she left, but Rob flung himself over her table. He was beating the table with his hands, yelling "No . . . No . . ." Punching the table for about ten minutes according to the gardener, until he pulled himself together and rushed back to the house. He remained in his office, pacing up and down. Then he left a message on tape for his secretary, telling her that he had changed his mind and they would purchase the fish from private operators as usual because he had gained new export markets. He packed an overnight bag and drove off. Evidently he is prospecting in the Namib. Do you know anything about these new markets?'

Angelo looked stricken. He stood up, stiff and proud and very sad. 'Lieutenant, you are a very devious man. You've brought me here to try to incriminate my grandson, Rob. You don't for one moment believe that I killed Rose or her son, do you? I will not answer any more questions until I am legally represented. You can go to hell.'

'But what if he really is Rose's son?'

'It makes no different. I love Rob. I always will. I do not believe that he murdered Ramona. He would never do that. Take me to the cells, or wherever you have in mind. You won't get another word out of me.'

He stood staring at the wall.

'You'll be held under guard at the military hospital,' Ari said. 'The guard is to protect you.' The old man made no sign that he had heard.

For seven days, Rob had endured the scorching heat of the high plateau in the moonscape region of the Namib desert, the oldest desert in the world. He was gaunt and his skin was tanned like leather, his hair was unkempt, and his eyes shone with a feverish light.

He had fled here after Ramona's revelation and only recently had he learned about his grandfather's arrest. This was the only place where he could cope with his trauma, he knew, for it was a place he loved and where he felt he belonged. Here, too, lay the fortune that was truly his, not Angelo's, nor Claire's. He had ventured here as a young geologist fresh from university and he had wrested a minor fortune from the sand, mainly living off the land, prospecting, staking his claims, and putting together consortiums to mine the claims. He was supposed to be prospecting now, but the truth was he had to get away from all ties and financial and emotional commitments, to think.

It was dusk: a strange, lingering desert dusk when the amber light bewitches the landscape and colours are mellowed and brightened, and the sand turns to a deep, dusky ochre.

Rob saw a Nama melon, cut it in half and sucked out the

bitter seeds and pulp gratefully. Then he sat under a fever tree and thought about his dilemma.

It seemed that he was at loggerheads with life. His unquenchable desire – for finance, for riches, for more power – seemed to have led him into a trap. That was why he had fled to the desert, his second home, to make a decision. Torn in two by the ferocity of his conflicting desires, he was suffering the hell of his own private purgatory.

Who knew his secret? Only Ramona, who was dead, and Frikkie, who was mad and incoherent – and who would believe that lunatic anyway?

What should he do? If he were to toil his guts out here in the Namib for his entire lifetime, he would only make a fraction of the fortune he stood to lose. Why should he be banished? He was Angelo's grandson, he was a Palma by blood, if not legally, he had the right to take what was morally his. *It would be so easy.*

And what was the alternative? He would be exposed as an imposter. His white status would be taken away. He would be scorned by Angelo, and known as the Septembers' coloured bastard, related to half the fishing village. He would lose the Palma home and estates, the fishing factories and ships, the du Toit's mines, the vineyards, his reputation, his power, everything!

And then there was Kate. He still hoped to woo her back, but as a small-time miner, a coloured, and a bastard, he stood no chance. Kate was made for better things than a mining camp in the Namib.

Fate had flipped his world upside down and he had to make a choice, good or evil, right or wrong, enjoy the fruits of his work and inheritance, or be utterly lost and destroyed. Surely he had the right to safeguard the position he had been reared to fill? He was his father's son. It was his birthright.

But he loved his grandfather, and his grandfather's life and liberty were at stake. He doubted the old man would survive long in prison. Only he could save Angelo. He was the living proof of the absurdity of his supposed crime. So what was he to choose?

Ari met Jean in the bar at nine. As usual he was serenading the barmaid.

'Ari, my friend, you're late,' he roared as he ordered Ari's beer. Ari sat studying him saying very little, watching him chatting up the new barmaid, a British blonde, a cockney from the sound of her voice. Despite her well-cultivated, naive manner, she was clearly adept at fending off the drunks and she was raking in good tips, Ari noticed. Jean was very taken by her. Ari said he was on duty and left after buying Jean a beer.

Willis was waiting at the yacht basin with a rowing boat.

'Stay here. If Jean pitches, fire your gun, and I'll row off pretty quickly. It's a dark night.'

It didn't take long to search *Tralee* and hide the tracking device. Ari felt inwardly furious. Sometimes he was so damn dense. He swore when he found the black and white snapshot of Rose pinned on the wall. She was smiling into the camera and she was very beautiful and very young. The size matched the hole on Ramona's pegboard and there was a small pin hole at the top of it.

Taking a glass, a lighter and a metal ashtray for finger-prints, Ari slipped over the side and rowed back to Willis. 'Get these checked against the prison prints of Jânek József,' he said. 'I want it by morning.'

'They're closed until morning.'

'Wake them up. Do it! You guys are half-asleep down here,' he grumbled.

It was 5 a.m. when the telephone rang. 'Jesus, Lieutenant,' the voice whined. 'What's so special about these damned fingerprints that I had to stay up half the night?'

'Sorry,' Ari said. 'It's an emergency. You guys have it easy most of the time. We're up most nights.'

'Says who?' the voice snarled. 'Anyway, listen! The prints are one and the same. That is, the prison prints of Jânek Jözsef match those on the lighter and the glass. The red smear on the picture is human blood, of the same type as the late Ramona September's. Looks like you're on to something.'

'Yes. Unfortunately the suspect might notice that a part of the picture has been torn off. That's why I needed the information fast.'

He replaced the receiver thinking, well, that lets Rob off the hook. Angelo will be pleased.

By 6.30 a.m., Ari was stationed at a vantage point behind the dunes. He waited for over an hour until Jean Graux sailed back from a north-westerly position to make fast at his moorings. This was his nightly ritual, but he was always back by six-thirty. He would probably go to work now. He was currently working as a carpenter at the boat building yard. Perhaps he couldn't cope with the long, but more remunerative fishing trips, with Mandy locked away somewhere and waiting to be fed and . . .

Ari gritted his teeth as he thought of what might be happening to the girl when Jean visited her night after night, but there was no point in getting morbid, he decided, as he forced his mind back to the job in hand.

Chapter 55

——— ▬ ———

Jean's yacht stole out of harbour at midnight and took a southerly course. There were no boats about, it was a moonless night and Ari was hopeful that they would not be detected as he and Willis followed the yacht in the police launch. The scanner was showing them the direction Jean had taken and there wasn't much chance they would lose him, unless he became suspicious and found the homing device. In case that happened, Ari was keeping the white sail in sight through his powerful night binoculars. The waves were rising and it was freezing cold with the south-easter blowing up.

An hour out of harbour, Ari thought he heard the sound of breakers on the stern side. They cut the engine and sat rising and falling over a heavy swell, listening.

'Is there an island hereabouts?' Ari asked.

'Several off the point. That's more or less where we are, I guess. More like rocky heaps than islands.'

Ari grabbed the night glasses and looked out at an expanse of glittering black waves. He panicked for a moment when he saw no sign of Jean's boat. Moments later it rose out of a trough of waves, like a macabre vision, as white became shimmering green through the nightscope.

Jean was a dim black shape obscuring the pale green

of the sail as he passed in front of it. Then the green disappeared; presumably Jean had unfurled his mainsail. They were too far away to hear if he had cut his engines, but he appeared to be dropping anchor.

'We have to get closer, but wait a bit first,' Ari said. Then came the unmistakable roar of powerful twin outboard engines and they saw the wake of Jean's inflatable, looking like a green trail cutting into the black sea.

'That's where he's got her,' Ari muttered. 'Stuck in some cave out there. Move in close, fast. He won't hear us against the noise of his engines.'

For a few minutes they sped in Jean's wake, skimming and bouncing on the wave crests. Ari leaned over Willis to cut back the throttle. Now that they were closer in, they could see the foaming surf smashing on jagged rocks that appeared to encircle the island. They heard when Jean cut his engines. Watching through the scopes, they saw his boat poised outside the reefs, rising and falling with the massive swell.

'He's waiting for the right wave,' Willis muttered. 'There's no channel to the island. He has to surf in.'

Moments later a large wave swept towards Jean. His engines came to life with a roar as he shot forward to surf in at high speed, skimming over the rocks, until he reached shallow water.

'Jesus!' Willis muttered. 'He's some sailor.' His blue eyes were glittering with alarm.

They watched Jean's tall figure dragging his boat out of the surf across a patch of sand, and disappear into the shadows.

'That place is impregnable,' Willis said. 'I've been here before. I tried to reach the island once. Penguins nest there. It's surrounded by rocks, bad currents, massive breakers and a dangerous undertow. We're near the southerly tip of the Continent. Two oceans meet here with a silent crash. The island's about sixty metres across. There are sheer rock-faces on three sides and a cave on the fourth side.'

'Tell me about the cave,' Ari said, tight-lipped with tension.

'I told you, I haven't been on the island. It appears to be about fifty metres up the rock-face with a dangerous ascent. If he knew you were coming, you'd be an easy target. There's absolutely no cover.'

Ari gazed at the sea feeling icy cold with fear. It was about the worst swim he'd ever contemplated. He longed for a good reason not to go.

Willis seemed to read his thoughts. 'Best thing would be to wait until he leaves and go in by helicopter to rescue her.'

Ari was locked in an awful premonition of impending disaster. He shook his head. 'The problem is, he might have seen us, in which case he'll have no alternative but to kill her and dump her body in the sea. We can't take that chance, Willis. Apart from her life, we wouldn't have a damn thing against him. That's if we ever saw him again. I reckon he would have exacted his revenge. We'd have failed and he'd have won. No, I'm going to have to get that bastard.'

He began to put on his scuba gear.

'You won't make it,' Willis said. 'It's suicide.'

'Not really. I'm a strong swimmer, I'll stick to the bottom.

'Listen, Willis. Take the launch to the yacht and tie up against it on the sea side. He'll get back on board about five o'clock. So you can hang on until four. Then you get back to base fast and bring in a helicopter. With luck I'll be hanging in there waiting for you.'

Willis refused to look at him. His moody blue eyes gazed over his shoulder, wide with disapproval. Ari set his course with his luminous direction finder, pulled on his mask and tipped backwards into the sea. He sank to six metres and set off towards the island.

At first the going was reasonably good. There was a heavy swell, and numerous swirling eddies and choppy side currents, some warm from the Indian Ocean, some icy cold from the south Atlantic. He was a strong swimmer, and he kept moving forward, pushing himself to go harder and faster for the next half-hour.

When he neared the island, conditions worsened. Suddenly the backwash took hold of him and swept him out faster than he had thought possible, whirling him round and over, tumbling him over the sea bed, pushing him up like a volcanic eruption, and back down onto the rocks. There was no way to fight this massive force of water. Then the incoming swell caught him in its ferocious grip and lashed him forwards, tumbling over the sea bed, hitting against rocks and stones, leaving him stunned and scared stiff. Four times he was buffeted in and out, and all his strength was like nothing. Then a sudden lurch sent him hard against a rock that was solid and still, and he hung on for his life. He felt battered, humbled and furious. He tried to check his equipment, but the force of the water was unbelievable. He knew he had lost his flippers, but he had his gun carefully wrapped under his wet suit and his knife was still strapped to his leg.

Another swirl knocked him hard against the rock, wrenching his mask off, but he grabbed at it in time, pushed it on with one hand, hanging on with the other, and blew out the water. Taking his torch, he shone the powerful beam around him. Ahead, across an open patch of sand, was a narrow channel through the rocks. If he could get there . . .

He waited for the next forward surge, but it took all his courage to let go of his precious rock. He was swept forward, powerless, but he struggled to keep down on the ocean bed, kicking and swimming with all his strength, trying to guide his direction, his terror of death giving him superhuman strength. Miraculously, he was rocketing down the narrow channel and wedged fast between two rocks. As the retreating undertow tore at him, he felt he was gripped by a giant vice that held him fast.

God help me, he thought, gripping his teeth harder on the rubber mouthpiece. The water turned again, pushing him onwards. Like a sea serpent he remained cautiously on the bottom, sliding on his belly, flicking his feet, allowing himself to surge forward from one safe handgrip to the next.

Then the channel came to an abrupt end. Flicking his torch again, he saw only sand ahead. He was too scared to leave the safety of the passageway. How could he? The swell was too dangerous and he was tiring fast. He was bruised and aching in every muscle and limb.

But he could not stay there, and he could not go back, so he would have to chance it. Waiting for the forward swell, he shot across the sandy space, surging fast, using every ounce of force he could muster in his legs and arms. He sensed the water was shallow, for the surf was smashing around his head. When the backtow sent him slithering and sliding back, he found a rock to hold and he hung on hard. Then disaster struck with a mighty slam against a rock that dislodged his tank and mask and nearly wrenched his mouthpiece out. This was it! He surfaced fast. There was no sign of an island, just miles of foaming water playing

around the rocks. Then he realised he was looking out to
sea and he whipped round. There was the island, a dense
blackness silhouetted against the night sky, hardly twenty
metres away. One more wave could get him there. He
fought against the backwash. Glancing over his shoulder
he saw a massive breaker bearing down on him. He began
to swim, shooting forward, praying, hoping to keep on the
crest. If he were tumbled here it would mean death.

The breaker caught him as if he were a cork and carried
him forward at a massive speed. He was out of control,
riding high. He kept on swimming fast, using every last
ounce of strength. Now he was falling. He was about to be
dumped. But where?

He landed with a smash that knocked the breath out of
him. He was only thigh deep in water, and the rocks were
cutting his feet. Ignoring the pain, he staggered to the
beach. He collapsed past the high water mark and dragged
himself behind a sheltering boulder.

Ari lay there, the breath knocked out of him, gasping for
oxygen, listening to the sound of the waves below. He felt
like a rag doll, his limbs heavy and powerless; he knew it
was a miracle he was alive. When he tried to sit up, he
could not.

'Ari,' he lectured himself. 'I'll give you ten minutes to
recover. Then you're going to climb up there and arrest
Jean Graux. The matter is not up for debate. You have no
alternative.' As he lay, calling up his resources, his strength
returned and his frozen limbs thawed.

At last he was able to peel off his wet suit. His shorts
and T-shirt would soon dry in the wind. He had his gun,
thank God. He unwrapped the plastic cover and felt for his
knife. Time to go!

Stealthily he crept barefooted towards the granite cliff

face. The clouds had blown away and the moon was rising. Damn! He'd taken too long. He thought he heard Willis' outboard engines starting up, but he wasn't sure since the breakers muffled all other sound. Did Jean hear? That was the problem.

If Jean were awake, he fretted, he would be silhouetted against the pale glow as he entered the cave mouth. With the gun clasped in his hand, he lay flat, holding his breath as he slithered along the entrance to the cave. Then he inched forward. Now he found he was facing a rough wooden door that blocked the wide entrance to the cave. Shit! He lay thinking for a while. Jean was heavier and stronger, and he was a trained killer. On his side he had youth, the element of surprise and speed, for he knew he was very fast.

The partition was hanging loose. He made a running dive at it, crashing it back with a strong kick. He landed in the cave on his knees, pointing his gun. 'Hands up,' he snarled.

It was so dark. He swung his torch around, but saw nothing except two old chairs and a table with a primus on it.

'Look out!' A woman's voice screamed.

As Ari threw himself sidelong, a crowbar crashed where his head had been a split-second before. It caught his arm, knocking his gun down somewhere in the dark. Jean fell heavily to the ground, carried by his own momentum, still holding the crowbar. For a second he lay spread-eagled. *Now*, a voice screamed silently inside Ari's head. He flung himself down over Jean, using his weight to pin him down, twisted one arm round his neck, tightening his grip, but his neck was like a wire rope.

Jean twisted his body like a whiplash, hurling Ari aside, but the effort left him breathless.

Ari leaped on to the crowbar, grabbed it and brought it smashing down on Jean's arm. A hard kick to the side of Jean's jaw knocked him out.

Was he shamming? Ari twisted his arm behind his back and lay over Jean, fighting to bring his panting breath back under control.

He called out: 'Mandy.'

There was a quiet sob. 'I didn't know what I would hear, Mandy or Rose,' she sobbed.

'Cut it out, Mandy. Pull yourself together and get down here. I need some rope. And I need help. You can cry later.'

'I can't,' she said plaintively. 'He heard the boat's engine. I'm handcuffed to the bed. The key is in his pocket.'

Ari slammed Jean's head hard against the ground. That should keep him quiet for five minutes. He fumbled for the keys, grabbed his torch and ran to the back of the cave. Mandy lay naked on a makeshift bed. Compassion surged and he almost cried out. He unlocked the handcuffs and ran back to Jean, who was groaning and moving. Despite his screams, Ari forced his hands behind his back and handcuffed them. Now he felt better.

Graux twisted his body round and slammed his foot against Ari's legs, but he couldn't do much with his feet, Ari thought. But he'd tie them anyway.

'You got sheets?' He looked up into huge amber eyes, set into a white face, with long black hair tumbling around. She had wrapped herself in a sheet and she looked scared and anguished.

He tried to quell her fears. 'I am Lieutenant Ari St John, of the SA Police, and I've been looking for you for a long time,' he said. 'I'm sorry it took me so long. Is there any rope here?'

She disappeared into the darkness and came back with a length of nylon rope.

Jean fought like a man possessed, until Ari flung himself over his legs to pin them while he bound them.

'Now, you bastard,' he said. 'Let's see what you can do now. Is he the only one here, besides you?' he asked.

'Yes,' she murmured. She had moved very close beside him, and he could feel her shaking. 'Can I get dressed, please?' she whispered. 'Can we get out of here? Can I go home now?'

'Yes. Everything's all right now. A helicopter's coming to fetch us. All we have to do now, Mandy, is to wait.'

She came back wearing shorts and a T-shirt. She was shivering, so he went down to the beach and brought back his diving suit. He took his knife and ripped off the bottom so that it looked like a short coat and helped her to put it on.

Then the tears came, as he'd guessed they would. A flood of past fears and the release from the awful tension of not knowing if finally she would live or die.

He cradled her in his arms, rocking her backwards and forwards. 'It's all right. It's over. You'll be home in no time.'

Jean Graux began to swear. 'Leave her. Don't touch her. I'll kill you, Ari – one day. I swear to God I'll come back for you, Rose.'

'Must I live with that voice? Will I never know just when he's going to get free and come after me?'

He took her down to the beach, as far away from the cave as they could go, gave her the torch and left her there. She was so scared, but despite her fears, she was exquisite. Just looking at her was a pleasure. Imagine spending your life looking at a vision like that. It would seem like paradise. He almost felt sorry for Jean. Easy for a girl like that to become an obsession, he thought, noting the way her breasts moved under the thin fabric of her T-shirt. He had seen how lovely they were. Her neck was long and perfect, her eyes large and set wide apart, her hair rose thickly from a widow's peak and her thick, black eyebrows seemed to accentuate the symmetry of her lovely, heart-shaped face.

He climbed back into the cave and dragged Jean out.

'Listen here, Jean. The helicopter's on the way. You may be hanged, but it's more likely you'll get life. You killed Ramona, and I can prove it. Quite apart from kidnapping and rape. Is this what you want? D'you want to be pushing eighty next time you face the world? I'm going to untie your ankles, but only for a short while. Make good use of the time, Graux.'

He untied his legs and sat watching him, holding his gun. Jean walked to the edge. He looked over his shoulder and said: 'Tell Rose . . .'

'I'll tell her nothing. Her name's Mandy and you know that damn well. Your game's over, Jean.'

Jean shuddered as he looked down. Far below the sea glittered with silver phosphorescence as it pounded the cruel rocks. He stepped forward into the black void.

As Ari ran back to Mandy he heard the drone of the helicopter.

Chapter 56

It was almost noon by the time Ari dispensed with statements to the prosecutor, formally identified the body of Jânek József and filled in the numerous, tedious forms. Then at last he was able to turn his back on death, but not on his own discomfort. He felt as if he'd had a close encounter with a steamroller. He was pretty sure a couple of ribs were cracked, every bone ached, his hands were raw and stung like crazy and his head ached intolerably because he had 'flu coming. *When this is over*, he promised himself, *I'll take a couple of days off.*

Back at the station he found half the fishermen and their wives clustered outside the building and filling the car park.

Willis hurried out to him. 'Watch out! Frost has called in the media. That bastard's doing a TV news broadcast right now in the Charge Office. He's stealing all the thunder.'

Willis looked upset, his blue eyes were burning with fury, his face looked brutish, his jaw was clenched, his cheeks flushed. Ari had never seen Willis lose his temper.

'Believe me, it's not important, Willis,' Ari said. 'The people who count know the truth.'

He looked into the crowded room towards the trestle

table where Gerber, Frost and their assistants sat facing
a barrage of journalists and flashguns.

'When did you first get on to the trail of Jânek József,
sir?' a journalist called to Gerber.

'About a month ago. But I had to be careful not to
alarm him until I discovered the whereabouts of Mandy
September.'

Gerber caught sight of Ari in the doorway and flushed
deep purple. 'I can't take all the credit,' he said. 'Police
work is team work. My staff did the leg work.'

Frost seemed anxious to get in on the act. Noting
Gerber's hesitation, he took over. 'Last week, acting on
a hunch, we succeeded in matching the fingerprints of one
of our yachtsmen, Jean Graux, supposedly from Mauritius,
with those of the deported criminal, József. From then on
it was plain sailing.'

Is that what it's called? Ari thought, smiling ruefully at
the memory of his underwater swim to the island.

'We almost succeeded a month back,' Frost went on
in his smooth, ingratiating manner, 'when I organised an
all-out search of the surrounding mountains. We spared no
expense or labour, and pulled in the full might of the SA
Police and Defence force to find this unfortunate young
girl.' Frost caught sight of Ari and turned chalk white. Ari
grinned nastily.

Gerber gestured that Ari should join them, but he
pretended not to see and pushed past a crowd of journalists
to reach the coffee machine. Moments later he gulped down
his coffee, wincing as it burned his sore throat. Retrieving
his file on Frikkie, he hurried to his car.

His annoyance faded as he drove towards the psychiatric
hospital in Wynberg. He was twenty minutes late for the
appointment, but Fink was not concerned. He was telling

Frikkie a funny story and, to his surprise, Frikkie was laughing.

'Let's get started,' Fink said, leading Ari to the corridor. 'You see, this drug ... well, basically it's a development of the old truth drug. Allied to hypnosis, it should have an explosive effect on Frikkie's memory. We'll know very shortly. Creative people are easier to hypnotise,' he went on quietly as he pushed the needle into Frikkie's arm. 'With Frikkie, I've been hampered by his inability to concentrate. His mind wanders and I can't fix it on anything long enough to get through to him.'

Once again Ari was struck by Frikkie's resemblance to Neanderthal man with his small eyes set close together under jutting brows, his wide nose, thick sinewy neck sloping forward, his broad shoulders and long arms which were lying limp on the bedspread. His eyes took on a relaxed, dreamy expression as the drug took effect. He was smiling softly.

Ari glanced at Fink and noticed his suppressed excitement as he tapped his finger on the back of Frikkie's hand.

'Relax, Frikkie,' he said. 'You're looking towards a bright light. You want to go down to the light, Frikkie, but there are ten steep steps. Hold on to the rail. D'you see it? Hang on and take the first step down. Move your thumb when you've made it. You ready? Down you go. That's it. That's it, Frikkie. Careful does it. Well done! Now the next step.

'This might take a while,' he whispered apologetically.

Ari's thoughts turned to Mandy. What a beautiful girl! He'd taken too long to find her and he blamed himself. Thank God she was safe at last. She was in hospital, but there was nothing physically wrong with her. With time and therapy she would recover from her traumatic experience,

the analyst had assured him. Ari was wrapping up his cases
because Colonel du Plessis was pushing for his return to
the Transvaal. He had decided to apply for a verdict of
accidental death for Rose and he had little doubt that the
court would support him. Patel was awaiting trial, but he'd
probably be free in less than ten years, or maybe sooner.
Ari was sick to death of seeing the criminals back on the
streets, sometimes within days of being arrested. That was
one of the reasons why he planned to leave the force. His
next move depended very much on Kate. He was going to
propose to her later today and this time he would press for
a straight answer. He was longing for her to say yes.

Ari was drifting along in happy daydreams when Fink's
voice brought him back to reality.

'Here goes, Ari,' he said quietly. 'Frikkie's in a deep
trance.' He leaned over the bed.

'Frikkie, do you remember the day Ramona gave you two
hundred rands? Why did she do that?'

'To drown the child for her.' His voice was odd. Almost
like someone's else's, it was so deep and gruff.

'Tell us what happened, Frikkie? I want you to go back
to that early morning when you rowed the child out in your
boat. It was March, 1967. You are standing on the beach.
What time is it?'

'It's early. Four o'clock or thereabouts.' Frikkie's hoarse
voice was hardly more than a whisper, now.

Ari trembled with anticipation.

'I've come out early before the others get here,' Frikkie
muttered. 'They mustn't see the child. Or hear it. Ramona's
handed it a bottle of milk to keep it quiet. It's hanging on to
the bottle with both hands, sucking as if its life depends on
it. It's half starved, I can see that. Poor child. Shame . . .
shame . . .'

Frikkie was breathing heavily and his body gave off a sickly smell of sweat. His eyes, rolling in their sockets, ran with tears.

'Skinny little thing. No one wants it,' he muttered. 'I've got to drown it like it's an unwanted puppy. Why me? They always give me the dirty work. They think I don't care. The child is sick, anyone can see that. There's some reason why Ramona's afraid to take it to the hospital. It will die anyway, so what's the difference?' He was speaking so indistinctly it was hard to understand him. 'I might as well drown it. She's up there watching me. She's sitting on the sand dune in a black dress and she looks like a witch. She is a witch! I'm afraid of her. If I don't do what she wants she'll beat me, or starve me, or stop my wine. All my life she's been nagging at me . . .'

He broke off and began to mutter incoherently. For a long time he gazed in silence at the wall, deeply involved in his other world.

'Where are the fishermen?' Fink prompted him after a while.

'Sleeping. They'll be here soon enough. By then old Frikkie must get out there and back again. Poor little child. Ramona has no mercy for those that get in her way. Like me. Everything goes to Bill. He has a boat and a house and I have nothing.'

He broke off and his cheeks became wet with tears while his hands clutched at each other. Moments later he gave a deep shuddering sigh and lapsed into silence.

'Frikkie! Frikkie! Can you hear me? Talk to us, Frikkie. Where are you?'

'I'm rowing . . . rowing out to sea. It's a pleasure to skim over the water. It's so calm, strange for this time of the year. No wind and so dark. There's no moon. The child is whimpering, almost as if he knows. Perhaps he does know . . .'

Frikkie began to shake violently. 'No . . .' he blurted out. 'No! How can he know?' His fingers tightened convulsively, and he sat up slowly and groaned, his eyes wide and sightless. Now he was rowing . . . flicking the oars effortlessly in the calm water . . . grunting occasionally. He paused and moved his arms as if he were pulling the oars into the boat. He leaned forward and hauled something towards him. 'Don't be afraid. It's quick. They say it's painless. What's the good of your life? No one wants you. You and me both. Please don't cry.' He made a quick, compulsive gesture as if pushing the child out. Then he pulled back.

'Oh God help me, I can't do it,' he cried. He was folding his arms around a vacuum of space, rocking softly from side to side. 'There . . . there . . . It's all right. Old Frikkie can't do it. You've got a right to your life. If Ramona wants you dead, someone else will have to do it. I can't. But what about Ramona? She'll kill me.' The spittle was running round his chin and his eyes looked frantic.

'Got to get back in,' he muttered. 'Before dawn. Got to hide you.

'Come here, boy,' Frikkie commanded, 'or you'll get tangled in the nets as I throw them out. Sit behind me in the stern. That's right. Keep right down. There's a good boy,' he growled. He began to sing an old Malay song: '*There comes the Alabama, the Alabama has come from the sea* . . .' crooning tunelessly to the frightened child, while he rowed and threw out the first section of the net which was attached to a buoy, and then the next one, buoy by buoy, until he had trekked the net a good distance.

It seemed so real. Tying both ends of the rope to the bows, he began the long, hard haul back, the weight of the rope dragging at the boat. Soon he was heaving and sweating with the effort.

'Look at that! Beads of perspiration,' Ari whispered. 'Look at his muscles tightening. That's amazing.'

'Sh!' Fink scowled at him.

'Hey!' Frikkie grunted. 'What's that?' He jerked forward, startling both of them. 'A dolphin! It'll mess up the nets, no mistake. I'll have to pull them in or I'll be mending them for days.'

He carried on heaving at the oars, taking long strokes, sweating and straining and groaning with the effort. 'Oh!' He exhaled with relief as he appeared to be beaching the boat on the sand. Moments later he was pulling the rope. It took a long time to heave in one end of the net, and Ari wondered if he'd die with the effort of all that straining and tugging. After all, he was twenty-six years older now.

'Oh my God! Here they come. I'll throw you into the net, boy. Stop it! Stop crying!' He clapped his hands over his ears.

A cunning look came into his eyes as Frikkie turned his head around the empty ward. 'Hi there, Jaapie. Hi, Cobus. I was rowing out there . . . far out to sea when I saw this boy riding on this dolphin's back. True as God! I saw it with my own eyes! They were going so fast. Like the wind. But the dolphin got tangled in the net and the boy started to cry. So I rowed back fast and here they are.

'Lying? No, never! I swear to God! Where else could the child come from? It's the truth, I tell you. You can see for yourself it's the truth. There's the dolphin and there's the boy.'

Frikkie lay down and closed his eyes. The minutes ticked by, but Frikkie seemed to be asleep. Eventually Fink bent over the man. 'And then, Frikkie? What happened then?'

'Nothing. Ramona never found out. Or if she did, she didn't say anything. Why should she? I'd got rid of the boy one way or another.'

'So what happened to the child?'

'Jaapie and a crowd of villagers took him to the priest up at the church. We never saw the child again.'

'Ask him what the priest's name was,' Ari said quietly.

'Why? I don't suppose he would know.'

'Ask – for God's sake!' Ari was shaking, but he made an effort to pull himself together.

'Do you remember the name of the priest, Frikkie? The one they took the child to?'

'A silly name,' he muttered. 'The kids called him moon-face. I remember him well because he came to see me many times. Mooney, his name was. He tried to find out where the boy came from. I never told him. Then he stopped coming.'

Ari walked out of the ward and saw a bathroom opposite. He went inside and locked the door. He sat on the floor, leaned against the wall and began to sob, smothering the sound with the hospital towel. He cried for Frikkie's compassion which had saved his life, and because he now understood his fear of Ramona and her cruel eyes, and the recurring nightmare of being buried alive in a deep dark hole. He cried for his loathing of cruelty and his aggressive desire to fight back, now that he was no longer a defenceless child. He cried for his disgust of the depraved farmfolk where he had been dumped. He cried, too, because he was in a state of shock, and because he did not know if his mother were Rose or Claire. He cried for Eunice and for Mandy and her ordeal, and lastly he cried for man's savagery to man. When he stood up, a wave of dizziness engulfed him, so he hung on to the towel rail.

Nausea rose from his stomach to his throat and he threw up in the lavatory for a long time. Eventually he pulled himself together, washed his face, straightened his shoulders and walked back to the ward.

Frikkie was spooning porridge into his mouth, dropping some of it on to a towel the nurse had tied around his neck.

'Clearly he's innocent of killing the child,' Ari told Fink. 'I shall release him as soon as you think he's well enough to go. He's harmless.'

'Hey there, sit down,' Fink said, grabbing his arm. 'You're as white as a sheet. What is it? What's wrong? All this means something special to you, doesn't it? I sensed that some time back. For you, it's not just another case.'

'I had thought it was important, but now I realise that it is not. Strange that,' he said, meaning it. 'Thanks, George.' He shook hands and left quickly before those compelling grey eyes wormed his secret out of him.

Chapter 57

——— ———

It was early morning and Kate was hard at work at her easel. She heard Dopey growling and looked up. A jolt of joy shot through her at the sight of Rob, framed in the doorway.

Taken by surprise, she ran towards him and flung her arms around him. 'Oh, Rob! Rob darling. I missed you.' Then she stepped back, remembering that they were getting divorced.

'Come in,' she said, loving the sight of him, but noticing that he looked tired. He must have driven back overnight, she thought. He was still wearing his desert gear, khaki shorts and vest and that was all. His hair was a mess. How quickly it had grown and his cheeks were covered with an inch of jet black beard.

'Come in. You look exhausted. I've just made some coffee,' she said. 'Sit down. Rob, I want to thank you for what you've done. I mean, the bird sanctuary. Well . . . thank you. What else can I say?'

'You could say: "What took you so long to come to your senses?"'

'I could,' she laughed. 'But then we'd be fighting again.'

'Not this time, Kate. I've come to say goodbye.'

A pang hit her like a blow in her solar plexus. 'Oh!' She bit back her disappointment.

'Where are you going?' she asked, pouring coffee from the filter machine.

'To the Namib desert. Kate, listen to me carefully, I don't have much time. I'm not the man you think I am, but while I'm still that man, I've instructed my lawyer to set up a trust for you. You'll be all right no matter what happens.'

'I am all right. Whatever are you talking about?'

'It doesn't matter.'

'It does to me. You see, Rob, I love you.'

'Sh! Don't say that. You don't even know me. I didn't even know myself.'

His story poured out starting with his shock when he had learned that the Palma fortune was not his. 'I don't own much that's truly mine. Just a couple of mines and a rough and ready camp. I shall start from there and build up,' he said. 'It's no place for a woman. I don't even know if we have to get divorced. Maybe we were never married. You married Rob Palma. I'm not him. Your lieutenant is the real heir.'

This time she was truly shocked. She backed into a chair and gazed at him blankly.

'And you are?'

'Rose's bastard son.'

Then we're free, she thought. We can live where we like. We don't have to live in Angelo's home.

'Rob, listen to me,' she said urgently. She sat on his knees and put her arms around his neck, covering his forehead with tiny kisses. 'I married *you*, darling. I married you with my heart, not with a piece of paper. I love you. You thought that I was influenced by money, but I never was.'

He didn't seem very convinced.

'Rob,' she said smiling. 'If we aren't married, will you marry me?'

'Jesus, Kate. It will take years to get back to what you're used to. Is this what you really want?'

'All I really want is you,' she said. 'Wherever you go, I'll go with you. It won't be the Namib forever. I have the greatest faith in you. Besides, I can make my own money. Look out, Rob Palma. I might keep you. Is that a deal?'

'It is,' he said solemnly. He stood up and folded her in his arms. 'It might take a while to sort out this mess, but I'll be back for you. I never stopped loving you.' He folded her in his arms and for a few seconds they clung to each other.

Ari found Kate in her studio, painting a lay-out for the Zimmermans' new sitting room. The sunlight was streaming on to her hair which shone brilliantly, her eyes were sparkling and she looked relaxed and full of joy. The past months' strain and anguish seemed to have drained away. That's success for you, Ari thought, watching her happily. But he was wrong.

'Oh, Ari! Dearest, dearest Ari. I have something to tell you,' she gushed. Leaving her easel, she rushed forward to hug him and kiss him on both cheeks. A sisterly kiss, he noted with dismay. 'I know you'll be so happy for me. Rob and I . . .'

Ari hardly heard the rest of her words: his ears were singing, his stomach churning and his legs had turned to stone.

'Rob told me he's quitting the Palma house and fortune forever. He's going back to the Namib to rebuild his own personal wealth. But first he has to speak to you and Angelo. He's gone to see Gerber to make a statement.

'When I saw him crushed, and hurt, and just a little

scared, I realised how much I love him.' She was brimming over with tenderness and womanly compassion – all that he had wanted for himself.

Ari wanted to say something meaningful, but he couldn't find the words. He wanted to say that Kate was more valuable than all the wealth and power in the world, but what was the point? He'd lost out.

Kate rushed around making him tea, pretending that nothing had changed and they were still the good friends they had always been, while Ari wondered what to do with the next fifty-odd empty years without the woman he loved by his side. And then he thought: nothing has changed really, only my expectations. I still love her. I always will and she can't take that away. I don't have to be loved in return, nor to possess her. It's enough that she is happy and I love her. I can live with that.

He gulped his hot tea and left. Funny how his feet seemed to have turned to lead, he thought as he drove to the station. It was time to leave Silver Bay. With a superhuman effort, he switched his mind off Kate and forced himself to consider his work and his many cases. What else was left to do? He couldn't think of a damn thing, except to release Angelo.

Angelo was sitting up in bed eating his breakfast. It smelled pretty good and Ari suddenly realised he was starving.

'Is this normal prison fare?' Angelo said. 'No wonder we have so much crime. I'm treated like a king here.'

'You know something, Mr Palma? There's a reason for that. I've discovered that everyone here loves you. They don't give a hoot what you've done. And the irony is, you think it's because you're rich. It's not. It's because you're you. You should get out more, with respect, sir.

'I've come to release you,' he said without beating around the bush. 'Frikkie was lying. The child was put up for adoption. I've checked it out very carefully. He went to a good home and he's happy where he is.'

Angelo was staring incredulously. 'You mean Rose's child still lives?'

'Yes. That's for sure. As I said, I've checked out every last detail. You can dress and leave.'

'No! Wait a minute!' Angelo was almost shouting. His hands were shaking and his eyes were shining.

'Where is he? I have to see him. I long to beg his forgiveness and start again. I want him back. I owe him.'

'I'm afraid there's no way you can see him. You see, it's too late. I've spoken to him, and he's perfectly content with his adoptive parents. He's well adjusted . . . in fact, sir, he's just fine. He doesn't need any of you. He told me to tell you not to search for him. He has his own family and his own roots. He wants to lead his own life.'

'So I can go?'

'Yes.'

'Just like that?'

'Why not?' Ari shrugged.

'And Mandy? I heard from the nurse that you found her.'

'That's true, sir.'

'And Jean Graux was the kidnapper.'

'Alias Jânek Jözsef, sir.'

'What about Rose's death?'

'I have convinced the prosecutor that it was an accident.'

'And Ramona's death?'

'Also Jözsef. He had embarked on a war of reprisals.

Fortunately he didn't get further. Your grandson is off the hook. My theory, such as it was, proved to be a load of nonsense.'

Angelo's eyes narrowed. 'You're a strange young man,' he said. 'You don't give a damn what anyone thinks about you. You only want to find the truth and punish the criminals. You seem to have a compulsion to do this. It's stronger than just a vocation.'

'All that may change, sir. I'm leaving the force.'

'I can always find you a good job on my estates,' Palma said. 'I have a talent for picking winners. You're a winner, Ari.'

He sighed. 'I have a lot of thinking to do, sir. Call the nurse and get dressed. It's all over and it's time to go home.'

There was a sound of footsteps in the corridor. Rob burst in with Gerber hurrying behind him. Rob was burned almost black by the sun and he was still wearing his khaki shorts and shirt. Ari had never seen him with a beard. It was black and bushy and his hair was long and there was something quite remarkable about the way his eyes burned and his teeth glistened white. Ari felt some of the intense personal magnetism of the man and realised why Kate had fallen in love with him.

'Grandfather,' he said, grabbing his hand. 'Are you all right?'

'Of course, of course,' Angelo said, patting him reassuringly.

'Lieutenant,' he said, turning angrily to Ari. 'Let him go. I am all the proof you need to release him from these absurd charges. I am Rose's son and I can prove it. What more proof do you need?'

He scowled at Ari. Some things never change, Ari

thought. He felt exhausted and he seemed to be reaching a point of unreality.

'You don't know my grandfather at all,' Rob growled as if he were spoiling for a fight. 'He wouldn't kill a living thing. Where's your heart pills?' he asked, turning back to Angelo with eyes that were so full of tenderness. 'You're going to need them.'

'Here!' Angelo touched his pocket. Watching him, Ari noticed that his eyes were glittering with amusement. The old devil. He's already worked it all out for himself. Now he's waiting to see how we handle the situation. Damn him!

'Grandfather, listen carefully. I love you, but I am the cuckoo in your nest – the bastard you fought so hard to keep out of your family. Ramona told me the night before she was killed.

'Grandfather, I'm ashamed that it took me so long to come to my senses. When you're out in the desert, away from all the wealth and power, you have the peace of mind to get back to what's real. That it's not money, nor power, nor being someone important, it's people that count. You can hang on to what's yours, Angelo. I've made enough in the Namib to give me a good start in life, but you owe me love. I'm still your grandson and you owe me that.'

Ari felt out of place and he was getting to feel lightheaded. Perhaps it was the swim, or a night without sleep. Or was it because he'd just realised that Claire was his mother? He'd felt such a warmth for her. Strange that. He sighed. He could have been Rob, over-defensive, introverted, unable to see himself as a real person beyond the power and the finance, lost in Angelo's shadow. Just what had it cost Rob to come here and say what he was saying? He had to sit it out now. He fiddled with a pencil while Rob painfully explained how he had contacted an industrial spy and set him to tracing the real heir back to Father Richard Mooney.

'It's him all right,' he muttered. 'Ramona as good as told me, but I didn't believe her.' He shot Ari a glance of pure loathing. 'He'd even checked his blood group.'

How he must have hoped it wasn't true.

'The point is, *I* am Rose's son. *He* is Claire's son. You didn't murder anyone and you can walk right out of here, right now. Let's go.'

'Exactly what I'd just been telling him when you blustered in,' Ari said. 'You blabbed it all out for nothing. I was keeping it quiet. Well, there's no harm done, Rob. You're the only heir he'll ever get, so he'd best make the most of you.'

'Just a minute,' Angelo said. 'Why do you say that?'

'Because I don't need you, nor your wealth. Because of what you did to Claire. She's wounded, scarred, you had no right. You see the world in terms of profits. My adoptive folks see it in terms of what they can put into it. I thank God Ramona swopped us round. I feel sorry for you,' he said to Rob.

'Ari? Why ever did they call you Ari?' Angelo asked distastefully. 'We'll have to change that.'

'Something to do with Greek mythology. I never did care much about the name. Something about a . . .' As he remembered, he broke off and burst out laughing. The old man was already taking over.

'Well, I guess you'd like to be on your way. I'll leave you two. To tell the truth I have other things to do.' He felt a world apart from the Palmas. 'As for our blood ties, forget it,' he said. 'Just leave me alone. I want nothing of yours. For some reason I wanted to find my roots. Now I wish to God I'd never started.'

'Ari, my boy,' he heard Angelo's anguished call behind him as he left them.

He strode out to the car park and turned the ignition key. A hand shot in, punching him on the cheek. The key was turned back and snatched out.

'You opened this can of worms,' Rob shouted. 'You came here. You can't just walk away from it. Angelo needs help . . . forgiveness! I can love him, but only you can forgive him.'

Then he realised that he could not run away. Angelo's wounds were festering and guilt is a hard act to live with. Reluctantly he walked back with Rob.

Epilogue

It was Ari's last morning in Silver Bay and he was both glad and regretful to be leaving. As he drove up the steep, winding cobbled streets of the fishing village he heard the muezzin's rich baritone voice calling the faithful to prayer. He parked and gazed at the harbour wreathed in a silvery mist that was stealing in from the south. The air was crystal clear, and filled with the fragrant scent of the sea and ozone. The mountains rose straight and majestic out of the white mist, each peak an island rising from a mystical snowy vista. The day was hot although it was autumn and the mist would soon disappear. Ari stood silently watching, trying to impress the scene on his mind. He knew he would miss Silver Bay.

He turned away and knocked on the Fernandeses' door. Emanuel was still in his pyjamas.

'I came to say goodbye, you lazy sod,' Ari said affectionately.

Emanuel hugged him with tears in his eyes. Since Silver Bay had learned about Ari's parentage, Emanuel had taken on the role of uncle, which was fair enough since he had been Trevor's close friend.

'I was working,' Emanuel protested. 'Come and see my masterpiece.' It was a boy on a dolphin, beautifully wrought in turquoise, blue and sea-green. 'It's yours when it's finished,' he said smilingly.

Ari was impressed. He ran his finger over the waves and the curved beak of the dolphin. 'It's beautiful,' he said.

Juliette came in with a tray of coffee. 'I heard your voice. I knew you'd never leave without saying goodbye.

'What next, Ari?' she asked. 'Are you leaving for good?'

'I don't know. I have so many offers I'm dazzled by them all. My father has found a post for me lecturing criminology at the university where he teaches. I'm leaving for Harare this morning. I shall stay with my folks long enough to make a few decisions.'

'And your other folks?' Emanuel prodded gently.

'Well, Claire wants me to run her game farm and hotel. I'm spending a month or more with her when I leave Zimbabwe. We aim to get to know each other, although quite honestly when I met her I felt I'd known her all my life.' At the time it seemed odd to feel so much for someone he did not know, but now it made sense.

'And Angelo?' Juliette asked. 'He won't let you out of his clutches.'

'He's backed off quite a bit in the past month. I think he's realised that I'm capable of running my own life and that I'm quite happy. He's got his guilt and bitterness under control. Of course, he'd like me to stay here. He's offered me the moon to do that, but I'm keeping my options open. Rob keeps insisting that he can't run the Palma holdings on his own, but quite honestly he was managing fine, so I don't believe him. He'll cope.'

He broke off and thought about Kate. For the past month he'd been learning to love her as a sister-in-law and he wasn't doing too badly, with a little help from Mandy.

'I hear you've been taking Mandy out,' Juliette said

intuitively, her eyes bright with curiosity. 'D'you realise it could be you and she who are supposed to fulfil Ramona's prophecy? Perhaps Ramona was in too much of a hurry.'

Juliette laughed as if she were playing the fool, but he guessed that Hannah and she had been plotting and wondering.

'I hardly know the kid and besides, she's much too young for me,' Ari said, deliberately concealing the truth. Mandy hero-worshipped him because he had rescued her. He found her madly exciting and excessively beautiful, but she had a lot of growing up to do.

He drained his coffee and stood up. 'Well, be seeing you,' he said. All at once he felt sad to leave them. He walked to the back door and peered into the yard. 'And you say my father planted that tree? I wish I'd known him.' For the first time he realised that he had fought the man who had killed his father. Fate? Coincidence? He'd never know and it didn't really matter.

He drove downhill to Tom's cottage perched on a ridge right over the harbour. The mist was clearing he noticed, and it was getting hotter. The old man was weeding his garden. Lately he had become adept at getting around on his new legs.

'Hi there,' Ari said. He walked inside and put a bottle of brandy on the table. There were two chairs instead of one and a brand new table to match, with flowers in a vase. The bed was made and the dishes washed and there was that indefinable sense of a woman's touch around the room. It gleamed and smelled different. Tom followed him inside.

'Looks good,' Ari said. 'You're looking great, too.'

'Now I can get around better I have a woman. Just a

friend, but she comes round and cooks for me. Sometimes we watch television together.'

'Life in the old dog, yet, eh?' Ari put his hand on Tom's shoulder and squeezed.

Tom gave him a searching glance. 'What's wrong, Ari?' he asked.

'Have a drink with me, Tom,' Ari said. 'I'm leaving today and this might be goodbye. I'm not sure if I'll ever come back.' He sat down and waited while Tom lit his pipe.

'Tom, there's something I want to ask you.' He drained his glass and shook his head when Tom picked up the bottle to pour another.

'It's crazy, but I was searching for the murderer of myself. I should have realised sooner. The truth is, I came here with some vague hope that I would find my real parents, my roots. But then I became obsessed with finding Mandy and the murders and it all seemed to belong to a different world to my own personal problems. I simply didn't put the two worlds together.'

He stood up and stared out of the window. The mist was almost gone and the bay was a deep, dark turquoise with purple reflections under the towering mountains. The valley was lush and green and Ari had a sudden longing for his own farm, maybe a vineyard, with grazing for cattle. A place where he could settle and grow and put down his roots. Making wine was an ancient dream of his. And why not here?

'You knew all the time,' he blurted out. 'But you're my friend. Why didn't you tell me, Tom? That's what's troubling me.'

Tom gazed at him with his remote blue eyes, which were always fixed on some further horizon. He didn't seem very perturbed.

'Listen, Ari,' he said eventually. 'You are yourself. Your roots are in you. They go far back, to the dawn of time. They are deeper and stronger than you realise. Your mind has evolved through the ages and through so many different lifetimes. It doesn't matter who gave birth to you. Your birth is merely accidental.'

'Do you honestly believe that?'

'Certainly I do.'

'Then I'll consider believing it, too.'

The old man frowned and gripped Ari's shoulder. 'Of course, many of us knew who you were,' he said. 'That's why you found yourself up against a conspiracy of silence. Look at it from our point of view. We had one of our fishing lads up there in the big house in a position of great power. From him we learned that we weren't second class after all, not when we had the right background and the right chances. Rob was our idol, our symbol, if you like. He was winning for all of us.'

He laughed without bitterness. 'Fate was against us. You were brought here to right a great wrong. And maybe you had to witness the tyranny of fate when man becomes a victim to his desires. But, Ari, if you're searching for yourself you still have a long way to go, my boy.'

Ari said goodbye and walked out, caught off-balance by Tom's words and the brandy.

Ten minutes later he was shaking hands with Gerber, who grovelled nowadays in the face of Ari's wealthy status, but Willis and Smit hadn't changed, thank goodness.

'You must come back soon,' Willis said, as he drove Ari over the mountain neck. 'This town will get back to normal. You'll see. It was an unusual summer.' Willis was an optimist, but Ari sensed that he was probably half right.

'You can say that again. Hang on here a minute, please.'

Ari got out of the car and gazed over the valley. Lately, Silver Bay filled Ari with awe. The townsfolk had pulled together to cope with their challenge and they had achieved a sense of togetherness and turned disaster into victory. The town had a soul at last, he thought. But not without pain. Vagrants still set light to the mountain bushes, and Saturday nights the valley rocked to the squatters' dance music. Mugging and housebreaking continued, but the crime statistics were improving.

Ari noticed now that the ugly gash on the mountain, where trees had been axed to make room for squatters' homes, was slowly healing. New trees had been planted, gardens were growing, the place was looking pretty good. Kate had won her battle and the new community was becoming integrated with great speed. A labour exchange and crèche and more jobs were pushing the ex-squatters into ratepayer status. The camp was called Lutuli Park Estate and it was thriving.

On Sundays, hundreds of pretty little black girls in white lace dresses came racing out on their way to church. And at weekends, a variety of pedigreed mutts and scruffy mongrels chased each other happily around the beach, despite the many signs prohibiting dogs. But everyone knew that the inhabitants of Silver Bay were a law unto themselves. They did what they liked with their own beach and lately half the dog-owners were blacks.

'Are you glad you came?' Willis asked as Ari got back into the car and they drove towards the airport.

What a question! He'd be leaving his heart here. The rest of him would have to learn to live without it.

'Did you know the birds are returning to the wetlands?'

Ari said, neatly dodging. 'The coots and terns and cormorants are back. I saw a heron and a stork there last week. Yesterday Kate told me a pair of water dikkops have moved in. The trees are recovering. It'll be great soon.'

'Kate's geese dropped into the police yard yesterday,' Willis said. 'Who's living at the lighthouse?'

'Only Frikkie, but he feeds them still.'

'Those lazy buggers are spoiled silly.'

It had been a momentous summer and not only for him, Ari thought. Rob had learned that he could be loved for himself, without his wealth, and he'd regained his wife. Kate had shaken herself loose from emotional dependence and learned to love her husband as an independent woman. And Angelo? He'd lost the massive guilt he'd been carrying on his back for years.

And I? Ari asked himself. He'd found his roots, or had he? Life had been so simple before he met Tom.

Then he thought of Mandy and Kate. Yes, he thought. The answer to your question, Willis, is yes.

Mandy would be joining him at Claire's game farm for her July holidays. He was looking forward to seeing her more than he should.

He remembered what his colonel had said. 'A long hot summer in the Cape will do you good.'

Yes, he thought. It has.

☐	Summer Harvest	Madge Swindells	£5.99
☐	Song of the Wind	Madge Swindells	£5.99
☐	Shadows on the Snow	Madge Swindells	£5.99
☐	The Corsican Woman	Madge Swindells	£5.99
☐	Edelweiss	Madge Swindells	£4.99
☐	The Sentinel	Madge Swindells	£5.99

Warner Books now offers an exciting range of quality titles by both established and new authors which can be ordered from the following address:

Little, Brown and Company (UK),
P.O. Box 11,
Falmouth,
Cornwall TR10 9EN.

Alternatively you may fax your order to the above address.
Fax No. 01326 317444.

Payments can be made as follows: cheque, postal order (payable to Little, Brown and Company) or by credit cards, Visa/Access. Do not send cash or currency. UK customers and B.F.P.O. please allow £1.00 for postage and packing for the first book, plus 50p for the second book, plus 30p for each additional book up to a maximum charge of £3.00 (7 books plus).

Overseas customers including Ireland, please allow £2.00 for the first book plus £1.00 for the second book, plus 50p for each additional book.

NAME (Block Letters) ....

....

ADDRESS ....

....

....

☐ I enclose my remittance for ....

☐ I wish to pay by Access/Visa Card

Number ☐☐☐☐☐☐☐☐☐☐☐☐☐☐☐☐

Card Expiry Date ☐☐☐☐